G000057215

# THE KEY OF ALANAR

## THE ALANAR ASCENDANT

Rory B Mackay

Copyright © 2017 Rory B. Mackay

Third Edition

Published 2017 by Blue Star Publishing

The right of Rory B. Mackay to be identified as the author of this work has been asserted by him in accordance with the Copyright, Designs and Patents Act, 1988.

All rights reserved. No part of this publication may be reproduced, distributed or transmitted in any form or by any means, without prior written permission.

dreamlight-fugitive.co.uk

Cover design by Damonza

The Key of Alanar / Rory B. Mackay -- 3rd ed.
ISBN 978-0-0000000-0-0

Dedicated to my Mum and Dad, with love and gratitude for everything.

# THE KEY OF ALANAR

"This world needs you in ways you can't even begin to imagine. You have no idea how important you are: how far you've come, and how far you will go..."

# The End

*It took only seconds for an entire civilization to perish.*

*Ardonis watched as the shockwave tore through the city, laying waste to the golden metropolis with devastating ease. The buildings collapsed into smoldering ash, scattered by the wind; the crowd of thousands incinerated in the blink of an eye.*

*Fire and cinders spiraled from the rubble; a rising cloud of smoke devouring every last trace of daylight. The only illumination came from the object of the city's destruction—the gateway. Towering above the ruins, its metal pillars stood unscathed; the pulsating whirlpool of blue-violet light raining down sparks of electrical charge.*

*His city was gone, but Ardonis knew the worst was yet to come.*

*He watched with a sense of dread as an object emerged through the gateway: an airship puncturing the thin membrane between universes. Closely followed by another, and then another, the black metallic craft soared over the ruins like carrion birds in search of prey.*

*A stream of ground troops followed; wraithlike reptilian creatures with gnarled, distorted faces, armed with rifles and blades. The metal-clad soldiers spilled into the dead city like an infestation.*

*Ardonis knew it was no coincidence these demonic creatures had arrived in the aftermath of such carnage. They somehow fed off the destruction around them; ingesting it as though death itself was a vital nourishment. He could sense their hunger. Finally freed after eons of captivity, they were ravenous and would not stop until their hunger was satisfied.*

*It wasn't just Ardonis's beloved city that had fallen. Death had been unleashed and the world of Alanar was but its first victim.*

\* \* \*

Ardonis awoke that morning determined that his day would begin as it always did. He stood upon the temple rooftop gazing across the horizon, where the first rays of sunlight shone above the mountainous peaks. Watching the sunrise from the rooftop was a ritualistic start to his day and something he had done for more years than he'd perhaps care to count. Today, however, was a day unlike any that preceded it. Today would be the last time he would ever see the sunrise.

As the twin suns of Alanar made their heavenward ascent, the High Priest looked down into the valley. Surrounded by forestland and a winding river, the sprawling City of El Ad'dan glistened in the morning light. Even from this distance he could see signs of activity as the golden city began to stir. In just a few hours people from all across the kingdom would gather at the central plaza for the activation of the gateway.

A new era, the king had promised; a new dawn for the people of Lasandria. It was a time of excitement and jubilation across the land. But while the gateway promised all the glories of the cosmos, it was about to unleash a force of evil beyond imagining.

Ardonis knew, for he had seen it—over and over again. For days now he'd been unable to close his eyes, much less sleep or meditate without being bombarded by visions of annihilation.

The hour drew close.

He'd accepted that. What he couldn't accept was that he was powerless to prevent this catastrophe. His people, at least those still loyal to the Priesthood, looked to him to guide and protect them, and in the past that was exactly what he had done. Only this time was different. This time he felt powerless to act.

"Ardonis."

Startled by the sound of his name, he turned to see his senior aide join him on the rooftop. "Jarado."

"Forgive the intrusion, High Priest."

"Not at all. You bring news, old friend?"

"The Council of Elders has sent word. They are ready to see you now."

Ardonis felt a tightening in his stomach. "Very well."

"You think they'll agree to help us?"

"We can but pray. It's the only option I see left to us."

The old monk had a look of desperation on his careworn face. "What about the king? What if you spoke to him again and tried to reason with him?"

"You were there yesterday, Jarado. Reason fell upon deaf ears. I did everything I could to get him to abort his plans. The harder I tried, the angrier he got. In the end all I did was make matters worse."

"Then you believe he'll dissolve the Priesthood as he threatened?"

"Dua-ron has been waiting years for the opportunity to strike me down and I finally gave it to him. The Priesthood is dead, Jarado. Not that it matters, for so too is our kingdom."

"The Council will listen. They have to!"

"Oh, they'll listen. But whether they act is another matter. The Guardians play by their own set of rules. Either way, we are soon to find out. I will head to portal chamber promptly. Go attend to your duties, Jarado. I will join you shortly."

With a bow, the monk departed, leaving the High Priest alone once more. Ardonis took one last look at the golden city in the heart of the valley. Rays of sunlight sparkled upon its towers, domes and rooftops as the suns climbed their way above the snow-capped peak of Mount Alsan.

El Ad'dan. A place of beauty, power, and history. It was here that the great Lasandrian civilization had been born all those millennia ago, and here that would see its demise. Unless, that was, one man could now change its fate and alter the destiny of an entire world.

Ardonis hurried through the temple, his footsteps echoing as he strode along the sleek sandstone corridors and down several flights of stairs into the very depths of the temple. Passing through an enchanted doorway accessible only to high levels of the Priesthood, he entered the portal chamber.

An elaborate crystalline cavern stretched before him: quartz clusters of varying size jutting out of the ground, walls, and ceiling. Pulsating with a blue-white light, they illuminated the cavern in a pale turquoise glow. A low-level hum permeated the chamber. The hot air tingled with electrostatic charge as Ardonis marched forward, his blue cloak swishing behind him.

At the center of the chamber he came to a platform upon which sat a particularly large crystal. Set into the base of the crystal was a large hexagonal mirror cast in a gleaming metal frame. A device built by the ancients with the ability to create inter-dimensional gateways, the Portal of Arazan enabled instantaneous travel throughout the cosmos.

Clearly, such technology carried with it great responsibility, which was why the portal lay buried deep within the temple, where it had been safeguarded by the Priesthood for millennia. Until recently, that was. Some time ago the portal chamber had been violated and nothing had been the same again since.

Coming to a stop before the mirror, Ardonis's crystal clear reflection stared back at him: that of a muscular bronze-skinned man clad in a loincloth and sandals, his neck and arms adorned with beads and talismans. With the traditional golden headdress of the Priesthood upon his crown, he had had all the regality and power befitting a High Priest, yet his soul was heavy and the strain etched upon his ageless face. Eyes fixed ahead, he inhaled deeply, bracing himself for the encounter ahead.

*"Bala'naron ista kar'on!"*

The moment the words left his mouth, the portal exploded into life. The towering amethyst sent waves of electricity surging outward. The mirror surface dissolved into a swirling pool of blue-violet energy. Ardonis could feel waves of kinetic force pass through him as he stood at the mouth of the portal.

"Take me to the Court of Shanadon."

Mustering all his fortitude, he stepped through the portal, disappearing into the vortex of light.

Exiting the gateway, Ardonis found himself again in the realm of the Guardians. He stood inside the Court of Shanadon, a cathedral-like structure built in multiple tiers. Far from solid, the crystalline walls, colonnades, and archways were translucent and swirling with an interfusion of rainbow color. Although often asked by his students to describe the place, he found it hard to convey the beauty of a world so unlike that of the physical realm. Here the constraints of physicality loosened; solidity giving way to fluidity and form dissolving into pure energy.

The gateway disappeared behind him. Ardonis hastened down the opaque, glasslike corridors until he reached the Council Chamber. An immense cylindrical room, the chamber was dominated by a pulsating pillar of white light reaching down from a high ceiling and plunging into a bottomless drop. Ardonis stepped forward, the quartz walkway beneath his feet leading to a platform encircling the beam of light at the heart of the chamber.

There, around a semicircular table, sat the Council of Elders; the twelve Guardians charged with overseeing the mortal realm. Dressed in white robes, their faces were shining and luminous, as though they were rays of sunlight that had merely assumed the visage of human form. The High Guardian Malkiastan sat at the head of the Council: a regal being with long locks of silver hair, glowing with a radiance that almost obscured his corporeal form.

Ardonis bowed before the Council. Malkiastan motioned for the High Priest to come forward. "Thank you for agreeing to see me," Ardonis said.

The Council spoke with a single, unified voice emanating from all around and echoing throughout the chamber. "*You are always welcome here, Ardonis.*"

"I'm sure you already know why I'm here. Indeed, I have a feeling it is you who are responsible for my visions..."

"*The visions were granted for a reason. It was necessary that you know what is to transpire.*"

"Then things will happen as I have foreseen?"

"*It is inevitable.*"

"I can't accept that. There must be something you can do."

There was silence.

"You can't allow this. You must intervene!"

"*We cannot stop what is to happen.*"

It was as he had feared. The Council could not—or would not—do anything. But Ardonis wasn't going to stand by and accept this. "I mean no disrespect, but how can that be true? You have the power. You could stop this from happening in an instant!"

*"These events were set in motion by the free will of the Lasandrian people. As you know, the Council is forbidden from direct intervention in mortal affairs. To do so would violate universal law."*

"I don't care about universal law. All I care about is the fate of my people. You yourselves have shown me what is to happen. Millions will die—an entire civilization annihilated! I implore you, you cannot sit by and allow that to happen."

*"This chain of events cannot be halted."*

Ardonis cast his eyes to the ground. "So this is how it ends?"

*"There are no endings. There are no beginnings. All that is, has been and ever shall be."*

"That's easy for you to say as you sit here in the Court of Shanadon, fearless and omnipotent. You're immortal! Nothing can touch you here. But what of those in the mortal realm? Such words are meaningless in the face of impending annihilation." Ardonis immediately regretted his words, which were disrespectful and ill-befitting a High Priest. Yet he was the one link between Alanar and the cosmic realms. It was his duty to bridge the two worlds and to speak for those that could not.

*"What is to take place cannot be averted. But with regard to the future, all is not lost. The Council has conferred at great length and has agreed to offer a dispensation."*

"A dispensation?"

Malkiastan rose from his seat at the center of the Council and addressed Ardonis directly. "We cannot change the rules," he said, his voice deep yet soft and melodious. "But we can bend them."

"Please, tell me what you have in mind."

"It is twofold. You must return to your world and gather as many people as possible: all those who remain loyal to the Priesthood and anyone else willing to listen. You are to take them through the portal. A place of safety has been arranged. They will be spared the impending upheaval."

Ardonis had considered this himself, although he was uncertain how many would be willing to leave Lasandria. It was a sad fact that the days when people paid heed to the Priesthood over the government and monarchy were long gone.

"Although your civilization may be lost," Malkiastan continued, "if even a handful of your people can survive and keep their spirit alive, the Lasandrian people will endure throughout time. Their legacy will continue. And there will come a time in your world's distant future when they will have the chance to rise up and reclaim all they had lost. Thus will the circle complete itself." The Guardian paused before continuing. "Darkness is coming, Ardonis. You know this. What you have foreseen will inevitably come to pass. But your people, and your world, have been granted the chance of a future. This future lies in the hands of another."

Ardonis felt his brow crease. "Another...?"

"Behold."

The fountain of energy at the heart of the chamber intensified. Growing ever brighter, an aperture formed at its center, sending rays of dazzling light shooting outward. Ardonis watched through squinted eyes as a figure emerged from the cascading light, coming to a stop beside the Council.

It was a man. No, barely a man at all—

It was a boy; an adolescent boy.

"Behold *Arran*, the timeless one," Malkiastan said. "He is your future, Ardonis. He alone has the power to save your world. Only he can safeguard your future."

Ardonis stared at the boy in astonishment. Who was he? Where was he from? And why had he been chosen to shoulder such a burden of responsibility?

The boy watched him with equal curiosity, his brown eyes betraying a weary knowingness that intrigued Ardonis. Whoever this boy was and wherever he was from, he had obviously suffered a great deal. It saddened him to see such pain in eyes so young. Yet beneath the surface, Ardonis could sense a reservoir of unfathomable inner strength. Moreover, there was something unspeakably familiar about him. He didn't know how or why, but Ardonis somehow knew this boy. He knew his thoughts, his dreams, and his pain almost as intimately as he knew his own reflection.

Ardonis was about to speak when Malkiastan raised his hand. Ardonis felt his body and mind engulfed by a wave of golden luminescence. His eyes closed. Time and space seemed to unravel as images flooded his mind...

*He was back on his world, several hours from now, standing amid the streets of El Ad'dan. The central plaza was filled with people, rife with excitement as they gathered to witness what they were promised was the crowning achievement of the Lasandrian people.*

*The countdown had begun—the countdown to annihilation.*

*All looked up in wonder as the gateway powered up. Towering above the buildings of the city center, the gateway comprised an enormous metal obelisk supported by two smaller pillars and connected by a metal wheel. Amid much excitement, the device was activated. The spinning wheel exploded into a vortex of blue-violet energy, stretching from the rooftops to the ground as it spewed out lightning-like sparks of electricity. The entire plaza lit up in a blue glow as the crowd reacted in awe.*

*"Behold the gateway," King Dua-ron called as he stood before the magnificent portal. "The gateway to our liberation!"*

*Ardonis knew what was coming next, for he'd been forced to witness it so many times before. Moments after the gateway opened, the portal exploded. A shockwave shot outward, pounding the city to rubble and killing every man, woman and child in a blinding flash.*

*Blackness pervaded. The only illumination came from the open gateway—all that now remained of the Lasandrian people.*

*In the aftermath of the blast, the invasion began, just as he knew it would. Air craft and ground troops stormed through the portal. These monstrous creatures, clearly from another universe, were driven by an unending thirst for death that would lead them to consume this entire world.*

*But there was more that Ardonis hadn't previously seen.*

*He saw himself back in the temple, leading dozens of his followers through the corridors into the portal chamber. In a race against time, he ushered the evacuees through the portal, promising that safety lay beyond the other side.*

*He was about to enter the portal himself—only it was too late.*

*A wave of fire blasted through the temple. With a force of fury, it consumed everything, tearing through stone, metal and flesh alike. All that remained of both he and his beloved temple was a wall of ash, and even that was soon dispersed by the wind. Ardonis had got his people to safety, but at the cost of his own life.*

*All hope now rested with a single boy: the boy known as Arran. Ardonis saw the boy racing through the rubble of El Ad'dan. Sent by the Guardians, he had been spared the destruction; his sole purpose to close the gateway and seal off whatever other horrors it would yet unleash. No matter the cost and no matter the sacrifice, he had to succeed.*

*Time had fragmented and the fate of multiple timelines—past, present and future—all seemed to converge upon a single moment in time. A moment that would determine the fate of not just this world, but possibly an entire universe.*

The dizzying stream of images subsided and Ardonis opened his eyes.

As he again aware of his surroundings, his gaze fell upon the teenage boy ahead of him. Rising from his place at the Council, Malkiastan stood by the boy, placing a hand upon his shoulder and motioning for Ardonis to come forward. "It has been decided," Malkiastan said. "The future now rests in your hands. It is time to go forth. Go forth and fight for it."

As Malkiastan's words echoed throughout the chamber, Ardonis turned to the boy, still curious as to who he was and why he had been brought here. This time, the moment their eyes met it all became clear to him.

Ardonis's kingdom would be destroyed, and the world of Alanar plunged into an abyss of darkness. But this wasn't the end.

*Hope.*

Even in the darkest of times, hope remained.

Whoever he was, this boy represented hope—a shining beacon of light amid an oncoming wave of darkness.

PART ONE

# AWAKENING

*"You're here for a reason, David. You have a destiny to fulfill and you have to see it through."*

# CHAPTER ONE

# The Stranger

*Year of Atahl, 14,999*

David was only eight years old when learned that his entire existence was a lie.

He stood upon the river's edge and gazed into the trickling water. It was a ghostly reflection that stared up at him—that of a young boy, confused, alone, and desperately trying to make sense of his world. Reaching down, he grabbed a rock and threw it at the water. The moment it hit the water surface his reflection shattered and vanished. He felt a strange sense of envy. Why couldn't he too simply blink out of existence? After all, what did it matter, and who would really care? It wasn't as though he belonged here.

He'd lived on the island of New Haven his entire life. It was the only home he'd ever known. Yet although it pained him to admit, he felt no real connection to the place, or to the people around him. From a young age he'd known he was different in some way. His parents cared for him deeply, and he them. But he'd long known there was something about him that made them uncomfortable—something had always set him apart from others. But what was it? What was it that was wrong with him?

Today was the day he'd finally learned the truth, and he now knew why he felt so innately like a stranger in his own world. It had happened after school. A chance encounter that brought his entire world crumbling down.

Situated on the edge of the Sharedo forest, the island school was just a short walk from the main town. Classes were finished for the day and David had been making his way home. While the other children gathered in groups to talk and play, David usually walked alone, often trailing behind everyone else. As the path forked to the right, he came across three boys playing an aggressive game of tagball. His heart sank upon recognizing them. Their ringleader was the notorious Dahn, a burly blonde-haired boy from two years above him, known throughout the school as a vindictive bully.

Over the years David had developed the knack of blending into the background, avoiding drawing undue attention to himself. While it seemed to work most of the time, there were occasions it didn't, and he'd very much become an object of Dahn's attention. Several weeks ago he'd come across Dahn beating up one of his classmates, a short, skinny boy called Antan. Unlike the other children, who knew better than to get involved, David found himself unable to turn a blind eye to someone in need of help. Mustering a courage that he never knew he possessed, David intervened, squaring up to Dahn and demanding that he leave Antan alone. Astounded that someone had the nerve to challenge him, Dahn released Antan and thereafter David became the focus of his attention.

Dahn hadn't resorted to physical violence but had adopted a subtler, more insidious form of bullying. Whenever they crossed paths at school, Dahn would fix David in his sights and glare at him menacingly, pointing him out to his thuggish friends; making jokes and jeering at him. David knew that this was merely the warm-up to a looming confrontation. Today, the moment he laid eyes on Dahn, he knew that his adversary was ready to move in for the kill.

Upon catching sight of David, the boys stopped their game and circled him like flies around a slab of meat. Dahn's sneering henchmen, Gerdan and Robb, made a grab for his schoolbooks. David pulled back, clutching the books to his chest. Dahn wasn't joining in but was watching with a dark glint in his eye. "So where d'you think you're going?" grunted Robb, his rounded face permanently flushed, accentuating his reddish freckles.

David said nothing, keeping his face neutral yet defiant.

"School's over," Gerdan cried, snatching the books from his arms. "You won't be needing these." The tall, stocky boy threw

the books to the ground and kicked them across the path, sending the pages flying.

David looked around helplessly. The other children were
far ahead, out of sight. There was no one to help. He felt his
heart pounding in his chest as Dahn's minions began pushing
him around, passing him to each other as though playing some
kind of bizarre ball game. He tried to break free but they were
stronger and easily overpowered him.

"Let him go," Dahn suddenly barked.

Surprised, Robb and Gerdan released David.

Dahn stepped toward him. "Don't mind them. Their moth-
ers obviously never taught them any manners." An insincere
smile played across his lips. "We've never really had the chance
to get to know each other, have we?"

David might even have believed this façade of friendliness
had it not been for the malicious glint in his eyes. "I think we've
been too hard on you," Dahn continued. "I mean, it must be
difficult for you. I don't know how I'd cope in your situation."

David eyed him suspiciously. "What situation?"

"You know, not having a real family. Not having real parents—not belonging here."

"What are you talking about? I have a family. I have parents!"

"Yeah, but they're not *really* your parents, are they?" Dahn
shrugged. "They just took pity on you. You don't have a real
family. I mean, how could you? You don't even come from the
island."

David stared at him blankly.

"They found you on the mainland when you were just a
baby. You were *abandoned* and they took pity on you..."

David stood still, numb with shock.

"You *did* know that...didn't you?" Dahn asked with mock
surprise. "I mean, surely they told you all this? After all, ev-
erybody knows it: that you're an orphan, an outsider, that you
don't belong here...that you're only here out of pity..."

Dahn's words cut through him like a blade. Unable to speak,
David found himself overcome by a barrage of emotion: shock,
anger—and sudden, blinding clarity. All he could remember

next was the sensation of something exploding inside him. He lashed out at Dahn, knocking him to the ground with such ferocity that his friends backed off in alarm.

After that, he ran. His mind numb and his senses blurred, David didn't even consciously know where he was going and was oblivious to both his surroundings and whoever he happened to encounter along his way.

As if pulled by instinct, he found himself in the depths of the Sharedo forest. The forest was a safe haven where he spent many hours enjoying the peace and solitude. Once certain that he was safe and alone, he stopped by the river. His knees buckled and he sank to the ground, engulfed by the storm of emotion he had thus far managed to hold at bay.

Initially he wondered whether Dahn's words were to be believed. It could have merely been a cruel joke on his part, yet something deep within him knew it was the truth. He'd finally been given the answer he'd sought his entire life. Everything made sense: his nagging, life-long inability to feel at home, the way other people treated him, and his yearning to be somewhere else; to find a place that he could truly call home.

He sat alone for what seemed like hours. He now had to accept the truth that he really was different to everyone else on the island. It was something he'd pretty much known his entire life and yet in spite of this, the eventual confirmation was no less painful. How many times had he wished and prayed that he could just be like everyone else? Fitting in and feeling as though he belonged here had been an elusive dream that was now forever dispelled by the light of truth. He had to accept that. And yet, if he didn't belong here, where *did* he belong?

Basically it came down to one simple question:

*Who am I?*

He threw another stone at the water with a force fueled by pent-up desperation. The stone landed with a splash, drops of water splattering onto his face. Wiping his face, he looked upward. Judging by the position of the twin suns in the mauve sky, he guessed it was now early evening. His parents would be worried about him. Although what did it matter? They weren't really his parents.

David found himself wandering through the forest. Birds cawed and cooed. The trees danced in the breeze as he climbed over fallen logs and tromped along the uneven terrain, his footsteps crunching in the twig-strewn undergrowth.

He came to the edge of the forest. A steep drop gave way to the rocky shoreline. Across the ocean, he could see the faint outline of land upon the horizon. He felt a pull toward it; a deep yearning. He now knew that his home was not here in New Haven but was out there, somewhere across the waters. If he ever truly wanted to know who he was and where he belonged, then that was where he had to go.

Looking down at the shore he saw a jetty at the edge of the cove with a small rowing boat bobbing up and down on the water. The moment he caught sight of the boat he knew that, come morning, he'd be on it. As this was a secluded spot, rarely used, he should be able to leave the island unseen.

His mind was set. The decision was made. He'd been lied to his entire life and he needed to know the truth. He needed to know where he belonged. Tomorrow he was taking the boat and leaving here. Tomorrow he was going home.

Bolstered by this grandiose conviction, he decided that it was time he went home and faced up to the wrath of his parents. He would need a good night's sleep, for he knew that tomorrow's endeavor would require as much strength as he could muster.

Turning to leave, he caught sight of something in the corner of his eye. It looked like a man standing at the edge of the forest, watching him. Yet the moment he turned in that direction, the figure was gone. Whoever it was had vanished. Or had he just imagined it? Puzzled, he nevertheless dismissed the incident and set on his way.

As expected, his parents, Jon and Jesanda, had panicked when he hadn't returned home from school. Despite being relieved to see him when he eventually turned up on the doorstep, they were angry at his 'irresponsibility' for having wandered off without notice. "Where were you anyway?" Jon demanded.

David didn't want them to know what had really happened. "I just went to play in the forest after school," he mumbled in response.

"Well, in future you're to let us know beforehand. Is that clear?"

"Yes," David sighed.

It was dark by the time they sat down to eat evening meal, and there was an awkward silence around the table. David wasn't hungry, but he knew that he had to keep his strength up for tomorrow. He ate somewhat laboriously, then excused himself and went to bed.

In spite of his tiredness, sleep eluded him. His mind continuously went over his plans for the morning. The day would begin as it always did. He would get up and leave for school, only he'd head for the edge of the Sharedo forest and set out on the boat. He knew it would be a long and difficult row. He'd been to the mainland before and it was at least a half day's journey from New Haven, and that was with adults at the helm. There was no telling how much longer it would take him.

He did feel a pang of remorse at the prospect of leaving his parents. He knew that they loved him. Yet they weren't his real parents. They'd lied to him his entire life. Perhaps it was a lie born of kindness, but that was beside the point. He needed to know the truth. The thought of setting out into the world alone was daunting, and he had no idea what he'd do once he arrived there. But perhaps it would all become clear to him. All he knew was that he had to do this. He'd never been more certain of anything.

Morning came, and with a yawn he pulled back the covers and climbed out of bed. He opened the curtain and looked out, disheartened by what he saw: an overcast sky, churning with raincloud. The island had enjoyed a long stretch of fine weather, which made this sudden shift all the more frustrating. But unfortunate though it was, he decided it wasn't reason enough to call off his plan.

He wasted little time in washing and getting dressed. His mother had laid out clothes for him: a pair of black cotton trousers and a sleeveless gray tunic. He tied up his boots and ran his hand through his short brown hair as he made his way through the hall into the kitchen, the smell of cooking wafting through the house.

The atmosphere had eased considerably following the previous night's drama. It was with a sense of sadness that David realized this would be the last meal he would share with his parents.

After they'd eaten and cleared up the dishes, Jon and Jesanda readied themselves to leave while David pretended to prepare for school. As she was about to leave, his mother reached out and hugged him goodbye as she always did, her wavy brown hair tickling the back of his neck as she held him. It was with a great sense of sadness that he said goodbye to them. As far as they were concerned they were just parting for the day, but David knew he might never see them again. Such a thought being too painful to reconcile, he made a pledge that someday he'd return to New Haven to see them again.

The moment the door clicked shut, he sprang into action. He packed several changes of clothing, filled a large water-skin flask and, raiding the pantry, stock-piled enough food to last several days. For sentimental reasons he also included one or two personal items, such as an engraving that his mother had created depicting the family. He stuffed them into a leather bag and slung it over his shoulder.

Stepping outside, the air was cool and the sky thick with ever-darkening cloud. Groups of children made their way along the path to school. David kept his head down, hoping to avoid anyone he knew.

Fortunately, he knew a detour enabling him to bypass the school lane and slip into the heart of the forest unseen. Traipsing along the forest path, the trees waving back and forth in the wind, he felt a knotted sensation in his stomach. He didn't know whether it was a feeling of excitement or fear, but he tried to dismiss it and kept on going.

Reaching the edge of the forest, he stopped and looked across the choppy gray waters to the horizon. Visibility was poor. He couldn't make out the headland at all.

He scrambled down the embankment onto the shoreline. The wind was picking up, blustering in gusts, forcing him to raise his arms to keep his balance as he stepped across the uneven rocks to the jetty. He climbed into the little red boat and laid down his bag. The boat lurched back and forth, banging against the side of the jetty. David awkwardly untethered the boat from its mooring, casting off the line as he sat down and took hold of the oars.

Continually buffeted by the tide, it took him a number of attempts to maneuver the boat away from the jetty. At one point he almost rammed into an outcropping of rock. Clearly this was more difficult than it looked. He eventually managed, with considerable exertion and a large measure of luck, to row the boat out of the cove and into the open expanse of the ocean. It was a moment that was in equal measure exhilarating and terrifying, and one in which he knew there was no turning back. He looked across at the island, the only home that he'd ever known, and with mixed emotion silently bade it farewell.

Had he not been blinded by the impetuousness of youth and the emotional turmoil that clouded his judgement, David would have known to heed the warning signs and at the very least postpone his departure. But instead, he turned a blind eye to the ever darkening skies and the imminent storm that was brewing.

The rain fell lightly at first, but it wasn't long before it lashed down in torrents, stinging his skin and soaking him from head to foot. He wasn't far from the island when the storm swept in and a blanket of cloud enveloped him. The wind howled and the waves took on a nightmarish life of their own, thrashing against the boat and further drenching the panic-stricken boy. He clung to the wooden hull, frozen by fear as the boat lurched back and forth. He didn't know what to do except hold on tight.

The storm only worsened; the wind howling as waves pummeled the boat. Nauseous and dizzy, David could barely see anything as the oars were snatched off the boat. He was helpless and entirely at the mercy of an opponent he could never have imagined would pose such a terrible threat: nature itself.

As the boat filled with water, David knew that it would only be a matter of time before it sank, capsized or was ripped apart by the waves. Whatever happened, he would surely drown, for there was no way he could hold his own against the might of this foe.

*Please. Someone help me...*

Wave after wave crashed over him. He choked, coughing up the salty water, still clinging with all his might to the battered vessel. Though unable to think clearly, one thought flashed through his mind and it was a thought of disbelief—

*This can't be the end. Can it?*

David was uncertain how long he spent clinging to the boat, eyes closed as the waves and rain lashed over him. Time blurred; each moment stretching into an eternity. He veered between hopelessness and desperation, praying—to who or what he didn't know—that he'd be okay. Pleading, begging, willing to do anything just to survive...

Perhaps someone or something was indeed listening to his prayer because something remarkable then happened. At first he thought it was his imagination, but he became aware of a light some way off. Yes, it was definitely a light—and it was getting brighter! It was soon accompanied by a voice, shouting above the roar of the storm—a voice calling his name.

He could barely believe his eyes when he saw a boat emerge through the screen of rain, mist, and water. It was one of the island's fishing boats; a vessel larger and sturdier than his rowing boat, but still taking a beating from the storm.

"David!"

This time he recognized the voice. It was his father, Jon. He'd come to rescue him! But how? What was he doing out here?

There were a handful of men on deck, frantic in their efforts to steady the boat. Two men stood on the edge of the deck, one brandishing the mysterious light that cut through the darkness like a knife. The other man, who David quickly realized was his father, called out to him: "David, can you hear me?"

"Yes!"

"Listen, David. I'm going to throw you a line. You have to catch it. Do you understand?"

"Yes," David spluttered, spitting out a mouthful of water as another wave crashed over him.

What sounded like a simple task was altogether more complicated in the eye of the storm. The first attempt to pass the rope was a misfire. Despite Jon's best effort to throw the line, the wind and rain deflected his aim and the rope doubled back and smacked against the side of the fishing boat. Jon tried to coincide his next effort with a lull between gusts of wind. Sure enough, it was a more successful throw, but he still missed his aim and the rope landed in the water. Jon reeled it in and made several more attempts before David successfully caught it.

"I've got it," he shouted to his father.

"Tie it to the mooring ring at the bow! Make it tight!"

David edged his way to the metal lock at the front of the boat. The waves continued striking the boat. He struggled to keep his balance as wall after wall of ice cold water crashed over him. By now the bottom of the boat was full of water. David knew the vessel wouldn't withstand much more of this.

His hands were numb and he could barely see through the stinging rain. He fumbled desperately as he tried to tie down the rope. He eventually managed to tie a knot. "I've done it!" he called, still incredulous that his father of all people had come to rescue him.

"We're going to pull you in," Jon shouted. Aided by the other men on deck, Jon was about to reel in the boat.

The storm, however, struck with its most brutal outburst yet. David bore the brunt of it. An immense wave exploded over the boat. Losing his grip, David was swept back as the boat split in two. His body slammed hard against the hull.

As the boat lurched again, David was rammed forward, his head colliding with the edge of the bow. The last thing he was aware of was a sharp pain and choking as water filled his lungs. His consciousness ebbed away and everything went dark.

# CHAPTER TWO

# Aftermath

He awoke with a sense of drowsiness and disorientation. His head was throbbing and his body aching all over. He had no idea where he was or how long he'd been unconscious. He found himself in an unfamiliar bed with a blanket draped over him. His water-soaked clothes had been removed and he was wearing an oversized shirt.

He propped himself up and looked around. The rocky walls were those of a cave, but this wasn't just any cave. Tapestries and fabrics of shimmering rainbow colors adorned the craggy walls, bringing what would otherwise have been a dank cave to entrancing life. An assortment of potted plants and flowers lined the chamber, providing dashes of green, blue and red. A stack of unpacked crates lay against the far wall alongside an old wooden table. David's eyes were drawn to the tabletop, which contained a number of exotic-looking artifacts including crystals of varying sizes and a collection of glass jars containing herbs and liquids. A dozen or so white candles illuminated the cave.

"I see you are awake."

David jumped, startled by the unfamiliar voice. A man stepped from the shadows into the flickering candlelight. It was someone he'd never seen before. Carrying himself with poise and elegance, the man was perhaps in his mid-forties; tall and of average build; his face rugged yet kind, a tanned complexion accentuating his emerald eyes. He had a neatly trimmed beard and his long, graying hair was tied back in plaits. His style of clothing was different to that of New Haven. He wore a navy tunic and trousers with a long dark gray cloak fastened at the neck by a gold broach. Whoever he was, he exuded gentleness, power and a foreignness that intrigued David.

"How are you feeling?" the stranger said.

"A bit dizzy...my head hurts," David croaked in response. "Where am I?"

"Somewhere safe." The man pulled an empty crate alongside the bed and sat down upon it. "Do you remember what happened?"

"The storm. I was caught in the storm..." It all came back to him. "But my father was there. He was trying to rescue me...I can't remember anything after that. What happened?"

"You lost consciousness. We managed to pull your boat in. By that time the storm had begun to subside and your father managed to get you aboard."

"So you were on the boat with my father?"

The man nodded.

David could stave off his curiosity no longer. "Who are you?"

"My name is Janir."

"Where are you from? I've never seen you before. And where *are* we?"

"This is my new home. I arrived on the island only a few days ago. Your island council granted me sanctuary. I came from a land far from here."

David felt as though he'd been struck by lightning. Could it really be true? Could he finally have met someone from the outer lands? What was he doing on New Haven? Where was he from? What was life like out there? He had a thousand questions...

As if sensing David's racing mind, Janir smiled and held up a hand. "There will be time to discuss everything later. I'm a healer. We brought you here so I could treat your injury. Your parents are waiting for you outside. I imagine they'll be eager to see you."

Janir stood up and was about to leave when David stopped him. "Wait. It was *you* I saw yesterday at the edge of the forest, wasn't it? You were watching me. I saw you out of the corner of my eye but when I turned a split second later, you were gone." He narrowed his eyes, his forehead creasing as he stared up at the stranger. "What were you doing there? Why were you watching me?"

Janir paused a moment. "Yes, I happened to be in the vicinity, and I noticed you standing on the hilltop. You seemed upset. I was concerned about you."

David knew that there was more to it than that. "You knew— you *knew* what I was planning! That I was going to leave the island. It must have been you that told my father and brought him to rescue me...?"

Janir said nothing. An enigmatic smile played across his lips and his eyes twinkled in the candlelight. "Your parents are here to take you home. You have a concussion and will need to rest for a few days, but you'll be fine."

"Will I see you again?"

"I'll drop by to check on you," Janir said as he disappeared back into the shadowy tunnel.

"Wait," David called after him, but he was gone. There was still so much he wanted to know. He couldn't believe it. Aside from the Alazan merchants that traded with the island, Janir was the first outlander that David had ever met.

"David," came his mother's voice. Looking up, he saw both her and his father entering the cave. Jesanda raced over to the bed and embraced him with such force that it almost knocked the breath out of him. "Oh David, thank the twin suns."

"David, we were worried to death," his father said. It showed on their faces too. His father looked particularly strained: his broad-set face pale and drawn and his sandy-brown hair disheveled and damp.

David felt a surge of guilt. "I'm sorry."

His father reached out and wrapped his arms around his son. "I thought we were going to lose you," he said, a slight wheeze in his voice. "You've no idea how scared we were."

"David," Jesanda began awkwardly. "What were you doing? In the boat, I mean. Where were you going?"

Part of him was tempted to lie. He didn't know if he had the strength to deal with this particular confrontation right now. Yet it had been ignored and denied for too long. Now was the time to finally get it into the open and deal with it. "I was leaving."

"Why?" Jesanda's eyes widened.

"Because I don't belong here."

It was his father who responded. "What are you talking about? Of course you do."

"No, I don't." David could feel a fire in his belly as he looked up at them. "Don't lie to me! I *know*..."

Silence followed. David averted his eyes, shifting his gaze to the silk tapestry on the wall across the from the bed. There was nothing more he could say now. All he could do now was wait for them to respond. Jesanda spoke first. "David..." she whispered, her eyes welling with tears.

Jon put his arm around her and looked down at David. "Who told you?"

"It doesn't matter. It's true, isn't it?"

Jesanda reached out to take his hand. "David, we never intended you to find out, not like this. Not until you were older."

"But I had a right to know. And in a way I always have known. I've always felt like I'm an outsider; that I'm not really welcome here..."

"That's not true. You're our son and we love you."

"No." He pulled his hand back from her. "I'm not your son—not really. I need to know the truth. I need to know who I am."

Again there was a silence in which the only sound David could hear was the beating of his own heart. It was almost a relief when the silence was broken by his father. "Very well, David. We were going to tell you this when you were older. But it seems the time has come sooner than we'd anticipated..."

"Jon," Jesanda interrupted, turning to him pleadingly. There was fear in her eyes; perhaps the fear of losing her only son. But she knew that the truth could be withheld no longer so she let Jon continue.

"Eight years ago I was part of a trade expedition to the mainland," Jon said. "We met the Alazan traders at our rendezvous in the forest of Senrah. Everything went as planned and we the exchanged goods as usual. Afterward, when we were on our way back to the shore we heard something in the forest. At first, I thought it was the call of some forest animal, but as it got louder we realized it was the cry of an infant. We followed the noise to its source and found, lying in a clearing and wrapped in a golden shawl...a baby."

"Me," David whispered.

"Yes. To this day we don't know who left you there or why. We spent hours searching, but there was no one within a radius of several miles. It started to get dark. We knew we couldn't leave you alone in the forest, so we took you with us back to New Haven. We returned to the mainland for the next few days, looking for signs of whoever might have left you. But there was nothing. It was a mystery."

"So someone abandoned me...? Why would they do that?"

Jesanda sat down on the edge of David's bed. "We asked ourselves that a thousand times, David. But the truth is we may never know."

"What happened then?"

"Well, obviously someone had to take care of you," Jon said. "Your mother and I longed to have children, but were unable..."

"Until fate delivered a beautiful little boy into our lives," Jesanda said, her face lighting with a proud smile. "It was the happiest time of our lives. We adopted you, pledging to take care of you and to raise you as our son. And David, in every way that matters, you *are* our son. I never want you to forget that."

Jon continued, "We knew this day would come. Maybe we should have told you sooner. Maybe that would have made it easier. We know how confusing this must be for you. We know that part of you will probably always be curious about your origin. And when you're old enough, if you still want to set out and discover the truth for yourself, if that's something you really have to do, we won't stand in your way."

"But for now," Jesanda said, "you have to know that we love you. That's all that matters. You mean everything to us."

David's vision blurred. A teardrop tickled his skin as it rolled down his face and dripped off the edge of his chin. He didn't know what to think anymore. But as his parents embraced him, he began to wonder if perhaps he'd been wrong. Perhaps this was his home after all, and he just hadn't realized it.

Just as the storm clouds dissipated, things outwardly appeared to settle down in the wake of that traumatic day. But the shock-waves continued to reverberate and in many respects, the most painful blow was yet to come.

David's concussion lingered for several days, which he spent in bed as Janir had advised. But whilst his body recovered, his mind was far from rested. The light of truth had altered his world in a way that could never be undone. He now had to come to terms with the mystery that surrounded his very existence. His parents hadn't mentioned it again. In a way, it was almost as though the revelation hadn't slipped out at all.

Daily life resumed and David returned to school a week after the incident. It was virtually impossible to keep a secret on such a small island and he knew that just about everyone would have heard about what happened. From the moment he set foot outdoors he was acutely aware of having been a major topic of conversation. He disliked being the center of attention at the best of times, so he detested the self-consciousness he now experienced. But after a few days interest in him began to subside, much to his relief.

Back at home, concern soon shifted to David's father. Jon was not as resilient as his son. He had developed a cough that had spread to his chest and was steadily worsening. Sania, the island's head physician, had tried administering several remedies, but they had failed to help. Although loathe to admit it, she was at a loss to help further. Much to Sania's chagrin, Jesanda sought out Janir. The mysterious incomer appeared to possess a medicinal skill that Sania, for all her good intentions, lacked. At Jesanda's request, Janir agreed to examine Jon.

David was excited to see him again, although he wished the circumstances were different. By the time Janir arrived, Jon's condition was deteriorating. He was now bedridden, having difficulty breathing and was coughing up large amounts of fluid. As Janir examined him, Jesanda and David waited outside anxiously. When Janir emerged from the bedroom, David noticed the solemnity of his expression and immediately realized that things were bad.

"He has an acute infection of the lungs," Janir said. "I would guess he contracted the infection when he was out at sea in the storm."

David felt a sharp pang of guilt. He knew that he was responsible.

"It's possible he ingested some form of bacteria from the water. His body is doing its best to fight off the infection. All I can do is to aid it in its struggle. I can try giving him some herbs and extracts known to have anti-bacterial properties."

"Do whatever you have to," Jesanda said, her voice filled with desperate resolve.

Janir immediately set to work preparing several remedies, including a salve that he applied to Jon's chest, a compress to reduce his fever and three different tinctures made with ingredients he claimed to have obtained from far-off lands. Jesanda was fired with the determination that with Janir helping, Jon would soon recover.

David tried to help his mother as much as he could, assisting her around the house and trying to bolster her resolve whenever she succumbed to the intense fear bubbling beneath the surface. He shared that same fear and looming sense of loss, but it was confounded by another emotion. Guilt. It was his fault his father was ill. If it hadn't been for his disastrous attempt to flee the island, Jon would never have contracted this infection. If his father died, it would forever be on David's conscience.

A week passed, with Janir a constant presence in the house as he tended to Jon day and night. It became increasingly evident that while the treatment was helping to make Jon more comfortable, the underlying condition was worsening.

That evening Janir gathered Jesanda and David in the main room. The moment he asked to speak with them, David saw the fear in his mother's eyes.

"As you know," Janir said, "I've done everything I can think of to cure Jon's illness, but his condition is not responding to treatment. The infection is spreading throughout his body and though I've tried, there's nothing I can do to stop it..."

"No," Jesanda gasped. "There must be something more you can do."

Janir knelt by her side. "Jesanda, I fear I've done all I can. His *zhian* is weak."

"His zhian?"

"His life force. When the life essence begins slipping away, there's nothing anyone can do to prevent it. If his zhian has decided it's time to withdraw from the physical sheath, then any measures to counter that will merely delay the inevitable."

"What are you saying?"

"You have to be willing to let him go. His time is nearing and there's nothing we can do to change that. We can only accept it and in so doing help ease his passage."

"How can this be happening?" Jesanda cried, pulling back from Janir. "He's young, healthy—he's never been ill like this before! What if it's *you* that's done something to him? How do we even know we can trust you? We know nothing about you! For all we know, you could have..." She broke down into sobs.

Janir placed a hand on her trembling arm. "I know the pain you're feeling. I too have lost people dear to me. But you have to be strong; for your husband and your son..."

As if suddenly just remembering that David was still there, Jesanda reached out to him and held him tightly. He felt her teardrops falling upon the top of his head. David was too shocked to cry. His mind and senses felt numb.

"How much longer does he have?" Jesanda's voice was but a whisper.

"There's no way to be certain, but I don't think he has long. Perhaps a day at most. Take this time to be with him. Sit with him. Talk to him. Make the most of this time together. It's more than many people ever get."

An ominous silence descended upon the house as they kept a deathbed vigil. Jesanda never left Jon's bedside and David spent long periods sitting with her, as his father drifted in and out of consciousness. When he was awake they would talk, although the conversations were distinctly one-sided, for he was too weak to say much, and when he slept they sat quietly by his side. Janir remained in the house, keeping a discreet distance but available should he be needed.

David couldn't bear the pain that was tearing him apart. His father was dying and it was his fault. How could he live knowing that? Confused and racked with guilt, he was sitting alone in his room when he heard a call from the other room. It was his mother, urgently calling for Janir. Fearing the worst, he hurried to the other room, to find his father uncontrollably coughing up blood. Janir arrived just behind him.

"Please, do something," Jesanda cried.

Rushing to the bed, Janir propped him up and asked David to pass him a cup sitting on the bedside table. Janir held the cup to Jon's mouth and helped him drink the liquid, amid much coughing and spluttering. Almost immediately Jon's coughing fit subsided but he was still having difficulty breathing.

"You can help him, can't you?" Jesanda pleaded.

Janir shook his head. He got up and indicated that he would leave them alone now. David understood the subtext: that these might well be Jon's last moments.

Somehow Jon himself also seemed to sense this. Still gasping for breath, he motioned for David to come closer. "David..." He looked pale and weak; so unlike the strong and vibrant man that David had known. "I want you to know...that...I love you."

"I know. I love you too, father."

Jon used what strength he had remaining to clasp his son's hand. "I want you to...look after...your mother for me. Promise me you'll look after her..."

"I promise," David said, tears spilling from his eyes, one of which landed on his father's pillow. David lent down and kissed him on the forehead, stepping aside to let his mother do likewise.

"Jon," she whispered into his ear. "I love you. I always will." As she bent down and gently kissed him on the lips, Jon drifted out of consciousness. His labored breathing continued until he made what sounded like one, last exhalation. All went silent.

Was that it? Was that the end?

Not yet. For Jon struggled to draw yet another breath. He wheezed, his body contorting as he struggled to breathe. Jesanda remained by his side, holding his hand and whispering occasional words of comfort.

Every so often there was a pause between breaths and each time David thought this to be the end. But Jon's body continued clinging to life, oblivious to the uphill nature of its struggle. It was bad enough that his father was dying, but for him to linger in such agony was almost more than David could bear. It wasn't much longer however before Jon finally breathed his last breath; emptying his body not just of air, but of life.

The room fell silent. David looked down at his mother. Her eyes were glazed and she seemed quite oblivious to his presence. She continued holding Jon's hand as she buried her head in his chest. David stood beside her, frozen to the spot. He felt as though his heart had been carved out of his chest. It was over. His father was gone.

David sat alone in his room. He stared blankly at the wall, his tears long since dried. He heard a noise and turned he saw Janir standing in the doorway. "May I come in?"

David nodded reluctantly.

Janir sat down beside him on the bed. "This isn't your fault you know. You're not to blame for this."

David was startled that his feelings were so transparent, and to a stranger no less. "I am. If it wasn't for me he wouldn't have got sick."

"You don't know that, David," Janir said. "If it's our time, if we've reached our journey's end, then the event that triggers it is merely the catalyst. As hard as it is to accept, this was the end of your father's journey and nothing could have altered that. If he hadn't contracted this infection, something else would have happened sooner or later to send him on his way." David said nothing, but listened as Janir continued. "Losing someone you love is one of the most painful experiences in life. This isn't going to be easy, but I promise you, you'll get through this. I'll be here to help you." He paused. "I'm curious, David. What do the people of New Haven believe happens to the individual after death?"

"What do you mean? When someone dies, that's it. They fall asleep and never wake up." David felt the words choke in his throat as his eyes moistened.

"That's not entirely true, David. I want you to know that no one ever truly dies. The physical body is cast off, yes, but something of us lives on."

"What?"

"My people refer to it as the *zhian*; our life essence. It is not of this world, and therefore nothing in this world can harm it. It was never born and thus it will never die."

"How do you know that's true?"

"Let's just say I have some experience in these matters. If you like, we can talk about it another time."

David nodded.

"For now," Janir said, "I want you to be strong and to know that although your father may no longer be with you physically, he'll live on in a different way, and in a sense he'll always be with you."

As Janir got up to leave, David had one last question for him. "Janir..." the words almost died in is throat. He had to force himself to continue. "You're from the outer lands. What's it like out there?"

Janir paused, his face darkening as he stood in the doorway. His response was a single word. "Dangerous."

He departed, leaving David overcome by a sudden sense of fear. It clearly wasn't safe out there and David's reckless attempt to plunge headfirst into the unknown had brought devastating consequences. His father was dead because of it.

From that day on, David's life changed. Every day that followed was different in that a large part of his old life was forever missing. Life went on, of course. The suns continued to rise and fall, and the grieving process took its toll as David and his mother struggled to accept their loss and move on from it.

David struggled to deal with his grief and the accompanying guilt. Setting aside his quest for answers, he vowed to try to make things right. The best way he knew to do that was to fulfill his promise to his father.

All the while, Janir's warning of danger stuck with him. Although Janir refused to elaborate, the more David thought about it, the more he could actually sense it somehow. He still felt a deep pull to the distant shores, but it was now confounded by the knowledge that there was some terrible danger out there; some dark force lurking in the shadows—watching, waiting.

He couldn't shake the feeling that he was connected to it in some way, and that at some point it would catch up with him. Whether it took months or even years, it would eventually find him—and when it did, nothing would ever be the same again.

# CHAPTER THREE

# The Gift

*Year of Alejan, 15,008*

David awoke on the morning of his seventeenth birthday in a state of shock. He sat bolt upright in bed, his skin covered in sweat, and his heart pounding in his chest. Disorientated, it took him a moment to realize where he was and what had happened.

A *dream*. It was only a dream. The same dream he'd had for several nights now.

It had felt so real; the images and sensations so intensely vivid. He put a hand to his throat. It felt tight and constricted as though someone had actually been trying to strangle him.

The images remained etched in his mind. As before, he'd been alone in a dark cavern; the air thick, cold and musty. He knew he was in mortal danger; being hunted like an animal. Though he couldn't see it, he could sense his enemy so clearly—some kind of ancient, primordial evil, and it was intent on finding him.

Desperate to escape, he ran, only to be chased by the enemy's minions: demonic corpse-like men staggering toward him from the shadows. He ran as far as he could until he came to abyss blocking his path. Forced to stop in his tracks, the shadow men were upon him, their claws digging into his skin as they grabbed hold of him and reeled him back. With twisted, malformed faces and pale, blistered skin, they swarmed round him, grabbing hold of his neck and choking him. He felt waves of darkness crawling over his skin, seeping into him and devouring him; until all that was left was an all-consuming blackness.

Wiping the sweat from his forehead, David tried to shake off the nightmare as he climbed out of bed.

*It was just a dream. It doesn't mean anything.*

He stepped over to the window and pulled back the curtain. The sky was still dark and twinkling with stars. Dawn couldn't be far off, however, for the horizon was lightening and the birds beginning to stir.

David made his way to the washroom. Splashing his face with water, he tried to wash away the sense of terror that clung to his skin. Looking up from the basin, he caught sight of his own reflection in the mirror. His shoulder-length brown hair framed a tanned, square-set face, illuminated by the lamplight. His glistening brown eyes seemed to draw him in, as if they were a gateway to a whole other dimension; a hidden world that seemed to promise answers to questions he hadn't yet dared ask.

Although he felt calmer and the specifics of the nightmare began slipping away, an ominous feeling remained; a low-level anxiety gnawing in the pit of his belly. He found himself unable to shake the strange feeling that something was different today—that something was about to change.

By the time he washed and dressed, the sun was shining through his window and the birds chattering contentedly as they welcomed the new day. He found his mother in the kitchen preparing first meal. The moment he entered the room his attention was drawn to a wooden box sitting upon the table. He'd never seen the box before. As his eyes settled upon it he felt an inexplicable sense of excitement and trepidation.

"David!" Jesanda bounded up to him, her face lighting with a broad smile as she embraced him. "Happy birthday."

"Thanks," he said with a smile, somehow struggling to take his eyes from the box.

"Seventeen years old," she said, "I can hardly believe it."

Of course it wasn't his real birthday, for that was as much an unknown as the place of his origin. Rather it was the anniversary of the day his father had found him on the mainland. "What are we having for first meal?" he asked.

"Your favorite: junjat with olak berries." Jesanda paused. "But first, I have something for you."

"Oh?"

Jesanda reached over to the table and picked up the box. David felt his chest tighten as she opened it. Inside was an amulet. It was a turquoise crystal shaped like a half moon, attached to a silver chain. The smooth, transparent stone was engraved with a symbol. It looked like half a star, suggesting the amulet was incomplete; that it had been broken in half.

"What is it?" he whispered.

"When you were a baby," Jesanda began awkwardly, "when your father found you in the forest of Senrah, this was the only possession you had with you aside for the blanket you were wrapped in. You were wearing it around your neck."

David was stunned. "Why didn't you tell me about it before?"

"Your father and I decided to safe-keep it for you until you were old enough. We both agreed that on your seventeenth birthday you'd have come of age to receive this part of...your inheritance."

David didn't know what to say. He was fascinated by this missing link to his past. He was also a little annoyed that it had been kept from him all these years. It was his, after all. But he could see how difficult this was for his mother. She'd never been comfortable when it came to discussing his true origin and this was clearly a difficult occasion for her. Deciding not to make it any harder on her, he set aside his grievance and nodded thoughtfully.

"Maybe I should have given it to you sooner, I don't know," Jesanda said. "It's been difficult knowing how best to deal with things. But you're seventeen years old. You're a young man now. And this belongs to you."

Jesanda held out the box. David reached out to pick it up. The moment he touched the amulet he felt a jolt of electricity surge through his body. He staggered back, dropping it the ground.

"What happened?" Jesanda gasped.

"I don't know." The amulet lay on the floor at his feet. "When I picked it up, I felt this...*surge*..."

"That's never happened before."

David reached down to pick it up. He was cautious at first, testing to make sure it wouldn't shock him again. Fortunately it didn't, but as he lifted it he noticed something strange. "Look, it's changed color!" Sure enough, the stone had changed from its original turquoise to a deep violet with dashes of sapphire.

"That's never happened before either..."

David held the amulet in his hands, feeling his entire body tingle with an almost electrical glow. Just setting eyes on this mystery object had rekindled a burning desire he'd set aside many years ago; the desire to know who he was and where he was from. He was desperate to know everything about this crystal—what it was, what it symbolized and why it had been left as his sole possession in the world.

Jesanda, for her part, seemed unnerved by it. It was alien to her and served as a pointed reminder that so too was her son. It represented a part of him that she'd spent many years trying to forget. "Do you want me to put it somewhere safe for you?" She held out the box.

"No, I want to wear it." He undid the clasp on the silver chain and handed it to her.

"Are you sure? What if it shocks you again?"

"I don't think it will."

With a barely concealed frown, she took the amulet and fastened it around his neck.

David looked down at the crystal hanging over his heart and felt a buzz of excitement. It was as though he'd been reunited with a missing part of himself. What he failed to realize, however, was that like every gift, it would come with a price.

The twin suns blazed against a cloudless lilac sky. The air was cool, fresh and scented with the sweet blossom of the tuanya trees lining the island's east side. David's boots scuffed against the ground as he made his way through the town and along the farm road. Once again he would spend the morning laboring in the fields. It wasn't a job he particularly enjoyed, but it was harvest season, a time in which the islanders worked together to assist the farmers, so he was happy to contribute.

It was the afternoons that David truly lived for. That was when he worked with Janir, training as his apprentice. From the moment he'd first met Janir all those years ago, David had been determined to spend as much time with him as possible and to learn all that he could about him. He'd been delighted when Janir had accepted him as his apprentice and his training had begun about a year ago.

He knew he'd wanted to become a healer from the time of his father's death, and Janir was the perfect teacher. Thus far his lessons had been fairly rudimentary. Janir had educated him in the uses of various herbs and roots in medicinal application and given him lessons in physiology, nature and methods of healing. All of this interested him, but David knew that the truly fascinating lessons were yet to come. He was convinced that Janir's knowledge extended far beyond the mixing of herbal remedies. He just wondered when Janir would see fit to entrust him with his secrets.

"David!"

He turned to see his friend Darien. Darien was about four years older than David and was one of the most popular young men on the island, a fact largely accountable to his roguish charm and lithe good looks. Taller and more muscular than David, Darien had long black hair tied into a ponytail, mischievous dark eyes and an air of confidence and bravado that people found either endearing or arrogant.

"You're actually on time for once?" David laughed mockingly. "What's farmer Doran going to think? Something must be terribly wrong with the world if Darien's on time for work."

"I wouldn't want to get myself a reputation for being predictable now, would I?" Darien laughed as he caught up with David. He slapped his hand on David's shoulder. "So birthday boy, how does it feel to be seventeen years old?"

"It feels good."

"What's that?" Darien motioned to David's amulet.

"A present from my mother. Apparently, this was the only possession I had when I was found in the forest of Senrah as a baby."

"Ah. Nice," Darien said, raising an eyebrow. "You know, you're bound to attract the girls' attention with that." He laughed, adding, "If you do, by the way—I want one."

David rolled his eyes. "As if you need it."

"Well, on occasion life does present its challenges." Something caught Darien's attention up ahead. "Speaking of which..."

David looked up to see a young woman carrying a basket appear from one of the side-paths leading from the farm house.

Darien's eyes lit up. "It's Janna!"

Janna was the life-long object of Darien's affections. It wasn't difficult to see why. Even when wearing only simple overalls she had the ability to turn heads, for she possessed a soft yet captivating beauty. With wavy blonde hair, her skin was smooth and her blue-green eyes alluring and mysterious. David didn't know that much about Janna other than the fact she was around Darien's age and worked in her father's bakery in the town square. David recognized some traits in her that he could relate to himself, particularly from his childhood. She seemed very reserved and spent much of her spare time alone. While friendly and polite, she clearly disliked being the center of attention and spent much of her time trying to fade into the background. Perhaps she would have been more successful had she not been blessed with a beauty that drew attention rather than deflected it.

"I'm going to ask her," Darien said.

"Ask her what?"

"What do you think? If she'll go to the Festival dance with me!"

"I'll believe *that* when I see it. You've been saying you're going to ask her for weeks now."

"And I will. I've just been waiting for the right opportunity," Darien whispered. He grinned boyishly as Janna approached. "Good day, Janna!"

"Good day," she replied.

"Beautiful morning, isn't it?"

David smiled politely and, taking Darien's lead, stopped to talk to her. Janna didn't seem particularly keen to engage in conversation, but nonetheless felt obliged to stop. "It is," she replied, looking up at the cloudless purple sky.

"I guess we need to make the most of it before Winter sets in, huh?"

"I suppose so."

"So what are you doing this morning?"

"Just some deliveries for my father. You?"

"David and I are on our way to the farm. We're working in the fields again today. It's been really busy with harvest and all."

Though David was by no means an expert on girls himself, he knew that such banal small talk was not the way to win a woman's heart, especially a woman who posed as much of a challenge as Janna. Darien was going to have to try a lot harder than this. "So, it's the Festival next week," Darien blurted. "I was wondering if you would...if you would like to go to the dance with me?"

There was an awkward pause as she considered her response. "Thanks for the offer," she said with a genuine smile. "But I never go to the dance."

Darien, however, was not going to give up without a fight. "But you really have to make an exception this year. You'll enjoy it! I promise you."

"Is that so? What makes you so sure?"

"Because *I'll* be with you!"

Janna smiled and rolled her eyes, which probably wasn't the reaction Darien was hoping for. "You never give up, do you?"

"Oh, I give up. Just not when I'm so close to achieving victory."

For a moment, David could see that Janna was actually considering Darien's offer, as if part of her was tempted to say yes. But ultimately something stopped her and whilst her final answer was delivered gently, it was nonetheless resolute. "I appreciate the offer, but the dance isn't my kind of thing. I hate big gatherings. I just get overwhelmed by all the noise and bustle. I'm sure you'll have no problem finding someone else to go with." She paused for a moment. "If you'll excuse me, I really have to get back to work. Have a nice day."

"You too," replied a crestfallen Darien.

Janna smiled apologetically and set on her way.

"Don't worry," David tried to console his friend. "She's right, you'll easily find someone else."

"But I don't *want* anyone else. I want her. And I haven't given up on her yet."

"Come on, we'd better get going."

"Have you found a date for the dance yet?"

"Didn't I tell you? I asked Cara yesterday and she said yes."

"So what do you have that I don't?"

David shrugged. "I guess I just don't set my sights on impossible goals."

"I don't believe in impossibility. I'll win her over in the end, you'll see. I think I just need to readjust my strategy."

"You don't *have* a strategy..."

"Yeah, and what would you know about anything?"

"What would I know? I'm the one with a date."

"Let's just get to the farm, all right?" Darien huffed as they continued down the road. "My day's off to a bad enough start without you making it worse."

The morning passed quickly, with David in high spirits. His thoughts kept returning to the amulet. It was a link to a world he had long dreamt of as a child. As he'd grown up and made a life for himself on the island, it was a dream he'd more or less abandoned. Yet this amulet served as a reminder of who he really was and had reawakened an old yearning to unravel the mystery of his existence.

Farmer Doran provided refreshments at midday, after which the morning workforce finished up and left to attend their other duties. All able-bodied islanders had a job; a person's vocation usually determined by the family line of work. For instance, Darien came from a family of fisherfolk and it was a job he loved. Indeed, he wasn't truly at home unless he was out at sea. Most people were happy to follow in the family tradition, although some opted for a different line of work. David was one such example. When Janir arrived on the island he quickly became renowned for his skills as a healer and following the death of Sania some years back, had been appointed the island's head physician. David was honored to be have been accepted as Janir's first and so far only trainee.

After making plans to meet up at night for his party, David said farewell to Darien. He hurried through the Sharedo forest and down to the eastern shore of the island, where Janir still resided in one of the caves. Although the island council had offered him a 'proper house' on several occasions, Janir had stubbornly refused, insisting that he was perfectly content with his current dwelling. The cave suited him well and was a home that he had made quite his own. He'd explained to David that it made him feel connected with nature and also provided him with a solitude he relished.

"Janir," he called as he entered the cave. He was eager to show Janir the gift from his mother, wondering if he might recognize its design.

Janir was nowhere to be seen. Assuming that he was in the back section, David peered through and found Janir standing at his workbench, a spherical metal object in his hands. It was the timepiece he had been working on for several weeks.

Janir looked up. "David, I'm sorry, I must have lost track of time." Seemingly aware of the irony, he placed the timepiece down.

"Is everything all right?"

"I don't know," Janir said, narrowing his eyes. "Something isn't quite right. Something has changed..."

"What?"

"I can't tell yet, but it's something important. I could see it in the stars and I can feel it in the air. It's subtle as of yet, but even the subtlest of changes can yield the most far-reaching of consequences..."

David recalled having experienced the same feeling earlier that day. He thought about quizzing him further but, realizing that Janir was unlikely to be any more forthcoming, he opted to change the topic. "Do you notice anything different about me today?"

It took Janir only a second to notice the crystal around David's neck. David watched as Janir's eyes fixed upon the amulet. He remained silent as he moved closer to inspect the talisman, cautiously lifting it, taking in every last detail. "David, where did you get this?"

Janir listened as David related the story behind the object. "So what do you think?" David asked. "Do you recognize it?"

"I don't know," Janir said, still unable to take his eyes off the amulet.

"Have you seen it before? Or anything like it?"

"No, I've never seen craftsmanship of the like."

David knew that he was holding something back.

Janir raised a hand to his head and ran it over his graying plaited hair. David studied his face, desperately trying to gauge what he was thinking. "How could I have forgotten," Janir whispered, his forehead creasing and his eyes distant. "David, I need some time to meditate on this. We will discuss it later."

"Why not now?"

"Because I must find the answers before I can possibly hope to share them."

"When will I come back?"

"Tomorrow afternoon, same time as usual."

"But you'll be at my birthday celebration this evening, won't you? It's in the town square. Everyone is coming."

"Yes, yes, of course. I'll try to make it," Janir responded. But David could see that his mind was elsewhere.

Without another word, David bowed before his teacher and departed, confused and discontented by his reaction. He hadn't known what Janir would say about the crystal, but he hadn't anticipated such a strange reaction. Janir seemed shocked, even scared by it—and David had never seen Janir scared by anything.

The taste was bitter. Nevertheless, Janir chewed and swallowed the perota root. It had been many years since he'd traversed the inner planes and he felt the need of a medicinal aid. He soon felt the effects of the drug as it coursed through his nervous system. He assumed his meditative posture and, closing his eyes, tried to focus his mental energy upon reaching the gates of Shanadon.

And, soon enough...

*His mind became the universe...*

*And the universe became his mind.*

*"Welcome back, Janir,"* came an echoing voice.

*Janir found himself on an endless stretch of beach. Beneath the cloudless sky the tide was far out, the water a glorious cobalt blue, the sand luminous golden-white, each grain shining as though a whole world of its own.*

*In front of him appeared Delei, his spirit guide. She looked just as he remembered her: radiant and ethereal, draped in flowing white robes, her silver hair cascading over slender shoulders. Yet there was something different about her. She exuded anxiety and concern, two emotions he would previously have thought as being antithetical to her nature.* "It has been a long time," *she said.*

"It has. For which I apologize..."

"You tried to ignore it. You tried to forget. Only now you can do so no longer. The time has come, Janir."

"For what...?"

"The final battle in a war that has been waged for countless eons. The end draws near. Victory or defeat will soon be decided."

"Then it's true, isn't it? The prophecies were correct. He is the one..."

"You already know this to be true."

"I suppose I've known it all along. As I settled into to life on the island it became all too easy to forget; to ignore what was standing right before me. But when I saw him with the Key, I knew I could no longer deny the truth, or hide from the inevitable. Please, Delei, tell me what I must do; tell me what I need to know..."

"Nearly ten years have passed since you left the outer lands behind. In that time much has changed..."

*Janir saw images flash before him: images of places and lands he had once known, including Taribor, his homeland. A black cloud engulfed the cities and towns in a pall of darkness. He saw the robotic soldiers of the enemy—bleak, terrifying and inhu-*

man—marching across the land; armies numbering in their tens of thousands. Massive airships loomed over the cities, obscuring the suns. Processions of troops trampled through the towns, weapons in hand, killing anyone who stood in their way. A feeling of terror accompanied the images: stark, primal fear, exacerbated by the helplessness of defeat.

"The Alliance has continued its conquest of the inhabited territories," Delei told him. "Its power has grown immeasurably in terms of territory, military strength and technological advancement. They stand on the verge of world domination. But as you know, world domination is not enough, and the Alliance is but the instrument of a much darker force. Alanar is being torn apart, Janir. There is only one hope..."

"David...?"

"The Key has been awakened—and they know it has. They have been silently lurking in the shadows for centuries, waiting for this moment, watching for this signal. Now they know that the Key exists, they will find it...and soon."

"What must I do?"

"Prepare. Events have been set in motion to assist you along your path. You must wait until you receive the appropriate signal and then follow the directions you are given. You must trust us implicitly, Janir. Everything depends on it."

David relied on the moonlight to guide him along the darkened forest path. His birthday celebration was over and everyone had gone home, their bellies full after a hearty meal and their spirits satisfied following a night of song and dance. Not every birthday was celebrated in such a manner but one's seventeenth was considered a significant occasion, marking the true onset of adulthood. It was customary for family and friends to gather for a big celebration.

Jesanda had pulled out all the stops to ensure that the party was a success and David had thanked her for such an enjoyable evening. He'd eaten all he could manage, drank perhaps a little too much wine and had fun sharing stories and laughter with his friends and fellow islanders. Not so long ago he'd have found being the center of such a social gathering uncomfortable and awkward, but the fact he had enjoyed it highlighted to him just how much he'd relaxed into island life.

His only disappointment was that Janir had failed to turn up. Given his puzzling behavior earlier that day, David was concerned. Something wasn't right. As his mother and the others headed home, David decided to go and check on him.

All around him the trees stretched up like tall sentinels. High above, the stars sparkled like fireflies in the sky, alongside the moon, a silver orb that bathed the forest below in a translucent glow. Aside for the rustling of the trees and the cooing of a distant owl, silence pervaded.

Striding through the forest, David began to feel as though someone was watching and listening amid the silence.

*It's just because it's dark,* he chastised himself. *Don't be such a child.*

But rationale failed to placate the uneasy feeling in his belly. There was someone nearby. Their presence was unmistakable.

David turned, scanning the area, but couldn't make out anything in the dark. Hastening his speed, he heard a noise behind—footsteps crunching on the leaves.

He was being followed.

As he began running, it became clear that he'd inadvertently strayed from the main path. Unable to see where he was going in the dark, and his senses dulled by one too many glasses of wine, he tripped on a stray log and came crashing to the ground.

Looking up, he saw his pursuer bearing down on him. David recoiled, but his assailant reached down and grabbed his arm, yanking him off the ground.

Pulling himself free, David staggered back. He stared at the man's face. A wave of dread swept over him. He'd never seen him before. Whoever this man was, he did not belong on New Haven.

# CHAPTER FOUR

# Harbinger

"Who are you?" David demanded.

"My name is Naranyan." A beam of silver moonlight washed over his face, revealing elaborate tribal markings across his forehead. No older than thirty, his skin was a shade darker than David's. Long black hair fell over his broad shoulders. He wore an animal-skin mantle and leggings, his muscular chest bedecked with necklaces made of shells and small bones. He was armed: a leather quiver strapped to his back containing a bow and arrows. David felt uneasy as the man studied him, his dark eyes gravitating to the amulet around David's neck. "You are David?"

"How do you know my name?"

"That is unimportant. I am here to bring you warning. Your life is in danger, as are the lives of everyone on this island. If you wish to live, you must leave here now."

A dozen thoughts raced through David's mind, but all that spilled out was a single word. "What?"

"You heard me. You are in great danger here. You must leave this place as soon as you possibly can."

"But why?"

"It is a long story. This is neither the time nor place to go into specifics. But know this: dark forces are at work and there are people out there who will stop at nothing to get their hands on you."

"Me—? Why me?"

Naranyan motioned to David's amulet. "Do you have any idea what *that* is?"

"It's just an amulet."

"An amulet?" Naranyan's tone was almost derisive. "It is much, much more than that. It is a *Key*. The most powerful key in all of Alanar."

"A key to what?"

"That you will learn later. For now, all you need know is that it yields a power unimaginable; a power sought by many. There are people out there—evil, twisted, ruthless people—that will go to any lengths to find this Key, and they do not care who or what they have to destroy along the way."

David felt a chill move down his spine. "Then they can have it. I don't want to cause trouble, I—"

Naranyan reached out and grabbed hold of the amulet. David tried to pull back but his grip was firm. "You must never give this Key to anyone, do you understand me?" His eyes seared through David, ablaze with indignation. David could only nod. "In time all will be explained. Until then you must make sure it never leaves your sight. It is yours, and yours alone."

Naranyan let go of the amulet. David let out a sharp exhale, taking a step back. "Who is it that's after this 'key'?"

"All you need know for now is that they are coming. That is why you must leave here now."

"And go where?"

"Head for the forest of Senrah on the mainland. I have been told that the enemy will strike within three cycles of the suns. You must be away from here by then. You may want to warn the others on your island, for no one will be safe when they attack. They will tear this island apart piece by piece as they search for the Key."

The silence was broken only by the sound of a hooting owl and the rustling of leaves in the breeze. David eyed him warily. "I don't know anything about you. How do I know I can trust a word that you say?"

"Because the only alternative is death. Death to you; to every man, woman and child on this island—death to us all."

"How do you know all this?"

"I have my sources. You must listen to me and listen well, for I speak the truth. I cannot overstate the danger you are in."

Naranyan turned and glanced around the forest, like a wild animal scanning for threats. "I must go now, but we will see each other again shortly…"

"In the forest of Senrah?"

"Yes. Remember, there is little time. Make plans to leave here as soon as possible. I bid you safe journey. May Hershala guide your way." With a nod of his head, Naranyan turned and strode off, disappearing into the darkened forest.

David was left alone, stunned and confused.

Janir. The first person he thought of was Janir. He'd know what to do.

Wasting no time, David raced along the moonlit path, his mind and senses a blur as he hastened to Janir's cave on the eastern shore. Upon arriving, he found Janir sitting cross-legged on the ground, deep in meditation. The air was still and tranquil, fragranced by the sprigs of flowers and herbs hanging from the walls; a dozen candles illumining the cave in a golden glow. Janir opened his eyes and looked up. Judging by the look on his face, David's arrival hadn't been unanticipated.

"Janir, I need to talk with you." Without waiting for a response, he related his story at breakneck speed. "I was on my way here when I met this stranger in the forest. I don't know where he was from but he knew my name and he seemed to know all about my amulet. He told me there were people after me; that they were going to attack the island and that—"

"Calm down, David." Janir got up from the ground. "I think you should sit down while I make you a cup of cadahn tea. It soothes the nerves."

"Janir, didn't you hear me? Someone's going to attack the island, and you're talking about *tea?*"

Janir held up his hand. "Try to relax. Use the breathing techniques I taught you. Once you've calmed down, you can tell me the whole story from the beginning. Yes?"

David sighed and nodded.

As Janir disappeared into the other chamber, David sat down on a wooden chair and, heeding Janir's advice, spent a moment practicing a breathing exercise to help regain his equilibrium.

Janir returned and presented him with a steaming cup of cadahn tea. Pungent and earthy, it was very much an acquired taste, but it did help ease his nerves. At Janir's prompting, David began his story again from the beginning, trying to recall every last detail of what Naranyan had told him. Janir listened, remaining silent until David had finished. "I should have been expecting this," Janir muttered.

"What do you mean?"

"I mean I've long known that this day was inevitable. I tried to forget; to convince myself that perhaps I was mistaken—that perhaps we'd be spared this ordeal..."

As often was the case, David was baffled by Janir's enigmatic response. "Do you know who this man was; what he was talking about?"

"Yes, I do."

"Then who is he?"

"He is a messenger sent by the Guardians."

"The Guardians?"

"Beings that exist at a different dimensional frequency. Our two worlds and countless other realms co-exist interdependently. The Guardians serve as custodians, overseeing the events of each realm, for each has an impact on the others, like ripples carrying across the surface of a pond. Whenever something threatens to disrupt the balance between realms, the Guardians must intervene to maintain the universal equilibrium."

"And they sent him here to warn me?"

Janir took a sip of tea and nodded. "These are dangerous times. Here on New Haven we live a sheltered life, tucked away from the outside world; a world that is unquestionably alien to you and to everyone on this island. There are so many things out there, David: magnificent wonders beyond description as well as nightmarish terrors that would chill you to your core."

This was the first time that Janir had spoken of the outer lands, in spite of the many years in which David had pressed him for information. His mentor's face darkened as he continued. "For aeons, there's been a delicate balance between the polarities of light and dark. But now the balance has tipped and darkness threatens to eclipse this world in a reign of terror. It's spreading across the planet and it infects like a disease." Janir paused. "This disease is personified by the Sevari Alliance, a tyrannical empire that seeks dominion over all: conquering and subjugating lands all across the planet, wiping out who or whatever stands in its path to supreme power. I've been told that the Alliance now holds two-thirds of the planet in its stranglehold of power."

"If this Sevari Alliance is so powerful, how come we've never heard of it?"

"As I said, we live a sheltered existence here. New Haven is but a pinprick on the map and of no significance to the enemy. Until now, that is."

"Then it's the Alliance that's after this amulet?"

Janir nodded.

"Why?"

Janir set his cup down on a nearby table. "It's a long story and we don't have time to go into it at this very moment. Suffice to say, what you now wear around your neck is no ordinary talisman."

"Naranyan said it was a key."

"Yes. The key to a power that must never fall into the hands of the enemy."

David got up from his seat and began pacing. "If it's so important, then what in the twin suns am I doing with it? How did it come to me?"

"It's not that simple, David. I don't think the Key came to you. Rather, I believe you came to it."

"What do you mean?"

"You'll find out soon enough, I promise. For now, we must heed Naranyan's warning. The Alliance is coming."

"Why now? The Key's been on the island, hidden in a drawer for as long as I've been here. Why is it only *now* they're coming? Why not five years ago, or ten, or fifteen?"

"As I understand it, the Key is alive. The moment you took possession of it, the long-dormant crystal awoke from its slumber, activated by your mere touch."

David stopped in his tracks. "When I touched it, something happened. I felt this surge of energy and the crystal changed color."

"Indeed. Dark forces have been lurking in the shadows for centuries, watching and waiting for this moment. They were aware the instant the Key awoke and it will only be a matter of time before they trace its location here."

Repressing a shudder, David resumed his pacing, struggling to reconcile all that he'd just been told. After a moment's silence, he stopped and turned to Janir. "I can understand the Key holds some kind of power that the Alliance wants—but why *me*? Naranyan specifically said they wanted me."

"Without you, the Key is of no use. It was you that activated the Key, David. No one else could have done it. And it is you—and you alone—who can use it."

"Me..."

"You are the Custodian of the Key. It's not a role you consciously chose, but it's a role the fates have thrust upon you and whether you like it or not, there's no way to change that. We can discuss this another time, but for now there are more pressing issues. Naranyan is correct, we must leave the island."

"Then we have to tell people. We have to get them to evacuate the island."

Janir stood, clasping his hands behind his back, the candlelight reflecting in his green eyes. "We shall go before the island Council tomorrow and inform them of the situation. When the Alliance strikes, no one will be safe. The Alliance abhors freedom; they see free people as either a resource to be exploited or an annoyance to be eradicated."

"What if the Council doesn't believe us? What if they decide to do nothing?"

"I pray they would not be that foolish. But whatever their decision, we must get you off this island as soon as possible. Naranyan said we have less than three days to prepare. We must, therefore, work within that timeframe. The Council will be in session tomorrow morning. I'll meet you outside the town hall first thing in the morning."

"First thing," David echoed.

"It's late. You'd best go home now." Janir placed a hand on David's shoulder. "I understand how overwhelming this is, David, but I'm relying on you to keep a clear head. Don't let this overwhelm you. Remain strong and steadfast and we'll get through this together. Now, go home and get some sleep. I'll see you in the morning."

They said farewell and David left the warmth and security of Janir's abode and began his journey home, up the cliffs and through the darkened forest, which had never seemed as sinister and lonely. Despite Janir's stipulation that he retain a level head, David's mind was racing as he struggled to assimilate all that he'd learned in what had been a long and eventful night. It was almost too much to take in: that people were hunting him for an object he hadn't even known had existed until that very morning.

When he arrived home, he crept through the house, undressed and climbed into bed. He lay awake for what seemed like hours, tossing and turning, his mind relentlessly replaying both his encounter with Naranyan and his subsequent discussion with Janir. It was some time before his exhausted mind and body finally gave in to the merciful release of sleep.

The following day started off like any other. David washed, dressed and joined his mother for first meal. He opted not to tell her about his encounter in the forest, at least not yet. He would wait until he and Janir had been to the island Council.

As they ate, Jesanda reminded him that she'd be helping out at the Festival in the afternoon. With all that had happened, David had forgotten about the Festival. It was set to commence in the afternoon with the Magistrate's opening address, followed by a grand feast in the evening. The festivities would continue for the next five days with a variety of events, displays, and banquets, culminating in the famous Festival dance. Although if Naranyan was to be believed, the Alliance would be here long before then.

After they finished their meal, David helped his mother wash up, said farewell and hurried off to the town center. As he walked down the streets, Naranyan's warning echoed through his mind: *"Your life is in grave danger...you must leave here now."*

David felt his world now shrouded by a veil of darkness. The island was a place of safety and comforting familiarity no longer. It was now the target of an unknown danger that threatened to destroy everything he'd ever known. For the best part of his life, he'd yearned to learn about the outside world and to discover the truth of his origin. Now that he'd had a taste of it, he realized the price of such knowledge—specifically, that he might learn things he didn't want to know.

Entering the main boulevard, David found the town center already a hub of activity. Even at this early hour preparations for the Festival had begun in earnest. As shopkeepers opened their doors for what would be a busy day's trade, people busily set up stalls and arranged street decorations. Streamers and lanterns hung from the white stone buildings and dangled from palm trees. Garlands and banners were strewn along the balconies, interspersed with blooming flowers.

David made his way through the town square, at the center of which stood the town hall, a marble two-story building nestled among a grove of ephrania trees; their wispy branches in full bloom with lavender flowers. David sat beneath one of the trees, beams of sunlight bathing him in a golden glow. He would wait here for Janir.

The Council members gradually arrived and filed into the hall. David watched as Magistrate Arick, the elected community leader—an overweight, grey-haired man in his fifties with a round, reddish face—haughtily strode down the street and up the steps into the hall without so much as a sideward glance.

Not far behind him was a smartly dressed woman in her late-fifties. It was David's former school mistress, Mariane, who now served on the island council. Her sandy-grey hair was tied into a bun, accentuating her penetrating eyes and lined face. Everything about her demeanor suggested an intelligent, forthright, and slightly austere woman. "David," she greeted him with a raised eyebrow. "What are you doing here?"

"I'm just waiting for someone," he answered with a slight shrug.

"I see," she said. She narrowed her eyes, evidently sensing that something wasn't quite right. "Very well then." With a nod, she carried on her way. If it hadn't been for the fact she was due at the council meeting she would probably have stopped to question him further. David watched as she marched up the steps and entered the arched doorway into the hall, closely followed by another two councilors.

Janir arrived shortly thereafter, looking elegant in his most regal garb: a patterned blue shirt, dark gray trousers and a flowing black cloak. As David watched him move, he was again struck by Janir's dual nature. While he was one of the gentlest and most compassionate people David had ever met, this sensitivity was balanced by an almost tangible sense of power and presence that pervaded his every word and action. David admired him greatly and looked up to him as a father figure. Indeed, he now considered Janir part of his family. But in spite of this, David still knew very little about him in terms of who he was and where he was from, for Janir had shared virtually nothing of his past. Despite having lived on the island for nine years, he remained an enigma. David got up to greet his mentor. "Good morning."

"And to you, David," he said, his face already set in an expression of utmost seriousness. It was clear that he had readied himself for the unenviable task of persuading the council to evacuate the island. "Let's get this over with, shall we?"

Ascending the steps, they entered the hall and made their way to a large door engraved with the words 'Council Room'. Taking a deep breath, Janir rapped his knuckles on the door, waited for a second and then pushed the door open.

David followed him inside. It was the first time he'd ever been in the Council room. Vast and elegantly furnished, the oak paneled walls gave rise to a high ceiling with wood beams interlacing the white plasterwork. The wall to David's right was dominated by a large window overlooking the town's houses, gardens, trees and parkland, the calm turquoise sea visible in the distance. Seated around a circular table at the center of the room, the councilors turned to the door, startled by the intrusion.

"Janir—?" Magistrate Arick exclaimed, his forehead creasing in annoyance. It was deemed most improper to interrupt the Council when it was in session.

"Magistrate, councillors: we must speak with you urgently," Janir said. "We bring distressing news that holds dire implications for everyone on New Haven."

There was a moment of silence. "You had better sit down then," Arick said cautiously, gesturing to some empty chairs stacked in the corner of the room.

Janir shook his head. "I'd rather stand, thank you." David stood by his side, unsure what, if anything, Janir expected him to say.

"So, what is this 'distressing news' that you bring?" David couldn't help but notice a look of skepticism, even antagonism, on Arick's face. He was a stuffy, middle-aged traditionalist, notoriously obstinate and set in his ways. David knew that Janir would have a difficult time making him listen.

"We must initiate an immediate evacuation of New Haven."

Arick's eyes narrowed. "What?"

"We've been warned of an impending attack on this island."

"An attack? By whom?"

"The Alliance."

A murmur erupted from the councilors, who shifted in their seats, exchanging concerned glances. "The Alliance?" one woman gasped, the horror evident in her voice.

"You *know* about the Alliance?" David asked. No one answered.

Arick lifted his hand and pointed at Janir. "Who told you this?"

"Someone who knows only too well the terror and destruction wrought by the Alliance."

"And where is this person now?"

"He is gone. He came only to warn us that the Alliance is on its way, and that it will strike within three days."

"That's preposterous! What reason would the Alliance possibly have to attack *us?*"

"What reason does the Alliance have to attack anyone? Power, territory, resources, domination! The Alliance will stop at nothing until it holds dominion over all of Alanar."

Sancho, one of the older councilors, ventured: "In all the years we've been on New Haven—several generations—we've been fortunate enough never to have heard the word 'Alliance' spoken in this hall..."

"Times are changing," Janir said. "The Alliance has not diminished in the years since the first settlers arrived in New Haven. On the contrary, it has grown! Your forefathers may have thought that a secluded island in the North Western reaches would be safe from Alliance encroachment; and back then, maybe they were right. But that is no longer the case. As I said, the Alliance is on its way as we speak. We must leave the island before they arrive."

"This is ridiculous, Janir," declared Arick. "We need firm, irrefutable proof if your claim is to be taken seriously."

"I've been given all the proof that I need." Janir took a step toward the council. "In deep meditation, I was granted a vision: a vision in which I saw the Alliance invading, conquering and destroying lands all across the world. They have amassed armies numbering in their millions and have acquired technology the likes of which Alanar has never before seen."

"You expect us to uproot the entire island on the basis of a *dream* you had?"

"It was no dream. It was a *warning*. And we must heed it..."

"Listen to him," David spoke up in an attempt to allay the helplessness he felt.

By now the council was in a furore. Arick, determined to regain control of the meeting, stood up and called for "Silence!" He then turned his attention to Janir and David. "We have lived here in peace for the best part of a century. In fact, this very day we celebrate the eighty-fourth anniversary of our arrival on this island! Eighty-four years of peace, safety and security—"

"Then what about the Kellian Raids?" Janir interrupted. "Surely you remember them, Magistrate? Because it demonstrated one thing: that although we think we're safe here, we have no defenses. If we just sit here waiting for the Alliance to arrive, we're all as good as dead."

Mariane stood up. "Magistrate, I agree that such claims seem somewhat outlandish. But I know Janir and I trust his judgment. He would not have come before the council without due cause and ample justification."

"Very well," Arick exclaimed in reluctant concession. "We shall consider Janir's...*claims*...but not today. It's the first day of the Festival and—"

"Did you not hear me?" Janir raised his voice. "The Alliance is on its way. We don't have time to deliberate! We have to leave *now*."

"And go where?" asked another of the councilors. "This island is our home. It's all we've ever known. If we're not safe from the Alliance here, then where will we be safe?"

Arick gave an exaggerated nod of agreement and sat back down, as if to rest his case. But as far as Janir was concerned, this was far from over. "We'd be best to split into groups and head in different directions. Some of us can journey to the mainland and into the uninhabited lands. The rest can travel north. There's a colony on the island of Chaneen. It's a voyage of several days, but the people of Chaneen are friendly and will welcome us."

"You propose splitting up the community?" said Sancho in dismay.

"Out of the question," Arick boomed.

"It may be our only hope," Janir warned.

"We are a community and we will not be split apart."

"Haven't you understood a word of this?" David exclaimed. "We're all in danger! If we don't act, then every man, woman and child on this island could be killed. And it'll be on *your* head, Magistrate."

"You're out of line," Arick barked, enraged at having his authority challenged by a mere boy. He rose from his seat, his portly body shaking with barely concealed rage as he turned his attention to Janir. "As I said, we will discuss your *story* another time, and frankly that's more than such ridiculous scaremongering warrants. But today is the start of the Festival and I will not ruin the occasion by proposing to tear apart the very community we have all sworn to honor and uphold."

Janir sighed in clear exasperation. "Magistrate, if you don't act now, if you don't pre-empt the Alliance, then I assure you, this community will be destroyed anyway."

"I don't believe you," Arick fumed. "And frankly I don't trust you. How can I? You may have lived here for a few years, you may even have made some friends here, but you are not one of us. We know *nothing* of who you are, where you come from or where your interests lie. For all we know, it could be that *you* that pose the danger to this island."

"Magistrate, I must object," Mariane cut in.

Arick ignored her. He kept his narrowed eyes fixed on Janir as he continued, his voice low and filled with contempt. "So I say to you, if you don't understand what this community means, then you have no right to be here..."

There was a long silence. "You fool," Janir exclaimed with subdued anger. "You don't know what you're doing..."

With that, he turned and exited the council room. David followed Janir out of the room, leaving behind the silent and stunned councilors.

"How dare Arick talk to you like that," David said as they left the building. "After all you've done for this island..."

"That's the least of it," Janir said. "I'm still an outsider, so they distrust me."

"But I can't believe that Arick is being so blind."

"He's scared. He's out of his depth and too stubborn and weak to act." Janir let out a frustrated sigh. "Alas the entire island will pay for his shortcomings."

"We have to do something."

"Agreed. But at the moment, I don't see what we can do." Janir came to a stop and turned to David. "I need time to meditate on this. I have to plan our next move. We can't afford to make a wrong turn at this stage."

"When will I see you next?"

Before he could respond, Janir's attention was drawn to the groups of people setting out tables, stalls, and marquees. "The Festival," he muttered. "Of course. It begins this afternoon with the opening ceremony, doesn't it?"

"That's right," David said, failing to see the relevance.

"Perfect." Janir was clearly beginning to formulate a plan. "I'll meet you here at the start of the ceremony."

Janir strode off down the street, leaving David alone in the town center, watching as the townspeople prepared for the celebration. The Festival was an occasion that everyone on the island keenly anticipated and David was no exception. But today he could feel nothing but dread. For as he looked across the town square, he was unable to shake the feeling that his entire world was about to come crashing down.

# CHAPTER FIVE

# The Festival

The air buzzed with excitement as the Festival got underway. Now a hub of activity, the town was vibrant with color; streamers, flags and garlands adorned the trees and buildings; an assortment of tents, stalls, and marquees lining the square. Musicians and street performers entertained the crowds as the people gathered to await the Magistrate's opening address. Following his speech, the islanders would enjoy a variety of performances, competitions, and recitals, as well as the annual feast, a communal meal in honor of those who first settled in New Haven. The island's best cooks had spent days preparing a feast plentiful enough to feed the island twice over. Mouth-watering aromas from the food tent carried across the square, more than whetting the crowd's appetite.

David kept his eyes on the boulevard, scanning the crowd and wondering when Janir would show up. After parting company this morning David hadn't known what to do with himself. Unable to figure out how they could convince Arick to evacuate the island, he'd gone home and sought solace in the quietude of meditation. Today it had been a fruitless endeavor, for he found his mind and thoughts altogether too turbulent.

He decided instead to keep himself occupied, assisting his mother and the rest of the Festival committee as they readied the town centre, setting up the necessary stalls, tables and chairs. But this still hadn't distracted him from his worries. Everyone he met seemed so happy and carefree—and woefully oblivious to the mortal danger that threatened them all. David felt like getting up and shouting from the rooftops. People needed to know what was happening.

He'd considered pulling his mother aside and telling her about Naranyan's warning. She deserved to hear the whole story from him. As he set one of the banquet tables, he looked over at his mother, who was helping at the wine stall with Darien's mother, Ana. Smiling warmly as she distributed glasses of wine and chatted with people, she was clearly enjoying herself. David didn't want to spoil that until he absolutely had no choice.

"David!" He turned and saw Darien pushing his way through the crowd along with two of his friends, Nartan and Rickos. David finished setting the last of the places at the table and made his way to join them.

"Where were you this morning?" Darien said.

David suddenly remembered he'd skipped work in order to join Janir at the Council. "Oh, yeah...something came up," he muttered.

"In other words, you slept in," Darien said with a laugh. "And you say I'm bad!"

"Guess you were feeling a little rough after the party last night?" Nartan winked.

"And if that wasn't bad enough, you got roped into helping out here," Rickos added.

"It's clearly not been your lucky day," Darien smirked.

David frowned. "You have no idea..."

Darien put his arm around David's shoulder. "Well, fear not. We've come to rescue you. You're finished here, right?"

"More or less."

"Good," Darien smiled, an exuberant glint in his eye. "Then let's get into the spirit of things." Plunging into the crowd, he led them straight to the wine stall. "Four glasses of your finest, please," he said, smiling at his mother expectantly.

Ana frowned. Her jet black hair was tied back with a few stray locks spilling down her attractive, slightly plump face. "Didn't you have enough wine at David's party last night?"

"Mother, you can never have enough wine."

"Oh yes you can—and oh yes you *did*! Or don't you remember stumbling home last night and waking up not only every-one in our house, but most of the neighbors as well? Let me tell you, we were not the most popular family on the island this morning."

"Oh, like the neighbors can talk! They're just as bad themselves. Anyway, it's the start of the Festival, a time for charity and forgiving. They'll get over it. Once they've had a few drinks, perhaps." He smiled at her expectantly.

With a long-suffering frown, Ana began pouring wine for the boys, decanting the dark red liquid into four large glasses. "Just so long as you behave yourself, young man," she cautioned as she handed him a glass.

"Oh mother, please. I'm twenty-two years old."

"Well then, maybe once in a while you might act like it."

Rickos and Nartan sniggered, much to Darien's annoyance. "Come on," he said. "Let's go see what's happening."

They took their wine and Darien led the way, maneuvering through the sea of people, followed by Rickos and Nartan. David tagged along behind, not feeling at his most sociable. He came across his mother collecting empty glasses. "David," she greeted him with a smile. "How are you doing?"

"I'm fine," he lied.

"You sure? You seem very quiet today; a little distracted."

"Yeah. Guess I'm just a little tired after last night."

"It was a good night, wasn't it?"

He smiled. "The best. Thanks again for everything."

"Oh, don't mention it. Everyone's seventeenth deserves to a memorable occasion."

"It certainly was memorable..."

"I'll see you at the feast later, right?"

David nodded. He heard Darien yelling at him from across the street. "I'd better go," he said with a roll of his eyes.

"Have fun."

David struggled to muster a smile. Something didn't feel right. Perhaps it was simply that he didn't like keeping her in the dark. As she got back to work, David tried to dismiss his feeling of unease.

He crossed the street, almost spilling his wine when some boisterous children bumped into him. Stopping to let them past, he caught sight of Magistrate Arick and two of his aides striding through the crowd. He and Arick locked eyes for a brief moment. David shot him a look of barely concealed contempt before turning his attention back to his friends. "She must be here," he heard Darien whine.

"Who?" David asked as he approached.

"Who do you think?" Nartan responded. "Who else does he obsess about endlessly?"

"David, have you seen Janna anywhere?"

"Um...yeah." David took a sip of his wine. "I think I saw her earlier."

Darien's brown eyes lit up. "Where?"

"She was helping her father set up the bakery stall."

"She still there now?"

"How would I know? I'm not stalking her, unlike certain people I could mention..."

Darien was about to reply when the sound of a gong reverberated through the square. The Magistrate was about to commence his speech. Conversation died down and all heads turned to the front podium. David watched as Arick climbed onto the stage to the jubilant applause of the audience. After a moment of basking in the adulation, Arick nodded his head and held up his hand. The applause gradually ceased. "Good day, my friends," he began. "And welcome! Welcome to this, the inauguration of this year's Festival."

The crowd was quiet as all listened to the Magistrate. Some of the children, however, particularly the younger ones, were less interested in hearing what Arick had to say and continued playing, much to the consternation of their parents.

"What a year it has been," Arick went on. "We have worked hard, we have worked steadily and have all played a vital contribution to the continued thriving of our community. We have achieved much—and for that we should be proud."

David shifted awkwardly as Arick continued. "That is why this is a time of celebration for us all. For the next few days, we take a break from our daily routine to celebrate the paradise we have built for ourselves in New Haven, and to honor our forebears who first settled upon the island. We pay our respect and gratitude for their achievements; for their spirit of exploration and adventure. We salute the courageousness and bravery of those intrepid explorers!"

A loud voice cut in: "Only they weren't explorers, were they, Magistrate?"

Arick, startled that someone would have the audacity to interrupt his speech, scanned the audience and quickly pinpointed the dissenter: Janir, moving through the crowd toward the stage. The Magistrate was clearly fuming at the interruption. Being a consummate politician, however, he tried to conceal his anger and responded in a carefully measured voice. "What are you talking about, Janir?"

Janir reached the front of the crowd and stepped onto the podium, much to Arick's chagrin. "I believe it is time to finally address a few commonly held misconceptions." He turned to the startled audience. "I have no wish to cause upset or offense, but there are some truths that must finally be acknowledged, for all our sakes."

An awkward silence was broken only by the distant cry of sea birds. The islanders stared at Janir, while Arick looked stunned and incapable of speaking. Janir continued: "With all due respect, I must point out that contrary to what you have been taught, the founders of this island were not explorers. They were *refugees.*"

The quietude was shattered as a wave of dissent erupted amongst the islanders. Arick tried to regain control of the stage. "That is ridiculous. Janir, I will not tolerate such lies, nor permit you to disrupt this event!"

"*You* will not tolerate it?" Janir roared, his voice filled with such ferocity that Arick stepped back. Janir turned to the shocked islanders. "Listen to me! Your grandparents were driven here as a means of escape! They sought to escape from the clutches of the Alliance, an empire of terror feared throughout Alanar: a conquering, devastating authority that seeks dominion over the entire planet. All that stand in its way are destroyed; entire cities wiped out in the blink of an eye! Their military arsenal is massive and their power is growing at an alarming rate." Janir paused. "It was the Alliance that this island's founders were running from eighty-four years ago. Their original home-land had been conquered, their people either captured or killed and their lives torn apart before their eyes. So what did they do? They *ran*—all the way here. They found a place as far from Alliance-held territory as they could and they sought to rebuild their home here, on New Haven..."

People looked at each other in confusion; no one quite sure how to respond. Arick stood behind Janir, his already-reddish face turning scarlet as he simmered with rage.

Having succeeded in getting the islanders' full attention, Janir went on. "They thought it would be safe here. For the past few decades it has been. But no longer! Over the years, the Alliance has only grown stronger and more deadly. I regret to inform you that we have received news: the Alliance has found us. They are on their way even as I speak. An attack is imminent. Which is why we must leave here now!"

The crowd finally erupted into chaos. David knew that this was exactly what Janir had intended. Raised voices filled the square as fear and confusion gripped the islanders. Darien leaned in close to David. "David, what in the name of Dalteen is he talking about?"

"I'm afraid it's true, Darien."

Arick tried to regain control of the situation. He summoned two of his aides, both burly, muscular men, and motioned for them to remove Janir from the stage. They bounded across the stage, took hold of Janir by the arms and led him off the podium. Janir did nothing to resist, but as they passed Arick, Janir told him sternly: "I've done what you could not. Now you must act, for you have no other choice."

Arick glared at him and turned to his aides. "Get him out of here," he snapped. As they complied and escorted Janir off the stage, David pushed his way through the crowd toward them.

Arick attempted to reassert his authority. "Can I have everyone's attention," he shouted, his face so red he could have burst a blood vessel, his chubby arm trembling as he raised it to silence the crowd. "There is no need to be alarmed!"

"Is this true?" someone shouted.

"There are one or two things we can discuss later, but there is no reason to be alarmed. Just listen to me—"

"Then he's right?" cried another voice.

"Please, just listen—"

While the Magistrate continued trying to restore order, his aides dragged Janir to the far end of the square where they deposited him by the old grocer's store. After muttering some kind of warning, they stomped off, returning to the podium. David pushed through the sea of people to get to his mentor. "Janir!"

Janir looked up, his face set with a look of grim resolve.

"What do we do now?" David asked, joining him beneath the arched doorway.

"We've done all we can here. It's time to gather our belongings and prepare to leave the island."

"Shouldn't we stay to help with the evacuation?"

"If Arick has his way there won't be an evacuation. But we warned everyone and hopefully those with the sense to heed us will leave of their own accord. We have to make our own plans, David. It's imperative that we get you to safety."

"I have to talk to my mother and friends. They'll listen to me; I can persuade them to come with us. I'm not going to leave them behind."

"Well, essentially it's their choice, but..." Janir looked up, distracted by a noise in the distance.

"What is that?" David said.

"No," Janir gasped, his face draining of color. "It can't be..."

"What?" David was alarmed by the look on his mentor's face. "What is it, Janir?"

The noise grew louder by the second: a deep mechanical rumble piercing the air; the vibration intense enough to make the ground tremble.

"Janir!" David had to shout to be heard.

Janir was silent, his eyes wide with terror.

David's attention was drawn upward. He could scarcely believe his eyes as something appeared in the sky above the town. It was a colossal black airship of some kind. With a tapered metallic body and outstretched wings, it looked like a killer insect of nightmarish proportions hovering above the town, ready to devour the terrified inhabitants. Another craft appeared alongside the first, eclipsing the sunlight.

"The Alliance!" Janir shouted.

But it couldn't be. Naranyan had said the Alliance wouldn't strike for three days...

The shouts and screams of the crowd were all that could be heard above the rumble of the airships. In a blind panic, the islanders gathered their families together, while others simply ran for shelter.

David stood rooted to the spot, overcome by shock as he stared up at the motionless predators in the sky. The Alliance was here—and they were here for him. The nightmare that had haunted him for the past day had finally come to terrifying life.

# CHAPTER SIX

# Shattered Dream

Hysteria gripped the islanders. Shocked and afraid, people tried to run, yet the town center was so congested that the crowd soon came to a virtual standstill. People shoved into each other, desperate to escape; many knocked to the ground and trampled amid the chaos.

Janir grabbed David's arm. "We have to leave now!"

"No, I have to find my mother."

"David, we don't have time."

David wasn't listening. Pulling himself free of Janir's grasp, he plunged into the crowd. While everyone was attempting to flee the town square, David moved deeper into it, pushing against the oncoming crowd, struggling to keep to his feet. He aimed for the general direction of the wine stall, the last place he'd seen her. He had to find her. He'd sworn to his father all those years ago that he'd always look after her, and he had to remain true to his word.

As he struggled against the relentless sea of people pushing into him, he became aware of a commotion ahead: screams of alarm followed by the sound of gunfire. Over the tops of people's heads, he saw a blast of energy slam into the town hall. The impact caused an explosion, sending debris flying as the building ignited in flames.

What was happening? That blast hadn't come from the airships overhead—it was from ground level.

Further shots were fired. Tents and marquees erupted into flames. The crowd reacted in heightened terror. As David struggled to push his way forward, he caught sight of Arick; his aides elbowing people aside in order to get the Magistrate to safety. Over the noise of the crowd and the continued droning of the ships above, he heard Arick scream at his men to retrieve weapons from the storage bunkers.

Unerring in his determination, David pushed forward, the town square rapidly filling with smoke from the blazing buildings and marquees. A burly man barged into him, elbowing him in the ribs. Gritting his teeth, he continued, looking over in the direction of the wine stall. Nothing could be seen but flames and smoke.

David's heart skipped a beat as he saw a figure emerge through the screen of smoke—a soldier of some kind, clad in grey-black metallic armor, brandishing a large rifle. It trudged through the rubble, kicking aside anything in its path. The soldier's body armor resembled a spiky exoskeleton. Its demonic-looking helmet was dominated by a red-tinted visor, with a grated mouthpiece and short metal horns sprouting either side of its head. Striding forward, it appeared to have him locked in its sights.

Overcome by terror, David turned and ran, following the other islanders as they tried to flee. Only there were more soldiers ahead, lining the rim of the square, advancing toward the hysterical townspeople. They were surrounded.

Glancing back he saw the soldier behind still lumbering toward him. He'd prayed it had been his imagination, but now it seemed that his fear was confirmed: he was indeed its target. He didn't know what to do. He was helpless. The crowd was at a standstill and the soldier was closing in on him.

Just when all seemed lost, he felt a hand grab his arm and yank him aside, pulling him through the crowd. Everything seemed to occur in slow motion as he was dragged through the crowd. At first, he didn't even know who was leading him away. For all he knew it could have been one of the attackers. But he recognized the back of Janir's head and knew that he was being led to safety.

Janir pulled David to the edge of the square, away from the crowd and at a safe enough distance from the nearest soldier. He unlatched a doorway and led David into the grocer's shop. "Come, we must leave," Janir barked. Closing the door, he slipped past the wooden counter, beckoning to a door at the rear of the store. "We have to get out of the town. I know a place we'll be safe."

"I'm not going without her."

"We have no choice, David." Janir pushed David toward the exit.

David relented, realizing that they wouldn't have a hope of rescuing anyone if they got caught themselves. "What are those things?"

"Eloramian Death Troops. Foot soldiers of the Alliance. Part man, part machine; ruthless, deadly. There's no telling how many there'll be on the island by now."

Janir unlocked the back door and pushed it open. Stepping onto the street, they froze in alarm. Two Death Troops were marching up the lane toward them, rifles aloft.

His reflexes lightning-fast, Janir reached into his trouser pocket, lifting out a spherical metal object. He threw it at the advancing soldiers. Exploding with a flash of light as it hit the ground, it sent billows of smoke spiraling upward, filling the lane. "Run!"

David did just that. Aware that Janir was right behind him, he raced down the narrow street. The sound of his feet against the cement was drowned out by the drone of the airships looming above the beleaguered town. As he ran he was unable to spare so much as a backward glance, but he was nonetheless certain that the soldiers were in close pursuit. Janir's trick may have provided a momentary distraction, but it wasn't enough to halt their pursuers.

David suddenly sensed that Janir was no longer behind him. Looking round, he was horrified to see that one of the armored attackers had caught hold of him. David didn't know what to do. His first impulse was to try and help Janir—but how? What could he do? The other soldier had him its sights and was gaining him. Realizing that he was helpless to assist, panic overwhelmed him and he kept on running. Taking a sharp right turn, he bolted down a side street.

This part of the town was eerily deserted; everyone having congregated at the square for the start of the Festival. David jumped over a fence into someone's garden, crossing the grass and trampling through a flower bed, making his way down the side of the house and onto the next street. Turning right, he was startled to see another of the mechanical men bounding toward him. He pulled back and turned to run in the opposite direction, only to see yet another soldier closing in on him from behind. They were everywhere!

David darted for the nearest house. The door was unlocked. He raced inside, bolting the door behind him. Unsure where to go, he raced up the stairs to the landing, tripping and falling as he did so. As he picked himself up he heard the soldiers smashing the door down.

He made for the room at the far end of the hall. Opening the door, he scanned the room in search of somewhere to hide. Of course he knew that nowhere would be safe; wherever he went his pursuers would find him. He could hear the clanking of their boots and armor as they marched up the stairs. He was out of time.

His attention was drawn to a balcony overlooking the street. He raced onto it, drawing the curtain behind him, coming to a stop against the steel railing. High above the adjacent rooftops, the airships hovered above the town, blocking the suns and casting a shadow upon the empty streets. Although there was no sign of any other soldiers in the immediate vicinity, he could hear the distant sound of screaming and shooting from elsewhere in the town.

This was all so hopeless. Where could he go now? Perhaps he could make it down onto the street? He climbed over the balcony railing, but lost his footing and found himself dangling over the edge. Holding onto the rail with all his might, he became aware that the soldiers were now in the room. It didn't take them long to tear down the curtains and find him hanging from the balcony.

One of the metal-clad troopers lumbered onto the balcony. David stared up at it. Whatever lay beneath that metal helmet, he could sense no trace of humanity. Overcome by a sudden chill, he realized that he was looking into the face of death itself. It reached out to grab him. David knew the only way was down. Just as the soldier was about to take hold of his hand, David let go of the railing.

Bam!

He collided with the ground. Although the hedge had broken his fall, his head struck the cement path at the edge of the garden. Everything receded into blackness.

How long a time he remained like that he was uncertain— hours, minutes or mere seconds? His mind and senses were numb as he drifted in and out of lucidity.

He was only aware of flashes of what happened next.

The enemy soldiers were upon him; striding toward him like silent machines of death. But something happened. Something repelled them. He was aware of a light and smoke, and felt someone scooping him from the ground and lifting him across their shoulders. He was certain it wasn't one of the machine soldiers, but a flesh and blood man, for he could feel the warmth of his touch as he carried him down the street.

He struggled to retain consciousness, his mind slipping in and out of wakefulness like waves lapping against the shore. His shoulder stabbed with a sharp pain and his head throbbed; his attention diffuse and scattered.

Who was it that had saved him from those soldiers? And where were they taking him?

Down winding avenues, past houses, trees, and parkland; all the while, the relentless drone of the airships above continued drilling through his head.

In and out of consciousness; in and out...

When David finally managed to focus his attention and retain consciousness for more than a fleeting moment, it was under a haze of disorientation. He lay upon the ground, his back propped against a wall. His head hurt and he felt a twinge of pain in his left shoulder.

*What...?*

He was in a warehouse of some kind. With no windows and the doors bolted shut, the light was dim. He saw a pile of crates stacked against the wall to his left and a couple of disused fishing boats upon the cold stone floor. High above, a few chinks of daylight streamed through gaps in the roof.

"David," a voice came from the other end of the warehouse.

A man stepped out of the shadows. Initially braced for the worst, David was surprised and relieved to see who it was. "Janir! What happened?"

"We were attacked."

"Yes, I remember. How did we get here?"

"I brought you here."

"But how? Those soldiers were everywhere. You were caught by one of them; I saw you."

"I managed to disable it and find you. You'd fallen from a balcony, hit your head and dislocated your shoulder. I carried you here, fixed your shoulder and treated your head injury as best I could, but you'll probably have a mild concussion."

"Where are we?"

"Down at the harbor. In one of the old warehouses."

David put a hand to his spinning head. "Won't they find us here?"

"Not as long as we remain in here. I placed a protective incantation around this building. We should remain hidden from the Alliance and shielded from their tracking devices."

"What about the others? What's going on out there?"

"Last I knew, the Alliance troops were ransacking the island, desperately searching for the Key...and for you..."

David's stomach lurched. "What will they do to everyone?"

"From what I know of the Alliance, they'll round everyone up for transport aboard their airships. It's Alliance policy for all citizens in conquered lands to be taken for processing at a designated outpost."

"Processing? What does that mean?"

"All able-bodied adults will be put into slavery, most likely sent to work in mines or construction facilities. The rest will either be dispensed with or put to other uses..."

"Other uses?" David echoed in horror. He wasn't sure he even wanted to know what that meant. "Janir, we can't let this happen. We can't just hide away here while everyone's being—"

"David, we have no choice. We have to stay here until the Alliance troops leave. Believe me, there's nothing else we can do."

"But we have to try." With a great deal of exertion and discomfort, David pushed himself up from the ground and stood to face his mentor. His head was still spinning, but he forced himself to focus as he fixed his attention on Janir. "I promised. I *promised* I'd look after my mother. How can I live with myself knowing I'd let her and the others be captured as slaves—or worse?"

"The moment it's safe to leave, we'll do all that we can to help them. But right now, we can't risk capture. We have to stay here."

David was unconvinced, but he could see that Janir was resolute on the matter and knew it would be futile to argue.

"I must enter deep meditation and try to contact the Guardians," Janir said. "I need their guidance. They'll tell me what's happening out there and how we can get through this. With their insight, we can plan our next move."

David stared at him blankly.

"I know how hard this is, David, but we have to sit tight for now. We really have no other option."

David didn't want to hear that, but he nodded, feigning agreement. Simpering with desperation, all he knew was that he *had* to rescue his mother and friends. And he was going to do just that, with or without Janir's approval.

He waited until the time was right. Janir readied himself to meditate; settling down in a corner of the warehouse and ingesting some kind of plant extract he claimed would help him contact the Guardians. David watched as he slipped into a state of deep trance and then, when he was convinced that Janir was oblivious to his surroundings, he quietly made his exit.

Slipping out of the warehouse and carefully closing the wooden door behind him, he looked around the deserted harbor. The boats bobbed up and down upon the water, their sails rippling in the breeze. There wasn't a soul to be seen, nor a sound to be heard. He'd expected to see the Alliance airships still hovering above the island, their relentless drone permeating the air, but there was nothing. Was it possible they'd now left the island?

He clambered up the road leading into town, troubled by the mere thought of what might be lying in wait for him. He could see smoke in the distance, rising ominously from the center of town. Approaching the outskirts of town, David was again struck by the silence. All he could hear was the beating of his heart and the scuff of his footsteps on the concrete paving. Even the birds were silent. There was no sign of life at all. Walking down the deserted streets and boulevards, he felt like he'd stepped into a ghost town. A short time ago there had been so much activity; celebration and excitement, followed by chaos and terror. Now there was nothing. New Haven was deserted and frozen in time, a sense of fear and shock hanging over the town like an invisible cloud.

David stepped onto the main street promenade. His heart froze as he saw the devastation. Just hours earlier the town center had been joyously decorated for the Festival—and now it lay in ruins. Buildings had been decimated and the stalls, marquees and tables upturned, smashed to pieces or set alight. The signs of struggle and violence were plentiful, as smoke billowed from the flaming houses and shops.

David drew closer and was horrified to see bodies lying amid the rubble—dozens of bodies. He'd walked into a mass graveyard.

In a state of shock, he stumbled over to the nearest body. It was Jattala, a school teacher, evidently shot in the chest by one of the soldiers. Next to her lay another motionless body, this one bigger, bulkier: Rit, the beloved old storyteller, a man who'd been like a surrogate grandfather to so many of the island's children. By his side were two young children, a boy and a girl. It looked as though Rit had been trying to protect the children, only to be killed along with them.

Dozens of other bodies lay scattered across the streets...

David felt an insurmountable rage swell inside him.

*How could this happen?*

He felt a hand touch his shoulder. He span round, ready to defend himself. But it wasn't a Death Troop that greeted him. It was Darien.

"David," Darien exclaimed. "You're okay?" His voice was hoarse and he looked disheveled and pale.

"Darien. Where's everyone else?"

"They're all gone. All except us."

Two others emerged from what had been the bakery: Mariane and Janna, both pale with shock as they surveyed the devastation around them.

"What happened, Darien?"

"Those *things* attacked us. They rounded everyone up. Anyone who resisted was killed on the spot. It was awful, David. Old people and children...they were grouped together and..."

Janna broke down into sobs. Mariane tried to comfort her as she looked over at David. "We should have listened to Janir," Mariane said, her voice filled with bitterness. "I should have made Arick take notice. Maybe this could have been avoided..."

David didn't know what to say. What *could* he say? Part of him kept hoping that this was all just a dream and that he'd awaken at any moment. "What happened to everyone else?"

"We think they were taken aboard the airships," Darien said. "But they're gone now, and everyone along with them."

"How did you manage to escape?"

"Sheer luck. We were all running, terrified. In the chaos I was separated from Nartan and Rickos—I don't know what happened to them. But I ran into Janna. I asked her if she knew anywhere we could hide. Turns out her father had a hidden basement beneath his store. It wasn't easy, but we managed to make our way through the crowd and into the bakery..."

Darien glanced over at Mariane, who was still trying to comfort Janna. "That's where we found Mariane," he added in a hushed voice. "They'd killed her husband."

David felt a pang of sorrow. He knew that she'd been married to her husband, Jadan, for almost forty years. Darien continued: "We were convinced they were going to find us. We could hear them above while we were hiding in the basement trying not to make a sound. We just had to wait it out, listening to all the screams, the shooting...feeling so helpless. Eventually everything went quiet. Still, we waited as long as we could. It was only just now that we ventured out. What about you? How did you escape?"

"I'll tell you later," David said. He then asked the question uppermost on his mind. "Darien, did you see my mother?"

Darien said nothing. He looked down at the ground as if unable to meet David's eyes.

"Darien, tell me."

"David, I'm sorry, I..."

"Where is she?"

"It was all happening so fast...but when Janna and I were trying to escape, I saw her, at least I'm pretty sure it was her. I don't know what was happening exactly, but I think she was trying to get some children to safety..."

"And—what happened?"

"They shot her."

No...

Darien was wrong. He had to be wrong.

David turned and raced down the street. Choking on the smoke, he was bombarded by images of the dead, many of whom he recognized as friends, neighbors, and acquaintances. Among them he saw Mariane's husband, Jadan...his elderly neighbors, Paal and Lishandra...Janna's father, Luan...his old music teacher Zahra...farmer Doran...

It was horrendous. Feeling the contents of his stomach lurching up, he pulled himself aside and vomited on the sidewalk. Dizzy and disoriented, he ventured further down the street, passing the water fountain into the center of the square. The buildings continued to burn, the fire spreading rapidly.

As he looked down at the ground, he was greeted by a sight that nothing could ever have prepared him for. Lying on the street, bruised and battered, was his mother. In an instant, he raced over to her. Falling to his knees, he tried to see if she was still alive, if she was still breathing...

She wasn't. Her eyes were still open and a stream of blood trickled from her mouth and down her chin.

"No." She couldn't be dead. She couldn't.

"David! Look out!" came Darien's voice.

David looked up and saw two Death Troops emerging through the smoke. The machine-soldiers strode through the rubble toward him, their armor clanking with each step. David stood up to face his adversaries. A rage such as he had never known burned within him. His blazing fury bypassed all reasoning and he was about to pounce at the soldiers when he felt Darien grab him from behind, restraining him.

"They did this," he shouted as he struggled to break free of Darien's grip.

"David, they're too strong," Darien said as he continued to hold him back. "We have to get out of here!"

But David wasn't going anywhere. The soldiers marched forward, rifles poised to fire. David stared at the soulless monsters that had destroyed his home and killed his mother and friends; his rage almost potent enough to strike a blow. But he knew that there was nothing he could do to defeat them. They were too strong, too powerful. He was defeated and he knew it. But he wasn't going to run this time. He was going to face them head-on.

Within moments the soldiers were upon them. Darien tried to pull him away, but David wouldn't budge. They ended up in a heap on the ground and Darien, not knowing what to do, backed off in terror.

David got to his feet and stared defiantly at the blank mechanical faces of his attackers as they lurched toward him. Just as one of them reached out to grab him, there was a sudden blast of light from behind. The soldier staggered and fell to the ground in a lifeless heap.

*What—?*

It was Janir. He stood amid the swirling smoke, brandishing one of the soldiers' own rifles.

The other Death Troop turned and took aim at Janir, but before it could open fire, Janir pre-empted it. The lightning-like pulse of energy from his rifle slammed into the soldier's armor, almost—but not quite—knocking it off its feet. The soldier returned fire. Janir, whose reflexes were as fast as David had ever seen, dodged the energy blast and it struck a building behind him. Janir fired again. Following another successive hit, he finally brought the soldier to the ground with a clanking thud.

David's eyes fell on Janir, who lowered his weapon and gave David a look of deep compassion.

"About time," Darien shouted with a mixture of shock and relief, adding in a somewhat embittered tone: "Where were you earlier?"

Ignoring Darien's comment, Janir called over to them— "Come, we must leave immediately. Although the Alliance ships have gone, it's standard procedure for them to leave a contingent to secure the area and ensure that all inhabitants have been captured. There will be other troops on the island and it won't take them long to find us."

David felt another wave of grief as he looked down at his mother's body. "I want to bury her."

"I'm sorry, David, but we don't have time. Look around you. This whole town is burning down. The fire will take care of the bodies." There was a moment's silence. "We have to go."

"Go where?" called over Mariane, joining them along with Janna.

"We'll take a boat to the mainland."

David looked up at Janir and then back down at his mother's body. "I want a moment," he said, his voice but a hoarse whisper.

Janir nodded and moved back to a respectful distance. Mariane, Darien and Janna likewise used the time to say farewell to their fallen loved ones.

David reached down and gently closed his mother's eyes and tried to wipe the blood from her face. Tears spilled from his eyes as memories flooded his mind. No matter what had happened, she'd always been there for him. She'd helped him through the darkest of times. He knelt down and cradled her body in his arms. He felt hatred burning inside him: hatred toward the Alliance for what they'd done to her. It was confounded by guilt. He'd promised his father all those years ago that he'd always look after her—and he'd failed. He held her limp and lifeless body to his chest. "I'm sorry...I'm so sorry..."

David laid down her body and forced himself to rejoin the others. Wiping the tears from his face, he tried to compose himself, but his body trembled. Spasms of grief extended from his belly up through his torso and throat; the muscles tight and knotted.

At Janir's behest, the somber group left behind the flaming ruins of what had been their home.

# CHAPTER SEVEN

# Whispers in the Dark

David stared across the ocean as the decimated island of New Haven receded into the horizon. Numb with shock, no one said a word as Janir rowed toward the mainland. As the boat rocked upon the ocean waves, the silence was broken only by the steady grinding of the oars and the rhythmic lapping of water against the hull.

It was dusk by the time they reached shore. Janir brought the boat into a rocky cove and everyone disembarked. After David and Darien helped Janir pull the boat ashore, they stood in silence, surveying the darkened shoreline. David could see that Janna had been crying, Darien looked shaken and whilst Mariane seemed outwardly composed, he knew this was simply because she wasn't the type of person to display emotion in front of others.

Janir ended the silence that had remained virtually unbroken since they'd left New Haven. "It's getting late. We'll find somewhere to camp for the night. There are some blankets and food rations stored in the boat. It's probably not much, but it'll suffice for the night at least."

With Darien's help, Janir unloaded a storage box from the boat and led the way through the forest, everyone else trailing behind as they traipsed through the undergrowth. Some way into the forest they reached a dip in the ground. At Janir's request, Darien set the box down against the roots of a large tree. "I think we all need some sleep," Janir said as he passed around the blankets. "But first, we should eat."

David shook his head. "I'm not hungry."

"I don't think any of us are," Mariane concurred.

"You really should eat something. We need to keep our strength up."

Again there was silence.

"It's been the darkest of days," Janir said. "I know we're all still reeling from the trauma of what's happened; from all that we've witnessed and all that we've lost. I wish I could say otherwise, but the pain isn't going to go away overnight. We must therefore endure it as best we can, for we must now turn our attention to the future..." He trailed off, perhaps realizing that words alone were insufficient to allay their grief. "Tomorrow we'll set off for a place of safety. For now, let's settle down for the night."

Janir began gathering sticks and branches to start a campfire. David could see Janna edging away from the gathering, distancing herself from the others. Darien and Mariane offered to help Janir set up the campfire, as if keeping busy would distract them from their pain.

David, feeling as though he could keep a lid on his feelings no longer, excused himself, stating he was going for a short walk. He stumbled off through the forest. Once clear of the others, he began running.

He raced through the darkened forest, as though running from himself and his own tormented emotions, trying desperately to leave them behind. But no matter how fast he ran he simply couldn't escape them—for there was no escaping himself and no escaping what had happened.

Eventually, realizing the futility, he collapsed on the forest floor. He rolled onto his side, head buried in his hands as images of death flooded his mind: the devastated streets of New Haven, the burning buildings, the Death Troops...and the bodies lying in the rubble, including his mother, unmoving, bruised and battered.

His eyes welling with tears, his whole body trembled, racked with an agonizing and intensely physical pain. He found his grief exacerbated by a crippling guilt that he simply couldn't shake. It had been *him* the Alliance was after. He should have been the one to die.

David lay in this state of torment for what seemed like hours, his mind replaying the whole nightmare over and over again, before eventually his exhausted body and mind succumbed to sleep.

*He awoke to find himself alone in the darkness...in a cavern of some kind; dark and dank, the air stale and musty. He didn't know how he got here, but it elicited a strange sense of familiarity. Although unable to remember when or how, he got the feeling that he'd been here before in the most distant of dreams or memories.*

*Standing alone, he shuddered in the cold, taking an uneasy breath of air. He felt naked and vulnerable, as though he'd been stripped of everything and was at the mercy of some unidentified predator. For someone—or something—was stalking him. He could feel it with every fiber of his being. He was being hunted.*

*David...*

*A voice echoing through the darkness, calling his name.*

*David...David...*

*It knew who he was and it knew he was here.*

*David...David...David...*

*This predator, whatever it was, lurked in the shadows around him. Nowhere was safe. Overcome by desperation, David started to run. The moment he started to move, his pursuers, wraithlike shadow men, leapt from the shadows and gave chase. There were too many of them and he knew that they were too strong and fast for him. There was no escape. Running was futile—why hadn't he learned that by now?*

*As it turned out, there was only so far he could run, for he soon came to a chasm splitting the ground in two, forcing him to stop in his tracks or else fall to his death. The moment he stopped, he felt the blistered hands of the shadow men reach out and tear into his skin. There was nothing he could do to fight them.*

*The shadow men pulled him back from the edge of the chasm. David felt a sense of dread as he watched a man step out of the blackness.*

*Dressed in a black and gray robe, the man was slim with olive skin, his face narrow and thin, long dark hair tied behind him; his emerald green eyes searingly intense. No older than his mid-thir-*

ties, he had an elaborate black tattoo stretching down the left side of his face.

David could feel waves of darkness reaching out from the man. He again tried to escape the firm grasp of the shadow men but found himself rooted to the spot, fixed in the intense stare of this mysterious stranger.

"David," the man greeted him, his voice deceptively gentle but devoid of warmth. Indeed, it betrayed a stark undercurrent of danger. "You have no idea how long I have awaited this meeting."

"Who are you?"

"My name is Zhayron."

"What do you want?"

"Only what is best for you."

David found that hard to believe. As he continued staring into David's eyes, David could feel waves of malevolence surround and engulf him, like an invisible snake coiling around his body. "You see, David, our fates are linked. They always have been. You are a part of me and I of you."

David was horrified. This man, whoever he was, was nothing to do with him. "You're lying..."

"I understand your confusion." Zhayron stepped closer. David tried to recoil, but was held firmly in place by the shadow men. "You've been through so much." Zhayron reached out and placed the palm of his hand on David's face. David flinched, feeling violated. He could feel Zhayron reaching into his mind, digging deeply into his innermost thoughts and feelings. Zhayron's voice was but a rumbling whisper. "I can feel your pain, David. So much pain...it clouds your judgment and obscures your true path. You have much to learn. But in time you will come to trust me, and embrace me as a brother."

"No..."

"It's inevitable. If you had seen what I have seen, if you knew what I know, you would have no doubt."

David shook his head and tried to pull back, his eye suddenly caught by a hazy figure appearing in the distance behind Zhayron. It was a girl—a teenage girl, with shoulder-length locks of brown hair, dressed in blue, exuding a sense of strength, determination, and regality. He didn't know who she was, but she seemed intimately familiar to him; as though he'd dreamt of her a million times before. She reached out and called to him, her face bearing an expression of concern and fear. But she was too far away—close enough to see, yet somehow a universe apart from him. He couldn't hear what she was saying...and she vanished as quickly as she'd appeared.

He looked up at Zhayron, who had evidently been unaware of the girl, his eyes continuing to burn through David. "Feel the darkness around you, David," he whispered. "Feel it within you. It is a part of you."

David made another valiant but futile effort to break free. He could feel Zhayron's words seeping through his mind like a poison. He couldn't let it take hold. He had to resist.

"Listen to me, David," Zhayron continued, his hand still pressed against David's skull. His eyes remained fixed on him like two black holes subtly drawing the life-force out of him.

"No," David growled. "Get away from me."

"Feel it consume you. Don't fight it, David. Let it happen. It is the only way."

Zhayron was somehow inside of him; peeling back every layer of his consciousness and choking his soul as the words echoed through his mind: "It will take away the pain...and all your suffering will melt away. But first you must let go...let it happen—embrace it!"

"No!"

David bolted upright, disorientated and distraught.

*A dream...*

It was just a dream.

It had felt so real.

He found himself on the forest floor; a few stars visible in the night sky. A faint light toward the horizon suggested an imminent dawn. The air was cool and the forest bathed in a serene quietude. His stomach knotted as the events of the previous day came flooding back to him—the attack, the destruction of the island and the death of his mother...

He'd gone from one nightmare only to find himself back in another.

With a pang of alarm, David realized that he was not alone. He spotted a lone figure leaning against a pine tree several paces away. It was a man, watching him intently. David was ready to make a bolt for it, but he quickly recognized him. It was Naranyan, the off-lander that had warned him of the Alliance's impending attack. "What...what are you doing here?"

"I came as soon as I realized what had happened," Naranyan said. "Our estimation of the Alliance attack was in error..."

"We noticed."

Naranyan lowered his head. "Their haste took us all by surprise. There was nothing we could have done to anticipate the timing of their assault."

"Who do you mean by 'we'?"

"I am *andala* to the Guardians," he explained, his voice deep and his tone solemn. "I am their messenger. I have been conferring with them for many years; living with one foot in this world, the other in theirs."

David narrowed his eyes. "How long have you been here?"

"A few hours perhaps. You were asleep when I found you. After all you had been through, I thought it best not to wake you. But it was not safe for you to be alone in the forest, so I decided to stay with you until you awoke."

"I see." David felt a little less awkward knowing that Naranyan hadn't seen him in fits of tears. "Have you seen Janir and the others?"

"No, but now that you are awake, I believe we should go find them."

"I don't know if I want to just yet," David admitted. "I'd like some time to be on my own."

"There will be time for solitude later. For now, we must move along."

"Move along *where?* There's nowhere for us to go."

"My people have a village not far from here. They will provide you and your friends with food, shelter and hospitality."

Although curious, the greater part of David remained beset by the black cloud enveloping him; the part of him that felt beaten and destroyed.

Sensing the boy's pain, Naranyan's demeanor softened. "I wish to show you something."

David looked up.

"Follow me." The enigmatic stranger turned and began marching through the forest. David felt obliged to follow. It grew lighter as they progressed, making the journey a little easier. The mossy ground steepened but Naranyan's pace never let up. He ascended an embankment, his every movement steadfast and surefooted, like that of a wild animal totally at one with its environment. He looked down, beckoning David to follow. David did so, although with a little less speed and grace than Naranyan.

Once he'd scrambled up the mound, David stopped to catch his breath. They were at the edge of the forest. Ahead of them was a sheer drop, below which the ocean lapped against the shoreline; the water a deep shade of indigo in the dim morning light. From here they could see for miles along the coast: sprawling headland silhouetted against the ocean; a vast region known only to New Haveners as 'the uninhabited lands'.

Naranyan motioned to the grassy cliffside. "Sit down, and watch."

With a sigh, David joined him upon the edge of the hilltop, his feet dangling over the cliff-ledge, the grass moist with morning dew. They sat in silence, their gaze settling upon the ocean.

David didn't understand Naranyan at all. After all that he'd been through, did Naranyan really think that a pretty view would make him feel the slightest bit better? Resigned to his frustration, David continued staring across the water. He couldn't help but think of New Haven. It was out there somewhere across the sea; devastated and lifeless, consumed by flames. He felt a wave of nausea as the images of death returned to his mind.

But something caught his eye upon the horizon. At first he wondered if it was a trick of the light, but as it intensified he realized it was the sunrise. As dawn slowly crept in, he became aware of an awakening taking place all around. The creatures of the forest began stirring from their slumber; the birds beginning to welcome the new day with song. The dormancy of the night was giving rise to the hopeful expectancy of a new day. David watched as the first of the twin suns began to peek above a bank of mist on the oceanic horizon, illuminating both sky and water with vibrant hues of gold and pink.

"Beautiful, is it not?" Naranyan said.

"It is."

"Do you know the legend of how the suns came to be?"

David shook his head.

"When I was a child it was one of my favorite tales." As he and David continued watching the increasingly spectacular sunrise, Naranyan began to relate the story. "It takes place many cycles ago, when the Great Creator, Hershala, was creating the heavens. It was a process that spanned many eons. One of the planets Hershala created was named Alanar: a jewel in the sky, created to serve as a beacon of light to all others."

"Our world..."

"Indeed. It was a world of majesty, wonder and magic; and a place with a special purpose. So important was Alanar that Hershala blessed it with not one, but two of His Sons. Named Mu and Næ, they walked upon the land as gods. They oversaw the creation of a world that would play a special role in the galaxy of Cha-Ra. Representatives from races from all across the galaxy were drawn to this new land. It was to serve as a meeting place; an outpost of peace and communion, overseen by the brothers Mu and Næ.

"They created a system of gateways that allowed instant travel to and from the planet. And they introduced much in the way of civilization: cities of crystal, advanced technology the likes of which the galaxy had never before seen, and a culture of deep spirituality. It was a time in which man and god alike walked upon the planet and beings from all across the universe came together in harmony. It was a grand experiment and one that spanned several million years."

"So what happened?"

"Things began to change. An element of corruption began to taint the purity of the land. As it spread like a slow and insidious poison, the planet began to change. A rot set in and continued to worsen until the gods could no longer walk upon on a land so rapidly descending into depravity. So they left."

Naranyan sighed, his face darkening as he continued the tale. "Following their departure, Alanar continued its decline until eventually the planet itself began to display symptoms of illness. Storms tore apart the land. Hurricanes and earthquakes struck with increasing severity. By this point, most of the races on Alanar had chosen to leave; and those that remained were at the mercy of a planet experiencing much change. Eventually, much of the civilization of the First Golden Age was destroyed. In the wake of this devastation, Alanar was consumed by an ice age. The planet froze and lay dormant for many thousands of years."

David was silent, eager for Naranyan to continue. "All seemed lost," Naranyan said, "and yet the gods never truly left. Although no longer able to stay upon Alanar, they would never forsake her. That is why they ever remain in the sky, shining down light and life upon all of creation: the twin Sons, Mu and Næ, forever supporting and sustaining our world, as they have since the very beginning."

David was unable to take his eyes from the two orbs of light as they continued their heavenward ascent, setting the sky alight with streaks of gold, orange and crimson; a kaleidoscope of color mirrored in the ocean beneath.

"Something about the grace and majesty of the rising suns has always been of comfort to me," Naranyan continued. "I never quite knew what it was until one day I was watching the sunrise with my old mentor. The sunrise, he told me, was an everyday miracle; a daily reminder that the rhythms and cycles of the natural world, and of life itself, are far out-with the control of man.

"Even in times of pain and strife, I have drawn comfort from the knowledge that each morning the suns will rise and each night they will set. Regardless of whatever might happen during the cycle, the cycle itself will never end. Darkness will inevitably descend, for such is the nature of life. But no matter how bad it might seem, the light *will* shine again. At daybreak, the gods will reappear in the heavens and pour their light upon us, dispelling the darkness and illumining our paths once more. The darkness will always give way to the light."

Finally understanding what Naranyan was trying to tell him, David felt moved by his words. Even the darkest night would eventually be superseded by dawn. Night had befallen David and he felt lost amid the darkness; his past obscured by pain and his future seemingly bleak. What he now had to do was find the strength to endure the night and the faith to believe that in time the light would shine again.

"David! Where have you been?"

"We were worried about you."

David rejoined the others, with Naranyan close behind. The moment his friends spotted the stranger, their reaction was one of alarm. "Who is that?" Darien demanded, stepping in front of Janna defensively.

"It's all right, Darien." David raised his hand. "This is Naranyan. He's no threat. He's here to help us."

Janir moved forward, greeting the newcomer with a bow of his head. "Naranyan, I'm pleased to meet you in person."

Naranyan nodded gracefully as he came to a stop before the gathering.

Not everyone was as welcoming, however. "Who exactly is he?" Mariane demanded.

"It is all right, Mariane, he's a friend," Janir assured her.

"How do we know that?" Her hesitation was only natural, for Naranyan cut an imposing figure. Tall, muscular and well-armed, he had the gait of a formidable warrior. "How do we know we can trust him?"

"Because I do," Janir said firmly.

Although Mariane trusted Janir, she still wasn't convinced; her expression tense and disapproving. On the other hand, Darien and Janna visibly relaxed. "Where are you from?" Darien asked the newcomer.

"You will soon see," Naranyan said. "I am here to take you to a place of safety. There is a tribe of my kinsmen not far from here. My people are known as the Enari."

"The Enari?"

"We are a simple, peaceful people; a race of hunter-gatherers, living off the land and honoring it accordingly."

"How many of you are there?"

"There are Enari tribes scattered across the length and breadth of Alanar. In these perilous times, most tribes are constantly on the run from aggressors such as the Alliance and the Kellians. We are forced to live a migratory existence."

"The Enari are a hospitable and noble people," Janir said. "I've had dealings with them in the past and have the deepest respect for their culture."

Naranyan acknowledged his words with a polite tilt of his head. "The tribe you will meet is called the Jasahn. I am born of the Tahlumar, a tribe from a distant land. But I have stayed with the Jasahn for some time and know them and their Chief, Deshonaan, well. They will be happy to provide you with respite, shelter and food."

"Such hospitality will be greatly appreciated." Janir turned to his comrades, seeking their response.

Darien and Janna nodded, but Mariane remained hesitant. "You're certain it's safe, Janir?"

"I am, Mariane. And, let's face it, our options are otherwise limited."

Mariane frowned, while the others remained silent.

"Let's get packed up and ready to go."

Without another word, they set to work. As Janir and Naranyan conferred at the edge of their makeshift camp, Mariane and Janna packed up the blankets and the remainder of the food rations. Darien gathered some earth and used it to conceal the charred embers of their campfire. It seemed a prudent move to hide any sign of their presence here. Clearly, the fear of pursuit wasn't only on David's mind.

While David knew that he ought to join in and help, he didn't feel like engaging with the others just yet. He watched from a distance as his friends readied themselves for departure. It had taken a degree of courage to come back here. He wanted to be alone right now; to deal with his feelings and to grieve in his own time and space. He felt the others deserved their solitude as well. Or perhaps that was being selfish. Maybe they needed each other right now?

That certainly seemed to be the case for Darien, who seemed eager to keep busy and get on with things. Janir was, of course, doing his utmost to hold the group together and support them through this painful time. David didn't know what they'd have done without him. But he could tell that Janna, like him, wanted to deal with her grief in privacy. An introvert at the best of times, she had retreated into herself, having barely spoken a word since the attack on New Haven, her misty green eyes filled with clear heartache. Mariane was a rigid, uptight woman who prized her dignity. She had obviously been hit hard by the loss of her husband, but refused to let anyone see the cracks in her veneer.

David now realized that this was no time for solitude. They had to stay together and work together no matter what. They remained in immense danger, for the Alliance was still after them; after *him*. He may have escaped them on New Haven but that certainly wouldn't stop them. They would be in pursuit again—assuming they weren't already.

As soon as they were ready, Janir gathered everyone together. "Let's get moving. According to Naranyan, we should reach the Enari encampment by nightfall."

The band of six set off. As Naranyan led them through the forest, rays of sunlight shone through the treetops, lighting the path ahead. The subtlest of breezes rustled through the leaves and the melodious sound of birdsong reverberated through the woodland.

Naranyan's direction was decisive as he tromped through the forest, using a knife to hack through dense areas of undergrowth. Darien and Janna followed some way behind. Darien had become particularly protective of Janna; always keeping a close eye on her, yet wise enough to allow her the space she needed. Mariane lagged behind them, uncharacteristically silent. David trailed behind the others along with Janir, who provided an unobtrusive but comforting presence nearby. At one point Janir stopped David and asked if he was okay.

"Not really," David replied.

"I understand," was Janir's gentle response. "I know the pain you must be feeling, David. But you must hold on and endure it, because it will get easier with time. That I promise you."

David wanted to believe him. But right now, in spite of the offer of hospitality from Naranyan's people, the future looked as bleak as the past and all he could see ahead was more terror, pain and suffering.

Looking into David's eyes, Janir could clearly see the pain there. He said nothing, but smiled compassionately, his emerald eyes communicating a mixture of tenderness and empathy.

They carried on walking, passing by a small stream and climbing over a fallen tree trunk; the others now some way ahead of them. The forest burst with life. The lush green trees reached heavenward, their branches swaying in the breeze. Amongst the shrubs and undergrowth the forest floor was carpeted with wildflowers. Yet amongst all the life, growth and beauty, the forest was also filled with death. Fallen logs and branches littered the ground, along with wet rotting leaves; the smell of decay intermingled with the fragrance of flowers and sap from the trees. Everywhere he looked he saw a tangled mix of life and death.

"It's ironic," David remarked, feeling the need to break the silence.

"What is?" Janir asked as he jumped off the tree trunk, his cloak flowing behind him and his boots crunching on the twig-strewn undergrowth.

"This place...the forest of Senrah. This is where my father found me as a baby, seventeen years ago. As far as anyone knows, this forest is where my life began." He paused before continuing. "Now my life, the life that I knew, is over...and here I am here again."

"One journey has ended," Janir said, "and you're back at the starting point, ready to embark on a new one."

Maybe he was on the verge of a new journey. In many ways this was what he'd dreamt of throughout his childhood: leaving behind New Haven and setting out into the wilderness, exploring new lands and finding his 'true' home and his 'true' family. Yet now that his childhood fantasies had become a reality—now that he was setting out into the world he'd so long dreamt of—all he wanted to do was to go back.

# CHAPTER EIGHT

# The Enari

Janir was adamant that they reach their destination by nightfall. For the most part the journey was made in silence; their stops were short and infrequent. By mid-afternoon, they'd left the boundaries of Senrah and entered what Naranyan told them was the forest of Dal. With the exception of Janir and Naranyan, this was the farthest any of them had ever been from New Haven.

A light mist pervaded this land, lending it an ethereal, otherworldly quality. It was accompanied by an almost tangible quietude, as though the forest itself was alive with a sense of hushed expectancy.

Naranyan continued leading the way with Janir not far behind. David plodded alongside Mariane, Janna and Darien. Overcome by physical and emotional exhaustion, he felt as though he was sleepwalking through the day, as though someone else was piloting his body.

His attention came into sharp focus when Janna suddenly stopped in her tracks, a haunted look on her face.

"What's wrong?" he asked.

"There's something here," she said. "Something here in the forest..."

"What makes you say that?" Darien said.

Before she could answer, a noise exploded through the forest, sending flurries of birds shooting up from the trees. It was an earth-shattering cacophony, unlike anything David had ever heard—like a thousand different voices screaming in unison. Turning, they were horrified to see a cloud of darkness rolling through the forest toward them.

"What the—"

Moving at an alarming speed, the black cloud thundered toward them, cutting across the woodland and spilling through the air like ink in water. Above the ear-pitching noise, they heard Janir shout to them—"Run!"

They did just that. Adrenaline surging, they raced ahead, desperately seeking escape from whatever it was advancing through the forest. They caught up with Janir, who motioned for them to keep moving. Naranyan was ahead of them, waiting to lead them to safety, or so David hoped.

Darien and Janna ran alongside him as they scrambled across the uneven forest floor. But someone was missing—where was Mariane? David glanced round and saw that she'd fallen behind. He stopped and watched in horror as the black cloud enveloped her like a ravenous swarm.

Just what *was* it? It wasn't a cloud, it wasn't a creature, but it was alive somehow. It was almost like an intermixed fusion of a thousand different people—ghostly entities enmeshed in a veil of darkness, twisting, contorting and writhing—all screaming in fury. Dozens of demonic hands reached out at Mariane, grasping, grabbing and pulling at her. She fell to the ground, struggling against the attacking entity.

As Janir ran to her rescue, Darien grabbed David's arm. "Come on! There's nothing we can do." Realizing that he was helpless to assist, David complied. Naranyan directed them to keep running ahead. Rather than joining them, the Enari turned and made his way toward the scene of the attack.

David, Darien and Janna sped through the forest, jumping over logs and trampling through the vine-strewn undergrowth. As they continued running, David became aware of a flash of light from behind. It was followed by another, and then another. The howling scream of the shadow creature grew louder. He didn't know what was happening, but he got the sense that a battle was being fought. He could only pray that Janir and Naranyan would be victorious.

Onward they ran, until a thunderous roar blasted through the forest, accompanied by an almost blinding flash of light.

David's senses were overloaded and for several long seconds, he found himself completely disorientated. He came to a stop and was struck by the sudden silence. The screaming was gone. Breathless and stunned, he turned to Darien and Janna. The silence lingered. The three of them stood rooted to the spot, no one daring to move.

What had happened? Had they defeated that thing—or had it defeated them?

David had to know they were all right. He needed Janir and couldn't bear the thought of losing him as well...

Without a word, he turned and ran back the way they'd come. His ears still buzzing from the cacophonous noise of only moments ago, he noticed a shift in the atmosphere around him. The air tingled with an electrical charge and the entire forest was bathed in a pale white luminescence.

He was relieved to find Janir and Naranyan helping a dazed Mariane to her feet. "Is she okay?" he called.

Janir looked up and nodded. "She will be. She's just a little shaken—understandably so."

"Janir, what was that thing?"

"Yes, that is something I should very much like to know," Mariane said, breathless.

"They're called the Jatei. Discarnate spirits unfortunate enough to be caught in Abidalos, the realm of the Shadow Lords. There they become restless demons; wraiths caught between two worlds."

"Why did they attack us?" David asked. "What did they want?"

"To eat," Naranyan said.

Janir nodded. "They must feed off the energy of the living in order to survive."

"Well, I knew there were dangerous things in the forest," Darien exclaimed, appearing alongside David, with Janna close behind. "But I figured it was things like wolves we had to look out for. Not man-eating *demons*..."

"We live in a predatory universe," Naranyan warned.

"There are certain places across Alanar where the magnetic grids are weak," Janir explained, "enabling demons like the Jatei to slip through the void."

"How did you manage to defeat them?" David asked.

"I've had to deal with such entities before. I—"

"You mean there are *more* of those things out there?" Darien cut in.

"Of course," Naranyan said.

"*Wonderful,*" Darien muttered.

"Fortunately," Janir continued, "there are several incantations that can drive them back to their own dimension. This was an especially powerful entity. It took a great deal of energy to ward it off. I couldn't have done it without Naranyan's help."

"We were lucky to survive the encounter," Naranyan said. "Not all are as fortunate when faced with the Jatei."

"Well, it's an encounter I for one do not intend to repeat," Mariane said, brushing the dirt off her trousers.

"Then I suggest we make haste," Naranyan said. "The Enari village is not far from here. It is safe there. The settlement is protected by charms and incantations to ward off predatory spirits."

"In that case," Darien said, "I'm officially sold on the idea. Lead the way."

With a curt nod, Naranyan set off, resuming his trek through the woodland. Janir and the others were set to follow, when Mariane pulled Janir aside. "Janir, I'm sorry but how do we know we can trust these people? We know nothing about them. For all we know, they could be—"

"Mariane," Janir cut in. "As I said before, if you can't trust them, then at least trust me. I have no hesitation in trusting the Enari. I would place my life in their hands. Besides, after all that's happened, I think it's clear that we need whatever help they can offer us." He turned to the others. "I know you all have unanswered questions, and I promise everything will be explained in due course. For now, it's getting dark. We have to get there by nightfall. So let's get moving."

They reached the Enari settlement by dusk. Situated amid a sprawling glade, the tribal village comprised an assortment of dwellings. There were tents of various shapes and sizes, along with dome-shaped huts covered with woven mats, mud-brick and bark. Lanterns hung from the trees and wind chimes tinkled as the breeze rustled through the leaves, sending blossom spiraling to the ground like pink snowflakes.

The travelers followed Naranyan into the heart of the forest dwelling. The tribes-folk watched the newcomers with hushed curiosity as they continued their tasks. Some were preparing food or weaving cloth or fabric, others were sharpening spears and arrows, while a few were arranging a stack of logs at the heart of the village. Children ran about playing, while animals, including goats and dogs, freely roamed the settlement. A number of old men sat watching all that was happening, inhaling puffs of smoke from long brown pipes.

"This place is amazing," Darien whispered to David. "Who'd have thought all this was barely a day's journey from New Haven?"

"I know." David had spent so many years dreaming about who and what lay out there, beyond the island—and here he was, in the middle of an Enari village.

They came to a stop outside a mud-brick hut decorated with red and gold paint. A man emerged from the entrance, his dark eyes narrowing as he studied the arrivals. Wearing a headdress of red feathers and robes patterned in red and brown, he was clearly someone of importance. He held a wooden staff in one hand; long locks of silver hair flowing down his broad shoulders. Although of advancing years, he bore the gait of a strong, agile man; a warrior. His voice was a deep, husky rumble as he spoke. "I am Deshonaan, Chief of the Jasahn."

Janir lowered his head. "It's an honor to meet you, Chief Deshonaan. I am Janir, and these are my friends: David, Janna, Darien and Mariane."

The Chief's eyes moved to each of the arrivals in turn. The moment their eyes locked, David felt as though Deshonaan was looking through him, as if gazing into his very soul. Unnerved yet not wishing to appear rude, he resisted the urge to look away. He noticed Deshonaan's eyes falling upon the crystal around his neck. Was it possible he recognized it?

"On the behalf of the Jasahn," Deshonaan said, "I bid you welcome. Our home is yours for as long as you wish. If there is anything we can do to make your stay more comfortable, please do not hesitate to ask. My people have greatly anticipated extending you their hospitality. We have known of your impending arrival for considerable time now."

Mariane's eyes narrowed with suspicion. "May I ask how?"

"The Oracle told us all."

"Who or what is the Oracle?" David asked.

Naranyan answered, "You will learn soon enough."

Deshonaan's face softened as he continued. "Allow me to offer my condolences as to the tragic events that brought you were. Your grief is our grief, for we have all suffered at the hands of the Alliance."

David felt a surge of pain at the mere mention of the Alliance.

"Thank you, Chief Deshonaan," Janir said. "Your kindness is appreciated more than we can ever say."

"We all have our part to play, do we not? I can see that you and your comrades are tired, and understandably so. I trust you will join us for evening meal. Then you are welcome to rest for as long as you wish." He seemed to be looking directly at David as he continued. "We will have the opportunity to confer tomorrow, for I know you have many questions and there is much to tell you. But first, you have had a long journey. You may wish to bathe down by the river and change into some fresh clothing."

At the wave of Deshonaan's hand, a group of young Enari women approached with fresh linen. "I will leave you in the capable hands of my people."

Deshonaan and Naranyan departed, disappearing into the hut. The Enari women coyly approached the arrivals. "I will take your clothes for you," the first woman said, gently pulling at Mariane's sleeve.

"I beg your pardon?" Mariane said.

The young maid smiled. "I will take your clothes for you," she said again, apparently expecting her to strip off on the spot.

"I'll take care of my own clothes thank you very much." Realizing she may have sounded rude, Mariane quickly added, "But I appreciate your kindness all the same."

Darien caught David's eye and they exchanged a smile. It struck David that this was the first time he had smiled since the attack. He felt a strange pang of guilt, as though he had no right to smile after all that had happened.

The Enari maids conferred for a moment, before handing their guests the towels and clothing. "Come with us," the first girl said, insisting that they follow as they led them down to the river at the edge of the valley.

It grew darker by the moment, with stars now visible in the sky. The maids departed, leaving the travelers to bathe in the crisply cool water. David was far too tired to be in the least bit bothered about undressing in front of the others, but Mariane was keen to retain her dignity and made an issue of securing privacy as she bathed. Drying off, they changed into their new clothes and made their way back to the settlement.

Evening meal was a communal affair. The entire tribe, over a hundred in all, gathered beneath the star-studded sky. A crackling campfire now dominated the center of the village. The travelers were seated as guests of honor upon log benches. David and his friends were objects of fascination to the Enari, many of whom stared without any pretense of subtlety. Prior to eating, the Enari began a prayer ritual involving chanting and casting squares of painted cloth into the campfire; an action done by the elders of the tribe with much gusto and to great applause.

"Please, enjoy," an elderly tribeswomen said as she ladled the newcomers generous portions of meat stew upon broad leaf plates. Although this was the first meal he'd had in well over a day, David wasn't hungry. He endeavored to take a few mouthfuls but his stomach was knotted and he found it difficult to swallow. He discreetly set his plate to one side.

The meal was followed by the tribe's customary evening ritual; a period of entertainment and festivity. The forest came alive with the pounding of drums and the reverberating echo of pipes. The entire tribe engaged in the revelry, with much singing, dancing and talking. A wooden jug was passed around, from which everyone took take a sip. When it came David's turn, he took a cautious sniff. Bright orange in color, the liquid smelt pleasant; sweet and fruity.

"It's delicious," Darien assured him. "I don't know what it is, but I could develop a taste for it."

David lifted the jug to his lips and tasted it. "Yeah, it's not bad." He passed the jug to Mariane. "Want some?"

She frowned.

David shrugged and reached out to hand the jug to Janir, who accepted it with a smile.

"So what do you make of this place?" Darien said.

"It's nice," David said, watching as the Enari sang and danced around the campfire. "They're certainly friendly."

"Maybe a little *too* friendly in some cases..."

One of the Enari girls, perhaps fifteen or sixteen, kept looking over and smiling. She seemed particularly keen on Darien. She'd already tried to coax them up to dance, as had one or two of the other Enari, but they had politely declined.

David suspected that, like him, the others were also far too tired and melancholic to appreciate the revelry. Just a day ago they'd lost their homes and families—it was clear none of them was in the mood to be dancing or partying.

"So," Darien began, "you don't suppose these people might be relatives?"

"Relatives?"

"Of yours! We're pretty close to the forest of Senrah, and that's where you were found as a baby, right?"

"Yeah."

"So for all you know, this could be your original home..."

"It's possible, but...I don't know." David shrugged. Although the possibility had crossed his mind, he'd always supposed that if he ever found his original home, he'd somehow *know* it—that there'd be no question in his mind.

Deshonaan sat nearby, smoking a pipe as he watched the festivity. Their eyes met, and the Chief smiled; his intense eyes drilling through David. David smiled back and awkwardly averted his gaze. Deshonaan seemed to know something; something about *him*. The question was, what?

David decided he'd had enough for the night. He tapped Janir on the shoulder, telling him that he needed to get some sleep. Mariane and Janna expressed a desire to do likewise. Darien, who was never far from Janna's side, agreed to join them.

Their accommodation was a dome shaped tent with five mattresses arranged around an oil lamp on the ground. David lay next to Darien and Janna, who along with Mariane, seemed to fall asleep quickly. Outside, the Enari revelry continued for some time. Janir arrived a little later, and also took little time to drift off to sleep.

David, however, lay awake for what seemed like hours, tossing and turning. Try though he might, he simply couldn't settle. Images of the attack on New Haven bombarded his mind—the robotic soldiers, the burning buildings, the bodies strewn across the streets...

Though exhausted and in desperate need of sleep, his thoughts would permit him no rest. The longer he lay, the more frenzied his mind became until he could stand it no longer.

Getting up from the bed, he made sure the others were still asleep and crept out of the tent.

A cool breeze swept through his hair as he surveyed his surroundings. The village was now asleep, with not a soul in sight.

With a sense of numbness, David trudged down the forest path. Leaving the village behind, it grew darker and the forest path more uneven. His way was illuminated by the tree lanterns and the glint of moonlight through the clouds. A silence pervaded the forest, broken only by the distant trickling of the river and the chirping of crickets in the undergrowth.

An owl, perched upon a nearby tree, let out an unexpected hoot. Startled, he glanced up to see two round yellow eyes staring down at him.

His mind a blur, he kept moving, as if driven by some unconscious instinct, one step in front of the other, until he stumbled upon a clearing.

There, among the trees, were dozens of graves; earthy mounds topped with headstones, the stonework glistening in the moonlight. Some of the graves looked old; covered in moss and foliage, while others had clearly been dug more recently. This must be where the Enari buried their dead.

What struck him was not only the universality of death, but the quietude that pervaded this cemetery. Stepping forward, he felt a strange sense of peace wash over him. He wasn't the first person to suffer a loss, and he wouldn't be the last. And someday he'd end up like this too; his body returned to the elements.

A noise in the undergrowth startled him. He turned to see a figure silhouetted beneath a pine tree. "Who's there?" he called.

"A friend," came a woman's voice.

David stared across at the shadowy outline. "I thought everyone was asleep."

"You are not..."

"I couldn't," he said. "I thought a walk might calm me."

"Interesting that you should find yourself here." Her voice was as melodious as the sweetest birdsong.

"I didn't really know where I was going..."

"Few mortals do."

David's curiosity was piqued. "Who exactly are you?"

"Someone who can sense your pain. You carry a tremendous burden of grief."

He said nothing.

"Why is it you grieve?"

David stared at the silhouette, still unable to make out who she was and unsure how to gauge the situation. Should he excuse himself and return to his tent or should he answer her? Something within him felt compelled to respond. "Because it's all over," he blurted. "The Alliance destroyed my home. They killed my mother, my friends, my neighbors. Just about everyone I've ever cared about is dead."

He cast his eyes to the ground. A long silence followed in which all he could hear was the sound of the wind dancing through the leaves. He actually wondered for a moment if the mysterious woman had departed. But he looked up and saw that she was still there. Finally, she spoke. "Tell me, what is death?"

"What is death?" David's astonishment turned to a flash of anger. "Everyone knows what death is." He gestured to the graves bathed in the moonlight. "This is death! It's the end—the end of life."

"That cannot be. There is no end to life."

"How can you say that? Look around you; these people are gone. And everyone on New Haven—they're all gone too."

"The forms may be gone, but the essence remains."

"What are you talking about?"

"Forms arise and dissolve every moment of every day. They are constantly fluctuating; constantly changing. In a sense, every moment is a birth and death. But there is no end to life. How can there be? There is a continuity; some factor that underlies and outlives all things."

David said nothing.

"On the level of form, all beings are but waves upon the ocean. Each wave arises, existing for a time, before dissolving back into the ocean—of which it was never truly separate. Was anything ever really lost?"

He frowned. "It's hardly the same though, is it?"

"In a universe in which the tiniest particles of our bodies mirror the dance of the stars and galaxies, everything is the same. How could it be otherwise? It is all a play of form. The source of your suffering is identifying too readily with the *form* and not the *essence*—with the wave and not the ocean."

"But when something's lost—"

"All that is lost is a body; a particular form..."

"But it's what we *are.*"

"*Is* it? You are witness to the body; you watch it function, you watch it act, you watch it change, grow old and eventually die. In order to witness a thing, you must be other than it. The perceiver cannot be that which is perceived. The body is but a sheath, temporarily enclosing your consciousness for a brief time, before it is cast off."

"This is some kind of Enari belief?"

"As taught to them by the Guardians."

"The Guardians..."

"Existing outside of space and time, the Guardians have an elevated perspective of reality."

"That must be nice..."

"One day you will understand."

"I'm not so sure," he said with a shrug.

"Perhaps not, but I am."

"How can you say that? You don't even know me."

"The question is, do you know yourself? What are you, David?"

He felt himself tense. "How do you know my name?"

"What *are* you?"

"Why are you asking me that?" He let out a frustrated laugh. "I don't know. I've never known. Not since I was a little child. Everyone around me seemed to know exactly who they were. But I didn't, and I still don't."

"They did not know what they were either. They simply assumed various masks, roles and identities. But we are all so much more than the sum of our parts." She paused. "You were right to question, as painful as it has been."

"It *has* been painful, and just look where it's gotten me."

"It has brought you here, which is where you needed to be."

"Every time I've tried to learn more about who I am it's caused disaster. There's a trail of destruction behind me."

"Knowledge often comes at a price."

He took a step back. "Then the price is too high! I don't want it—not if so many people have to die because of it."

"The moment each wave rises from the ocean, David," she said, "its trajectory and momentum is *set*. It cannot be halted."

Her words struck him with an almost tangible force. He took an intake of air. "So you're saying it was all inevitable..."

"Inevitable, yes."

"Then there's no going back? And there never was..."

"What happened cannot be undone. All you can now do is accept it and turn your attention to the future. You must keep questioning, for the answers will come, and the way forward will be revealed. Only knowledge can set you free."

"What kind of knowledge?"

"Self knowledge." She remained in the shadows, the faintest of silhouettes against the nocturnal woodland. "Your grief is a natural one; the inevitable pain of loss felt by all beings. I can only offer you comfort in the knowledge that you are part of something greater; a grand tapestry of unbelievable beauty and magnitude. Your journey is only beginning now, David. You must not let your pain cripple you. You must accept the past and look to the future. For death, seen from the perspective of Infinity, cannot be more than illusion. Your true essence, and the essence of all beings, is untouchable yet ever present—and it is eternal and limitless."

She fell silent. Her words swept over him like a warm wave, taking the edge of his pain and igniting a flame in his heart; a subtle flame of hope. "Who are you?" he asked again.

"You will learn soon enough."

"All that you've just told me, about life and death and our true nature...you speak with such certainty. How do you know all this?"

"Enough questions for tonight. It is time that you returned to your tent and got some rest. You must be refreshed for the morning."

Although about to protest, David knew that she was right. Overcome by a sudden wave of tiredness, it was clear that he needed sleep. "Will I see you again?"

"You will, and sooner than you might think."

David was glad. Whoever she was, she had done the seemingly impossible and helped ease his burdened mind.

He stepped forward, ready to thank her, only to find she was gone. Tired but strangely at peace, he made his way back to the Enari village, hopeful that he would finally get some sleep.

David awoke the next morning to find Janir kneeling by his bed, nudging his arm. "David..."

"Janir...what's wrong?"

"Nothing's wrong." His voice was hushed. "But it's time."

"Time for what?"

There was no answer. Rubbing his eyes, David looked around the tent. The others were still asleep. Naranyan stood at the mouth of the tent, his arms folded, watching pensively.

"What's happening?" David asked again.

"You have to get up, David. We're all waiting for you."

Who was waiting for him—and why?

David pulled back his blanket and climbed to his feet, stifling a yawn.

Janir and Naranyan led him out of the tent. It was early morning. A thick mist had descended over the forest. Ahead of them, a figure emerged through the veil of white. It was Chief Deshonaan, staff in hand, purposeful in his gait, his expression solemn. "Good," he said. "You are ready. Balaska will see you now."

"Who's Balaska?" David said.

"The Oracle," Deshonaan answered, as if that was supposed to mean something to him.

David turned to his mentor. "Janir, what's going on?"

"It's time for you to learn the truth, David."

"About what?"

"*Everything.* Had I not been so blind I'd have told you long before now." He motioned to the crystal amulet around David's neck. "The Key, David..."

"What about it?"

"It's time you learned what it is, why you're here, and what you were born to do."

# CHAPTER NINE

# Balaska

David followed Deshonaan through the mist-filled forest. He was unable to see more than a stone's throw ahead for the cloud of white engulfing the land, but Deshonaan appeared to know precisely where they were going.

It took little time to reach their destination: a solitary tent pitched some way from the rest of the village. Like many of the other Enari tents, it was cone-shaped, rising to a pointed apex, constructed of long sticks and woven fabric.

Deshonaan turned and beckoned for David to enter. "Balaska will see you now."

David felt his stomach tighten. He looked to Janir for reassurance. Janir motioned for him to do as Deshonaan said. David approached the tent, cautiously pulling back the opening flap before stepping inside, uncertain what to expect.

The first thing he noticed was how much larger it appeared to be on the inside. He didn't know how it was possible. It must surely have been an optical illusion, but it had a sense of vastness and spaciousness. Wreaths of flowers and herbs lined the inside of the tent, alongside animal skulls and feathers.

A woman sat cross-legged upon a fur rug in the middle of the tent. Her eyes closed, she was seemingly deep in meditation. With jet black hair cascading over her shoulders, she wore white robes emblazoned with gold. Her olive-skinned face shone with an immortal beauty transcendent of age. At once she seemed as youthful as a child yet as old and enduring as time itself.

Although David had never before laid eyes on her, there was something strangely familiar about her presence. Even as she sat in silence, she exuded an alluring sweetness; an otherworldliness that enraptured him. A dozen candles burned around her. The spiraling smoke of incense filled the air with a sweet floral fragrance. Just one inhalation was enough to make David feel lightheaded.

Janir and Naranyan entered the tent behind him. David looked at them questioningly. Neither met his gaze, their eyes fixed upon the woman.

Just as David turned, she opened her eyes. The moment their eyes met he felt himself somehow melting—as though dissolving into an ocean of light...

He suddenly realized his mind was slipping from him. Unnerved, he sought to regain control of his thoughts.

What was happening? That smoke, that incense—it must be doing something to him. Either that or it was *her*. Although serene, she radiated an almost tangible sense of power and presence.

"Welcome," the woman said. "Please, sit. Make yourselves comfortable." David's heart jumped at the sound of her voice. He recognized it immediately. It was the woman he'd encountered in the forest the previous night, at the Enari graveyard.

Following Janir and Naranyan's lead, he sat down upon the floor, which was carpeted with reeds. With a smile upon her lips, she answered the question uppermost in David's mind. "I am Balaska. Did I not tell you that we would soon meet again?"

David nodded. "What are you?"

"I am what in the ancient world was known as an Oracle. I serve as a bridge between this world and the higher dimensions; living with one foot in the mortal realm, and the other in the formless realms of eternity. This I have done for many years. But my time upon this world shall soon come to an end. My mission here nears completion."

Naranyan's dismay was clear. "You are leaving us?"

"Even my stay in the mortal realm is but a temporary one. But regardless, I will always be close by." She turned back to David. "Do you know why you are here, David?"

"Not really..."

"You are here neither by accident nor by chance. The fates conspired to bring you here for a reason. I have known of your coming for many years—from the moment of your birth, as it happens. For this meeting is a pivotal step in your journey."

David waited for her to elaborate.

"The Key," she said. "May I see it please?"

With only momentary hesitation, David lifted the chain from around his neck and handed it to her. She took the crystal in her hands and examined it. "Ah, I recall its creation as though it were yesterday..."

"You were there when the Key was created?" Janir said.

She looked up and smiled. "Oh yes, I sat upon the Council of Elders which presided over its creation."

"But it's the Guardians that sit upon the Council. Which would mean that you're—"

"A Guardian."

"In physical form?"

"From time to time, my people assume physical embodiment. Not very often, but on occasion, when necessary. But that is a discussion for another time." She turned her attention back to the Key, running her finger along the outer rim. "The Key of Alanar," she said. "But only one-half of a whole."

"What do you mean?" asked David.

She held up the half moon-shaped amulet, the amethyst crystal glistening in the candlelight. "This is but *half* of the Key of Alanar."

"Of course," Janir exclaimed. "It's broken in two! That explains the prophecy of the two Keys becoming one..."

David again felt his head begin to spin. The conversation had leapt ahead as far as he was concerned. "Wait a moment. I first want to know what this Key is, what it has to do with me and why so many people have been killed because of it."

"And that is precisely why you are here." Balaska handed him the amulet, which he placed back around his neck.

"I believe we should start at the very beginning. Your friends here are both already familiar with the history of the Key. You too must learn this vital piece of Alanar's history. And what better way than to show you? David, please give me your hand."

Surprised, he nevertheless did as she asked. She placed the palm of her hand atop his. The moment their skin touched David felt a surge of energy shoot through his body. Letting out a gasp of shock, his eyes closed—and this time he truly did lose his mind.

# CHAPTER TEN

# The Fall of Lasandria

*Balaska's gentle touch had opened the floodgates of Infinity itself.*

*David found himself swept away by the unrelenting current of a universe folding in on itself. Translucent colors flashed before him, cascading and melting into his consciousness.*

*Everything he knew was slipping away from him—the present dissipating, the past relinquishing and the future dissolving into an expanse of both nothing and everything.*

*Distinction seemed meaningless and boundaries obsolete, as the limited yielded to the limitless...*

It took him what felt like an eternity to regain his sense of self—to disentangle himself from the rest of the cosmos.

Thoughts began returning to him, and they were thoughts of confusion—

*Where am I? What happened?*

"I have given you your first taste of Infinity," Balaska's voice echoed. He looked around in astonishment. No longer in the Oracle's forest tent, he found himself standing on a mountain-top with Balaska by his side. The suns shone amid a violet sky, illumining the mist-shrouded mountains.

"How did we get here? A moment ago we were sitting in your tent..."

"And we still are. Our physical bodies are still comfortably seated in my dwelling. Our astral bodies, however, have jour-neyed a great distance, across time and space."

David saw that his body had a transparent, semi-visible qual-ity to it. "Is this a dream...?"

"Think of it as more of a vision; a glimpse into the past."

She stepped to the edge of the mountaintop plateau and raised her hand, beckoning to the land beneath. "Welcome to the Kingdom of Lasandria."

Nestled beneath the tree-covered mountains was a lush and fertile valley, sprinkled with patches of mist and intercut by a winding river sparkling in the sunlight. To the right of the valley, one mountain dwarfed all the others. It reached toward the sky like a pillar holding the heavens aloft, its peak obscured by a band of cloud. From the foot of the mountain, an ancient-looking city stretched across the valley. Lined with magnificent towers and walls, its golden buildings were interconnected by walkways, bridges, and courtyards. With lavish temples, dome-shaped observatories and pyramidal structures, it was a remarkable, dreamlike city, and the energy of the land vibrant and invigorating.

"Lasandria..." It was a name he recognized, for Janir had mentioned it once or twice—something about an ancient civilization, supposedly destroyed millennia ago. "Why have you taken me here?"

"Because there is much you must learn. I understand that Naranyan has already taught you something of Alanaran history?"

"He told me some legend about two sons being sent to look after the planet. Something about a golden age...only the planet became corrupt and they were forced to leave..."

"This world was originally a melting pot of cultures from across the stars; a grand experiment conducted by a semi-mythical race known only as the Creators. Alanar, however, fell into darkness and disarray when the Creators vanished into obscurity. For millennia, the planet was gripped by an ice age, during which many, if not most of its inhabitants were wiped out. Those that survived the freeze lived in a world of grave disorder. Various factions arose, each seeking power and dominance. Where once Alanar had been a land of the gods, it had degenerated into a place of darkness, famine and war."

As she spoke, images flashed through David's mind. He saw disparate tribes scattered across the land, the living conditions arduous and food scarce; every day a struggle for survival. He witnessed battles fought with the crudest of weapons; bodies strewn across battlefields and men, women and children running through forests and valleys desperately seeking escape from rival tribes.

"This age of darkness lasted for many cycles of the sun," Balaska said. "Until help arrived from the stars..."

In his mind's eye, David beheld the night sky, and he saw magnificent starships sailing across the ocean of the heavens. He witnessed their arrival upon Alanar; greeted with a mixture of fear and fascination by the planet's inhabitants. The pilots of these space vessels were tall, elegant beings, long-limbed and hairless with pale silver skin, shining with the luminescence of moonlight.

"They were called the Lasan, or the Preservers; an advanced race of explorers," Balaska's voice echoed in his mind. "Desirous of helping a world in chaos, the Lasan single-handedly rebuilt civilization: constructing glorious cities, teaching the lost ways of agriculture and industry, technology and diplomacy."

In a flash of images, David witnessed the construction of the golden city, created with the advanced technology of the Lasan.

"They brought peace and prosperity and a deep spirituality to the people of Alanar. Although many divisions still existed, the people generally came together in peace under the Lasan, heralding an age of brotherhood and kinship. Thus was born the civilization of Lasandria. Its people, the result of interbreeding between the Lasan and the Alanaran natives, were known as the Lasandrians."

"What happened to them—the Lasan?"

"Content that this civilization would endure and flourish without them, they departed as mysteriously as they arrived." The scene shifted and he watched as the city's inhabitants gathered at nightfall, watching in wonder and sadness as the Lasan starships shot into the sky, vanishing into the stars. "They left behind their children, the Lasandrians, under the partnership of a monarchy and the Sacred Priesthood of Lasandria."

The images subsided and David opened his eyes. Balaska stood alongside him on the mountaintop, gazing down at the city in the valley. "This is the City of El Ad'dan, the capital of Lasandria."

David nodded. He'd just witnessed the birth of an entire civilization. He had an ominous feeling that he now was about to witness its death. "What happened to it?"

"There came a division at the heart of Lasandrian society."

Balaska motioned to a hill overlooking the valley, upon which stood a golden temple. "The Sacred Temple of El Ad'dan," she said. "This was the heart of Lasandria's spiritual life, serving as a portal to the higher realms."

"A portal—?"

"The Lasan had recovered the ancient technology of the Creators, including a system of inter-dimensional portals allowing instantaneous travel to and from Alanar. The Temple of El Ad'dan was built around one such gateway. This technology was entrusted exclusively to the Priesthood, enabling the High Priest to commune directly with the Guardians; serving as a bridge between your dimension and mine.

"A partnership between the Priesthood and the Ranorian royal lineage ruled Lasandria for millennia. But toward the end days, this allegiance disintegrated until, on the eve of Lasandria's demise, the last of the Ranorian kings, a man named Dua-ron, annulled it altogether."

At the mention of his name, David saw the image of a large, bloated man dressed in regal robes, adorned with a crown and all kinds of gold and silver jewelry. With reddish-brown locks of wavy hair and a graying beard, he had a rounded, almost pig-like face, with pasty skin and small narrow eyes without a hint of warmth or kindness. Everything about his demeanor suggested a grasping, covetous nature; a man who possessed everything yet still craved more.

"The story behind Dua-ron's accession to the throne is a contentious one," Balaska said. "He was the last of four children born to the previous king and queen. However, a mysterious illness tragically killed all three of Dua-ron's siblings and he became sole heir to the throne. The Priesthood justly suspected the involvement of Mailyn, a mysterious woman who ingratiated her way into the palace and became instrumental in raising Dua-ron. In actuality, she was a dark sorceress, an enchantress who manipulated the royal family, and in particular Dua-ron, for her own sinister motives."

David restrained a shudder as he saw a middle-aged woman dressed in a long black dress, slim and slight, with grey hair falling down her shoulders and back. With searing black eyes, the narrow-faced, pale-skinned woman had a cold, calculating feel about her, exuding an aura of icy dispassion.

"Raised under the influence of the sorceress Mailyn, Dua-ron grew up a dark and twisted man. Encouraged by Mailyn, Dua-ron became obsessed with pushing technological boundaries, driven by a burning desire for power and conquest. Under Dua-ron's rule, the people turned away from the teachings of the Priesthood in favor of a more tantalizing god—that of technology.

"It was the ancient technology of the Priesthood that most fascinated Dua-ron," she continued. "Specifically, the ability to create inter-dimensional gateways. When the High Priest Ardonis refused to share this technology, Dua-ron had his troops and scientists storm the temple in an attempt to discover the secrets of the temple gateway. His head scientist, Lian-andon, eventually managed to deduce how the technology worked and a grand scheme commenced to create a super-gateway, the likes of which Alanar had never seen."

Balaska waved her hand and their surroundings changed. They now stood in the heart of the city, amid a plaza packed with people. Thousands of men, women and children lined the streets, gathered around an ominous-looking metal structure. Comprising a colossal metal obelisk and two smaller pillars linked by a large wheel, the imposing structure cast a shadow upon the land as it eclipsed the suns. "The gateway," David whispered.

Balaska nodded. "It was a time of celebration for the Lasandrian people. Dua-ron convinced them that they stood upon the brink of a bold new era; that the gateway would bring Lasandria immeasurable power."

"I'm guessing it didn't..."

Balaska shook her head.

David had expected their sudden appearance to cause consternation among the city inhabitants, but it seemed both he and Balaska were invisible to those around them. Indeed, much to his astonishment, one woman even walked right through him as though he was nothing more than a ghost.

Beneath the gateway, Dua-ron stood center stage upon a raised platform, the waif-like Mailyn by his side. Power generators and control panels lined either side of the platform. A dozen scientists and technicians manned the controls, overseen by the head scientist Lian-andon; a drab-looking middle-aged man with a mane of gray-speckled hair.

The crowd began chanting in anticipation as Lian-andon prepared to activate the gateway. The excitement was tangible. But while thousands of people were swept up in a euphoria of anticipation and wonder, David could only feel a sense of dread. These people didn't know what they were doing.

Following a theatrical wave of Dua-ron's hand, Lian-nandon activated the gateway.

The city shook underfoot as the gateway powered into life. Waves of electricity surged up the obelisks, setting the wheel into motion. It spun slowly at first, but soon rotated with such speed it was barely visible to the eye. As it spun, a spiraling vortex of energy formed at its apex. Rapidly growing in size and intensity, the swirling pool of light stretched all the way from the sky to the ground.

"Behold, the gateway!" Dua-ron called to the bedazzled crowd, his voice amplified by a loudspeaker. "The gateway to our liberation!"

All eyes were fixed upon the sheer magnificence of this, the pinnacle of Lasandria's technological glory.

It was then that something went terribly, terribly wrong.

The portal exploded.

David recoiled as an immense blast tore through the city.

Although spared from the annihilation, he watched in horror as the crowds were seared to ashes in the blink of an eye. A shockwave rippled outward, tearing the buildings to rubble as if made of nothing more than sand.

All went dark and the scene again shifted. David found himself back on the mountaintop alongside Balaska. This time a cloak of darkness had swallowed the valley and surrounding mountains.

Breathless and disorientated, all he could now see of the city were flames and billowing black smoke. The city was gone—completely obliterated—its inhabitants killed in the merest flash. Trembling, he looked up at Balaska. "What happened?"

Balaska's eyes met his through the darkness, and her face was filled with sadness. "Mailyn sabotaged the gateway's encoding system. She herself but a pawn, she deliberately locked the coordinates onto Abidalos, the dark dimension. The moment the gateway opened, the membrane between their realm and yours was breached, causing a catastrophic explosion. As you just saw, the city was reduced to rubble and the shockwave rippled across an entire continent and beyond."

"And it was over just like that..."

"That was not all."

"There's more?"

"The door was now open and a ravenous dark force was ready to pass through it. Death was unleashed."

In his mind's eye David saw a series of airships shooting through the mouth of the portal. They hovered over the ruined city, closely followed by ground troops. These were creatures unlike anything he'd seen in his worst nightmares: monstrous reptilian beings clad in armor, brandishing rifles and knives. They pored over the wreckage like scavengers, clearly delighting in the death and desolation around them.

"They are called Narssians," came Balaska's voice. "Parasitic demons—they feed off the life force of living beings and of entire worlds."

David was overcome with horror as he saw the alien creatures advancing through the dead city.

"The Kingdom of Lasandria was destroyed in a matter of hours. Within days, the whole of Alanar had been decimated. The Narssians left this world and spread across the stars, feeding on whatever worlds they encountered. They became a scourge, feared throughout the galaxy as the destroyer of worlds."

The images faded from David's mind. He looked up at Balaska. A single teardrop rolled down her cheek. "The Narssians left Alanar but a withered shell of a planet," she said. "It was the catastrophic end to another great Age of Alanar. There were some survivors, but they had to adjust to living in a twilight world of darkness and disorder. They sought to rebuild, but civilization had been lost. Alanar was reduced, once again, to what it had been prior to the arrival of the Lasan: savage, war-torn and primitive. Only this time, things were immeasurably worse."

"How long ago did all this happen?"

"Ten thousand years before you were born."

"And these people, the Lasandrians, were essentially responsible for their own destruction."

"Yes, and that is the saddest, most tragic thing of all..."

David looked down at the amulet around his neck. "You said you were going to tell me about the history of the Key. What does all this have to do with the Key of Alanar?"

"Before the cataclysm, the High Priest Ardonis foresaw what was to occur. He tried to warn Dua-ron and the science ministry but his warnings fell upon deaf ears. He even appealed to the public themselves, but few paid heed. There was nothing Ardonis could do to prevent the imminent catastrophe. However, acting at the behest of the Council of Elders, he gathered anyone who would listen and led them through the temple gateway to a place of safety. Thus, a handful of Lasandria's people were spared the annihilation."

"Didn't you say that you were on the Council of Elders?"

"Yes. We were aware of what was to happen. Though we could not directly intervene, we knew that we had to do something, for as bad as things were, they could have been infinitely worse."

"How could they have *possibly* been worse?"

"It was but a scout force of Narssians that emerged through the gateway; no more than sixty in total. And *this* is the destruction they wrought." She glanced down at the scorched ruins of El Ad'dan. "If the portal had not been sealed thereafter, an endless stream of Narssians would have poured through the gateway, unleashing the full force of Death upon the mortal realm. The consequences would have been unimaginable; the scale of destruction simply inconceivable. In time, this entire universe would have been overrun by Narssians. The Guardians could not allow this to happen. We knew they had to be stopped, and that was why the Key of Alanar was created."

"For what reason?"

"The Key of Alanar is just that—a *key*. It has the ability to lock and unlock inter-dimensional gateways."

"Like the one that destroyed Lasandria?"

"Precisely. Once the gateway was opened, only *one* thing could close it again." She paused. "The Key was created by the Guardians and given to a man known as Arran. It was his mission to enter the ruined city of El Ad'dan and use the Key to seal the gateway, preventing any more Narssians from entering this dimension. Arran accepted this dangerous task—and he succeeded, albeit at the cost of his own life."

"So the Key has been used before," he said. "Thousands of years before I was born?"

She nodded.

"How did it come to be in my possession?"

Balaska glanced down into the valley, her eyes coming to rest upon the burning embers of the dead city, now barely visible through the curtain of black smoke. "I believe we have seen all that we need to see here." She turned back to him. "The rest we can discuss another...*time.*"

She reached out and took hold of David's hand. The moment her hand touched his, reality once again disintegrated...

*His surroundings melted and David felt his body and mind dissolving—his consciousness surging into and through the timeless currents of Infinity.*

*Time was again fluidic; the centuries passing like grains of sand through an hourglass.*

# CHAPTER ELEVEN

# The Choice

David came crashing back to reality with such force it took a moment for him to adjust to being back in his physical body. The last thing he remembered was—

"Lasandria..."

"That was ten millennia ago," came Balaska's voice.

As his senses came back into focus, he realized that he was still seated in Balaska's tent alongside Janir and Naranyan. Both seemed oblivious to his inexplicable journey through time and space.

"David has now seen firsthand the destruction caused during the final days of the Lasandria," Balaska told them.

Janir nodded solemnly.

"So what happened," David said, "after Lasandria was destroyed and the Narssians left?"

"The survivors strove to rebuild in a world of darkness," she said, "a world stained with blood and haunted by the memory of a grievous holocaust. The people of Alanar were deeply scarred; a scar that remains to this day."

"Did they manage to rebuild?"

"It was a tumultuous process. Even when communities managed to form some semblance of order, the incessant warring and conflict hindered any real progress. Civilizations rose, but beset by conflict, they eventually fell again; and so it was for millennia. It was from this vacuum of power that a coalition eventually formed; a coalition that called itself the Sevari Alliance."

"The Alliance?" The mere name was enough to make him shudder.

"Yes," Balaska confirmed. "The Alliance began as a means of stabilizing the world order. It was an institution of peace: its mandate to end the fighting that was tearing Alanar apart and to bring tribes, cultures and whole continents together in peace."

David frowned.

"Hard to believe, isn't it?" Janir said.

"The Alliance was certainly born of the noblest of ideologies," Balaska said.

"Yet noble intent is often cast aside as men grow ever hungrier for power," Naranyan observed.

"Over the centuries," Balaska said, "the Alliance fell into darkness and depravity, until it eventually became the tyrannical empire it is today. That, however, is a story for another time." She stood up, her face darkening as she looked down at David. "What you need know is this: the Alliance is now working with the Narssians."

David felt a chill run down his spine. He turned to Janir and Naranyan, whose grim expressions seemed to confirm her words. "The Narssians—*why?*"

"Death is hungry," Balaska said. She began pacing, her graceful form illuminated by candlelight. "These demonic creatures have spent eons trying to escape the dimensional prison of Abidalos; desperate to free themselves and satiate their unending hunger for life. Even from the confines of the dark dimension they are able to manipulate susceptible minds. As indeed they did with Mailyn, the sorceress who sabotaged the Lasandrian gateway, unleashing the scout force of Narssian troops.

"Although immortal, those very Narssians have been unable to procreate in this universe. On a deep cellular level, their physiological makeup is incompatible with this realm. Their numbers were always limited to the few dozen that made it through the gateway prior to Arran sealing it. But heeding the call of their brethren, they have now returned to Alanar, determined to tear down the barriers between universes."

"So they're trying to release the rest of their kind?"

"Imagine it, David. An open doorway to hell, allowing Death to flood this realm—consuming, devouring all. And they intend to do more than just reopen a gateway to their universe. They want nothing less than to converge this universe with their own, enabling them to reign supreme in both."

David rose to his feet, overcome by a sense of dread.

"World after world will fall as the infection spreads; system after system, galaxy after galaxy. This entire universe will eventually be destroyed, if not by the Narssians, then by the resulting *pralaya.*"

"Pralaya?"

"The Great Dissolution. By tampering with the fabric of reality they will cause irreparable damage, triggering a fatal chain reaction. Eventually, the entire multiverse will collapse, consumed by irreversible entropy."

David shook his head. "What does this have to do with the Alliance?"

"The Narssians don't possess gateway technology themselves. But knowing that such technology once existed on this world, they have returned, and are working with the Alliance to find it."

"Why would the Alliance ally themselves with the Narssians?"

"The Alliance hierarchy have long been under the influence of the Narssians and their incorporeal counterparts, the Shadow Lords. In addition, the Narssians have provided the Alliance with technology, aircraft, and weaponry far in advance of anything they previously possessed. In the short term, it is an equitable deal for them. Driven by a hive mind, the Narssians know only how to use brute force. The Alliance, however, has been working on more insidious levels, scouring the ancient texts and using dark sorcery in a desperate bid to recover the technology. Thus far their efforts have proven in vain."

"Why?"

"Because they have come to realize that there is only one thing on Alanar still capable of opening or sealing an interdimensional gateway. And that, David, is the object that now hangs around your neck."

"The Key of Alanar..."

"They cannot reopen the gateway without the Key. They need it."

"And they need you, David," Janir added, rising to his feet. "For only you can use the Key."

"So that's why they've been pursuing me; why they attacked New Haven." He turned to Balaska. "What am I supposed to do?"

"What you must do is resist them. It is essential that you find and reunite the Key with its missing half. That is now your mission."

"Why would you want me to find the other half of the Key? Surely as long as it's broken in two it's useless to them?"

"Were it that simple, we would have destroyed the Key long ago. But as you will learn in time, the Key was created for a specific purpose; a purpose that has yet to unfold. For now, all you need know is this: the Key of Alanar must be made whole. Everything depends upon it; past, present, and future."

David shook his head. "So what you're saying is you want me to find the other half of this Key, while trying to escape not only the Alliance, but these demonic monsters capable of destroying entire universes..."

"You must," Naranyan said with cutting bluntness. "If you do not, it will be the end of all things."

Janir placed a hand on David's arm. "David, I know this is an overwhelming burden, especially for one so young. If I could change it, I would. But I can't. You, David, are the Custodian of the Key, a role prophesied in the ancient scriptures millennia ago."

"Prophesied?" David echoed. "You're saying this is somehow my *destiny*—that I have no choice in the matter?"

"There is always choice," Balaska said, "even within the boundaries of prophecy. This is the path the fates have laid out for you. Yet no one can force you to walk it, for it is a dangerous one, rife with peril. If you so choose you can walk away from it, but—"

"Then I choose to walk away." This was like some kind of twisted nightmare and he didn't want any part of it. David took a step back. "I'm sorry. But you must have made some mistake. I can't do this. I can't..."

He'd made his decision, and in that moment the entire course of history was changed.

Unable to face them any longer, David exited the tent, marching into the surrounding woodland. Still shrouded in mist, the forest remained eerily still. He came to a stop beneath a large pine, its outstretched branches barely visible through the vaporous mist. Simmering with pent-up desperation, he briefly considered making a run for it, leaving this place and all this insanity behind. But he had nowhere to go; and besides, try though he might, he could never escape himself.

Hearing someone approach, he turned to see Janir appearing through the mist. "I'm sorry," David said, "I just needed to get out of there."

"I understand how overwhelming this must be," Janir said.

"Overwhelming doesn't begin to cover it." David snatched the Key from around his neck. "I never asked for *this*."

"And yet the fates have given you it."

"Well, the fates can have it back." He wanted to throw it away; to get as much distance from it as he could, yet something stopped him. He stared ahead, his eyes as misty as the forest. "I just want to go back to the way things were."

"I know. But there's no going back, David."

"No, I don't suppose there is..."

"All we can do now is look forward."

"Balaska said I had the choice to just walk away from this. But I don't, do I? Not really..."

"The choice is there. But if you do walk away, you must still face the repercussions. The Alliance will still be after you, and no matter where you tried to hide, they'd eventually find you. They'd catch you, break you and use you to achieve their goal; the consequences of which would be unimaginable."

"And it would be my fault..."

"For every choice that we make, there's a consequence. When deciding upon a course of action, we must gauge all likely consequences of that act. If you try to walk away, the Alliance will find you nonetheless; and they will win. But if you choose to accept the challenges ahead, and embrace your destiny, then there's a chance you can defeat them."

David said nothing.

"You know, you got what you wanted, David."

"I did?"

"You wanted to know who you are and why you're here. Few in life ever truly fathom their reason for being. They drift like leaves in the wind, never realizing the truth of their existence. You'll never be like that. You've been chosen by the fates to undertake a mission of importance at a time of great need. You can't let fear obscure your judgment. You have all the strength you need in order to undertake this task. Indeed, you've been prepared for it in ways you can't even begin to imagine."

"I spent most of my childhood feeling as though my life was wrong somehow," David admitted. "I often had this overwhelming sense that I was meant to be someplace else and that there was something important I had to do. I just didn't know what."

"Your entire life has been leading to this. You may not feel ready, but I can assure you that you are. The question is whether you are willing."

David felt his body tense as he stared into the mist.

"Because if you're not," Janir continued, "you need to be aware of the consequences. One way or another, the Narssians will find a way to create a gateway and they will tear this universe apart from the inside out. They'll strip this realm apart piece by piece, feeding off entire planets; entire galaxies. And once they've totally consumed our universe, they'll grow hungry again, and seek other dimensions in search of more conquest, more prey, more destruction."

"So I can either let this happen, or I can fight to stop it..."

Part of him was struggling to see beyond his own personal grief in order to even care what happened to the rest of the universe. But then it struck him. Something clicked into place inside him. He would do it. "I have to make things right," he said, a flame of indignation igniting within. "They killed my mother, my friends, my family, and it was because of me. I can't let their deaths be for nothing. I can't just sit back and let this happen or run away and hide like a frightened child. I have to fight—I have to fight to make things right again."

In that moment he made a vow that the deaths of his mother and the others would not be in vain. He now had a reason to live. The Alliance had destroyed his life. He would now fight them with whatever strength remained—and he would destroy them. Knowing that Janir would disapprove of such a vengeful thought, he sought to banish it from his mind, for Janir often displayed an uncanny ability to read his thoughts.

"It is decided then," came Balaska's voice. They turned to see she and Naranyan appearing through the mist.

David nodded.

"Your quest is to find the City of Lorden. There lies the other half of the Key of Alanar."

"I always thought the City of Lorden was a myth," Janir said.

"It is no myth," Balaska said. "It exists, and you must find it."

"Where is it?" David asked. No one answered. He turned to Janir and Naranyan. "You must have some idea where it is?" Judging by their expressions, they did not.

Balaska smiled. "Hold the Key in your right hand. Direct your attention to it, and inwardly ask it to point you to its missing half."

Although he thought it to be an odd instruction, he did as she said. Looking down at the crystal, he was astonished to see the farthest tip light up with a silvery glow.

"The Key will serve as your compass," she said. "Follow it unerringly and it will lead you to the City of Lorden."

"And once we get there?"

"The Key will be made whole; ready to use to save this world and defeat the enemy."

"How?"

"One step at a time. Rest assured, you will be guided by the Guardians. You are not alone and will not be forsaken."

"Balaska's right," Janir said. "You won't be alone. I'll be by your side, David."

Naranyan lowered his head. "I also pledge myself to your cause. I offer to accompany you on your mission, guiding you through these lands and assisting in any way I can."

David nodded. Although Naranyan remained something of an enigma, he was reasonably certain he could trust the Enari messenger. Besides, he would need all the help he could get. "What about the others?" He turned to Janir, suddenly remembering Darien, Janna and Mariane. "What will they do?"

"I'm sure Deshonaan would allow them to remain here with the Enari. It'd certainly be safer for them to stay, but it's their choice. We can discuss it with them later."

Part of him hoped they'd agree to join him, but he knew that Janir was right. There was no telling what dangers lay ahead and he couldn't bear the thought of losing anyone else dear to him. He'd already experienced firsthand the devastating might of the Alliance and even that would pale in comparison with the terror of the Narssians. He found it hard to shake an ominous sense of dread about the journey ahead. But the decision was made, and he knew there was no going back.

If he had any doubts as to the dangers ahead, Balaska was about to dispel them once and for all. "The mission is set," she declared. "I suggest you rest for the next few days. You have a long journey ahead of you, and it will be an arduous path. Though many times the odds against you will seem insurmountable, you must be strong; you must endure, and fight for victory. For the fate of this, and countless other worlds now lies with you."

PART TWO

# THE DARKNESS AND THE LIGHT

*"In spite of all that's happened; all that you've done and all that's been done to you, you have still have something to offer this world—something they want and are determined to take from you..."*

# CHAPTER TWELVE

# Ascension

Five days had passed since arriving at the Enari settlement. In some ways, it seemed longer. There were moments when David felt separated from his old life as if by a vast eternity, while at other times it seemed only a heartbeat away. He and his comrades had spent the time resting and recuperating. The initial shock following the destruction of their home and the murder of their families had dissipated, leaving each struggling with the bitter intensity of their bereavement.

David's grief was far from the only thing he had to deal with. The day he met Balaska his life had changed forever.

Following their fateful encounter that misty morning, he, Janir and Naranyan had returned to the village and spoken with Darien, Janna and Mariane. They told them of the Key, the reason for the Alliance's pursuit and their impending quest to find the City of Lorden.

Understandably, it had elicited a great many questions. David tried to answer as best he could, but he often had to defer to Janir and Naranyan. It had been clear from the offset that the pair of them knew far more than he did.

"There's a reason for that," Janir had told him. "We've both been in communion with the Guardians and are well versed in the ancient texts and prophecies." David couldn't help but wonder just how long Janir had known about his role as 'Custodian of the Key'. He'd known Janir since childhood. Had Janir harbored this secret all that time?

His friends seemed to accept all they'd been told. Outlining the dangers, Janir suggested they would be better put remaining with the Enari. However, Darien, Janna, and Mariane unanimously agreed that their place was with David, and they would accompany him on his mission regardless of the dangers. Even Mariane seemed resolute in her decision to join them.

David was relieved by their decision. After all they'd been through in this short time, a bond had formed between them. They were his family now.

It was late afternoon, and with an overriding sense of apprehension he and his comrades prepared to set off the following morning. While Janir and Naranyan conferred, carefully planning their route ahead, David and the others, assisted by several Enari, prepared supplies for the journey. They packed as much food as they could carry, for no one could say how long they would be traveling, nor indeed where their journey would take them.

Earlier that day, the Enari had provided them with some weaponry, including spears, daggers and bows and arrows. The tribe's hunters had given David, Darien and Janna rudimentary instruction on the usage of the weapons; Mariane having refused to participate. David couldn't shake the feeling that such primitive weapons would be entirely useless against the enemy.

No one was looking forward to leaving. David had started to feel at quite home among the Enari. They lived a simple, contented life, seemingly far from the rest of civilization. But as Janir pointed out, the longer they stayed, the greater likelihood their presence would endanger their hosts.

The decision to leave had been made, and David would stand by it. He was still struggling to reconcile all that Balaska had told him about his supposed role as some kind of savior of the planet. "What if you've got this wrong?" he'd asked Janir. "What if it's all some kind of mistake?"

"Infinity doesn't make mistakes," was Janir's response.

David wasn't sure he believed that.

He aired his misgivings with Darien, who had simply tried to make light of it, as only Darien could. It was probably the only way he knew to help. Mariane had been uncomfortable talking about the subject at all. She'd been his tutor when he was a child and it seemed that even after all these years they had difficulty relating outside of their teacher-pupil relationship. Then there was Janna, who, an introvert at the best of times, was becoming so increasingly distant that David couldn't gauge her opinion.

As he and Darien packed the last of the food supplies into leather backpacks, David heard a voice call his name. He turned to see Deshonaan standing behind him, staff in hand. "I bring word," the Chief said. "Balaska wishes to see you."

David nodded. Balaska had told him that she would see him one last time before he left. It was just as well too, for he had something important to ask her.

Deshonaan led him through the forest. The suns had disappeared from the sky and dusk set in. Arriving at Balaska's solitary tent, Deshonaan beckoned toward it with a smile and departed. Taking a deep breath, David stepped inside. Before he'd assumed that it had just been his imagination, but this time he was certain—the tent was larger on the inside!

Balaska stood before him. David again found himself mesmerized by her ethereal beauty; only this time her otherworldliness seemed even more pronounced. Her form glowed with a radiance that somehow shone through her skin, reflected in her twinkling dark eyes.

"I was hoping I'd see you again before we left," he smiled.

"I said you would," she whispered, "and do you know why I said that?"

He shook his head.

"Because I saw it. As a Guardian, I see a great many things. Some are things that have happened in the past; some are happening now, and some will happen in the future—or at least *may* happen. The future is not always set in stone. But this I do know for certain: I must now leave this world."

"And go where?"

"Home, David. My stay in this realm is at an end."

"I kind of hoped you'd come with us." If anyone could help them along their journey it would surely be Balaska.

"In a sense, I will. You need only ever close your eyes, call my name and I will be there."

The warmth of her smile and the sweetness of her voice touched David's heart. In her presence, his pain and anguish seemed to temporarily melt away. But there was something urgent on his mind. "You seem to know just about everything. So please, Balaska, tell me this—who *am* I? Where am I from, and why was I abandoned as a baby?"

"These questions I cannot yet answer for you."

David found that hard to believe.

"Some answers cannot simply be given," she explained. "They must be discovered for oneself and sometimes even fought for. The journey you now embark upon will eventually yield the answers you seek. For you seek not only the City of Lorden and the Key—you seek yourself."

"I don't understand..."

"In time you shall. The path on which you now set out is a path of initiation. You will learn much, you will experience much and you will *become* much. Only then will you find answers to your questions. It is not an easy path, but it is a necessary one, for it is a journey to wholeness."

This wasn't the answer he wanted, but it was somehow an answer he could accept, for now.

Balaska placed her hand upon his cheek as she gazed into his eyes. "There is much pain within you. You must be strong. You must not let it cloud your judgment. You have been through much and much yet lies ahead of you. Be brave, David, and have faith in the knowledge that you are not alone. The power of Infinity itself is supporting you. But you must reach out to it; you must allow yourself to open to it. We can only help you to the extent that you help yourself."

She withdrew her hand and he immediately missed the warmth of her touch. "You will face adversity along your way. You will have choices to make...and you must be careful, for you will be enticed to make the wrong decisions. And there will come a time; a time when you must be willing to sacrifice *everything* in order to achieve your goal..."

Her words struck a chord of fear in him. "Acknowledge your fear," she said, "and move beyond it. You must master the inner world before you have any hope of mastering the outer world.

It is imperative that you relinquish your doubt, your anger, and hatred; for that is what will ultimately destroy you."

She took a step back. She was about to leave; he could feel it.

"Remember I am with you always," she said. *"Remember..."*

She closed her eyes and raised her arms. David was astonished by what happened next. Waves of rippling golden light cascaded down from above, enveloping her. The entire tent lit up as Balaska's form began dissolving into the light.

The radiance continued intensifying, forcing David to shield his eyes. He felt as though he was at the center of a star about to go nova. He could feel it building in intensity—building and building—until it eventually peaked in an explosion of light. And then nothing.

She was gone.

The very tent in which they'd stood had disappeared and he found himself alone in the forest.

The suns had set and darkness was creeping in. Looking upward, he saw a few dim stars dotted across the sky. One star stood apart from the others. It shone brightly; a beacon sparkling amid the heavens. For some reason, he stood transfixed by it, still able to sense Balaska's comforting presence.

*Remember...*

# CHAPTER THIRTEEN

# Quagmire

"Janir, when are we going to stop? My feet hurt."

"We're all tired, Mariane..."

"I didn't say I was tired, I said my feet hurt. They're covered in blisters! Perhaps you'd care to see them?"

Clearly speechless, Janir said nothing. It was Darien that responded. "Mariane, you knew it would be a long road before we set out; and you volunteered to come along—no one forced you to be here!"

"I was talking to *Janir*," Mariane barked.

"Lucky Janir," Darien muttered. He and Mariane had been at each other's throats ever since they'd left the Enari settlement two days ago. It had already been a long and exhausting trek and they were all on edge.

"Just a little farther, Mariane," Janir assured her. "Then we'll stop for the night."

"How much farther?"

Janir motioned to Naranyan, who was some way ahead of them, hacking his way through the undergrowth with a large knife. "As soon as Naranyan has determined we're at a safe enough distance from the nearest Kellian tribal grounds. Because believe me, the last thing you want is to be woken up in the night by a gang of Kellian raiders."

Mariane grunted and fell silent. The travelers had now entered the borders of Kellian territory. The Enari had provided maps of the area. That, coupled with Naranyan and Janir's experience of having previously traveled in the region, would hopefully be enough to ensure they avoided any entanglement with the Kellians.

The day began to draw in. Waning sunlight glimmered through the trees. The scent of wildflowers mixed with the

earthy aroma of moss and decaying leaves as it carried upon the faintest of breezes. The sound of running water alerted the travelers to a nearby river, which they followed until they came to a waterfall. Naranyan decided this would be a good place to stop for the night.

After setting up camp, preparing evening meal was thankfully an easy task, for they still had ample food rations. The group sat around the campfire as they ate, glad of the warmth as darkness fell. "So where are we actually going?" Darien asked.

"Wherever we must to avoid the Kellians," Janir said.

"Which will be no easy task," Naranyan warned, stoking the campfire with a stick as the rest of them ate. "This region alone is home to dozens of tribes and there is no way around it."

"We're taking the safest route we can," Janir assured them. "Unfortunately, it'll take us through the marshlands. It won't make for pleasant walking, but after that, we should be at a reasonably safe distance from the nearest Kellian settlements."

"Where do we go from there?" asked Janna, speaking up for perhaps the first time that evening.

"As David will tell you, the Key is pointing us due east." Janir took a sip from his waterskin flask and continued. "According to the Enari maps, that will take us to Port Llanyeau on the East coast. From there, we'll have to find passage across the sea to Sekyr."

David looked up. "Why Sekyr? What's there?"

"Sekyr is the most westerly port on the continent of Ardesha. As for what's there—let's just say that we'll be going from the so-called 'uninhabited lands' to a land that is very much inhabited..."

"So what's the story with these Kellians?" Darien asked. "I mean, we've heard all about the Kellian raids on New Haven. But that was before I was born, and I'm pretty sure the old folk on the island exaggerated those stories. So..."

"Are the Kellians really as bad as we've been told?" Janna finished his sentence.

"I do not know what you have been told," Naranyan said, throwing his stick into the fire and taking a seat opposite them.

"But I do not believe it is possible to overstate the savagery of the Kellians."

"Their entire culture is rooted in conquest," Janir said. "They burn and pillage their way across the land, stealing whatever takes their fancy and destroying all else. From what I understand it was about forty-five years ago the raids on New Haven took place, is that right?"

"Yes," Mariane said. "It happened when I was a child." She shot Darien a withering glance. "And I can assure you that myself and the other 'old folk' were not exaggerating. It was a terrifying time for the island. I suppose we'd assumed we were safe in our seclusion, so the arrival of the Kellians was an immense shock for all of us. But although initially unprepared for the onslaught, we eventually managed to fight them off—though not without losing a great many of our own. It was brutal; so brutal. But having demonstrated that we were capable of defending our home, the Kellians eventually left and never returned."

"If only all were as lucky," Naranyan said.

"It's unusual for the Kellians to surrender," Janir noted. "Whenever they do encounter a race capable of fighting back, they weigh up the reward of conquest against the cost of war. Occasionally they resort to more civilized means of interaction, but that's more the exception than the rule."

"All in all, they sound like a nasty bunch," Darien concluded as he finished off his meal.

"Indeed," Janir said. "They used to be feared throughout the entire planet."

"Used to be?" David said.

"The Alliance has wiped out dozens of Kellian tribes. The Kellians have sworn revenge, but it's a war they can't possibly win. To the Alliance, the Kellians are nothing more than an inconsequential menace; a nuisance to be eradicated."

"However," Naranyan warned. "If we are unfortunate enough to encounter them, you will find it hard to dismiss them so brazenly."

"Is it true they eat their own dead?" Darien asked with a grimace.

"Yes," Naranyan said. "And they would just as happily eat you—only they may not be so merciful as to wait until you are dead..."

"Let's just leave it at that," Janir suggested, registering the horrified expressions on the others' faces. "Suffice to say, we'll be doing our utmost to avoid them." He stood up, brushing the crumbs off his lap. "Right, it's getting late. We all need sleep, so let's get cleared up and settle down for the night."

No one was in the mood to argue. Janir distributed the blankets and they gathered down around the campfire, endeavoring to get as comfortable as they could upon the cold, hard ground.

They agreed to take turns to keep watch. Naranyan volunteered to take the first watch. Armed with his spear, he paced the perimeter of the camp while the others tried to get some sleep. Aside from the hooting of owls and chirping of insects, all that could be heard was the sound of the fire as it slowly consumed the logs and branches; crackling, hissing and occasionally popping. David found it strangely soothing and, such was his exhaustion, it took him little time to drift off to sleep.

Another nightmare. The same nightmare he'd been had been having since leaving New Haven—a dream that shook him to the core, leaving him anguished for hours after. He shuddered as he tried to shake it off.

David sat up and looked around. Everyone else was asleep around the campfire; now but a pile of dimly glowing embers. David knew that he ought to try and get back to sleep himself, but his mind was still racing and his stomach knotted.

Bracing himself against the nocturnal chill, he got up and wandered to the waterfall. A lone figure stood silhouetted on the riverbank. It was Janir. It must have been his turn to keep watch. "Shouldn't you be asleep?"

"I had another nightmare," David said. A misty spray from the waterfall caressed his skin as he gazed into the moonlit water.

"It's hardly surprising you're having bad dreams. I think most of us are."

"I've had bad dreams before, but nothing like this. I don't know how or why, but they're *more* than just dreams somehow."

"Tell me about them."

"It's the same dream over and over again, night after night. First of all, I'm back in New Haven after the Alliance attack. The streets are full of bodies and I come across my mother, lying in the rubble. Then it shifts and I'm being chased. These creatures are after me. I try to run, but there's a big chasm ahead of me blocking my escape. The creatures grab hold of me and I can't break free. They take me before this man. He's their leader I think. He makes my skin crawl, Janir. I don't know how or why but he's trying to *get* to me somehow—trying to manipulate and coerce me—" David saw the look of alarm on Janir's face. "What's wrong?"

"I don't know..."

"Janir, if it's about my dream, I want to know."

"It's probably nothing, but let me know if the nightmares continue."

"Why?"

"Just a feeling I have. No reason for you to worry right now."

David wasn't entirely convinced. He felt unnerved by Janir's reaction. Sensing David's unease, Janir changed the subject. "You'd better try to get some more rest. We all need to keep our strength up."

"I'm awake now, so I might as well take the next watch."

"Very well. As soon as you get tired, get someone else to take over from you."

David nodded. Janir placed a hand on his shoulder before going off to join the others around the remnants of the campfire.

As David paced the riverbank, keeping watch over his sleeping comrades, his thoughts kept returning to his dream, and in particular, Janir's reaction to it. Janir seemed alarmed by it—but why? David hated the way Janir often withheld things from him, particularly when it came to matters that clearly involved him.

David stayed up for as long as he could and then, when tiredness finally got the better of him, he coaxed up a reluctant Darien, for it was his turn to keep watch. He returned to his spot on the ground and, huddling beneath his blanket for warmth, he soon fell asleep once more.

That morning the travelers bathed in the crisp water before first meal. Wasting little time, they then packed up their supplies and readied themselves for another day of hiking.

Around midday, they reached the edge of the forest, beyond which lay a seemingly endless stretch of marshland. The going was tough and wading through the swamp slowed their pace considerably. Darien had already slipped and fallen into the marsh and—along with Naranyan, who had plunged in to pull him out—was covered in mud from head to foot.

The marshland was a dark and dank place; an interminable expanse of deadness and decomposition. Aside from the precariousness of the marshy ground, the swamp smelled rancid and a grimy mist clung to their skin and obscured all trace of sunlight. Matters were made worse when Naranyan happened to mention something in passing about avoiding 'swamp creatures'.

"Swamp creatures?" Mariane spluttered in disbelief.

"Wait a moment, no one said anything about swamp creatures," Darien added, his face draining of color.

"What kind of creatures...?" David asked, not entirely sure that he wanted to know the answer.

Janir frowned at Naranyan, evidently having told him not to mention this to the others. "It's nothing to worry about."

"I think we'll be the judge of that," Mariane said. "What exactly do you mean by *creatures?*"

"Swamp serpents," Naranyan answered with his trademark bluntness.

"How wonderful," Darien muttered as he nearly slipped in the mud again.

"I first encountered one when I was only five years old," Naranyan said, an almost nostalgic tone slipping into his voice as he continued wading through the putrid marsh. "Luckily, it was but a small one and I was with an adult who managed to slay the creature. But even then, it was not a pleasant experience. They can grow quite large."

Darien's eyes widened. "How large?"

Naranyan stopped and pointed to a gnarled old tree. "Do you see that tree?"

Darien nodded.

"Well, about four times that size."

Mariane turned to Janir. "Janir, why didn't you tell us about this?"

"I didn't want to worry you unnecessarily. They tend to be quite rare so I felt it best not to—"

"I want out of this place, now! I'd never have set foot here if I'd known anything about serpents."

"Remember, we're here to avoid the Kellians. If we'd carried on the way we were going we'd have strayed too close to the nearest Kellian settlement."

"So the choice is between being killed by the Kellians or killed by a giant serpent!"

"No one is going to be killed by *anything!* Now, let's keep moving. We'll get out of here as quickly as we can. It may not be an ideal route but it's a necessary one given the circumstances."

That was his final word on the matter and with that, they resumed their plod through the marshland, albeit rather more nervously than before. The subject of swamp serpents had been quelled for the moment, along with any further mention of the Kellians. They were all on edge enough as it was.

The afternoon seemed to stretch on without end, much like their dismal surroundings. Eventually, to everyone's relief, Janir decided that it was time to stop for evening meal, after which they would find a place to settle for the evening. While Naranyan and the others began preparing the rations, Janir pulled David aside. He led him away from the others, through the muddy, moss-filled ground to a rocky clearing surrounded by dead trees. "What's wrong?" David asked.

"Nothing's wrong. But it's time I took your training to the next level; something I should have done long before now. As Balaska told you, this is a path of training and initiation; one that's necessary to prepare you for what lies ahead. It has fallen upon me to direct and supervise your training, and time is of the essence. What ordinarily takes initiates many years to learn, you must now learn in a matter of weeks."

"What kind of training are we talking about?"

"Everything. Every aspect of your being must be brought under mastery. This begins with the mental and emotional levels. You recall I taught you to meditate as a means of calming the mind and balancing the emotions?"

David nodded. "Can we discuss this over our meal? I'm kind of hungry."

"There will be time for food later," Janir said firmly. David was unnerved by his manner. Janir's normally unflappable demeanor had started to slip and for the first time he could see the strain showing in his mentor. "The power of meditation cannot be overstated. It is a weapon by which we can conquer the greatest foe we will ever face—ourselves."

"How can we be our own greatest foe?"

"Precisely because we lack mastery of our mind and emotions. We fall victim to our thoughts and feelings over and over again. They control us, shaping how we interpret life, what we believe and what we desire and fear. In many ways, they drive our every action."

"So how do we control them?"

"It's not so much a matter of controlling them as dis-identifying from them. We must learn to disengage from the perpetual flow of thoughts and emotions as they pass through our mind and allow them to drift by like clouds in the sky."

"Okay..."

"To cease identifying with the content of the mind is a key to immense power. In consciously disengaging from the mindstream, we shift our identification from the clouds to the sky; the ever-present substratum; that which is always there, boundless and free. In doing so, we realize our essential oneness with Infinity."

"I've heard you speak of 'Infinity' before. What exactly is it?"

"What is it not?" Janir said with a half smile. "Infinity is the totality of all that is. It is both the creative force of the universe and that which is created. It sustains and infuses all of life, binding together all that exists. Appearances notwithstanding, there are no boundaries, David. All is part of the dance of Infinity."

"Where does it come from?"

"The unmanifest aspect of Infinity is beginning-less and timeless. It is *existence* itself. From it, the manifest forms of life rise and fall like waves upon the ocean."

"Why don't people know about this, about Infinity?"

"Oh, Infinity has many different names across different cultures. The Enari call it the Great Spirit, or Hershala. Others refer to it as the First Source, or the Creator and represent it with a whole host of gods. But words and concepts are insufficient. They place limits upon that which is limitless. To the sorcerer—those who actively engage with this creative principle—it is simply referred to as Infinity."

"Is that what you are? A sorcerer?"

"This is not the time to discuss me, David. It is time for you to listen and learn to apply this knowledge. It is necessary that you learn to tap into Infinity and eventually learn to use it."

"Use it? How?"

Janir smiled. "Let's not get ahead of ourselves. We'll start at the beginning." He beckoned for David to sit on a nearby rock. David did so and Janir began to guide him into a state of meditation. "Close your eyes and relax. Allow your mind to settle upon the breath as it flows in and out of your body." David followed his instruction as Janir continued, "Allow any thoughts to simply drift by. Don't hold onto them. See them as transient clouds, passing through the mind; fleeting and insubstantial..."

David had practiced meditation many times under Janir's tutelage. Over the years he'd even become quite proficient at it, finding it easy to reach a deep sense of peace as his mind began to settle. This time, however, he was engulfed by a wave of panic.

His eyes snapped open. "Janir, something's wrong! We're in danger here—"

A sudden scream shattered the silence of the swamp.

It had come from the vicinity of the others.

Bolting to his feet, David followed Janir as he raced through the mud. His heart froze upon seeing a gigantic serpentine creature rising from the swamp, towering over his friends. The creature hissed as its winding body thrashed about, sending waves of mud flying; its cold reptilian eyes fixed upon its prey. Letting out a piercing wail, its jaws opened to reveal a set of dagger-like teeth.

Darien, Janna and Mariane stood motionless on the marsh bank, frozen in terror. Naranyan reached out and pulled them back, shouting at them to run for cover. Roused from their petrified stupor, they did just that. But running on such slippery, uneven ground was easier said than done. Within seconds Janna had slipped and fallen headfirst into the mud. Darien, who'd been just ahead of her, stopped and went back to help her. But it was too late, for the creature was upon her.

David felt helpless. There was nothing he could do but watch in horror as the serpent lunged down at her. But just as it was about to snatch Janna in its jaws, a metal arrow slammed into the creature's neck. The serpent arched upward, recoiling in shock.

Another metal arrow impaled the creature between the eyes. It thrashed about, howling in agony. Another round of projectiles punctured its neck and head, until eventually, it fell to the ground, displacing a wall of mud in its wake. David watched, his heart pounding as the unmoving serpent submerged into the mud.

"What just happened?" Darien cried as he helped a shocked but relieved Janna to her feet. "Who killed that thing?"

"That's a good question." David turned to Janir.

Janir had caught sight of something. Following his line of vision, David saw a figure standing some way across the swamp, only just visible through the grimy mist.

With horror, David realized it was a Kellian. He'd never seen one before, but the description was unmistakable. Tall, broad and extremely muscular, the Kellian was built more like an animal than a man, with coarse gray skin and boney ridges stretching from the top of his hairless head down his face and neck. He wore little aside from a loincloth and studded leather buckles across his rippling chest. His most obvious adornment was his personal armory, which included various sheathed blades and a metal crossbow aimed directly at them. It was the Kellian that had killed the serpent. He had saved their lives.

No one moved a muscle. All eyes were upon the Kellian, who stared back at them, expressionless. Janir broke the uneasy silence. "I take it we are your prisoners now?"

The Kellian lowered his weapon. "Go," he boomed. "Now, while you still can."

David didn't understand. Why would he just let them go?

Without another word, Janir turned to his comrades and motioned for them to leave.

But they were too late. David's heart sank as he saw a dozen other Kellians emerging through the swamp alongside the first. With a roar of glee, they congratulated their comrade. "Good hunting, Chari! Who would have thought a lowly Null would end up with such a catch. Maybe there is hope for you after all."

Their gruff, animalistic faces tightened as they began closing in on their prey, knives drawn and crossbows poised to fire. David knew there was no point in putting up a struggle. Outnumbered and outmaneuvered, there was nothing they could do to resist. They were prisoners of the Kellians.

# CHAPTER FOURTEEN

# The Kellians

The Kellians dragged their captives, bound in chains, through the swamp and back into the forest. Sturdily built creatures, they made no concessions to their exhausted prisoners as they stormed through the forest. Whenever any of the captives happened to slow down or stumble and fall, they were harshly yanked up and dragged along.

His body covered in cuts and bruises, David's legs ached with increasing pain as he was forced onward, the friction of the shackles against his wrists drawing blood. He knew the others were in equally as bad a state. He had no idea what the Kellians were likely to do to them. Given the stories he'd heard, it was something he dared not contemplate.

It was nightfall by the time they reached their destination: a Kellian settlement upon the edge of a quarry. Lit by a number of campfires and flaming torches skewered into the ground, the ramshackle settlement comprised dozens of shabby huts and buildings cobbled together with scraps of wood and metal, all in varying states of decay and disrepair. It was filthy and overpopulated, with Kellians as far as the eye could see.

Dragged through the settlement, David was struck by the death around them. Animal carcasses hung from hooks on the side of buildings; the smell of rotting flesh mixing with smoke from the fires. A number of the carcasses lay strewn upon the ground, being carved and gutted by Kellian women, distinguishable from the males only by their bare breasts. The other Kellians sat around eating and drinking, conversing in grunts and shouts. Entertainment seemed to comprise Kellian males engaging in hand-to-hand combat, vigorously fighting each other as groups of spectators cheered them on.

Upon catching sight of the arrivals, a horde of Kellians swarmed around them. They laughed and jeered as they surveyed the captives; jostling, pushing and pulling at them, yanking at the chains; some even reaching out and snapping their jaws. Horrified, David and the others tried to recoil from the animalistic creatures.

Led through the boisterous crowd, they were taken into one of the bigger buildings. A rickety wooden hall, the fire-lit interior was decorated with bones and skinned animals. The prisoners were lined up and ordered to stand while they awaited the Chieftain.

The Kellians talked amongst themselves, a conversation of which David was only able to pick up snippets. They were evidently excited about the promise of reward for their 'catch'. David noticed that one of the Kellians stood apart from the others, noticeably more subdued. It was the Kellian that had saved them from the swamp serpent.

He looked around at his friends. Their faces were understandably grim. Janir's expression was unreadable, his eyes fixed ahead. David could only pray that he had some plan up his sleeve; some means of escape.

Their captors hushed as an imperious Kellian wielding an animal skull scepter strode into the room, flanked by two guards. With the self-important swagger of a monarch, he was large by even Kellian standards, his bulging arms, legs, chest and shoulders so muscular his body almost looked set to explode. Rags of animal hide were draped over his waist and shoulders, along with studded leather straps. An assortment of blades was tethered to a silver belt around his substantial waist. "Why do you disturb my rest?" he barked.

Visibly shrinking in his presence, the Kellians lowered their heads in deference and stood aside to reveal their prisoners. As the Kellian leader set eyes upon them, a malevolent sneer stretched across his coarse-skinned face. "You have done well."

David repressed a shudder as the Kellian leader stepped forward, studying them intently; his small, black eyes drinking in every last detail. "I am Tchyan," he rumbled, "leader of the Kellian Yarta."

Janir spoke up, his voice confident yet earnest. "My name is Janir. There seems to have been—"

Tchyan walloped him across the face; a blow of such force that Janir stumbled back, almost falling to the ground.

"I do not care who you are," Tchyan growled, towering over Janir. "You are *nothing*—nothing but my prisoners. And this you will be till the day you die. You exist only to serve me." Looking down at Janna, he added with a salacious smile, "In *whatever* ways I deem necessary..." He grabbed hold of her, pulling her toward him with a smile. Janna tried to recoil, but he was too strong to resist.

"Leave her alone!" Darien cried, making a lunge for Tchyan.

Tchyan let go of Janna and turned his attention to Darien. "Do not dare speak to me like that." Punching Darien across the face, the Kellian sent him flying to the ground, the metal chains clattering against the stone floor. Looking down at him with repugnance, Tchyan kicked him in the ribs, causing him to cry out in pain.

Tchyan turned to the rest of them, his face contorted menacingly, his voice but a low rumble. "The next time any of you show me or my men such disrespect, you will be torn apart limb by limb. And we will force you to watch with your dying breath as we devour your carcass before your eyes."

Now disenchanted by his prisoners, Tchyan turned his attention to his men, ordering them to "lock them up with the other slaves" and promising them due reward for their bounty. With that, he stormed out of the hall.

David and Naranyan helped Darien to his feet. Although clearly in pain, Darien wavered their concerns, assuring them that he was all right.

With a grunt and a yank of the chains, two of the Kellians set them moving, leading them out of the hall, back through the noisy, smoke-filled settlement. They soon came to a disintegrating wooden shed; evidently some kind of jailhouse.

Inside the dingy building was a cell lined with thick metal bars, already home to a couple of prisoners. The first Kellian bundled them into the cage, closing it with a clatter. "I suggest you get some rest. You will need it." With a sadistic snigger he turned and exited the building.

The other Kellian remained. He stood watching them in silence. David again recognized him as the Kellian who had saved them from the serpent. If he recalled correctly, the other Kellians had called him Chari.

Janir clearly recognized him too, for he approached the bars and looked into his eyes, as if trying to make a connection with him. "We won't survive here," Janir said. "You know that. I don't know why, but you were willing to let us escape earlier. I know it's a lot to ask, but we need your help again now..."

Chari stared at him blankly. "There is nothing I can do. Jaltah was correct. You had best get some rest. Tomorrow you will be put to work mining chelridium ore. You will need your strength." Before Janir could say anymore, Chari turned and left, the door clanking shut behind him.

David turned to his mentor in anguish. "What are we going to do?"

"I don't know yet, but we will find some other way to escape."

"If there *was* a way to escape," said one of the other prisoners, "then I can assure you that we would *not* be sitting here now."

David and the others turned. In the dim light streaming through a glassless window, they saw two men sitting on a metal bench. One was tall and muscular in build, his skin a light shade of gray. He wore a tattered tunic and leather waistcoat, with dark trousers and knee length boots. Middle-aged and rugged, he had thick locks of black hair tied in a ponytail. "So glad you could join us," he muttered, his voice gruff but with a hint of irony. He glanced down at the man sat next to him. "Amongst other things, the company around here has been sadly lacking."

The second prisoner was far smaller in stature, his legs barely reaching the ground from where he sat. Portly, with a roundish face, his skin had a notably reddish tone, as did his sparse auburn hair. He wore what once may have been finely tailored clothes; an elegant shirt and trousers, but which were now torn, tattered and covered in mud. The little man's expression was one of barely concealed repugnance. "It's about time they brought in someone else. It's hell enough being kept prisoner by those Kellian *savages*, but to be stuck here with only this Alazan oaf for company..."

"Watch your tongue, little man," the first man growled, jabbing him in the chest with his elbow.

"What did I tell you," the red man snapped, his face twitching with rage. "I told you never to touch me! I am royalty, I will not be defiled by some menial Alazan brute."

"Royalty my 'hind." The gray-skinned man turned to the arrivals. "See what I've had to put up with? If we should never make it out of here, please put me out my misery...and kill him."

"How did you end up here?" David asked.

"I'm an Alazan trader," he replied. "Dhjtak's the name. Captain of the Aurora Restan, flagship of the Alazan Lentai trading corporation. Least it was. My ship was sabotaged by a rival trading corporation; infected with bodan eggs. Once they hatched, the damn things killed my crew and tore the ship apart. I was lucky to make it to land alive. My luck, however, was short-lived. Barely a day later I was captured by the Kellians. I've been here ever since." He looked down at the little red-skinned man. "As for this little delight here..."

"My name is Devlan," the man boomed, the self-importance clear in his voice. "That's all you need know for now."

Djhtak rolled his eyes. "Oh, he's cagey at first, but he's certain to tell you his whole story. Over and *over* again..."

"How long have you been here?" Naranyan asked.

"Nearly two months," Djhtak said. "His Lordship here a bit longer by all accounts."

"Just the two of you?"

"When I arrived, there were others; a couple of Enari. But they fell ill and died. The Kellians make no attempt to keep their prisoners healthy."

"Why would they?" Devlan growled. "They don't need slaves. The very idea! They're far stronger than we are. There's nothing we can do that they can't in half the time. We're only kept alive because we amuse them in some perverse fashion. But don't be under any illusion. The moment we cease to amuse them, we'll be dispensed with."

Darien had heard enough. "Janir, we have to get out of here," he exclaimed, holding a hand to his ribs, clearly still in pain following Tchyan's assault. "There's no telling what they'll do to us. You saw the way that animal was looking at Janna..."

"Indeed, there must be something you can do," Mariane implored as she collapsed on one of the benches. "Before, in the forest, you saved me from those Jatei wraiths. If you could defeat them, then I'm sure you must have some way of—"

"That was a different situation altogether, Mariane," Janir cut in. "The Jatei were incorporeal entities. The Kellians, on the other hand, can only be defeated by sheer brute force; something we don't possess."

"But back on New Haven you rescued me from the Alliance troops," David said. "If you could do that, then surely—"

"What I did was the result of careful orchestration and a significant degree of luck." Janir paused for a moment before continuing. "Listen, we *will* get out of here. But we must wait for the right opportunity and be absolutely certain that we can succeed in the endeavor. For if we're caught in the attempt, I have no doubt we'd be killed on the spot."

"I told you, there *is* no escape," Devlan declared. "I suggest you get used to the fact that you'll be here for the rest of your short and sure to be miserable lives."

"The Kellian that just left," Janna began. "I think they called him Chari...the one that saved us before. He's quite different to the others..."

"He's what the Kellians call a *null*," Djhtak explained. "You can tell by the circular symbol branded on his forehead."

"What does it mean?" David asked.

"Means he failed his warrior's initiation in adolescence. That's something no Kellian wants to do. The stigma follows them for life. Basically, among the Kellian hierarchy, he's the lowest of the low."

"If that's true then why did he save us before?" Darien asked. "By capturing us he might have been able to prove himself as a warrior?"

"I don't understand it either," Janir said. "But in spite of his refusal to help us now, I sense we may have an ally of sorts."

"You're deluding yourself if you think *he* will help you," Devlan exclaimed. "There's no way one of those filthy, savage animals would risk their life to help us! You may have only just arrived, but it's time to face the reality of the situation. We're stuck here! Clinging to false hope is only a waste of precious energy."

"Here we go," Djhtak exclaimed. "Our chief motivational officer has spoken."

"Everyone, listen to me," Janir called. "We're going to get out of here! I promise. We've come too far and been through too much to simply to give up now."

David was heartened by Janir's determination. If Janir had conceded defeat, then he really would have known that it was all over.

"And if you do, what of us?" Djhtak's eyes narrowed.

"You're free to come with us, of course; both of you. We're getting out of here as soon as the opportunity presents itself. For now, though, let's try to get some some sleep. I think we all need it, and it appears we have a busy day ahead of us tomorrow."

"Oh, you have no idea," Devlan muttered darkly.

Lying upon the dirty, uneven ground, it was one of the most miserable nights of David's life. Like the others, he was still bound by chains, which dug into his bloodied wrists. Yet his exhaustion soon gave way to a restless sleep. Again he experienced the recurring nightmare he'd had ever since leaving New Haven. Whether awake or asleep, his life now seemed a succession of nightmares.

Come morning, they were unceremoniously awoken by the Kellian jailor, who opened the cell door and threw in a bucket of slops. The bucket landed on its side, its contents spilling across the floor. Evidently, this was to be shared among them. Feeling nauseous just looking at the rancid scraps of raw meat, David decided he wasn't hungry and declined the offer. His friends did likewise, but Devlan and Djhtak, who were clearly used to eating little else, ate what they could.

Naranyan sat at the edge of the cell, cross-legged upon the ground, meditating as he always did first thing. David paced the cage like a trapped animal, overcome by a growing sense of desperation as he contemplated what might lie in store for them.

It wasn't long before he was to find out. Two Kellian men arrived and led the prisoners out by their chains, dragging them across the settlement to the quarry. The towering reddish-grey rocks formed sharp peaks, the minerals in the rock sparkling as the morning suns shone down from a clear crimson sky. It was here that they were put to work for the day. Equipped with crude pickaxes, the newcomers were instructed to break the rock into fragments that were to be gathered and deposited in a large metal crate.

As they began hacking away at the rock, the Kellian supervisors lazed around in amusement as they watched their slaves, often shouting aggressive and lewd comments. One of them brandished a long whip and wasn't hesitant to use it if someone wasn't working fast enough for his liking.

From the moment his axe first struck the rock bed, David knew that this would test their physical endurance to the limit. He was particularly concerned about Mariane and Janir, for they were by far the oldest of the group. If he was finding the work grueling, he could only imagine how Mariane was coping.

None of them spoke as they worked, for they simply didn't have the energy. All of their effort went into the grinding of axe against rock as they mined the ore. Under the blazing suns, it was hot, heavy, backbreaking work. Seldom allowed breaks, the brutality of the guards exacerbated their misery. The Kellians didn't care that their new prisoners were unaccustomed to such labor and made no concessions, even for Mariane, who was struggling immensely. David winced each time he heard the vindictive guard lashing the whip at one of his friends. When he fell victim himself, he was unprepared for the pain of the whip as it cut through his shirt and skin alike, leaving his back raw and tender in the blistering sun. By midday just about every muscle in his body pulsated with pain. Sweltering in the heat, he found himself several times close to collapse.

At one point something triggered a small landslide. A wall of rock crumbled, crashing down where David was working. He stumbled and fell, spraining his ankle as he landed on the ground, the chains clattering against the rock. Janir went to his aid and tried to help him to his feet. His act of kindness angered the guard, who lashed him with a crack of the whip. Infuriated, Darien protested and became the next victim, the guard lashing him several times, bloodied streaks appearing across his chest, arms and face. "Last warning," the Kellian roared. "Another word out your mouth and you will pay for it with your life."

"We would take great pleasure in disemboweling you here and now," the other guard added with a sadistic smile.

David forced himself to his feet. His ankle was painful, but he had no choice but to bear it and struggle on. Should there be even the slightest dissent, he had no doubt that the Kellians would be true to their word.

It seemed like an eternity later when the Kellians finally decided that work was finished. Although relieved that their ordeal was over for the day, David knew that tomorrow it would begin all over again. The guards rounded them up and grabbed hold of the chains, dragging them back through the quarry, toward the settlement at the edge of the forest. The noise from the shantytown carried through the air: the sound of shouting, laughing and fighting. David's ankle throbbed with pain, making every step difficult, the chains clanging as they trudged along.

It was then that something unexpected happened.

The first thing David heard was a twanging noise: first one, then another—coming from behind. Initially stunned, it took him a moment to realize what was happening.

They were under attack.

The Kellian guard ahead of them collapsed, sending a cloud of dust flying upward as his body hit the ground. A metal-tipped arrow punctured his neck and another protruded from the back of his ridged grey head. Brownish-red blood spilled across the ground.

The other Kellian released the prisoners' chains and drew his axe. But he was unable to see their attacker for the rising dust cloud. As the dust began to clear, their ambusher was revealed. Much to David's astonishment, it was another Kellian. It was Chari. He stood facing them, his crossbow raised.

"Chari?" spluttered the other guard. Although momentarily stunned, he quickly seemed to realize what had happened. Chari had betrayed them.

Raising his axe, he lunged at the traitor. Naranyan, however, stopped him before he could strike. Looping the metal chains around the guard's neck, he pulled him to the ground with a heave. The Kellian grunted; the axe flying from his hand as he fell. Chari moved forward and looked down at the fallen guard. Without a word, he took aim with his crossbow and fired. At point-blank range, the arrow struck his forehead, penetrating his thick, scaly skin as easily as a knife through butter. The Kellian howled, his whole body contorting. After a few seconds, he went limp as the life drained from his body.

Chari unlocked the prisoners' chains. He reached down to retrieve the guards' axes, handing them to Janir and Naranyan.

"Why are you doing this?" Naranyan asked as he suspiciously accepted the weapon.

"There is no time to talk. Come!" He gestured for them to follow him as he lumbered off. Only momentarily hesitating, they followed as Chari led them back through the quarry and into the surrounding forest. Though every step was painful, David tried to block out the discomfort as he focussed on the promise of escape.

"I don't know what to say," Janir said as they sped through the forest.

"Then say nothing," came Chari's blunt response. "You must get away from here as quickly as possible. It will not take the others long to learn what has happened."

"What will happen to you?" David asked.

"I will tell you what will happen," a voice boomed.

With a sense of dread, they turned to see another Kellian striding through the undergrowth, crossbow trained on them. "You will be made to suffer a long, slow and humiliating execution." His narrow eyes were fixed upon Chari. "A death befitting a traitor!"

Chari clearly recognized their ambusher. "Bruhta."

"Why, Chari? Why betray your own people? In the long and proud history of our tribe there has never been an act of such treachery. Even by a wretched *null*..."

"Our people have lost their way," Chari said. He and Bruhta had their weapons trained on each other. "Our race is dying. The old ways no longer work; the Alliance has seen to that. We can no longer pillage our way across the planet like mindless barbarians. There has been enough mindless killing. If we are to survive, our people must find a different way—a better way..."

"You are a disgrace to all Kellians," Bruhta spat. "And for that you will die."

Bruhta made a move to fire, but Chari beat him to it. A metal-tipped arrow shot through the air like a bolt of lightning, striking Bruhta in the chest. Chari again fired, this time hitting him between the eyes. With a cry of pain, Bruhta stumbled and collided with the ground. His body writhed as he frantically tried to dislodge the poison-tipped arrows, but the life force soon ebbed from his body and he went deathly still.

Chari stared down at the body, a look of bitter remorse upon his face. "Bruhta is the Chieftain's son. When Tchyan finds out what has happened, that the prisoners have escaped and his son killed, he will be on the warpath. He will not rest until he has hunted and slaughtered you. And it will not take him long to deduce my involvement."

"Then you must come with us," Janir said.

Clearly, it was a difficult decision, but realizing that it was his only option, Chari nodded.

"Wait a moment!" Devlan said. "How do we know we can trust him?"

"He just saved our lives," David exclaimed. Indeed, for whatever reason, Chari had sacrificed everything for them.

"If you want to stay behind then please feel free, Devlan," Djhtak said. "Been a real delight knowing you..."

Devlan averted his gaze, his lip protruding in a childish pout. In spite of his protestation, the diminutive red-skinned man had no intention of remaining behind.

"Come, let us make haste," Naranyan said, ushering them forward.

Chari concurred. "We should head to the mountain pass to the north of here. But we must move quickly."

Although exhausted, bruised and bloodied, the escapees leaped into motion, gritting their teeth to bear the pain as they hurried through the forest, knowing that at any moment the Kellians would be upon them, this time with a thirst for revenge.

# CHAPTER FIFTEEN

# On the Run

Led by the wayward Kellian, Chari, the escapees made their way through the forest with haste. Although there had been no immediate sign of pursuit, they knew complacency could be ill-afforded. They had to avoid recapture at all costs, for they knew they would never survive a second encounter with the Kellians.

As night crept in, the weather took a turn for the worse. Rain lashed down, pooling on the ground and forming rivulets along the forest floor. By the time they reached the mountain pass, the red-stone peaks were obscured by churning cloud. The downpour had soaked the travelers from head to foot, making their journey all the more miserable. Exhausted after their day of forced labor and bruised and bloodied from their treatment at the hands of the Kellians, every step proved a challenge. David's injured ankle continued to cause pain, making it difficult for him to keep up with the others as they climbed the mountain path.

By the time they reached the summit of the first mountain, darkness had set in and they could see no more than two paces ahead. It was an altogether wretched journey but fear of what lay behind them hastened them to keep struggling onward. Janir assured them that they would stop as soon as they found somewhere to shelter from both the elements and their pursuers.

At the foot of the mountain, they found themselves in a rocky canyon interlaced by a network of craggy caves cut deep into the mountainside. Janir conferred with Naranyan and Chari. They agreed this would be a suitable place for them to stop and get some rest before daybreak.

Venturing into a large and suitably concealed cave, they were fortunate to find some scattered branches spared from the rain outside. Gathering the twigs and branches, Naranyan set about lighting a fire, chanting an invocation to the Enari fire spirits as he rubbed two stones together. They were all ravenous and immensely relieved that Chari had possessed the foresight to bring a small supply of food with him before mounting his rescue. "There is not much," he admitted as he distributed the scraps of meat.

"There's barely a morsel here," complained Devlan as he looked down at the offering. "How are we to survive on scraps of meat that wouldn't even feed a dog?"

"It's better than nothing," snapped Janir, growing weary of Devlan's continued belligerence.

They settled around the fire, attempting to warm up and dry off their rain-soaked garments. After devouring their meager portions of food, they endeavored to make themselves comfortable as they huddled around the fire.

Janir had promised to take a look at David's ankle. Kneeling at David's feet, he took the ankle in his hands and whispered a healing incantation. His hands warmed and a surge of heat passed through David's foot and leg. Within moments, the pain had eased considerably and, as Janir got up, David thanked him.

Everyone was clearly exhausted, but David sensed an atmosphere of tension lingering over the group. This feeling of unease was perhaps only natural. It would no doubt take the extended company some time to grow comfortable with each other, particularly now there was a Kellian in their midst.

Perhaps hoping to dissipate the undercurrent of tension, the travelers took the opportunity to learn more about each other. David had taken a liking to Djhtak, who he found to be an affable, larger than life character. "I've been a trader all my life," the Alazan told them. "Worked my way through the ranks of Lantei trading corporation and been Captain of my own ship for twelve years. Can't believe she's gone."

"You said you were sabotaged by a rival company?" David asked.

Djhtak nodded. "I took on a new member of crew. His name was Arshnat. Turned out he was a saboteur from Drendal merchants. The bastard infected my cargo with bodan eggs."

"What are bodan?" Darien asked.

"Be grateful you don't know. They're savage, deadly crea-tures—originally created in Alliance laboratories as a means of population control."

"Population control?" Mariane grimaced.

"The Alliance invade the territories they want, right? Well, the territories they don't want, and those that may be a potential threat, are infected with bodan. The eggs start off pretty small, so it's easy to sneak them through the borders. But once the damn things hatch and grow, they consume and destroy pretty much everything in their path. They also breed at a phenomenal rate. In a matter of days, they can overrun and decimate entire cities. Took them only a few hours to kill my entire crew and cripple my ship."

"What happened?" David said.

"I did the only thing I could. I knew there was no way to save my ship and I couldn't risk the damn creatures getting to shore. The death toll would have been catastrophic. So I set ex-plosives. Made it to the lifeboat, and barely escaped with my life. Then I had to watch as my beloved ship went up in flames and sank beneath the waves."

"I can't believe a rival company would do that," Darien said. "There's competition and then there's cold-blooded murder..."

"Times are hard," Djhtak said. "Alliance levies are basically crippling us. Non-Alliance regions are becoming few and far be-tween. The Alliance occupies the rich and powerful regions and the smaller ones are simply crushed. It's only a matter of time before the Alazan traders cease trading."

"What will you do now?"

"Go back home, I suppose and wait for the inevitable Alliance invasion."

David looked around at the others. Janna seemed to be asleep, lying by Darien's side on the cave floor. Mariane's inces-sant complaining about her tired and aching body had finally subsided, so David presumed that she too had fallen asleep.

As David curled up, trying in vain to make himself comfort-able on the cavern floor, Devlan began to tell of his capture by the Kellians. There was something about him that made David uneasy. He was a belligerent and obnoxious little man, his red skin quite matching his fiery temperament. "As you may or may not know," Devlan began, "I am the prince of Sekyr."

Sekyr. David recognized the name. That was where they'd been headed before being captured by the Kellians.

"The prince of Sekyr?" Naranyan echoed, disbelievingly. "What would the prince of Sekyr be doing in a Kellian jail cell?"

"I was tricked and betrayed. By my own brother, no less. Just prior to my coronation, I was usurped by my treacherous sibling. I always knew he had ambition, but to kidnap me in the middle of the night and take me from my royal palace..."

"What happened?" Janir asked.

"Oh, please don't get him started," Djhtak muttered.

Ignoring him, Devlan continued, "Why, my dear brother had his men bundle me onto a merchant ship. I was taken across the sea and abandoned here in this godforsaken land. It was surely no coincidence that they happened to deposit me right on the outskirts of a Kellian settlement. So while my brother was ascending to the throne of Sekyr, I was being forced to endure all manner of indignities at the hands of those Kellian beasts. Let me tell you, all that kept me going was the thought of returning home, reclaiming my throne and having my dear brother executed outside the citadel for all to see."

Djhtak rolled his eyes, having clearly heard the story many times before. He looked over at Janir. "What about yourselves?" he asked. "Where do you come from?"

Janir seemed to carefully consider his response. "We're from an island to the east of the mainland. It was attacked and destroyed by the Alliance. We were fortunate to escape...the rest of our people were not so lucky."

"I have never heard of the Alliance striking so far east."

"Times are changing," Naranyan said.

Janir turned to Devlan. "Sekyr is an Alliance-controlled territory, isn't it?"

David felt a shiver run down his spine. Janir hadn't mentioned that Sekyr was in Alliance territory.

Devlan nodded. "Yes. The Alliance invaded Sekyr twelve years ago. As you can imagine, it was a time of great fear and uncertainty for my people. But the occupation was nowhere near as bad as we had feared. The Alliance left us with a reasonably free rein to conduct our affairs. Why do you ask?"

"Because that's where we're going."

"You've just escaped the Alliance," Djhtak said. "Why would you want to head into Alliance territory?"

David was confused and disturbed by this himself. But he didn't wish to air his concerns in front of everyone else. He would wait until he could speak to Janir alone.

"We live in dangerous times," Janir said. "Nowhere is safe. Even these so-called 'uninhabited lands' are filled with danger as we have all seen."

David noticed that Janir had decided not to divulge the fact they were looking for the City of Lorden. Clearly, he was sharing information on a need-to-know basis.

"I take it you intend to return to Sekyr?" Janir asked Devlan.

"Of course I do," Devlan grunted. "It's *my* kingdom and it's time I returned to make my brother pay for his treason!"

"In that case, we will accompany you."

"Very well then. But upon arrival we shall promptly part ways." He raised a suspicious eyebrow. "The last thing I wish is to be seen with dubious off-landers and fugitives from the Alliance."

Rather than being offended, Janir seemed to find this rather amusing and let out a somewhat wry chuckle. He turned to Djhtak. "What about you, Djhtak? What do you intend to do with your freedom?"

"I guess I'll accompany you to Sekyr," he said with a shrug. "Awful place, don't get me wrong, but it is the nearest point of civilization. From there I'll get transport back to the Alazan territories and make those bastards at Drendal merchants pay for what they did to my ship and crew."

Janir nodded. After a moment's silence, his attention turned to Chari, who stood in a darkened corner of the cave. Silent since they arrived, the burly Kellian stared into space, his mind clearly elsewhere. "What of you, Chari?" he called over. "What will you do?"

The Kellian looked up. "What *can* I do? I cannot return to my people. I have nowhere to go…"

An awkward silence followed before Naranyan spoke up. "I still cannot believe you risked your life to save ours. It seems inconceivable. It goes against everything we know about Kellian culture."

"The Kellians are but aggressive, uncivilized brutes," Devlan declared. "Why should *he* be any different?"

Chari remained motionless and silent. Tension had just about reached its zenith when Mariane—whom David had presumed was asleep—made matters worse. "I have to agree," she announced. "For all we know this could be an elaborate hoax… some kind of perverse hunting exercise. How do we know we can trust him? How can we be sure he won't kill us all as we sleep?"

"You were there when Chari rescued us," Janir said. "You saw what happened. He sacrificed everything to save us. He's one of us now, without question."

The silence was broken only by the crackling of the fire and the sound of the rain pattering outside and dripping down the entrance of the cave. Janir said, "I assure you, we're most grateful to you, Chari. It's to you that we owe our freedom. That said, it's difficult for some of us to understand why you were willing to sacrifice so much to help us."

Chari's face was largely obscured by the shadows. "They are right. For all you know, I could kill you the moment your backs are turned. I am Kellian after all. The blood of my people flows through my veins." He paused. "But I am not like them." This admission was clearly difficult for him. "I was born among them. I was one of them. Yet I lacked something. I lacked my people's thirst for blood. I had no appetite for conquest and violence. I suppose I thought too much, and I asked questions that no one else dared ask. As I grew up, I came to think of myself as somehow defective." He raised his hand and pointed to the symbol burned onto his forehead. "This proves it. I am a failure as a Kellian warrior and an embarrassment to my family and kin. In their eyes, I have always been nothing. Less than nothing! Do you have any idea what that was like?"

Janir shook his head. "No, I can't say that I do."

"In some ways being an outsider has its advantages. It made me question things, and see things that others could not."

"Such as?" Naranyan asked.

"I came to realize that my race is in decline; that my people are paving the way to their own extinction. The only way for them, for us, to survive is to change. But they are too rooted in tradition and hierarchy to do that. So I took the first step."

"Which was what?" David asked.

"I saved you."

"Why?"

"Because there has been enough senseless violence. I knew what would happen to you. I could not let your deaths be on my conscience—and you would have died, without question."

Djhtak let out an incredulous snort. "Who would have thought it! A Kellian with a conscience."

"I did not just do it for you, or even my own conscience," Chair said. "I did it for my people—for their future. By my actions, I have changed things. I have done something radical and broken down the hierarchy. I do not know what will happen next, but it may cause my people to question assumptions they have held for generations."

David felt an empathy for Chari. He'd grown up feeling he didn't quite belong himself, and Chari had experienced this to a far more dramatic degree. There was one thing he didn't understand, however. "After all your people have done to you," he said, "making you feel like an outsider and a nobody, why do you even *care* what happens to them?"

"Because although they despise me, they are still my people and I do not want to see them destroyed. I may never be able to return to them, but perhaps my actions will force them to change. Maybe that will enable them to adapt and survive in a rapidly changing world."

Naranyan shifted uncomfortably. "My mother was killed by Kellians when I was just a child," he ventured, a sudden vulnerability puncturing the Enari's stoic demeanor. "I grew up despising your people. I never imagined I would encounter a Kellian capable of anything other than violence and savagery. Yet I now sit alongside something I long would have considered a contradiction in terms—a noble Kellian."

Janir nodded. "You may not be able to return to your people, Chari, but you don't have to be alone. You are more than welcome to accompany us on our journey."

The Kellian remained silent. He had said all that needed to be said. David now understood the enigmatic Kellian a bit more. Like Naranyan, he was touched by the sacrifice he'd made—all for the love of a people that had continually ostracized him. The thought of a Kellian joining them on their quest was somewhat strange, but like them, he too had lost his home and his people, albeit under very different circumstances.

Overcome by tiredness, the travelers settled down, endeavoring to get the rest their bodies so desperately needed. It had been a long and traumatic day; first spent laboring under a Kellian whip and then on the run from their captors.

Although he craved sleep, David had also come to dread it, for he was almost guaranteed to be plagued by that same nightmare. The man in his dreams, the one named Zhayron, seemed to be getting clearer and more vivid with each passing night—a pervasive specter lurking in the shadows of his unconscious.

Whoever he was, he was calling to David; his voice somehow permeating the boy's consciousness. *Don't fight me,* the voice implored. *Give into me, David. It's the only way.*

It seemed he'd barely gotten to sleep and it was time to get up. Wasting little time, the ragtag band resumed their hike through the canyon.

David used the Key to guide them along their way. Serving as their compass, it was still pointing due east. Using the map given them by the Enari, Janir and Naranyan plotted their course. It would take them beyond the mountain pass to the most easterly point of the continent; a place called Port Llanyeau. There they would have to seek passage across the sea to Sekyr.

David had an ominous feeling about this. As he'd learned last night, the moment they reached Sekyr they would be entering Alliance-controlled territory.

The first opportunity he could, he pulled Janir aside to air his concerns. "What's troubling you?" Janir asked as they continued through the canyon; the sky overcast and the uneven ground wet and muddy.

"Quite a few things," David said. "For a start, perhaps you would tell me why we're headed into Alliance territory?"

Janir seemed taken aback by David's forthrightness. "I know the path we tread is far from ideal, but given the options, we have no other choice. We have to find the City of Lorden—and the Key, as you know, is pointing us east, toward the continent of Ardesha. The only way of getting to Ardesha from here is to travel via Sekyr."

"But surely the moment we enter Sekyr we'll be signing our own death warrants! The Alliance is desperate to find us—and we'll be walking straight onto their doorstep."

"It's a risk, I know. But we'll keep our eyes and ears open and we'll proceed with the utmost caution. Sekyr is by no means the heart of Alliance territory. By sticking to the peripheral regions and staying clear of the citadels we should manage to avoid any entanglement with the Alliance."

Janir may have found some way to rationalize this, but try though he might, David was unable to shake the feeling that something terrible was lying in wait for them—and for whatever reason Janir was leading them straight toward it.

# CHAPTER SIXTEEN

# Exile

Dusk fell over the valley. Four days on from their escape from the Kellians, and the exhausted travelers found themselves lost amid a seemingly endless stretch of forestland. Morale continued plummeting, but they had no option but to keep pushing onward. Despite no overt sign of either Kellian or Alliance pursuit, they dared not labor under the delusion they were safe.

Like the others, David found himself struggling. Their unrelenting pace, the constant exhaustion and the continual threat of recapture were pushing him to the brink physically and emotionally.

His grand mission to find the City of Lorden and the other half of the Key almost seemed like a hazy dream now. Their immediate concern had become survival. Had it been foolhardy of him to imagine he could ever possibly have achieved such an objective? He'd seen the overwhelming might of the enemy, and they'd only just set out on their journey when the Kellians had captured them. How many other, potentially worse dangers lay out there?

The farther they went, the more he could feel hope slipping from him. Yet just when he was on the brink of despair, something was about to change their fortune.

The forest grew darker until the only source of illumination was the moonlight shining through gaps in the cloud. Chari, leading the way through the undergrowth, suddenly stopped in his tracks and called back to the others. He had found something. Catching up with him, they saw that ahead, amid a vast clearing, stood the remnants of an ancient town.

They approached the ruins, intrigued yet cautious. Clearly, at one time, this had been a thriving metropolis, but time had stripped it of all life. All that remained were roofless skeletons of houses, crumbling walls and fallen pillars; cracked, scattered and covered in grass and moss.

"Who do you think lived here?" David asked as they wandered down what appeared to have been one of the town's central walkways.

"I'm not sure," Janir said, "but they clearly haven't been here for a very long time."

"According to the map," Naranyan said, "this must be Numaria, an ancient Lasandrian province."

"Lasandrian?" David echoed.

Janir nodded. "Yes, quite possibly. They had outposts all across Alanar."

They came to the edge of a courtyard. The silver moonlight cast a dreamlike glow upon the ruins. David imagined he could almost see, hear and feel the shadows of an ancient, long forgotten past. It was an eerie, disquieting feeling; as though they were walking through a city of ghosts.

"What happened to the inhabitants?" Darien wondered aloud.

"Same as happens to everyone eventually," Djhtak said as he marched along with his typical swagger. "They died."

"Such an erudite historian," Devlan grumbled.

"Lasandria was wiped out by a cataclysm thousands of years ago," Janir said. "It was one of the watershed moments of Alanaran history."

David repressed a shudder. The memory of Lasandria's demise remained etched in his mind.

Janna came to a stop at the foot of what had evidently once been a water fountain. Her body tensed, her face straining as she turned in alarm. "There's someone here," she warned.

"What makes you say that, lass?" Djhtak said.

"I can sense someone nearby; a presence."

"You're sure?" Janir said.

She nodded.

"What you mean you 'sense' someone?" snapped Devlan. "What nonsense is this?"

"Don't speak to her like that," Darien growled.

"I just *feel* it," Janna said. "There's someone nearby—I'm certain of it."

"Be on your guard everyone," Janir cautioned.

Chari and Naranyan drew their weapons, glancing suspiciously around the courtyard.

"What should we do?" David asked.

"May I suggest we get out of here," Mariane said, "and the sooner the better. I just *knew* this place would be dangerous."

"Then why didn't you say anything?" Darien shot back.

"Frankly I didn't see the point since people rarely seem to listen to what I have to say anymore..."

"Please don't worry," came an unfamiliar voice. "There's no danger here."

David felt a surge of alarm as a figure emerged from behind one of the buildings, stepping into the moonlit courtyard. Much to his relief, it wasn't a Kellian, but an old man; well-built yet somewhat frail.

"Identify yourself," Chari snarled, his crossbow trained on the man.

"There's no need for alarm," the stranger assured them. Wearing clothing of a similar style to the Enari, with a patterned gray poncho draped over his shoulders, he carried a glowing lantern in one hand and a wooden cane in the other. A wolf trotted alongside him, coming to a stop at the man's legs, eying the strangers warily.

Janir motioned for Chari and Naranyan to lower their weapons.

"My name is Anaskaban," the old man said with a tilt of his head. "Oh," he added, looking down at the wolf by his side. "And this is my good friend Nahnto."

Like Devlan, Anaskaban had a reddish tint to his skin, but he was a good bit taller than the Sekyrian prince. His rounded, chubby face was a kindly one, with twinkling dark eyes exuding a warmth and gentleness that immediately put David at ease. He had a grandfatherly quality, although David sensed an undercurrent of sadness in him.

Janir introduced himself and his comrades. As they spoke, the wolf grew bolder, stepping forward and sniffing the newcomers. David reached down and stroked its head.

"I don't think I've ever seen a more diverse group of travelers," Anaskaban remarked. "Let's see—Alanarans, an Enari, a Kellian, an Alazan and a Sekyrian."

Devlan stepped forward imperiously. "I see you are Sekyrian as well."

"Indeed I am."

"Then you must surely recognize me?"

"I can see that you're of the royal lineage, but I'm afraid I don't—"

"I am Devlan, prince of Sekyr, and rightful heir to the throne! You claim to be from Sekyr, yet you do not recognize its sovereign...?"

"Oh, I've not been in Sekyr for a number of years. When last I was there, the reigning monarch was King Autalan."

"My father. He died not even a year ago."

David was curious. "How did he know you're one of the royal lineage?"

Devlan glared at David. "Because of my noble *stature*, boy."

"What do you mean?"

"Must I explain everything? It's all a matter of height! The Sekyrian royal lineage is of the same compact stature as myself. The proletarian class are taller; much the same height as the rest of you..."

"Oh," Darien remarked. "I thought you were just short."

"Short?" Devlan echoed, his face twitching with anger.

"It's true what they say about Sekyrian royals," Djhtak remarked with a laugh. "Little men with big tempers."

"And it's true what they say about Alazan," Devlan retorted. "Ignorant oafs with neither culture or decorum."

"I'll show you *decorum*, your lowness—"

"Please, enough bickering," Mariane groaned. "It's like being back at school. I knew there was a reason I retired."

"If I may ask," Naranyan cut in, addressing Anaskaban. "What are you doing here? We are far from Sekyr."

"Oh, now that's a long story, my friend," the old man said. "How about I tell you over supper? You are all hungry, I presume?"

"Starving," David said.

"Well, please allow me to extend you my hospitality."

"If I were you," Djhtak remarked, "I doubt I'd so readily invite us for supper. After all, you know nothing about us. Personally, I'd take one look at us and run the other way."

"Indeed, and we know nothing about *you*," Devlan added.

"He's Sekyrian," David said. "Isn't that enough for you?"

"It's highly irregular for my subjects to leave the borders of our territory. Something clearly isn't right here."

Janir stepped in to ease the undercurrent of distrust. "I apologize, Anaskaban. I assure you, no offense is intended. Recent experience has simply made us somewhat cautious."

"Oh, I understand only too well," Anaskaban said. "These are dangerous times. Caution is advisable. All I can do is assure you that you have nothing to fear from me. I'm but a humble old man living in exile from my homeland. I don't get many guests as you can imagine, so I'm only too happy to offer you some food and shelter."

"Then we graciously accept," Janir said.

"Hold on," barked Devlan. "You say you were *exiled* from Sekyr. Why?"

"As I said, it's a long story. I'll tell you everything over supper. Now, my home isn't far from here and I already have some food on the stove. Let's go, shall we? It's late, and getting darker by the moment."

Lantern in hand, Anaskaban turned and began hobbling through the ruins. David looked to Janir, who nodded, prompting everyone to follow. While he'd had taken an instant liking to the old man, and was immensely grateful for the offer of food and shelter, David could understand Djhtak and Devlan's reticence.

Something didn't seem entirely right. What had the old man been doing here in the dark? It was almost as though he'd been expecting them. While hopeful that his fears were unfounded,

David couldn't shake a feeling of apprehension as they followed him through the valley.

The old man had more stamina than initially appeared to be the case. Leading them through the valley and up a mountain trail, they came to a sandstone temple perched upon the hillside. Although more intact than the ruins in the valley, the temple was clearly an ancient relic of a time long gone. "You live here alone?" Mariane asked as they climbed a flight of well-worn steps to an arched entrance.

Anaskaban nodded. "It's just Nahnto and myself."

Lanterns hung from the walls, casting dancing shadows upon the brickwork as Anaskaban led them down the long and drafty corridors. David found himself fascinated by the temple. Clearly, it had been a sacred place during the Lasandrian era; a holy shrine overlooking the town of Numaria in the valley.

They came to a large kitchen. Lit by oil lamps, the room was furnished with a table and chairs, and shelving containing crockery, flowers, and sprigs of herbs. Unlike the rest of the crumbling temple, it had a lived in, homely feel. A stewpot sat above a crackling fireplace. The smell of cooking wafted through the air, reminding David just how hungry he was.

The wolf lay down on a blanket by the fireside as Anaskaban seated them at the table. Chari opted to stand, as his considerable size and weight would probably have broken the chair. Anaskaban ladled generous servings of vegetable stew onto earthen plates and distributed them to his guests. It was the first proper meal David had eaten in days. He devoured every last bite and was happy when Anaskaban offered him a second helping. As he ate, he found it curious that although Anaskaban apparently lived alone with his pet wolf, he had prepared enough food for all of them.

"How long have you lived here, Anaskaban?" Janir asked.

"Oh, it must be close to nine years now," the old man said. "Yes...nine years since Ekara passed away. It hardly seems possible!"

"Who was Ekara?" David asked.

"She was my beloved wife."

"What happened to her?" Darien said.

Anaskaban cast his eyes to the ground. "Oh, now that is a long and painful story."

"You said you were exiled from Sekyr," Devlan interjected. "I should like to know why."

"If you don't mind our asking, that is," Janir added.

"No, not at all." Anaskaban looked up; a distant expression upon his face, as though his mind was somewhere else altogether. "I was once a priest, you know."

"In the Ministry of Sekyr?" Devlan said.

The man nodded. "I served in the Ministry for decades, alongside Ekara; my first and only love. I eventually became one of its elected leaders. It was a great honor and privilege to serve in the Ministry, bringing our people together under the glorious teachings of Hershala; spreading his message of love and unity. But I don't suppose anything lasts forever. All things change. And Sekyr certainly changed when the Alliance invaded.

"I remember the day they came as though it were yesterday. We were in temple services at the time. Someone came running in to raise the alarm. We went outside to see what the commotion was, and were horrified to see a legion of Alliance troops storming down the streets; the skies overhead blackened by their huge air vehicles, looming over the citdael like storm clouds."

"I remember that day too," Devlan said. "Their arrival was so sudden we could offer little resistance."

"It was a dark day for our people."

"It could have been worse. As invasions go, we were fortunate. The bloodshed was minimal."

"Only because we literally handed power to the Alliance! Instead of fighting for our freedom, our leaders sold us out."

"What would you rather have had my father do? Risk a full-scale massacre? We were fortunate to avoid such a thing. We've all heard tales of entire cities being blasted to the ground by the Alliance."

"Yes, we've seen what the Alliance is capable of," David remarked.

"Besides," Devlan continued, "our lives have not been adversely affected by the Alliance. The Sekyrian monarchy has been kept in place and Sekyrian subjects are free to go about their daily business."

Anaskaban's brow furrowed. His tone changed to one of indignant bitterness. "It may have been nine years since I last set foot in my homeland, but I've no doubt that Alliance soldiers still patrol the streets; that freedom of expression is curtailed and that anyone speaking up against the Alliance is imprisoned and executed. I mean no disrespect, but everyone knows that the monarchy was only left in place to implement the dictate of the Alliance overseers."

Devlan's face flushed an even deeper shade of red. His hands clenched with barely contained fury. "Remember to whom you speak! I am your Prince, and heir to the throne of Sekyr. The Alliance has brought power and prestige to Sekyr. Whereas once we were a small and impoverished nation, now we've rebuilt the citadels and have a place on the map."

"But at least before we were *free!*" Anaskaban slammed his hand against the tabletop.

"Perhaps we should avoid political discussion," Janir suggested. It was clearly unwise to provoke their host, who had thus far been exceptionally kind and hospitable.

"You still haven't told me why you were exiled," Devlan said.

"The Alliance sent me into exile," Anaskaban said.

"Why—what did you do?"

Anaskaban turned to David and the others. "Although the Alliance have massive armies of soldiers and troops," he explained, "their main means of controlling the people is not by force, but by fear and manipulation. They infuse every component of a conquered society with their carefully distilled poison, whether it be government or educational or religious institutions. The Ministry was compromised in little time; the ancient teachings twisted and distorted to reflect the Alliance's agenda, enabling them to insidiously gain control of the hearts and minds of the people."

Devlan let out a disgruntled sigh.

Anaskaban continued, "Not long after the Alliance arrived in Sekyr, they placed several of their Eloramian missionaries—ambassadors from the Alliance hierarchy—into our Ministry, where they began to rewrite the ancient teachings and rearrange our order." He shook his head. "Oh, I was horrified at the damage they perpetrated. It wasn't long before the extent to which they were destroying our spiritual life became clear."

"In what way?" David asked.

"It was no longer Hershala, the great creator that was being worshiped," Anaskaban said, his voice trembling. "Rather I believe they had invoked the Shadow Lords of Abidalos; the ravenous dark ones of ancient times. I tried to stop this monstrous distortion of our Ministry. I tried so hard! But they were too strong. They had eyes and ears everywhere. They knew I was trying to subvert them and save that which I held so sacred. What happened next came as little surprise. They arrested Ekara and myself on charges of sedition."

"What happened?" Darien asked.

"They punished me in the most severe way they could." A teardrop rolled down his puffy red cheek. "They killed her. They killed Ekara. Right before my eyes, forcing me to watch..." It was clearly a struggle for him to continue. "Rather than make me share her fate, which at that point I would have welcomed, the Alliance commandant decided that to kill me would not be punishment enough. No, he wanted me to live with my pain for the rest of my life. So, they exiled me from Sekyr, making me serve as an example to all other would-be dissenters."

"That's awful," Mariane exclaimed.

Anaskaban's husky voice wavered as he continued. "With nothing but the clothes I was wearing, I was taken to the port, given one last beating by the Alliance soldiers and bundled onto an outbound freighter. It was headed to the Northern territories via Port Llanyeau. That was where the captain was ordered to leave me; right on the edge of the uninhabited lands."

"So that's how you came to be here," Naranyan said.

He nodded. "I began wandering the forests, hills, and mountains, quite lost in my grief. I was a broken man; so lost and utterly alone. I even considered taking my own life." He paused. "I recall standing at the edge of a mountain, and I very nearly jumped. All I wanted was to be free of the pain, and to be with my beloved Ekara again."

"What stopped you?" said Janna, her eyes filled with compassion.

"Now this is where it gets interesting." Anaskaban tried to muster a smile as he wiped his eyes. "Standing upon the mountain, I beheld a vision. A multitude of radiant beings appeared before me—the Guardians!"

"I'm sure they did," Djhtak scoffed.

Janir frowned at Djhtak. He urged Anaskaban to continue. "Go on..."

"They told me that my journey through the mortal realm was not yet over," Anaskaban said, "and that I had something important left to do. They led me through the mountains and forestlands all the way here—to the ruins of Numaria, and this temple in which you now sit."

"Why here?" Darien said.

"The temple belonged to the ancient Lasandrian Priesthood. Although I found it in a state of decay, one thing did remain intact, buried deep within its walls—a gateway."

"Gateway?" Astonished, David looked at Janir, who nodded thoughtfully.

"And what's a *gateway*?" Djhtak said.

"An ancient device enabling travel throughout the cosmos," Anaskaban said. "Apparently once there were many such portals across the planet, all connected to a central gateway in the temple at the City of El Ad'dan. These gateways were destroyed when Lasandria fell. All but one, that is. The gateway here, at Numaria, is the only one remaining—and it has to be guarded, lest it ever fell into the wrong hands."

David could hardly believe it. Why hadn't Balaska told him there was another gateway still on Alanar? The implications were staggering. What if the Alliance learned of it? That was precisely what they and the Narssians were after.

"I've never heard such nonsense," Devlan muttered.

Anaskaban ignored him. "It's been my great honor to make this my new home and serve as guardian of the gateway. And here I've been the past nine years, along with dear Nahnto, of course."

"You made this ruin habitable all by yourself?" Naranyan asked.

"Not entirely. I've made some friends over the years, including a group of your people, the Enari. Such a wise and wonderful people! They helped me turn this old temple into something resembling a home."

"I'm glad you managed to find a new life for yourself following your loss," Mariane said, clearly touched by his story.

He smiled at her, perhaps sensing the pain she herself carried. "Oh, that I have. It's a solitary one, yes, but one with purpose. When tragedy strikes, often all we can do is seek to reinvent ourself—to find a new purpose, a new reason for living."

"When you found us down in the valley," David said. "You almost seemed like you were expecting us."

"Oh, but I was." Anaskaban rose from the table, carrying some of the empty plates to the adjacent wash basin. "The Guardians told me of your coming." He seemed to be looking directly at David as he continued. "They want you to know that in spite of all that's happened, they are watching over you and guiding you from afar. You have not been forsaken, nor will you ever be."

David couldn't help but think of Balaska. She'd told him much the same thing prior to her departure. Although they'd spent little time together, he missed her.

"So where is this 'gateway'?" Darien asked.

Anaskaban pointed to the ground. "Right beneath us."

David was about to speak when he let out an involuntary yawn.

"Ah, I can see you're all tired," Anaskaban said. "Not at all surprising. Why don't I show you to your room? Get a good night's sleep. We can talk more in the morning."

"No argument from me," Darien said.

"Nor I," Mariane added.

Anaskaban smiled. "It's been a long time since Nahnto and I have had company. Please feel welcome to stay as long as you please."

"You're most kind, my friend," Janir said, "but I'm afraid we can't stay long. We're being pursued by both the Kellians and the Alliance. The longer we stay, the more I fear our presence will put you at risk."

"It does seem we're a little bit cursed," Darien muttered.

Devlan leaned forward, his little black eyes bulging from his red face. "You say you are being *pursued* by the Alliance. Why is that?"

"That's not your concern," David spoke up.

"I beg to differ. I have a right to know what's going on, especially if you expect to enter *my* country!"

Janir let out a sigh. "We'll be happy to answer whatever questions you have, Devlan, but now is not the time."

"I disagree! Now is as good a time as any."

"We will not discuss this now," Janir snapped. "Anaskaban is correct. It's been a long and exhausting journey and we all need some rest. We'll discuss whatever questions you have at a more appropriate time."

Devlan folded his arms and shot Janir a petulant glance, clearly unhappy at being spoken to in such a manner.

"My apologies, Anaskaban," Janir said. "Tempers have been flaring of late. As I said, we won't stay long, as I wouldn't want our presence here to endanger you in any way."

"You needn't worry about me, my friend," the old man said. "Now, come! I suggest you all get some sleep. Let us deal with tomorrow when it comes, shall we?"

Lantern in hand, Anaskaban showed them to their room, where he'd already laid out nine beds comprised of leaf mattresses and blankets. It seemed he truly had been expecting them. The benevolent host left his guests to settle down for the night.

"Well, it's nice to have a bed to sleep in again," Mariane said.

"Even if it is flimsy." Devlan stood over his mattress, nudging it with his foot.

"No pleasing some people," Darien said with a yawn.

"Can you believe there's a gateway here?" David whispered to Janir.

Janir shook his head. "I certainly didn't expect that."

"Maybe we're here for a reason, Janir. Maybe we can use it—maybe it can take us to the City of Lorden..."

"I don't know if we should be using it, David. If anything must be destroyed."

"Destroyed—?"

"If it should fall into the hands of the Alliance, they'll use it to reopen a gateway to the Narssians' realm. This universe will be invaded—and it'll be the end of everything."

"But maybe we can use it. Use it to stop them."

"I'd feel happier knowing it didn't exist. We'll talk about it tomorrow, David. Let's get some sleep. Things will seem clearer in the morning."

David hoped he was right.

Removing his boots, trousers, and shirt, he lay down on his bed. Above him, the room's sole window had been crudely boarded up. Thin slivers of moonlight streamed through cracks in the boarding, shining down upon him as his mind drifted into a restless slumber.

*He should have known he'd have to face the same nightmare once again. He again found himself in New Haven in the aftermath of the Alliance attack. Wandering the corpse-filled streets, David watched as the flames consumed what remained of the lifeless town. He found himself standing over his mother's body as it lay upon the blood-spattered walkway. He reached down and cradled her in his arms.*

*Why was he forced to relive this agony over and over again? If only there was something he could have done for her—some way of preventing this whole tragedy.*

*Something caught his attention.*

*He looked up to see a figure appearing across the street—a teenage girl with dark hair and fiery eyes, dressed in blue-violet, her entire body bathed in a white luminescence.*

*She reached out and called his name.*

*He didn't know who she was, yet she was so strangely familiar to him, as though he'd seen her face before in a thousand forgotten dreams. She again called out to him, a look of urgency and alarm upon her face.*

*Why did he get the feeling she was here to warn him about something?*

*Standing up, he moved toward her, but she disappeared.*

*The scene around him dissolved into blackness.*

*Alone in the dark, a voice echoed around him—a voice that was by now intimately familiar to him. It was the voice of Zhayron, and it was calling to him—"I'm coming for you, David. I'm coming for you..."*

# CHAPTER SEVENTEEN

# The Attack

Despite having had a full night's sleep for the first time in days, David felt little refreshed when he awoke. The dark images of his dreams lingered in his mind as he wandered down the ancient corridors. He could almost still hear the voice of Zhayron calling his name. While the others had gathered in the kitchen for first meal, David felt the need for solitude.

Venturing outside the temple, he made his way to edge of the mountainside. The twin suns shone amid a clear lilac sky and birds chattered and chirped. Gazing into the valley, he saw the ruins of Numaria visible through patches in the forestland. High above stood the green and blue mountains, encircled by wispy trails of mist.

It was a tranquil scene, but it did little to calm the boy's turbulent mind. Not only troubled by his dreams, he found himself filled with trepidation about their mission. For some time now he'd been questioning Janir's judgment on certain things, particularly his willingness to lead them straight into Alliance territory.

"You are not having first meal with the others?"

Startled, David turned to see Naranyan approaching through the trees. "No," he said. "No, I wasn't that hungry."

"You need to keep your strength up."

"I know. I'll get something later. How about you? Have you eaten yet?"

"I will shortly." The Enari came to a stop alongside David. "I wanted to find a secluded spot to do my morning meditation first."

"How was it—your mediation?"

"It was beneficial."

"I admire your discipline. I've seen you do it every single day now, morning and night, even in the worst of conditions, like when we were imprisoned by the Kellians."

"I make it a priority. It is all too easy to lose ourselves to the push and pull of outer events. Forfeiting our oneness with Infinity, we become enmeshed in not only the outer world—the world of events, problems and challenges—but also the inner world—the world of our thoughts, feelings, and interpretations. Meditation is the blade with which I cut these bonds."

"Janir taught me to meditate."

"You should put his teaching into practice."

"I know. I just haven't found it easy lately, especially with all that's been happening."

"Turning inward is not for the faint of heart. It requires not only diligent perseverance but also great courage, for it is there we must confront our demons."

"Demons?"

"Our fears, pain, and regrets. We tend to bury them within. But although painful, but we must eventually find the courage to face and resolve our darkest shadows. If we do not, they devour us from within until, eventually, nothing remains."

David said nothing.

Naranyan's voice softened. "I regret that we have little chance to speak, just you and I. I never told you this, but it was during my meditations that the Guardians directed me to leave my home and set out across Alanar. I was embroiled in this great quest not of my own volition, but because destiny so decreed it."

"Destiny?"

The Enari nodded. "I never questioned my destiny. I trusted and yielded to it, though often the path ahead seemed impossible. My trust never wavered, even when called upon to leave my home and my betrothed and to journey halfway across the world; all to find a stranger in a land I knew nothing of—to find you."

"You were to be married?"

"To the one love of my life; the keeper of my heart. I still miss him with each day that passes. But I had to leave. The Guardians were quite clear. My destiny was linked to you, David. My mission was to find you and warn you to leave New Haven before the Alliance could get to you."

"If you hadn't come, I'd be—"

"You'd be in the hands of the Alliance, and quite likely, this would all be over."

"I never thanked you..."

"There is no need. I did it because I had to; because I surrendered myself to the tides of fate." He took a deep breath and continued. "But now I sense a change in that tide. Something is going to happen, and I fear our ways will soon part."

"What do you mean?"

Naranyan opened his mouth to answer, but before he could speak a sudden noise shattered the calm—a piercing mechanical rumble. David watched as a shadow rolled across the valley. Its source: a black airship shooting through the sky. He immediately recognized the predator-like craft.

"The Alliance," Naranyan growled.

David felt a chill grip his soul. They were coming—coming for him.

"They must be sweeping the area," Naranyan said, "searching for signs of life."

"We have to warn the others!"

They turned and made for the temple. But as David ran, a wave of darkness bombarded his mind and senses. Stunned, he stopped in his tracks, frozen in terror. He could feel a malevolent presence seeping through his being, penetrating his mind. Immersed in a suffocating veil of darkness, a voice echoed in his mind—

*Don't try to escape, David.*

It was the voice of Zhayron; the man from his dreams.

*Don't resist me. You have nothing to fear.*

Trembling, David lifted his hands to his head, desperate to free himself from this pernicious presence. It had invaded his mind and he had to be free of it—

*I told you I was coming for you, David. There's no escape. Let it happen...*

No! He would not succumb to it! He couldn't.

It took all of his strength but David managed to shake off the dark presence.

Snapping back to reality, it took him a moment to regain his senses. He stood at the foot of the temple steps. Naranyan was looking down at him from the entrance, calling for him to hurry.

Still shaken, David sprinted up the steps, following Naranyan into the temple.

The others, having heard the disturbance, joined them in the hallway. "What's going on out there?" Darien called. "We heard a noise—"

"It's the Alliance," David said. "They're here."

"The Alliance?" echoed Djhtak.

"How did they find us?" Mariane gasped.

"It was only a matter of time," Janir said grimly.

"Why would the Alliance be doing chasing you the likes of you?" Devlan demanded.

"I don't believe they are here by chance," Anaskaban said. Nahnto circled the old man's legs with an anxious whine.

"What do you mean?" Darien said.

"They've been *led* here," Anaskaban said. "Someone among us has been touched by the darkness. The Alliance now sees through *their* eyes."

David felt the color drain from his face. It was him. It had to be him. He noticed Janna staring at him, a look of alarm on her face. *She knows,* he realized with a growing sense of despair. *She knows it's me.*

"The question is, what are we going to do?" Naranyan said. "With their technology, it will take them no time at all to find us."

"They'll be quick to send down the Death Troops, as they did on New Haven," Janir said.

"So we're sitting targets here," Darien exclaimed. "We have to do something!"

"The gateway," Anaskaban said.

David felt a flash of hope. "Yes, the gateway!"

"Anaskaban," Janir said. "Can we use the gateway to escape here?"

"Why, of course. I knew this would happen all along. The Guardians told me the Alliance would follow in your wake. Before you even arrived I readied the gateway as a means of escape should it be required."

"Then, please, by all means, lead the way."

Anaskaban ushered them down the torchlit corridors with haste, hobbling as he leaned on his cane. David's heart pounded as he followed alongside Janir and the others. He was still reeling from whatever had happened to him outside the temple, and fearful it might happen again.

"This is madness," Devlan grumbled as Anaskaban led them down several flights of stairs into the heart of the temple.

"Oh be quiet, you obnoxious little man," Mariane panted as she followed behind.

"No, I will not be quiet. And kindly remember to whom you are speaking, woman. I am royalty!"

"You're certainly not royalty to me. Now, stop talking and hurry up."

"I can't 'hurry up'. My legs will only carry me so fast."

"Well that's your problem for being short," Darien grunted.

"I am *not* short!"

Once they reached the bottom of the stairway, Anaskaban led them down a corridor into a spacious underground chamber. He bolted the door shut behind them. Lanterns hung from the crumbling sandstone walls, revealing a large hexagonal mirror at the center of the chamber. Standing upon a raised platform, the mirror was set into a glistening crystalline base.

"That's the gateway?" David asked.

"That's the gateway," Anaskaban confirmed. Nahnto trotted by his side as he climbed the platform steps and stood before the mirror.

"I hate to break it to you, Anaskaban, but that's a *mirror*," Darien said. "Something for doing your hair in front of—"

"Let's just trust him," Janna urged, placing a hand upon his arm.

"Behold," the old man said. Leaning upon his cane and gazing into the reflective surface, he uttered some words that were unfamiliar to David. Almost immediately the crystal encasing the mirror began glowing with an immense white radiance. Dancing with sparks of electrical charge, the mirror surface dissolved into a swirling pool of blue-violet light. Anaskaban turned, beaming with pride. "This is, I believe, the last gateway of its kind on Alanar. It'll take you to a place of safety."

"Where?" Chari asked.

"Let's just say that it will hasten you along your journey."

This was all too much for Devlan. "Not so fast! I demand some answers, now! What in the twin suns is that thing?"

"I'll tell you what it is," Janir said. "It's our only way out of here."

"I've never seen anything of the like. How do we know it's safe?"

"There's only one way to find out, isn't there?"

"Do you really think I'm going to risk my life stepping into that—*contraption,* without the slightest idea what it is?"

"It's our only option," David said. "We either go through the gateway or remain here and end up in the hands of the Alliance."

"So what if we do? I'm the rightful monarch of Sekyr. They'll be obliged to return me to my homeland, problem solved!"

Djhtak pushed past him as he marched toward the gateway. "Well, why don't you stay here, little man, while the rest of us leave?"

"Sounds like a plan to me," Darien said as he took Janna's hand and made for the gateway.

A sudden noise alerted them to a commotion above the chamber. "They're here," Anaskaban said.

"No doubt ransacking the temple in search of their prize." Janir's eyes met David's. "They can't find you, David—we have to get you away from here now. And they must not find this gateway."

Anaskaban ushered them toward the spinning vortex of light. "Come, my friends, you must leave now."

"What about you, Anaskaban?" David said. "You are coming with us, aren't you?"

The old man shook his head.

"But you can't stay here—who knows what they'll do to you."

"I'd hoped this would never happen, but the Alliance is here, in this temple. They'll find the gateway—and as your wise friend said, that cannot be allowed to happen. The Guardians made it clear to me that my purpose is to guard the gateway and prevent this technology from ever falling into the wrong hands."

He was right of course. If the Alliance were to find the gateway, all would be lost. This was what he was fighting so hard to prevent. But the Alliance was here, now—how could they possibly stop them from finding the gateway?

As it happened, Anaskaban had everything planned. "Once you pass through the gateway, I will destroy it."

The noise outside grew louder: crashing, clanging and the marching of booted feet.

Anaskaban stepped over to a wooden crate, retrieving a rectangular mechanical apparatus. "What is that?" Darien asked.

"A detonator. This entire chamber is laced with velitrium explosive."

"Where did you get velitrium?" Djhtak demanded.

"I obtained all the necessary components from my Enari friends and passing Alazan traders such as yourself. I've long planned for this day. At the press of a button, this room and likely half the temple will be obliterated—and along with it, all trace of the gateway."

"Surely there's another way," Mariane exclaimed, her eyes welling with tears.

"I'm afraid not. But I do not fear death, my dear. For I know I'll finally be with my beloved Ekara again. I only ask that you take Nahnto with you. Look after him, and he'll certainly look after you." Anaskaban knelt down and put his arm around the wolf, who lovingly licked his master's cheek.

They could hear the drumming of footsteps along the corridor. Anaskaban motioned for them to enter the portal. "Please go, my friends! We have so little time."

"Anaskaban, I don't know what to say," Janir began.

David felt overcome by emotion. Someone else was about to die because of him. He had to force himself to look in the old man's eye. "I promise your sacrifice won't be in vain," he said.

Anaskaban opened his mouth to respond when the chamber door burst open. A dozen Death Troops spilled through the doorway, rifles in hand.

Nahnto reacted by leaping at the intruders with a fearsome growl. One of the metal soldiers opened fire, gunning the wolf down in midair. The wolf whimpered as he fell to the ground.

The metal device fell from his hand as Anaskaban ran to Nahnto and sank to his knees. Holding the wolf's limp body in his arms, he looked up at the soldiers. "You killed him," he cried, his voice broken. "You killed Nahnto."

Releasing the wolf's body, the old man forced himself to his feet. Overcome by blinding grief, Anaskaban leapt at the soldiers, screaming with rage. His mind had snapped. They'd taken everything from him—everything and everyone he'd ever cared about.

The Death Troops opened fire.

David watched as Anaskaban was struck down by the barrage of electrical fire. In seconds, he lay motionless upon the stone floor, smoke rising from his chest. His eyes were wide open, filled with a mix of shock, rage and grief. He was clearly dead by the time his body hit the ground.

Wasting no time, Naranyan reached down and grabbed hold of the detonator. "Go," he cried. "I'll destroy the gateway once you are through!"

"Naranyan," Janir cried, "you don't have to do this."

"Yes, I do. There is no time for discussion. You were right— the Alliance cannot have this gateway."

The Death Troops advanced, rifles aloft.

"Go," Naranyan shouted. "Now!"

"You heard him," Janir cried, ushering everyone to the gateway.

Mariane was the first to enter, albeit reluctantly; her form disappearing into the swirling violet light as she stepped forward. Despite his initial protestation, Devlan was next, followed by Djhtak.

Just as the rest of them were about to enter the portal, one of the Death Troops opened fire. Janna was hit by the blast. The lightning bolt struck her left shoulder, electrifying her entire torso. She doubled over, crying out in pain.

"Janna!" Darien grabbed hold of her.

Chari returned fire. The bolts from his crossbow shot toward the attackers, only to be deflected by the metal armor. With a guttural roar, he shot again and again as the soldiers closed in.

Determined to get them to safety, Janir pushed Janna and Darien through the gateway. "Chari, we have to go," he called. With some reluctance, the Kellian stepped back, weapon still raised as he plunged into the swirling pool of light.

"Come on," Janir took David's arm and led him through the portal. As David entered the portal, he looked back and saw Naranyan standing at the mouth of the gateway, detonator in hand, surrounded by Death Troops.

The scene vanished.

Swallowed by the gateway, David felt the solidity of three-dimensional reality collapse into a fluidic tunnel of light and energy, pulsating like the heartbeat of the universe. Aware of Janir next to him as he passed through the corridor of energy, it was only a few seconds before he found himself hastily exiting it with a sharp bump.

Colliding with the ground, the first thing David was aware of was—

Sand.

He was lying in sand.

He could feel it over his skin, and in his hair and mouth as he struggled for breath. His ribs felt bruised as he pushed himself up and looked around, desperate to gain his bearings.

Where were they—where had the gateway taken them?

To his astonishment, they'd been deposited on a beach. Ocean waves lapped upon the shoreline; the sky above covered with thick cloud.

His attention was drawn to the gateway. The portal span in mid-air, almost like the fabric of the universe had been carved open. With a pang of dread, he watched as another figure emerged through the opening. It was one of the Death Troops. The metal-plated soldier stepped onto the sand, seemingly unperturbed by its transit. Scanning its new surroundings, the soldier zeroed in on its prey, raising its weapon.

Pre-empting it, Chari took aim and fired. The metal bolt from his crossbow sliced through the air, impaling the soldier's visor. Blinded, the Death Troop staggered forward, dropping its rifle.

Chari lunged at the attacker, knocking it to the ground. He reached down and grabbed the soldier's neck, twisting it clear off its body. With a growl, he tossed the decapitated head to the ground and stood over the corpse. A gruesome combination of wires and blood spilled from the cyborg's neck and head.

Before anyone could react, a blast of light erupted from the gateway. The portal exploded with a brilliant flash, forcing them to shield their eyes. As the light subsided, David opened his eyes. It was gone.

"Naranyan," David whispered.

"He did it," Janir said. "He succeeded in destroying the gateway."

"Then he's gone," Mariane gasped.

"I'm afraid so. But he took the Death Troops along with him." He paused. "Is everyone all right?"

"No," came Darien's voice. He was kneeling by Janna's side. She lay unmoving on the sand. Janir rushed to assist.

The others looked around, startled at having instantaneously traveled from Anaskaban's temple to—a beach, of all places. David found himself staring down at the decapitated Alliance soldier. Although their ordeal was over, he found it hard to relax.

Grabbing the Death Troop's rifle, Chari began pacing like a caged animal, restless and on edge. Despite lacking his people's taste for violence, the impulse to fight clearly ran strong through his veins; an impulse he often had to restrain.

Devlan had worked himself into a frenzy. "I demand to know what's happening here! Why are you people being hunted by the Alliance? Surely you must be criminals or outlaws of some kind? I have a right to know..."

"What are you complaining about?" Djhtak said, the disdain clear in his voice as he stared down at the pint-sized prince. "You're *alive*. Which frankly confirms my suspicion that we're cursed."

"What's that supposed to mean?"

"You work it out, your most exalted majesty."

"This isn't the time for petty bickering," David snapped. "Naranyan's dead! He died to save us." He felt the bitter sting of grief at his friend's loss. It had taken him a while to see beyond the Enari's brusque exterior, but he'd come to admire and respect him as an honorable, noble man. Naranyan had saved his life more than once. It seemed impossible to believe they'd never see him again.

Overcome with despair, David joined Janir as he examined Janna's shoulder. Darien remained by her side, holding her hand as her body twitched and trembled. Mariane looked on in concern, clearly wanting to help but unsure what to do. Barely conscious, Janna's face was contorted with pain.

"You have to help her," Darien pleaded.

"She got hit at point-blank range," Janir said.

"But it's just her shoulder, right? They didn't hit any of her vital organs."

"Doesn't matter where she got shot, kid," said Djhtak. "You don't want to get hit by one of those Alliance weapons."

Janir concurred, "Those electro-pulse rifles are terrible weapons. It's not so much the wound that's the problem. If we get the proper supplies I can treat that..."

"Then what is the problem?"

"The chemical compound in the blast contains a deadly nerve toxin. It quickly spreads throughout the body. Unless treated promptly, it's almost always fatal."

"Then how do we treat it?"

"The only antidote I know of is tocah serum."

"But it's got to be administered as quickly as possible," Djhtak said. "By the look of it, fever and delirium have already set in. As the toxin spreads, it'll cause madness and excruciating pain. I've seen men die of this—and believe me, it'd be preferable to end the girl's suffering now."

"Don't speak like that," Darien growled. "We're going to save her. Right, Janir?"

Janir nodded, but he didn't seem confident.

"You'd better hurry then," Djhtak said. Folding his arms, the Alazan shook his head slowly. Clearly he didn't hold out much hope.

"We have to do something," Mariane said. "We have to help her!"

David stepped forward. "Where can we find this serum?"

"Depends on where we are," Janir said. "We could be anywhere."

"Not anywhere," Devlan exclaimed, his eyes fixed ahead. "I'm back...I'm finally back!"

"Back where?" David said.

"Back home, of course!" Devlan's face lit with a smile. "Look over there, upon the shore—why, it's the town of Akyron, and beyond it, my citadel! I don't know how that contraption worked, but praise the royal dynasty, it's taken me all the way home—to Sekyr!"

# CHAPTER EIGHTEEN

# A Dangerous Game

"Sekyr," David exclaimed. "If this is Sekyr—"

"Then the gateway just saved us weeks of traveling," Janir said. "Anaskaban did say it would hasten us along our journey."

David, however, felt little in the way of relief. He looked across the port at the far end of the beach. Filled with boats, ships, and freighters, it was clearly a focal point of activity for seafarers, mariners and traders. Above it, a ramshackle town sat upon the hillside, with a pristine granite citadel rising from its heart.

David's first thought was of the Alliance. They were here. He could almost sense them. He recalled Anaskaban's warning that one of them had been touched by the darkness. David knew it was him. They were in his head; first in his dreams and now in his waking consciousness. The enemy wasn't just hunting him—they were inside of him. He'd inadvertently led them to Numaria, and both Anaskaban and Naranyan had paid the price. Looking down at Janna, barely conscious on the ground, he swore that no one else would die because of him. "Janir," he said, "can we get the medicine we need here?"

Janir looked to Devlan, whose eyes were fixed upon the glistening citadel. "Devlan, is there anywhere we could find tocah serum?"

"I don't know," the Sekyrian shrugged. "Perhaps in the marketplace."

"Will you take us there?"

"I can point you in that vicinity, yes. But then I will take my leave of you. Now that I'm back in my kingdom, it's time I returned to the citadel to depose my traitorous brother. My throne awaits me."

"By the twin suns," Mariane exclaimed, "how can you leave us when we're in such a predicament? Perhaps you're forgetting who rescued you from the Kellians?"

"Not at all. But now that I'm home I wish to resume my affairs immediately. And frankly, I don't wish to be seen with the likes of you."

"What's that supposed to mean?" David said.

"Clearly you're outlaws of some kind—and if I, prince of Sekyr, am seen to be associating with such dubious characters, my reputation could be irreparably be damaged."

"You need only to open your mouth for that to happen," Djhtak barked. "You're an obnoxious, self-serving little—"

"That's enough," Janir said. "We need that serum, and we need it now. Devlan will show us to the marketplace. But we have another problem. We need currency, or we won't be able to buy *anything.*"

"I still have some." Djhtak reached into a hidden pocket in the folds of his trousers, producing a handful of gold coins. "It's not much, though. We'll need more. But I have an idea how we can get some. I'll accompany you to the market."

"You mean you're willing to associate with us outlaws?" David grunted.

"Well, until I get passage back to the Northern Territories, I haven't got anything else to do. Besides, I've always had a soft spot for outlaws!"

"Now there's a surprise," Devlan muttered.

"Then what are we waiting for," Darien said. "Let's *go.*"

Janir said, "Mariane and I will remain with Janna. David, you stay here as well. The rest of you can get ready and—"

"No," David interjected, annoyed that Janir had made the decision for him. "I'm going with them."

"David, it would be safer if—"

"I'm going." David was resolute. He felt responsible for what had happened and he wanted to make sure they did everything in their power to help Janna.

Janir could see it was pointless arguing. "Very well, but be careful. Watch your backs, and try to get back by nightfall. Janna needs that serum as quickly as possible."

"We'll be back soon," David promised.

Darien stroked Janna's face as he leaned down and whispering something in her ear. Mariane sat down by her side, taking the girl's hand. "We'll look after her," she assured Darien. Although their relationship had been largely frosty, Darien smiled in appreciation.

"Remember this is Alliance territory," Janir cautioned as they departed, "keep a low profile and be on the lookout for trouble at all times."

"Relax," Djhtak said, looking round at Chari, who strode alongside him, rifle in hand. "We got our own personal Kellian bodyguard. What could possibly go wrong?"

David half-expected a squadron of Death Troops to be lying in wait for them. But, upon arriving at the harbor, he was relieved to see no immediate sign of the Alliance. Filled with ships and bustling with activity, the old working port had clearly been in use for centuries.

It seemed to be a melting pot of people from many different cultures. There was a number of Sekyrians, recognizable by their red-tinted skin. The tall Sekyrians comprised the workforce—fishermen, laborers, and technicians—while a group of shorter men, resembling Devlan, appeared to be the administrators of the port. Dressed in drab uniforms, they flitted about with clipboards, bearing an air of indignant authority. In addition, David saw a number of Alazan traders strutting about, and several Alanarans, or 'humans', such as David and the islanders. He watched as a heated argument broke out between a group of red-robed reptilian creatures and two men with furry, animalistic features and thick manes of brown hair—something to do with 'trading rights'.

"Don't speak to anyone," Devlan said. "In fact, don't even *look* at anyone! Just follow me—but not too closely. I don't want it to look like we're together."

Climbing down the harbor wall into the port, they kept their heads down as they moved through the crowd. There was an overpowering smell of fish from crates along the pier along with the odor of oil and grease. Devlan led them through the harbor, past a shipyard and up a steeply inclined road lined by warehouses. At the top of the hill, they reached the outskirts of the city.

"Ah, Akyron," Devlan beamed, a little breathless from the ascent.

"Haven't been here for a while," Djhtak said, "but it's just as miserable as I remember."

David was astonished by how squalid the town was. Dingy gray tenements overlooked the winding, congested streets. Thick reams of smoke spewed from the chimney pots and most buildings were in varying states of disrepair. In sharp contrast, the elegant citadel stood at the heart of the city; its towers rising high above the shabby metropolis, no doubt visible for miles in any direction. Constructed of granite and built in levels, the citadel was a monument of grandiose architecture. Yet it seemed so curiously out of place, as though it belonged in a different world to the decaying city sprawled around it.

"Glorious, isn't it?" Devlan exclaimed.

"Who decides who lives up there and who lives down here?" David asked.

"Sekyrian society is governed by a strict caste system," Devlan explained as they made their way into the heart of town. "The ruling class live in the citadels. The working classes reside in the surrounding cities and towns, and in villages and farms in the country provinces. The land is leased to them by the monarchy. They, in turn, live and work for their keep."

This seemed unfair to David; a society based on blatant inequality. "And what do the ruling class do exactly?"

Devlan stopped, narrowed his eyes and shot David an imperious glare. "We *rule*, obviously."

"At least there doesn't seem to be any sign of the Alliance," Darien remarked.

"Not yet," Chari cautioned, constantly on edge as he kept a close eye on the crowd.

"As far as I know, the Alliance is stationed in an underground base beneath the citadel," Djhtak said.

"That's correct," Devlan said. "However, the First Guard regularly patrols the streets, so consider yourselves warned."

"So where's the marketplace?" Darien asked.

Devlan pointed ahead. "Follow that street and take the first lane to the right. You can't miss it. It's one of the busiest markets in all of Sekyr."

Djhtak nodded. "Yeah, I've been here before. I know the way from here."

Devlan straightened up, puffing out his chest and running his hands down his tattered green suit. "Now, I wish you well I'm sure, but I must take my leave of you. It's time I returned to the citadel to reclaim my throne."

"You're leaving us so soon?" Djhtak said with mock sorrow. "Well, it's been an absolute delight knowing you, your supreme highness! We'll miss you immeasurably."

Devlan glared at him. "I'm *sure.*" Clearly happy to be rid of them, the pint-sized prince turned and pushed his way through the crowd, promptly disappearing from sight.

"You think they'll be glad to have him back?" Darien said.

"I very much doubt it," David said. "Would *you* be?"

"Point taken."

"Right," said Djhtak. "Now we've finally got rid of his lordship, let's get down to business. Follow me, boys."

They soon arrived at the marketplace—an explosion of noise, color, and activity. The densely packed promenade heaved with people as they flitted about the stalls and shops, of which there were hundreds. David found the noise initially overwhelming: the sound of so many people talking, laughing and shouting; as well as music, sirens, the rumble of machinery and the cries of seabirds as they searched for scraps of food.

"Don't get lost," Djhtak warned as they edged forward.

David marveled at the variety of things on offer: from just about every food imaginable to clothes, jewelry, cosmetics, precious stones, mechanical hardware, plants and religious artifacts. One vendor, a peculiar obese man with large yellow-flecked eyes and bluish skin, sold caged animals: chattering monkey-like creatures packed into small metal cages.

David found himself both allured and disturbed by this most alien of places, but Darien hadn't lost sight of the purpose of their visit. He turned to Djhtak, having to almost shout to be heard above the noise. "Where will we find the medicine we need?"

Djhtak put his hand on Darien's shoulder and smiled. "First thing's first, boy—we need more currency. I have only six cretnas to my name and believe me, that won't get us far."

"So how are we going to get more?" David asked.

"Oh, that shouldn't be too hard." Gesturing for them to follow, Djhtak turned and pushed his way through the crowd. Some way along the edge of the marketplace they came to an old two-story building. A crooked sign hung above the entrance, inscribed in a language David couldn't read. With a smile, Djhtak entered and the others followed.

They found themselves in a smoky tavern. David immediately felt his hackles rise. In keeping with pretty much everything else he'd seen in the Sekyrian city, the building was centuries old and in a state of disrepair. Lanterns hung from the walls, but the lighting was dim and the place stank of stale smoke and liquor.

"A bar," Darien muttered to David. "He's taken us to a bar..."

The patrons, mainly men, were a motley assortment. There were some Alanarans, working class Sekyrians, several Alazan and another of the gruff, brown-maned men they'd seen at the harbor. A plump, purplish-skinned man sat slouched at the bar with tentacles protruding from his head. The barman, a tall, middle-aged Sekyrian, stood behind the bar polishing a set of glasses, eyeing the strangers warily as they entered.

Chari was unimpressed. "Why have you taken us here? We have no time for this."

"Relax, Kellian," Djhtak said. "We need more currency, don't we? Well I'm about to show you how to take six cretnas and quadruple them! Now, watch and learn."

Djhtak strode to the other side of the room and the others hesitantly followed. A log fire crackled at the far side of the tavern; two swords mounted upon the wall above it. Most of the tables and benches were occupied. The patrons looked up at the new arrivals as they passed, paying particular attention to Chari. In spite of the diverse nationalities that congregated in Sekyr, it seemed Kellians were far from commonplace.

Djhtak led them to a gaming table in a corner of the room. Half a dozen men stood around the table, cards in hand, taking turns to spin a metal wheel. One of the men, a bald, brown-skinned man in a purple robe, appeared to have won this particular round. With a groan of frustration, the other players passed him their coins.

"This is your plan?" Chari grumbled. "To waste what little money you have gambling?"

"Listen Kellian, when it comes to Kahjika, I am a master. Take my word for it, I'm going to wipe them out—the lot of them."

Chari grunted, unimpressed. Djhtak turned to David and Darien and tossed them a gold coin. "Here! Go buy yourselves a drink."

"Shouldn't we be saving whatever money we have?" David said as he caught the coin.

"Don't worry so much, kid. You'll have yourself a heart attack by the time you're thirty. We'll soon have more money than we know what to do with."

With a confident swagger, Djhtak approached the gaming table. He introduced himself and laid his money on the table. The other players looked him up and down, gauging him suspiciously, before agreeing to deal him into the next round.

"I hope he knows what he's doing," David said.

"He'd better," Darien said. "Because Janna's life depends on it."

David looked down at the coin. "You want a drink then?"

"Well, we're here. I guess we might as well."

"Chari?"

"No," the Kellian said. "I will remain here and keep an eye on Djhtak."

"What kind of stuff do they serve in here anyway?" Darien asked.

David shrugged. "I don't know. I'm not exactly a regular."

They approached the bar. The bartender hadn't taken his eyes off them since they'd entered. "What do you want?" he barked.

David looked down at the purple-skinned tentacled man slumped across the bar. He was nursing a half-finished glass of orange liquid. "What's he drinking?"

"Rasnat."

"I'll have two of those."

The bartender produced two small glasses and poured the drinks, his eyes trained on them the whole time. Had it not been for Anaskaban's kindly nature, David would have assumed the man's belligerent manner to be a characteristic of all Sekyrians. The bartender slammed the bottle down, muttered something and held his hand out for payment. David gave him the gold coin. He examined it closely before reaching into his cash register and practically throwing David his change with an indecipherable grunt.

They took their drinks and joined Chari, who stood in a darkened corner of the room overlooking the gaming table. "Djhtak better be winning," Darien said as they sat down at the nearest table.

"Well, he's certainly confident," David said. He looked down at his drink, swirling it about the glass and taking a tentative sniff. Darien seemed similarly reticent. "After you," David said.

"Oh, no. We do this together..."

In unison, they lifted their glasses and took a mouthful of the drink.

David slammed the glass down on the table. As he swallowed he felt the liquid leave what felt like a trail of fire down his throat. That was to say nothing of the taste. Both began coughing.

"That is...vile!" Darien exclaimed.

Chari turned and frowned. "You should not touch anything in a place like this. You do not know *what* you might be drinking."

"Why didn't you warn us before we drank it?" David said, putting a hand to his burning throat.

"You never asked."

Although they soon recovered from their experience of rasnat (one they vowed never to repeat) David and Darien grew ever more impatient and uptight as Djhtak's game dragged on. They knew time was of the essence. Chari said nothing, keeping his attention fixed on proceedings as if anticipating looming trouble.

Darien rapped his knuckles on the table anxiously. "I hope she's okay."

"She will be," David assured him. "She's in good hands with Janir. We'll get the money, buy the medicine and she'll be fine."

"I can't lose her, David." Darien's usual bravado was slipping and for the first time David could see his true vulnerability. "The Alliance took my family—who knows where they are now. Janna's all I've got. I can't bear the thought of losing her..."

"You really care for her don't you?"

"I love her."

"You do?"

"I know it started off as some kind of schoolboy crush, but it's so much more than that. I can't imagine my life without her."

"You think she feels the same way?"

"I don't know. I mean, I hope so, but we haven't spoken about it. With all that's been happening, there's never been a right moment to tell her."

"I know what you mean. These past weeks have been hell." He paused. "Darien, have you noticed something about Janna..."

"What?"

"She seems to know things before they happen—as though she can sense things the rest of us can't? It's happened several times now. Like when we encountered the Jatei in the forest of Senrah, or Anaskaban in Numaria...?"

"Yeah, I noticed. I don't know, she's maybe just more perceptive than the rest of us?"

David nodded, although he was certain there was more to it than that. When the Alliance arrived at Numaria, he'd seen the way Janna had looked at him. It was as though she knew what was going on inside him. He'd been trying not to think about that, or the deaths of Naranyan and Anaskaban. He still felt a sense of guilt. It was him that had drawn the Alliance to Numaria—him they were after. Why had so many others had to die because of him? All he could do was make sure their deaths would not be in vain. Maybe that way the pain and suffering would be bearable in the end.

A cry of triumph erupted from the gaming table. Djhtak had won. "Good game," the Alazan called to his opponents with a gleeful smile. "You played well, my friends—just not as well as me."

The players conceded defeat and passed their money to Djhtak. Unfortunately, one of his opponents—another of the gruff, animal-like men David had first seen down at the harbor—was unwilling to accept defeat so readily. Tall and muscular, with a coat of gray fur and a thick mane of brown hair, his face was wild and animalistic. His narrowed black eyes blazed with anger as he glared at Djhtak. "You—play again," he growled.

"Not today," was Djhtak's brusque response. "If you'll just pass me my winnings, I must be going."

"No! Game not over. You—play *again!*"

David knew trouble was brewing. He got up from the table and leaned toward Chari. "That man, what race is he?"

"Nitralian," Chari said. "A proud race of warriors; ancient adversaries to the Kellians. They are fiercely protective of their personal honor. It motivates their every action. The Nitralians are not a people to be crossed."

Unfortunately, Djhtak was about to do just that. "Listen, my furry friend. The game is over! Finished! You lost. So give me my winnings please, because I'm leaving now."

"No," snarled the Nitralian. "You—cheat!"

"I never cheat!" Djhtak shouted, squaring up to the Nitralian.

"You—lie!" The Nitralian drew his sword from its sheath.

Djhtak stepped back toward the fireplace, grabbing one of the swords from the wall. The other players backed off. All attention in the tavern was upon Djhtak and the Nitralian. Everyone could sense an imminent fight, and this caused a perverse stir of excitement. Chari bristled, raising his rifle, ready to render assistance should it be needed.

"Let's not overreact here," Djhtak said. "I'd never cheat; you have my word on that. I've simply played a lot of Kahjika over the years...and I never lose a game."

"Because you—cheat!" With a snarl, the Nitralian took a swipe at Djhtak. Raising his blade, Djhtak deflected the blow. Angered, the Nitralian launched an all-out offensive. Djhtak more than held his own as the pair clashed swords, knocking over tables, breaking chairs and smashing glasses as they fought. The spectators cheered and shouted in boorish delight, enthralled by the excitement. The bartender was less impressed. Although hesitant to leave the relative safety of the bar, he shouted at them to stop before they completely tore apart his establishment.

"We do not have time for this," Chari grumbled. Rifle raised, he stepped forward.

By this point the Nitralian had Djhtak cornered. His back was hard against the wall as he desperately deflected his opponent's strikes.

Chari took aim and pulled the trigger, sending a shot of lightning blasting from the barrel, slamming into the Nitralian's torso, electrifying his body. With a cry of pain, the Nitralian stopped and fell to his knees. His sword dropped with a clatter as he slumped to the ground.

Djhtak looked down at the body then up at Chari. Rather than being grateful, he seemed angry. "You shot him in the back!"

"I could not stand by and allow the Nitralian to kill you."

"I had it under control. I could easily have defeated him—and I would have!"

"That did not appear to be the case. Now, pick up your winnings. We must leave. You can thank me for saving your life at a later time."

Clearly raging, Djhtak marched over to the gaming table and snatched up his winnings, stuffing the impressive stack of coins into his trousers pockets.

They made for the exit; the crowd readily standing aside to let them past. The tavern was now a mess. Tables and chairs had been upturned and destroyed—and of course, a dead Nitralian lay upon the ground in a smoldering heap. The bartender, who had been a less than gracious host to begin with, was understandably livid. "And don't come back!" he bellowed as they exited.

"We'd best hurry," Djhtak said as they stepped back into the marketplace. "When that Nitralian's friends find out what's happened they'll no doubt want revenge..."

"You should have thought of that before you got involved in a fight with him," Chari said.

"I got us the currency, didn't I?"

"Only by cheating."

Djhtak shrugged and smiled.

"You mean the Nitralian was right?" Darien said. "You *did* cheat?"

"I'm an Alazan, of course I cheated! But, hey, I got us our currency. That's all that matters."

David was astounded by Djhtak's gall, but there was little time to debate the merit of his actions. The suns were lowering in the sky and they still hadn't found what they'd come for. Time was running out. They all knew that if they didn't get back with the medicine soon, Janna was as good as dead.

# CHAPTER NINETEEN

# Betrayal

"Right, be on the lookout," Djhtak said. "There's bound to be a witch doctor here somewhere."

There surely had to be, for there was just about everything else imaginable. As they wandered through the marketplace, David again found his senses besieged by so many foreign sights, sounds, and smells. A man inadvertently elbowed him in the ribs as he stopped to look at a food stall serving steamed rice dishes and other exotic cuisine. The enticing smell drew his attention to his own empty belly. It had been almost a full day since his last meal. He only hoped they'd have some money left over from Janna's remedy to buy some food for themselves and the others.

Although some of the vendors had now begun packing up their goods and dismantling their stalls, the market seemed as busy as ever. It was packed with people of all ages, sizes and description, including a fair number of nefarious-looking characters. He was glad that aside from the crystal Key around his neck he didn't have anything worth stealing, for the market clearly abounded with thieves, pick-pockets, and other criminals. Given the squalor of the Sekyrian city, this hardly seemed surprising.

While Djhtak and Chari led the way, David and Darien lagged a little behind. The Alliance remained uppermost on David's mind. Although there had been no sign of any Alliance activity, he knew they couldn't afford to relax for a second.

Just as it began to seem as though they were hopelessly wandering in circles, Djhtak turned and called to the boys, beckoning them to a stall tucked away in a relatively quiet corner of the market.

Comprising an upturned crate covered with a threadbare cloth, the stall was laid out with an assortment of herbs and potions, along with some trinkets, bracelets, and amulets. An exceedingly old woman sat behind the stall, her wizened face rapt with curiosity as she studied her potential customers. An odd-looking woman by any standards, she had a thick mop of unkempt white hair cascading over her shoulders and down her back; her bronzed, paper-thin skin lined with deep-set wrinkles and crevices. Thin and slight, she wore emerald green robes patterned with circles, her ears, neck, and wrists bedecked with beads and bangles. "Welcome," she said, smiling at them with a somewhat manic glint in her misty, cataract-ridden brown eyes. "Can I interest you in a reading?"

"No," Chari said.

"Are you a witch doctor?" Djhtak asked.

"I prefer the term *healer,* my dear. So...who would like a reading?"

"We were hoping you could help us," Darien said.

"Do you have any tocah serum?" David continued.

The woman seemed uninterested in Darien but she studied David intently, her crazed eyes drinking in every last detail as she scanned his face. David felt unnerved. "Well, do you?" he asked finally.

"Why, yes of course," she said in a tone of disinterest.

Darien's face lit up in relief. "That's great!"

The woman finally managed to take her eyes off David and she looked round at Darien, smiling to reveal a row of craggy, damaged teeth, several of which were missing. She began stroking her tangled mop of hair in absent-minded fashion as she muttered, "Yes, I have a wide variety of herbs, roots and plant extracts hand-gathered from all across the world..." She picked up a small jar filled with red berries and unscrewed the rubber cap. "I particularly recommend these. Oh yes! Tridalan berries, gathered from the rainforests of Ustabor. You simply must have one."

She emptied a handful of berries into the palm of her claw-like hand and reached out to David. "Try!"

David took a couple of berries and looked at them warily.

"Oh you must try," the woman exclaimed. "Chew slowly. They are delicious! Tridalan is a fine delicacy, worth significant currency—but a free sample I offer to you."

Feeling obliged to comply, David put the berries in his mouth. To his surprise they actually tasted quite nice; a delicate, sweet flavor that helped take away the taste lingering in his mouth from the vile beverage he'd drunk in the tavern. But almost the moment he swallowed the berries, he was overcome by a wave of dizziness. He staggered back, nearly falling to the ground, only to be steadied by Darien.

"Are you all right?" Darien asked.

"I don't know. I feel light-headed..."

"You should refrain from eating anything unless you now exactly what it is," Chari admonished.

"Again, I wish you'd said that before I ate it," David said. The temporary dizziness passing, he now felt able to stand unassisted. "I'm fine."

"Of course you are! I would not give you anything dangerous," the old woman said. "Only good things do I sell here, that I can assure you. Now, I've got the cards right here—can I interest you in a reading?"

"No," Darien said impatiently. "We're only here for the serum. Do you have it or not?"

"Of course I do." She reached beneath the counter and produced a small glass vial. "Tocah serum. Made from fresh extract of tocah root. I sell only the finest of products!"

"How much is it?" Djhtak asked.

"That'll be twelve cretnas, please." She opened the vial, took a sniff of the potion and let out a violent sneeze.

"Twelve cretnas for that tiny vial? That's extortionate."

"Like I said, I sell only the finest of products," she retorted, wiping her nose and sealing the vial. "And the finest of products naturally fetch the finest of prices."

"We'll take it," Darien said. He turned to Djhtak and gestured for the Alazan to pay her. With a roll of his eyes, Djhtak delved into his pocket and produced a handful of coins, counting out twelve cretnas and reluctantly passing them to the old woman.

She grinned as she surveyed the money and set it aside, handing Djhtak the vial. "Now that we have that out the way," she said perkily, "can I interest you in a reading?"

"No!" Djhtak barked. He turned to the others and motioned for them to leave.

Just as they were about to set off, the old woman issued a sudden warning that made David's heart freeze. "You must hurry. Danger is closing in fast. If you are to escape, you must run *now!*"

Filled with a sudden dread, David knew she was right. They *were* in danger. He didn't know how or why he knew this, but it was an unshakable knowing.

"Looks like we have company," Djhtak said.

David turned to see a dozen Alliance Death Troops marching into the marketplace.

The Alliance had found them, and David could see precisely how. Alongside the machine-like soldiers was the pint-sized Devlan, conferring with the lead soldier and pointing across the market in the direction of David and his comrades. He'd sold them out to the Alliance. David had always suspected the Sekyrian prince wasn't to be trusted.

The Death Troops began shoving their way through the crowd, sending startled patrons flying to the ground and crashing into stalls.

"Run," Chari barked. The muscular Kellian led the way as they raced through the market.

"Out of the way," David yelled as he pushed through the crowd, almost tripping over a basket of fruit. He couldn't let the Alliance get him. He'd been through too much for it all to end here.

In his frenzied haste, the startled teenager soon realized that Darien and Djhtak were no longer by his side. And where was Chari? He'd somehow lost them. Still, he couldn't afford to stop now.

He was aware of the Alliance Troops closing in on him. Fueled by surging adrenaline, David found himself exiting the market and racing down a side-lane. The cobbled road was lined either side by rickety stone houses, with washing strewn from the balconies.

Though he didn't know where he was or where he was going, he knew that he had to keep going. This was the third time he'd encountered the Alliance Death Troops. As before, they elicited in him a potent mix of terror and hatred: terror because what they were capable of doing and hatred for what they had done.

He reached the bottom of the street, which forked in two directions.

Which way?

He hadn't noticed how dark it was getting. Daylight was fading, making the deserted streets ever more dark and dismal. He stopped for a moment, hiding behind an outhouse to catch his breath. He glanced down the road he'd come. To his relief, there was no sign of his pursuers. He must have lost them in the market. The problem was he'd lost everyone else as well.

Looking around in dismay, he was struck by how quiet this part of the city was. He couldn't even hear the noise of the market or the sounds from the streets and harbor here. Why was it so quiet—and where was everyone? The rest of the town was packed full of people, yet there wasn't a soul to be seen here.

Crouching against the wall, he lifted his hands to his head. What was he going to do? *Think!* He couldn't go back the way he'd come. The Death Troops would find him for sure. No, he had to find a way back down to the beach. He had to warn Janir. Devlan had no doubt already told the Alliance of their whereabouts.

The sound of footsteps alerted David to someone nearby. Fortunately, it wasn't the clanking thud of Death Troops, but quieter, more delicate footsteps, echoing across the street. David cautiously peered out from the side of the outhouse.

It couldn't be...

A girl, no older than he—and one he recognized in an instant. It was the girl he'd seen in his dreams so many times before. Dressed in a blue-violet tunic with trousers and boots, she had shoulder-length dark hair and an aura of power and regality.

She stood at the road end looking straight at him, beckoning him to come closer. David could hardly believe it. She wasn't just a figment of his imagination after all. She was a real, flesh and blood person—and she was here, in Sekyr. How was that even possible?

He walked toward her, hypnotized by her beauty. Coming to a stop in front of her, his eyes melted into hers. Beautiful and alluring, they were the eyes of a young woman of immense power and stature, yet someone who had suffered much, fought much; and perhaps had to sacrifice much just to be here.

"Who are you?" he whispered, feeling an immediate and intense connection with the girl.

"My name is Eladria."

"What are you doing here?"

"I've come a long way for you, David. I'm here to help you. You're in danger here. Come!"

She turned and began running down the road. David knew he had to follow. He needed to know who she was and why she was here. She ran so fast; far faster than he'd expected. "Wait," he called. Although overcome by a growing dizziness, he kept on running.

The road led them to a hilltop at the edge of the city overlooking the harbor and surrounding shoreline. The girl stopped at the edge of the cliff. She opened her mouth to speak, but to David's astonishment it wasn't the girl's voice that issued from her mouth—"Can I interest you in a reading?"

David blinked. The figure before him had somehow transformed. It was no longer the teenage girl standing before him. It was the old woman from the marketplace.

"I don't understand," he gasped. "What are you doing here?"

The old woman smiled. "It was you that sought me, remember?"

"Why have you taken me here?"

"Clarity. It was not just the serum you sought. It was clarity. And clarity you will now get."

The old woman pointed down to the shore.

David stepped toward the crumbling edge of the cliff. Looking down, his stomach lurched upon seeing dozens of Death Troops spreading across the beach. His comrades were at the center of the commotion. Djhtak, Darien and Chari had made it back to the beach, but they'd all been caught by the Alliance. As he'd feared, Devlan had led the Alliance straight to them. He watched helplessly as the Troops surrounded them at gunpoint. He knew this was the end. There was no way that he alone could save them.

The biggest shock was yet to come. While the others were chained and carted off by the soldiers, Janir stood casually talking to one of the soldiers. He pointed down to Janna, who still lay unconscious on the sand. The soldier raised its rifle and shot her. The energy discharge electrified her body. There was no way that she could have survived that shot, especially at such close range. Reeling from the shock, David watched as Janir folded his arms and stared down at her unmoving body.

This couldn't be—Janir was working for the Alliance?

It was the only explanation.

He'd pretended to be their friend and trusted leader, while all along he was marching them to their deaths at the hands of the Alliance.

David had believed in him. He'd trusted him. He would have done anything for him—and all this time Janir had been double-crossing them.

He turned to the old woman, whose face was blank, her expression unreadable.

A force of rage swept through David's mind and senses like a tornado, and something inside of him snapped.

He began climbing down the embankment to the beach below. He didn't care if the Alliance caught him now. He was going to confront Janir and make him pay for his betrayal. But as he scrambled down the hill, the rocks gave way beneath his feet, crumbling like sand. He fell, bashing his head against a large rock, his body ensnared by gravity's unyielding pull.

# CHAPTER TWENTY

# Severence

David opened his eyes. He lifted a hand to his head, his vision misty and senses dulled. He found himself indoors, in a dimly lit room, lying upon a creaky old bed.

"David," came Janir's voice. "Thank Hershala you're awake."

David bristled at the sound of his voice. He propped himself up and looked around.

Janir sat on a wooden chair by his bedside and the outline of Chari loomed in the shadows behind him. A spiraling cloud of smoke drifted across the room, catching in David's throat. Following it to its source, he caught sight of Djhtak sitting in a darkened corner of the room puffing on a pipe.

"Where am I?"

The room was small, the wallpaper faded, stained and peeling, and the only illumination came from a narrow skylight on the sloped ceiling. Starkly furnished, a number of old boxes lay stacked against the far wall and a series of uneven shelves lined the adjacent walls, packed with assorted bottles and jars. A stale, musty smell permeated the room, along with the pungent taste of tobacco smoke.

"Somewhere safe," Janir said.

David felt himself inwardly recoil from Janir; an involuntary reaction due to the fact he'd just witnessed Janir betraying them all to the Alliance. Or had he? The memory now seemed vague, distant and dreamlike. Overcome by disorientation, David wasn't sure what to think anymore.

"How do you feel?" Janir asked.

"My head hurts," he said. "What happened?"

"You've been unconscious for nearly a day."

"A *day...*?"

"What's the last thing you remember?"

"We were in the marketplace, running from the Alliance soldiers. I got separated from the others..." he trailed off, deciding not reveal what he'd seen next.

"David, none of that happened."

"What...?"

Chari said, "We *were* in the market. That much you remember correctly. We found the old woman's stall and asked her for the tocah serum."

"That's right."

"Do you recall she gave you something to eat?"

"Yes—those berries..."

"Which," Janir said, "were actually some kind of psychotropic compound."

"A drug?"

"You collapsed and fell unconscious," Chari said. "There was nothing we could do to wake you."

"And we tried just about everything, believe me," Djhtak said, expelling a lungful of smoke.

"Oh, for the great maker's sake, I told them you would be fine," interjected another voice.

David saw a small, hunched figure with an untamed mop of white hair shuffle into the room. It was the old woman from the market. "I am a master healer," she said. "I knew precisely what I was doing. But did they listen to me? Why, of course not..."

"What's she doing here?" David asked.

"We did not know what else to do," Chari said. "So we demanded that she take us to a place of safety until you woke up. She took us here, to her home."

"If you can call it that," Djhtak said. "It's more of an apothecary than a home."

"Djhtak stayed here with you while Darien and I took the medicine to the others," Chari said.

"I administered the serum to Janna," Janir continued. "And as soon as she was able to move we made our way here to join you."

"How is Janna?" David asked.

"She's doing well. Her condition is steadily improving. She's through in the other room with Darien and Mariane."

David nodded. His head was still sore and his mind scattered and disorientated. He found himself struggling to take this all in. "So I've been unconscious for a whole day..."

"That's right."

"Then everything I experienced, or thought I experienced after the marketplace was just a dream."

"More of a drug-induced hallucination."

"The old woman drugged you," Djhtak said, clearly amused by the whole incident.

"The old woman has a *name,*" she said with a frown. "You may address me as Letanta, world-renowned healer of outstanding repute; known across the lands as a leading expert on the knowledge and application of plant-based healing modalities."

"Whatever you say." Djhtak took another puff from his pipe.

David looked over at the woman, barely able to keep his eyes in focus. "Why did you do that to me?"

Letanta approached his bedside and smiled, a deranged glint in her wild, dark eyes. "The moment I saw you, young David, I could sense the anger within you—the bitterness, confusion and sadness. So much of it unexpressed—held back! You needed to express those feelings lest they obstruct your clarity. So I gave you extract of tridalan, hand-picked from the rainforests of Ustabor. Now it's not an inexpensive compound I might add, but a free sample you were given!"

"What did it do to me?"

"Think of it as a psychic laxative! Enabling you to explore your inner doubts and fears; casting them into the open where they might be vanquished."

Janir was unimpressed. "You had no right to interfere like that. There's no telling what damage you could have done. These drugs are unpredictable and come with all manner of side effects."

"I am a healer," Letanta responded cheerily. It seemed unclear whether the woman was simply eccentric or bordering on senility. "When I see someone in need, I endeavor to help by whatever means I can. And in young David I saw a very great need."

David said, "Then the things I dreamt were just my fears and doubts rising to the surface?"

Letanta smiled and snapped her fingers. "Exactly! Rise to the surface they must, before they can be healed! We all carry so many burdens, so many unexpressed fears and sorrows. They must be surmounted or in time they will consume and destroy us."

This wasn't the first time that David had heard this. He recalled Naranyan telling him pretty much the same thing the morning he died at Numaria. He could hear rain starting to fall against the skylight, a rhythmic patter he found strangely soothing. "So what happens next?" he asked Janir. "We made it to Sekyr and we've cured Janna. What now?"

"Both you and Janna need some time to recuperate before we move on."

"You are welcome to stay here as long as you wish," Letanta beamed. "I do not get many houseguests."

"I can see why," Djhtak remarked, looking around the tattered room.

Ignoring Djhtak's comment, Janir thanked Letanta for her offer. "We are most grateful. But we cannot stay any longer than is absolutely necessary. It's imperative that we move on as soon as possible."

"Where is it you people are going anyway?" Djhtak asked.

"We're on a quest, as it happens. In search of the City of Lorden."

"The City of Lorden?" Djhtak echoed with an incredulous chuckle. "Are you serious?"

"Very much so."

"Then I hate to disappoint you, my friend, but there *is* no City of Lorden. It's a legend; a myth—a story they tell children."

"I can assure you, it does exist, and we're going to find it."

"How exciting," Letanta said, letting out a mirthful giggle. "Indeed, why doesn't it say in the Chronicle of Alanar: '*the time-*

*less one shall unlock the gates to the city amid the final battle of the heartland'."*

"You know of the ancient prophecies?"

"Oh yes, I am quite familiar with the ancient texts! *'At the crossing point of time, what was broken shall be repaired. The two keys shall be made one and time shall be restored'...*"

"Superstitious nonsense," Djhtak scoffed.

"Then why not come with us and see for yourself?" Janir offered.

"Alas, no. As entertaining as this all sounds, your search will be a fruitless one. I say it again: the City of Lorden does not exist. And there's little profit wasting time in search of fairytale cities. I'm a businessman. Business is what I do. It's in my blood."

"What business? I hate to remind you, but you lost your ship, Djhtak. You're a trader without a means to trade."

"A problem to be sure, but I'll find a way around it. No obstacle is insurmountable to an Alazan."

"Perhaps not, but I think what you need is a change of career—a new direction. Why not join us, Djhtak? You're a good man, and I can promise you this will be the adventure of a lifetime. In spite of your protestations, I know it's not really money you're after, but adventure; excitement."

"Even if that were so, there are other considerations to be taken into account."

"Such as?"

"The fact you're on the run from the Alliance does not bode well. Now, I despise the Alliance as much as anyone, but I have no desire to cross them. The last thing I want to do is end up in the Arkan complex."

"The Arkan complex?"

"You've never heard of the Arkan complex?"

Janir shook his head.

"It's an underground processing center beneath the royal citadel."

"Processing center?" David asked.

"Rumored to be where all Alliance prisoners are taken in this region. No one quite knows what happens to them. They all go in, but few ever come back out."

"Wait a moment, you say all Alliance prisoners are taken there?"

"All prisoners from the Western territories, that is. Those nearer the Eastern borders are taken directly to Eloramia, the heartland of the Alliance."

"Janir, do you hear that? All Alliance prisoners in the West are taken here, and we're right on the doorstep of the citadel."

Janir looked at him blankly.

"Don't you see? The survivors of New Haven, all those that were taken by the Alliance—they were surely taken *here*."

Janir said nothing.

"We can rescue them, Janir!" David pushed himself up off the bed. Although light-headed and weak on his feet, he forced himself to stand. "We can rescue them and go back. We can rebuild New Haven!"

Janir did not share his enthusiasm. "David, we can't simply stroll into the citadel, break into this Arkan complex, sift through however many thousands of prisoners might be there and then sneak them back out. We'd be caught in an instant."

"But we have to try. We owe it to them, Janir. They took Darien's family, and so many others. They're our people; our friends, neighbors, and family. They got caught and we didn't. It's our duty to do whatever we can to save them."

Djhtak shared Janir's reticence. "It'd take an army to liberate the Arkan complex. By all accounts, it's a heavily fortified base, the focal point of all Alliance activity in Sekyr. You can bet there are entire legions of Death Troops stationed there. What you're proposing is very noble, boy, but it's suicide."

"We can't just leave them there."

"David, you're forgetting something," Janir said. "We have another mission to complete."

"It can wait!" David shouted.

Janir stood up and turned to the others. "Could you give David and I a moment alone, please?" In compliance, Djhtak,

Chari and Letanta cleared the room, leaving Janir and David alone.

David began pacing the room, his legs and knees still weak and unsteady. The sound of rain continued rattling against the window as the sky darkened. Janir's expression was one of concern and weariness. "We can talk about this, David. But first, you need to calm down."

"I'm perfectly calm." The moment he uttered those words, a tad more sharply than he'd intended, he heard a voice echo in his mind:

*Don't let him get the upper hand. That's what he wants. Don't give in to him.*

"We don't even know for sure the captives from New Haven are there," Janir said. "It's been weeks since the attack. There's no telling where they might be now."

David stood to face Janir. "But if there's even the slightest chance they're here, we have to try and rescue them."

"Be reasonable, David. You heard Djhtak. Even if this Arkan complex does exist, we simply don't have the means to stage a rescue. Make no mistake, we'd be caught in an instant."

"But we have to try. Don't you see? It's *my* fault they were caught..."

"Is that what this is about? You feel guilty?"

David said nothing.

"Guilty that you survived and they didn't?" Janir took a step toward him. "David, you can't blame yourself for this. You're not responsible for what happened."

"Yes, I am." David lifted the Key from around his neck. He held it aloft, the crystal dangling from its chain. "They were after *this*, weren't they? It's because of *me* that so many people have been killed. Well, I can't bring them back, but I can save those who are still alive and enslaved by the Alliance."

"We don't even know if they *are* still alive, David..."

"Well, I intend to find out."

Janir reached out to place his hand on David's shoulder, but David pulled back.

"David," Janir said, "you've lost sight of the bigger picture. We have a mission. We have to find the City of Lorden and retrieve the other fragment of the Key. It's the only way we can stop the Alliance and the Narssians. If we don't the consequences will be catastrophic. You know that. You saw what happened to Lasandria, and that's a pale shadow of the horror the Narssians will unleash on this universe if we don't stop them now."

"Whose word do I have to take for all this—yours? The Enari's? The Guardians? I don't know *what* to believe anymore, Janir. According to Djhtak, the City of Lorden doesn't exist! What if this is one big joke and we're chasing shadows—running after legends and mythical cities that don't even exist."

"David, please calm down. You're being irrational now."

"I'm not the one being irrational."

Again David heard that same voice in his mind: *Don't give in to him. That's what he wants.*

"Listen to me, David." Janir was beginning to sound desperate. "The drug Letanta gave you has done something to you. It's clouded your mind and obscured your judgment. You're not seeing things clearly right now."

"No, it feels like for the first time I *can* see clearly—and you know what I see? I see a nightmare!" He threw the Key to the ground with such force he hoped the crystal would just smash, ending their problems. He didn't want this burden any longer. "I just want to make things right," he whispered.

Janir knelt down to pick up the amulet.

*See,* the voice said, *he doesn't care about you. He just wants the Key of Alanar. He's only in this for himself. He's been using you all along.*

Janir handed the Key back to him. David eyed him warily as he reached out and grabbed hold of it.

"I know this has been difficult," Janir said. "It's pushed us all to the brink. But we must keep on going. We have to heed the word of Balaska and the Guardians. We have to find Lorden and the other half of the Key—and then, when this is all over, I promise we'll return here and search for our captured friends."

*Don't believe a word he says. You can't trust him. Just look at the way he speaks to you.*

"You've been treating me like a child, Janir; as though I'm incompetent and incapable of knowing my own mind. You've been making all the decisions, but this whole thing—the Alliance, the Key—it's not about you. It's about me."

"David, I've only been trying to help you. That's why I'm here. All I've ever tried to do is share your burden and make things easier for you."

"Well, maybe I don't need your help. I'm an adult now and I can make my own decisions. And I've decided that since we're here, on the doorstep of the citadel, we're going to find a way to rescue the survivors of New Haven."

*That's right. You tell him.*

"That's not going to happen, David. It's a suicide mission and I will not sanction it."

*It's not for him to sanction.*

"Then I'll go without you," David shot back, feeling a volcanic force of anger and frustration exploding within him. "I can do this alone. I don't need you or anyone else…"

*You're better off without them, David. They're only holding you back.*

"David, you're in no fit state of mind to make such a choice." Janir paused. "I suggest you get some sleep. I pray that you'll have a clearer head in the morning. We can talk about this when you're feeling calmer."

With a sigh, Janir turned and left the room. He closed the door behind him, and David was left standing alone in the dark, listening to the patter of the rain against the glass.

*He always has to have the last word. You were right. He does treat you like a child. You can't let him continue to demean and control you.*

David sat on the edge of the bed, his body shaking with pent up anger. That was it. It was over with Janir. He was on his own now. Janir was wrong—wrong about so many things. Why waste their time searching for some mythical lost city when they were duty-bound to rescue their fellow islanders? It was his fault they'd been captured and it was, therefore, his responsibility to free them. Why couldn't Janir see that?

David lay down, curling up on the bed, succumbing to the exhaustion that gripped his mind and body; no doubt lingering after-effects of the drug in his system. Although he lay awake for some time, his mind spinning round in circles, he eventually drifted into a tormented sleep in which the voice in his head grew louder and louder. It was calling to him—calling him home. Its pull grew ever stronger until he knew he could ignore its call no longer.

# CHAPTER TWENTY ONE

# Into the Dark

David awoke with a start. It was night, and amid the darkness, he could just make out three bodies lying asleep with blankets on the floor—Janir, Chari, and Djhtak.

*It's time to go,* the voice in his mind implored.

David got out of bed. Finding his boots at the foot of the bed, he put them on, trying hard to not to make a sound.

He looked down at Janir. He'd known him for so long. He'd placed so much trust in him and loved him as a mentor and surrogate father.

*You have to leave,* the voice continued. *He'll only hold you back. He wants the Key for himself. He's blinded by his own lust for power.*

Could it really be true?

*He's dangerous. You're better off without him. Leave now, while you still can.*

David crept past Janir and made for the door. It was slightly ajar; a glimmer of light shining through the edge of the doorway. He opened it, wincing as it let out a slight creak, but evidently not enough to stir them from their slumber.

Slipping through the doorway, he crept along the landing in search of an exit. There only appeared to be two other rooms. One room was an apothecary filled with all kinds of exotic plants, herbs, berries, and potions.

He peered into the adjacent room and found the others asleep. Janna lay on the bed, with Darien, Mariane and the old woman sleeping on the floor. He knew this would probably be the last time he'd see them. He'd miss them. But it was necessary that he leave. He knew that.

*Hurry, it's time to go.*

At the end of the landing, a flight of stairs led down to a door. Descending the creaky wooden steps, David prayed that the noise wouldn't wake the others. He came to the exit and unlocked and opened the door, stepping out into the cool night air.

Departing the witch doctor's house, he found himself walking down the long and dismal Sekyrian streets. Although the rain had stopped, the streets were wet and filled with puddles; droplets still falling from the edge of rooftops and windows. Aside from the dim red glow of the street lamps, the only source of light came from the moon and stars shining in the heavens, sparkling like jewels amid the inky black sky.

David knew precisely where he was going. He had an almost irresistible compulsion to go to the citadel. He knew he'd potentially be walking into the hands of the Alliance, but that was a risk he was willing to take.

The streets were largely deserted. When he did happen to encounter anyone along his way—drunks, the homeless or prostitutes who eyed him expectantly—he ignored them and continued marching onward.

Before long, however, it became clear to him that he was lost. It was then that he caught sight of a pale-skinned, raven-haired woman standing at the bottom of the cobbled lane. Dressed in a flowing black gown, the elegant figure exuded a mysterious, ghostlike quality. She raised her arm, beckoning him to follow as she turned and began walking in the opposite direction.

Compelled to follow, he called after her, determined to find out who she was, but she didn't respond. She kept on gliding down the streets and alleyways; a ghostly silhouette barely visible in the consuming darkness.

No matter how hard David tried to catch up with her, he never quite succeeded. Yet his determination grew. He wanted to know who she was, where she was taking him and why she seemed so oddly familiar.

*Keep going, David,* the voice in his mind impelled. *You're nearly there.*

David's surroundings became a blur: the winding streets, the maze-like town with its ramshackle houses and buildings, the homeless and staggering drunks littering the streets. All the while the citadel loomed over the city, imposing and omnipresent—and they were getting ever closer to it.

Rounding a sharp bend, they came to a granite wall stretching in either direction. The fortified wall cut through the heart of the town; a dividing line beyond which the citadel stood in all its opulent glory.

The sprawling fortress was unquestionably the most extraordinary feat of architecture David had ever seen. Constructed in levels, it was lit from the outside by reddish spotlights and dotted with thousands of windows illuminated from within. As David stood before the citadel, all fear left him and he felt strangely at peace. He was meant to be here; he could feel it.

The woman in black led him through a silver gate on the wall. David followed, surprised by the lack of guards or security on patrol. The gate led into an expansive courtyard. There were no signs of life at all.

She soon stood at the entrance to the citadel: a colossal archway that stood open like a gigantic mouth ready to devour incomers. He followed as she disappeared into the citadel.

Once inside, he found himself in a corridor illuminated by red ceiling lamps. The walls were sleek and smooth, adorned with endless portraits of Sekyrian monarchs and noblemen—all red-skinned and absurdly short in stature.

His mind was curiously placid as he followed the ghostly figure through the passageways, the echo his footsteps ricocheting against the walls, floor, and ceiling. Odd that the woman seemed to make no sound as she moved, as though her feet barely touched the ground at all. With a slight smile, she turned and began ascending a flight of stairs. Again, without hesitation, David followed.

*Nearly there,* the voice whispered.

Reaching the top of the stairs, of which there were six full flights, David stopped to catch his breath. Ahead was a narrow corridor, at the end of which a single doorway stood open. The woman stepped through the door, her black gown trailing behind her as she disappeared into the shadows.

David stepped through the door. He found himself in a rectangular, windowless room. Candles burned upon a table against the wall; the flickering flames piercing the darkness, casting dancing shadows upon the high stone walls.

"Welcome, David," a voice came from the shadows.

It wasn't the woman who'd led him here. She was nowhere to be seen. This was a man's voice. Deep, resonant, yet softly spoken, the voice was already intimately familiar to him—for it was the same voice he could hear in his mind—the voice that had guided him all the way here.

A man stepped out of the shadows. Slim with olive skin and penetrating emerald eyes, his jet black hair was tied behind his neck. He wore a gray and black robe with body armor. Obscure symbols were tattooed in black all the way down the left side of his narrow face and neck. He had an air of controlled confidence about him; a dark charisma that David found strangely magnetic. The man's thin lip curled in a slight smile. "I've been waiting for you."

"Who are you?" David said.

"Please, David, you know who I am."

"Zhayron." David paused, struggling to think. "I've seen you before—in my dreams. And I've heard your voice in my mind. How's that possible?"

"Because we're connected. There's a seed of me within you, David; planted deep in the recesses of your mind. It's been growing all this time—until now, when it's finally led you here... to me."

Unsettled, David stepped back. "You told me your name but you haven't told me who you are."

Zhayron remained silent but continued watching him intently. David felt a strange sensation, as though something was crawling over his skin and seeping through him. After a long pause, Zhayron finally spoke: "Do you know why you are here, David?"

David struggled to answer. It felt like his mind was being pulled apart like a piece of fruit. Memories of his past and the events that had led him here were slipping away from him. It took considerable effort to piece it all together. "I'm here to rescue the survivors from New Haven." His voice was wavering. "They were captured by the Alliance and taken here—to the Arkan complex."

"There *is* no Arkan complex. It's but a myth; one of countless that have been invented to slander the Alliance."

"Then where are they? The prisoners from New Haven..."

"I'll find out for you and make sure they are unharmed. But first, it's imperative that you realize something. In spite of what you may have been told, the Alliance is not your enemy."

"How can you say that? They're cold blooded killers. They invaded my home and destroyed everything I ever cared about."

Zhayron began circling him, his hands clasped behind his back. "Mistakes have been made. But you must not believe all that you've been told. You've been lied to and manipulated. Your losses are deeply unfortunate, but in truth, the Alliance was only ever trying to save you."

"Save me? How—by destroying my life?"

"Your life has not been destroyed, David. Indeed, it's only just beginning. You've been through so much. But your anger and hatred are misplaced." Zhayron came to a stop, his eyes locked upon David's. "You must not resist me. Embrace me and I promise I will take away your pain." Zhayron's gaze had a hypnotic effect, as though his eyes were melting David's mind. "You are here because you are meant to be," he continued. "I know you have many questions. But they are for another time."

He placed his hand on David's forehead.

The moment Zhayron touched him, David felt a surge of energy pass through his body. He experienced a burst of dizziness followed by a sleepiness so intense he found it almost impossible to keep his eyes open.

"Because first you must rest," Zhayron whispered. "Much rest is needed..."

Zhayron guided him to a bed in the corner of the room. David flopped onto it, his whole body relaxed to the point of paralysis. Through heavy eyes, he saw Zhayron standing over him, arms folded, a satisfied smile upon his face.

Unable to fight off the drowsiness, David found himself slipping into a deep, enforced state of sleep. His consciousness slipped away from him, supplanted by an all-consuming void of darkness. All he was aware of was Zhayron's voice echoing through his mind in endless reverberation:

*Welcome home....*

# CHAPTER TWENTY THREE

# Conduit

The moment Janir woke up he knew that something was wrong. He looked over at the bed and his suspicions were confirmed. David was gone.

He bolted up from the floor and hurried through the house. The others were still asleep in the adjacent room. He found Letanta in her kitchen-apothecary. A slab of meat was roasting on a spit over the fire, while Letanta hunched over the counter, chopping vegetables. Djhtak was reluctantly assisting, washing a sprig of herbs in a basin.

"Have you seen David?" he called.

"No," Djhtak said. "Why?"

"He's not here."

Djhtak shrugged. "Well, he can't be far away, can he?"

"How long have you both been up?"

"Not long. I found the old woman cooking. She bribed me into assisting."

Letanta smiled. "I told him that if he does not help, he does not eat! And a fine assistant he makes too."

"What about you?" Janir asked the witch doctor. "Did you see David leave the house?"

"Why, no, I saw nothing."

"Damn!" Janir slammed his fist against the wall. "Given the state of mind he was in last night, there's no telling where he is and what he's capable of doing."

"Come on," Djhtak said, "he surely wouldn't have done anything stupid."

"You saw him last night, Djhtak. I've never seen him like that before. He was irrational, paranoid and delusional. He'd lost all sense of perspective."

"So where do you think he's gone then?"

"He kept talking about going to the citadel—to this Arkan complex—to rescue the captives from New Haven."

"That was just talk! Even if he tried, the entire perimeter's patrolled by guards. He wouldn't get within ten meters of the place."

"I hope not. Because if he did, he's now in the hands of the Alliance and everything we've fought for is over."

Janir woke the others and the explained the situation. The moment they were dressed and ready, they left to search for David, leaving Letanta behind to look after Janna.

Stepping outside, they were greeted by a stream of rain lashing down upon the buildings and cobbled streets. The sky, heavy with cloud, promised no respite from the downpour. Soaked from head to foot, they marched down the streets with Janir in the lead. He walked at such a brisk pace that the others, aside from Chari, had to sprint to keep up with him.

Upon reaching the city center, they decided to split up in order to cover as much of the city as possible. "Remember to be on the lookout for trouble," Janir warned. "Keep a low profile, and try not to get lost."

"That may be easier said than done," Mariane grumbled, not entirely happy at being paired with Darien.

"Relax, Mariane, we'll be fine," Darien said. "What's the worst that can happen?"

"I daren't imagine," she muttered as the pair set off.

Janir, Djhtak and Chari began scouring the eastern side of Akyron. They entered the marketplace, which was still busy in spite of the rain. "I am certain David is fine," said Chari as they stopped to let an old man past.

"The Kellian's right," Djhtak said. "The kid had a tantrum and went off in the huff. He'll be back as soon as he's cooled off. I've got kids myself. I know how it goes."

"I wish I shared your optimism."

Janir's attention was drawn above the rooftops to the citadel towering above the city. He felt a chill as he was struck by a sudden realization. *David was there.* He was in the hands of the

Alliance. "Djhtak, tell me more about the citadel. Is there any way to get inside it?"

"Absolutely not! It's a hive of Alliance activity. Believe me, you don't want to go anywhere near the place."

"That may be true, but I fear David already has."

"I very much doubt it. Like I said, there's no way Alliance security would let him through."

"On the contrary, the Alliance would have welcomed him with open arms."

"And why would they do that?"

"Because they want him. They want him more than anything."

"But he's just a boy! What could the Alliance possibly want with him?"

"I am curious myself," Chari added.

"It's a long story. I promise I'll explain everything later."

"Frankly, I'm not sure I want to know," Djhtak said, holding up his hand. "The less I know the better. As I said before, I've no intention of getting on the wrong side of the Alliance. Because there's a word for that—suicide."

Janir was about to respond when he heard someone call his name. He turned to see Darien and Mariane rush through the marketplace toward them, clearly disturbed. "Janir," Darien called. "We think there's a problem. You know how you told us to be on the lookout for trouble? Well, it seems that trouble is on the lookout for *us*."

"What do you mean?"

Darien motioned to a group of six uniformed men marching into the marketplace. Armed with Alliance electro-pulse rifles, they were clearly soldiers of some kind, although Janir hadn't seen their like before. With deathly white skin and long silver hair, the tall, muscular men were clad in military boots and black body armor embossed with silver. Janir watched as they tromped through the market, shoving aside anyone who happened to be in their way. "Any idea who they are?" he asked Djhtak.

"The Eloramian First Guard," Djhtak said grimly.

"Alliance soldiers?" Chari asked.

"For a Kellian, you're pretty smart. They're stationed in all Alliance-occupied territories. The First Guard serve as the local policing force. Basically, it's their job to keep the local population under control. Little gets past the First Guard."

"I'm pretty sure they're looking for us," Darien said. "They were stopping people and asking if they'd seen any unusual strangers."

"What makes you think they were referring to us?" asked Chari.

Djhtak raised an eyebrow. "Paranoia perhaps?"

"If you'd been through all that we have, you'd be paranoid too," Darien said.

Janir watched as the soldiers scanned the crowd and appeared to catch sight of them. The lead soldier pointed in their direction and ordered his men to pursue. "I don't think that's paranoia," Janir said. "Let's get out of here!"

They got moving, pushing their way past the various stalls and shops and through the meandering crowd.

The sickly pale soldiers clearly didn't want them escaping. Raising their rifles, they opened fire, sending a volley of electrical shots flying toward them. The blasts slammed into nearby stalls. Tables and goods went flying; canvas tarpaulin igniting in flames. The crowd reacted in terror, with screams and shouting as several people were gunned down by the weapons fire.

Fueled by adrenaline, Janir and the others raced through the crowd. More shots were fired—one only narrowly missing Chari and hitting a woman by his side.

While the congestion provided a degree of cover, it also slowed their escape. They managed to exit the market square, racing down a narrow cobbled road. Although not once daring glance back, Janir knew the enemy was in close pursuit.

A sudden blast of weapons fire struck the building ahead of them, sending rubble flying, obstructing their escape. The screaming townspeople fled for cover as the firing continued. The First Guard had evidently been ordered to catch them alive.

At this range they could easily have gunned down the escapees had that been their intent.

Chari returned fire. It provided some cover as Janir led them down another side street. The street was lined with houses; ropes tied between them pegged with washing. The hanging clothes flapped in the breeze like bodiless ghosts, dripping with rain.

Rounding another corner, Janir surprised them all by stopping in his tracks, coming to a standstill. "What are you doing, man?" Djhtak cried. "We have to move! Those bastards are right behind us. They'll be on us in seconds!"

Janir ignored him. Raising his hand, he focused his mind as he recited an ancient shielding incantation. Once satisfied he'd implemented the spell as best he could, he turned to the others. "They won't be able to find us here. I've put them off our trail. We're safe, at least for now."

"I don't understand," Mariane said, hand on her chest, heaving for breath.

"I cast a protective incantation. This whole street is now invisible to them. It should hold just long enough for us to flee the vicinity. Now, let's go!"

They continued on their way; their feet splashing in the puddles as they raced down the lane. Every so often Janir glanced behind to look for signs of pursuit, but thankfully it appeared they'd managed to evade the First Guard. For now, at least.

"That was a close one," Darien exclaimed as they arrived back at Letanta's house.

Janir bolted the door behind them. "We're not safe here."

"Clearly," Mariane said.

They climbed the stairs to the landing. "If it is David the Alliance is after," Chari said, "and they now have him as you believe, why would they still be pursuing us?"

"Unless they don't have him after all," Djhtak suggested.

Janir shook his head. "They do. I'm certain of it. But they don't want to risk losing him. They know we're out here and they see us as a potential threat."

"Wait a moment," Darien said. "David's been caught by the Alliance? How do you know that?"

"I just do, Darien. Last night David was determined to get to the citadel."

"Why in the name of Dalteen would he want to go there?"

"He'd come to believe the captives from New Haven were being held there."

"But even if that were true," said Mariane, "how did he propose to rescue them?"

"The kid wasn't thinking straight," Djhtak said. "I blame the old witch. She poisoned his mind with her drugs."

Janir shook his head. "Letanta's drug certainly didn't help matters, but I fear David's mind has already been poisoned in an altogether different way."

"What do you mean?" Darien said.

"For some time I've sensed something going on in his mind—some kind of inner struggle—a battle being waged inside of him. Something dark was taking root in his consciousness and now I fear it has finally overpowered him..."

"Surely not," Mariane gasped.

Janir cast his eyes to the ground. He'd suspected what was happening and he'd done nothing to stop it. He'd ignored what was happening before his very eyes. "I've failed him," he whispered. "And in so doing I've doomed us all..."

"Don't speak like that," Darien said. "You can't blame yourself for whatever's happened. It wasn't your doing."

"It's not often I agree with Darien," Mariane said, "but he's right, Janir. We're all struggling through this as best we can and you're no different. All we can do now is decide what we're going to do next."

Janir didn't have a clue what they should do next. He knew everyone was looking to him to lead them—to assure them that everything would be okay and to rally them forward. After all, that's exactly what he'd done until now.

He was incapable of doing that any longer. He knew it was only a matter of time before the Alliance found them. And when they did, cheap magic tricks like protective incantations would be of little use. There would be no escaping. Not that it truly mattered what happened to them anyway. Because with David now in the hands of the enemy, it was all over.

Letanta appeared from one of the other rooms. "For the great maker's sake, what a cloud of gloom has descended upon my home!"

"With good reason," Janir said darkly. "It's all over. Everything we've fought for..."

"Oh no," the old woman said, shaking her frizzy head. "No, no, no! If I have learned anything in all these years, it is to never give up. Never! The path is long and hard and it pushes each of us to our limits, but we must never, ever give up."

Djhtak glared at her. "This is your fault, old woman. You messed up the boy's mind with that drug."

"Oh, but I only endeavor to help."

"Some help!"

"I do what I must. Just as I have now done with young Janna."

"What?" Darien asked in sudden alarm. "What about Janna?"

The old woman smiled. "So young and beautiful she is, and so gifted, too. Only she has blocked herself from expressing this gift and spent a lifetime denying who she truly is. I have done what I can to clear those blocks! Only once she has been set *free* will she fully recover from her malady."

Darien pushed past the old woman and hurried to the bedroom to check on her.

Janir said, "What do you mean when you say Janna is gifted?"

"Young Janna has the gift of sight and perception. Such latent power she possesses. With proper training, she will be capable of untold, wondrous things!"

"Janir, what in the twin suns is she talking about?" Mariane said.

"I'm not sure." Prior their departure from New Haven, he hadn't known Janna that well, but he'd always sensed there was something different about her. He could sense that beyond her demure exterior lay an untapped reservoir of power. Quite what that power was he didn't know, but he knew she was somehow withholding it and denying her own nature. The question was, what had Letanta done to her? He only hoped that her interference would not bode ill, as it had for David.

He entered the bedroom. The others followed. Blankets and cushions, used as beds by the others, lay strewn across the floor. The only proper bed sat against the far wall. A small window above let in muted daylight through partly drawn curtains.

Darien sat on the edge of the bed. Janna lay partially propped up, her head resting against the wall. She seemed conscious but delirious, muttering strange words under her breath. Her eyes were open, but her mind appeared to be someplace altogether different. Darien stroked her face gently, whispering words of comfort.

Janir grabbed Letanta's arm. "What have you done to her?"

She smiled, her exuberant eyes sparkling with excitement. "I have cut the cords that bind her. She is now free to function in her true capacity—as a conduit."

"A conduit?"

"Yes!"

"I swear if you've done anything to harm her..."

To everyone's surprise, Janna suddenly spoke up: "It's all right."

Janir turned in surprise.

She appeared to be quite lucid now. "I must speak with you, Janir," she said. "Alone."

Darien was clearly affronted by this, but he didn't argue. Something about the way she spoke was a little unsettling. She sounded distant and detached, her eyes shining with an unworldly radiance. Alarmed by this change in her, Darien looked to Janir, who nodded in reassurance. "It's okay, Darien. Give us a moment alone, please."

Darien left the room along with the others. Janir knelt down by the bed and took Janna's hand, gazing into her shining blue-green eyes. "Janna, what did she do to you?"

There was a curious mixture of serenity and apprehension upon her pale face. "She told me I have a power within me—a gift, she called it. Something I can no longer deny. She gave some kind of potion...and it opened the floodgates. It was as though my mind expanded and opened up. I began to see images, places, people, flashes of insight and..."

She fell silent. She seemed to be looking beyond Janir, as though she'd caught sight of something or someone else in the room. "What's wrong, Janna?"

"I can sense them," she whispered. "I can feel them. I can almost even see them..."

"Who?"

"They call themselves the Guardians. They're here with us. It's as though our two worlds are somehow intersecting. Can't you see them?"

"No, I'm afraid I can't."

"It's extraordinary." Her eyes were filled with wonder. "They're speaking to me; telling me they have a message for you."

"Please, go on."

She squinted, as if struggling to concentrate. "They say the mission is over."

"Yes, I know. The mission failed."

"No. Listen carefully, for this line of communication can only be sustained for a short while. They say you must not presume to judge the outcome. David may be in the hands of the enemy, but do not indulge in notions of failure or defeat. It is as we have foreseen, and it is far from over."

Janir felt a surge of hope. He once again had a direct line of communication with the Guardians. He had to take advantage of this opportunity, for he so desperately needed their guidance. "Please," he began, "tell me what we must do next."

"Leave Sekyr at once. Nothing more can be done here and you are in danger as long as you remain."

"But what about David? Surely we can't just leave him here?"

As Janna spoke it was clear that she was merely relaying the words; whispers echoing across an infinite void. "Heed our words. You can do no good for him by remaining here and being captured by the Alliance. Leave as soon as possible and travel eastward. Head through the mountains and across the desert of Draas to Rastayan. Plans are in motion and once at Rastayan your next move shall be clear."

Although reassuring, Janir had one question that begged to be asked. "Please, tell me. I've felt a certain presence for some time now." He paused, almost having to force the words out. "It's Zhayron, isn't it? He's the masterminding element behind all this."

"You are correct. Although Zhayron and the rest of the Alliance Hierarchy are but instruments of the Shadow Lords."

Janir felt a wave of emotion at the mere mention of Zhayron's name. It was a name he'd not heard spoken for many years. A name he'd tried so hard to forget.

Janna continued relaying the words of the Guardians: "You must not let Zhayron's involvement blind you. He is your weak spot and the enemy knows that. In fact, they are counting on it. They will try to break you. You must not let them."

"I won't," Janir said. "I promise." The burden he'd been forced to shoulder and the momentousness of their quest had been overwhelming. The loss of David to the Alliance had pushed him to the brink of defeat. But in spite of confirmation of Zhayron's involvement, the words of the Guardians were of great solace to him.

"Leave Sekyr as soon as you can. Once you cross the border, travel to Rastayan where the next part of your journey will be revealed." A slight smile played across Janna's delicate mouth; her eyes still shining with a radiant otherworldly light. "Keep your faith and know that in spite of all that has transpired, this is not the end. Your journey now begins anew."

"So you're really going?" Djhtak stood in the doorway with Letanta.

Five days had passed and, having made a swift recovery, Janna was now strong enough to travel. Janir and the others had packed some bags, having spent the past few days gathering food, water, and basic supplies. It was now dawn, and they were ready to depart. Following his communication with the Guardians, Janir felt ready to face whatever lay ahead with renewed vigor and determination. "We have to," he said. "The Guardians were clear—we must travel to Rastayan. All will become clear there."

"You're a trusting sort, aren't you?" the Alazan replied.

"You're sure you won't join us?"

"Oh, I'm sure. What with spending two months as a Kellian prisoner and our little altercations with the Alliance, I think I've had enough adventure for now. I'm going to arrange passage back to the Northern Territories. I guarantee within a month I'll have a new ship and be trading again."

"I wish you all the best, Djhtak."

"And you. Good luck finding this lost city you're seeking. And I hope you find a way to help the boy..."

"We will," Darien said. "We're gonna get David back, aren't we, Janir?"

"I don't know how yet, but we will. This isn't over yet."

"That's what I like to hear," Letanta beamed. "Good old fashioned fortitude!"

Darien hovered around Janna anxiously. "You certain you're well enough to travel?"

"I'm fine, Darien. Really."

"If you're sure..."

"I am. Stop worrying."

"I'll try."

"Goodness knows there's plenty of other things left to worry about," Mariane said.

"Well," Djhtak said, "before you go, I have something for you." He reached into his pocket and pulled out some folded parchment. He handed it to Janir.

"What's this?" Janir asked.

"A map. Got it for you in the market. Thought it would help you along your journey."

"Why, Djhtak, thank you—I must confess we'd be a little lost without one."

"I figured as much. With the luck you've been having, you need every advantage you can get. Consider it a parting gift—and a thank you. If you hadn't come along I'd probably still be incarcerated by those stinking Kellians." He looked up at Chari. "No offense, big man."

Janir unfolded the map. It looked clear and comprehensive, covering the entire continent of Ardesha. "I hope it didn't cost you too much."

"Ah, don't worry, it's only money. I can easy get more. I might hit the Kahjika table later!"

"In which case," Chari rumbled, "May I suggest you stay away from Nitralians."

Djhtak let out a snort. Darien looked up at the Kellian. "Was that a joke, Chari? I didn't think Kellians made jokes."

"We do not."

"Right," Janir said, turning to his friends. "Let's get going before the town gets too busy. We need to get past the citadel, leave Akyron and make for the borders of Sekyr. Rastayan awaits us."

"Do travel safely," Letanta said.

"We will," Janir said. "Thank you for your hospitality and assistance—both of you." He smiled and bowed his head. Perhaps he was getting sentimental after all that had happened these past weeks, but he would miss them—even the unhinged old witch doctor.

They exchanged goodbyes and prepared to set off down the dismal streets of Akyron.

"One last thing before you go," Letanta called after them. "I meant to offer earlier! Can I interest you in a reading?"

"No," they all replied together.

# Valley of Dreams

*David was lost in a void of unconsciousness.*

*Drifting amid a sea of tangled dreams, he found himself bombarded by images of past and present—transient, intangible and ever-shifting. Try though he might, he was unable to reach out and grasp hold of anything. There was nothing to hold onto.*

*There were brief moments of lucidity. But just as quickly as he began to stir, the spell again took hold and dragged him into ever deeper states of unconsciousness.*

*This continued for an indefinable amount of time. Time had no meaning in this kaleidoscopic dreamworld. A second might as well have been a decade; a minute a lifetime.*

*All the while, there was something insidiously creeping over him. As he slept—his mind trapped in a purgatory of restless dreams—some dark force was seeping through every level of his being.*

*Most of the time he was quite unaware of it. His mind had been forcibly shut down and there was nothing for him to do but passively observe the images appearing before him.*

*In a flash his entire childhood would unfold before him: sharing meals with his parents, being at school, playing ball, sitting alone in the forest, looking across the sea, dreaming of his true home...*

*All too readily the memories became nightmares. To his distress, he had to relive the death of his father and all the heartache and guilt that came with it.*

*The years flashed by until he found himself standing amid the ruins of New Haven in the aftermath of the Alliance attack. As the town burned around him, he stood over the lifeless body of his mother. Blood trickled from her mouth, her eyes wide open in shock.*

Why—why must I keep seeing this?

*He sunk to the ground and lifted her in his arms. It was because of him that she'd died. If only he could have gone back and some-*

*how stopped this from happening. He'd have sacrificed himself to save her and the others in an instant.*

*He became aware of a girl in the distance.*

*In her late teens, she was dark-haired and beautiful, with the gait of both a warrior and a princess. He'd seen her before, but he didn't know where or how. A name flashed through his mind—*

Eladria. *She was called Eladria.*

*But who was she? And what was she doing here?*

*"David," she called to him from across the rubble. "You're in danger. You have to get out of here. You to have to leave here now! He's trying to get to you—you mustn't let him. You have to—"*

*Before she could finish, she vanished; the decimated streets of New Haven disappearing into the blackness along with her.*

*David found himself alone in a darkened cavern. It was a grim, lifeless underworld; a place devoid of light, life, and hope. Shuddering in the cold, he became aware of something stirring around him: some kind of presence—a silent, malevolent predator.*

*It called to him—a lone voice reverberating through the blackness—*

David...

*Knowing he had to escape, David began running.*

There's nowhere to run, *the voice echoed.*

*It was right. Ahead the ground gave way to a chasm; a gaping abyss obstructing the path ahead. Aware that his predator was behind him, David stopped and turned.*

*A figure stepped out of the blackness.*

*"Zhayron."*

*"Don't run from me, David," Zhayron purred. "There's nowhere to go and nothing to do; nothing except embrace me and accept your destiny."*

*Upon seeing him, David's fear quickly vanished. He found himself strangely compelled by the dark figure. Zhayron exuded a forceful power and magnetism. In his presence, David's fear and apprehension melted like ice in sunlight. Pulled by some inexplicable draw, he approached Zhayron. With a smile, the dark figure placed his hands on David's shoulders.*

At that moment, David began to stir from his slumber.

The dream dissipated and, gradually regaining conscious-ness, he became aware of his surroundings: a small room, illu-minated by candlelight and filled with thick, scented smoke. He found himself lying on a bed, his unclothed body anointed with some kind of fragrant oil.

*"Nas Dar Niquanta ru'mahna estiva nousyata."*

Chanting reverberated through the room like an ancient incantation from a long-forgotten world. There were people standing around the bed, five or six in all, barely visible in the shadows. One of them, an ageless woman with flowing dark hair and a black robe stepped forward. She slipped her hand beneath his head and lifted a chalice to his mouth. "Drink."

David had little choice. The sweet-tasting liquid had a warm-ing sensation as it filled his mouth and passed down his throat.

*Is this real,* he wondered, *or just another dream?*

The woman laid his head back upon the bed and withdrew into the shadows.

David's head began spinning. Struggling to focus, he became aware of Zhayron stepping toward him, his face and body illu-minated by the flickering candlelight. It was Zhayron that was chanting the mantra which echoed through the room like a hyp-notic lullaby:

*"Nas Dar Niquanta ru'mahna estiva nousyata."*

He reached down and placed his hand upon David's fore-head. David felt a rush of kinetic force sweep through his mind and senses.

Another wave of profound, unshakable sleepiness overcame him. Though he tried to resist it, consciousness once again slipped away from him.

*He drifted into another deep sleep, the mantra continuing to echo through his mind.*

*This time the only thing that David was aware of in his tor-mented dream state was Zhayron. All he could see before him was the shadowy figure of Zhayron and all he could hear was his deep, resonant voice as he continued chanting.*

"Nas Dar Niquanta ru'mahna estiva nousyata..."

*Whatever these strange words meant, they gradually saturated David's mind.*

*Zhayron had penetrated his very being. David's mind was no longer his own. It belonged to Zhayron, and Zhayron alone.*

"Nas Dar Niquanta ru'mahna estiva nousyata..."

*On some level, he was entranced and soothed by the hypnotic chant. But another part of him—perhaps the last vestige of his ability to question and discriminate—was struck by a terrible realization:*

What have I done...?

# CHAPTER TWENTY FOUR

# Shelter

Sekyr seemed but a distant memory as they trudged through the desert. Arid and blisteringly hot, every step they took was grueling. Their journey was made even more arduous by the frequent dust storms.

In spite of the adverse conditions, Janir knew they'd been fortunate thus far. They'd managed to navigate their way through Sekyr, bypassing the inhabited regions and avoiding any further entanglement with the Alliance.

Their relief at leaving the borders of Sekyr had been short-lived, however, as they realized just how difficult the way ahead would be. Alas, crossing the desert of Draas was the only viable way of reaching Rastayan—and that, according to the Guardians, was where they had to go. So onward they went, enduring the heat, thirst, and discomfort as best they could.

It was always a relief when the suns lowered toward the horizon. This particular night the sky was a striking magenta. The two orange-red orbs bathed the landscape in a pale red-dish glow. Chari found somewhere to stop for the night: a hollow beneath an outcrop of red rock, lined by wiry desert trees. As the others unpacked their supplies—sleeping mats, blankets and food and water—Chari gathered some branches and, with a single blast from his rifle, started a campfire. The moment the suns set over the horizon, the temperature plummeted.

"So, if I understand this," Chari said, watching as Janir warmed his hands over the fire. "The Alliance sought David because he has the power to open gateways, like the one that took us from Numaria to Sekyr..."

Janir nodded. He'd decided it was time to finally tell Chari the whole story behind their mission. "The Alliance themselves are controlled by the Narssians and Shadow Lords—terrible parasitic beings, determined to break free of their dimensional prison. Should the Alliance succeed in reopening a gateway to their realm, these creatures will invade our universe and strip it of all life."

"Kellian legend speaks of such creatures. We call them the Gr'noth—invisible shadow creatures that feed off the living."

"That doesn't surprise me. The mythologies of many cultures across Alanar speak of these beings."

"Clearly they must be stopped. The question is, how?"

"According to the ancient prophecies, David alone is capable of stopping them."

"And he is now in the hands of the enemy."

Darien stepped forward. "What do you think they're doing with him?"

Janir felt himself tense. "He's in the hands of a dark and powerful sorcerer—a man named Zhayron. He'll be doing everything in his power to corrupt and distort David's mind. He'll try to gain David's trust and use him to open a gateway to Abidalos, the realm of the Narssians."

"But he can't do that until he finds the other half of the Key, right?"

"And Zhayron knows this. As soon as he has David's compliance, he'll get him to lead them to the City of Lorden. There the Key of Alanar will be made whole—and ready to unleash armageddon."

"I still don't know why the Guardians sent us here, through this dreadful desert," Mariane said. "I don't understand what good we'll be able to do from this 'Rastayan' place."

"Yeah," Darien said. "Presumably David's still back in Sekyr? And we're headed in the opposite direction."

"It's not for us to second-guess the Guardians," Janir said.

Janna, who'd said little about it since her inexplicable communion with the Guardians back in Sekyr, agreed. "They were clear," she said. "Rastayan is where we need to be."

"But why?" Darien said.

"And just how much can we trust these Guardians?" Chari said. "They are invisible beings just like the Gr'noth. For all we know they could be working in league with them."

"No," Janir said. "I trust the Guardians implicitly. They're a benevolent force dedicated to protecting the mortal realm. Existing outside of space and time, they have a much wider—and wiser—perspective. They see things that we cannot, and that's why I unquestioningly heed their guidance."

"I hope your trust is not misplaced," Chari said.

"It isn't," Janir assured him. "We must have faith; faith that there's an unseen hand guiding us, and that all is not yet lost."

"Is that faith or hope?" Mariane mused. "I sometimes wonder if there's really a difference."

"Whether you think of it as faith or hope," Janir said, "it's something we can never afford to lose."

Having eaten, Janir gazed across the darkened desert. A crescent moon shone amid the star-filled sky as an icy chill consumed the land beneath.

He noticed Chari sitting on one of the rocks some way off. He had proven himself a remarkable ally and a trustworthy friend, but the Kellian disliked socializing and spent much of his time alone. Janir often felt a sadness for him. He was no longer part of his own tribe, but he wasn't quite fully one of theirs, either. He always kept himself at a slight distance.

Janir returned to the warmth of the campfire. Janna and Darien were nearby, engaged in what appeared to be a heated and emotive discussion. Mariane joined him by the fire. "It's so cold," she said.

"The desert certainly is a place of extremes."

Mariane nodded, letting out a sigh as she gazed into the flames.

"Are you all right, Mariane?"

"No," she admitted after a pause. "I don't suppose I am." Her normally assertive, assured voice was wavering. "And I haven't been in what seems like a very long time."

Mariane had been uncharacteristically withdrawn the past few days. Janir sensed that the trauma of all that had happened had finally caught up with her. As the eldest of the New Haven survivors, Mariane had been the most settled upon the island and had been married to her husband, Jadan, for many years. His death had obviously hit her hard. "Mariane, it's all right to grieve, you know. You've experienced a tremendous loss. I know the pain you must be feeling."

"Do you?" There was a hint of bitterness in her voice. "Do you really?"

"Yes, I do. I've never spoken of this to anyone, but I too have lost people dear to me; people I've loved with all my heart. So I know what you're going through. I know that it's the hardest, most painful thing in the world..."

Her eyes welled with tears. While ordinarily not one to show emotion in front of others, she now seemed unable to hold it back. "I'd known him my entire life. I can't remember a time when Jadan wasn't there. I just—I can't bring myself to believe he's gone. And though I've tried, I really don't think I can go on without him..."

"Yes, you can, and you must. You owe it to Jadan. What would he do in your place? Would he give up?"

"No." She wiped the tears from her eyes. "But he was stronger than I am. Everyone always thought I was the strong one; and I know I can be outspoken and forthright, but Jadan had a true inner strength to him; a strength that always kept him going, no matter what." She shook her head. "I shouldn't have come with you. I should have stayed with the Enari when I had the chance. I really don't know what I was thinking; how I thought I'd be able to endure this never-ending nightmare of a journey—being hunted, captured, chased, attacked and always on the run. I'm tired, Janir. I'm so tired."

The exhaustion was plain to see on her face. Like the rest of them she'd lost weight and the skin stretched over her face, accentuating her age, making her look weary and fragile. "I'm too old for this," she continued. "Perhaps Darien and Janna can handle the pace, but I'm old enough to be their grandmother. And I must admit, for the first time I'm starting to feel my age."

"Maybe so, but you're stronger than you think. You only have to look at how far you've come, and how much you've been through. You, Mariane, are one of the strongest people I know. You must have faith in yourself. Because I do."

"Thank you, Janir."

"This certainly isn't your fight. I'm grateful you've come this far, but I won't lie: we'll be stepping into even greater danger in the days to come. When we get to Rastayan, if there's a suitable and safe place for you to stay, I'll understand if you decide not to join us."

"Right now that seems like the best option. But let's take one day a time. You were right about Jadan. He would never have given up and although he never left New Haven, he was an adventurer at heart. Part of him would have relished this journey in spite of the perils. I lack his temperament and sensibilities, but if he were here, he certainly wouldn't allow me to give up."

Janir was about to respond when he was distracted by the sound of raised voices. Darien and Janna were now locked in a heated argument. "That's most unlike them," he said. "What could they be arguing about?"

"There's been discord between them ever since we left Sekyr. I'm not entirely sure why. I decided it was best to stay out of it."

By now it was impossible not to overhear the conversation: "You're wrong," Darien shouted. "I *do* know you—better than you realize and probably better than you even know yourself!" He stormed off, leaving Janna alone.

"I'd better go speak to them," Janir said, excusing himself. Morale was at an all-time low, and it had again fallen to him to attempt to restore it.

By now Darien was out of sight, having wandered off into the darkness. Janir invited Janna to join him by the campfire. They took a seat on the rocks in front of the flames. "What was all that about? "

Janna shrugged. "He's been trying to get me to talk about this, but...I can't. Not yet. I'm at a point where I don't know what to think, or how to comprehend what's happened to me."

"You mean back in Sekyr?"

"Letanta told me she was helping me become who and what I truly am—but what is that? *What am I?*" A teardrop trickled down her cheek. She reached up, wiped it away and dried her eyes, seemingly ashamed at having displayed her vulnerability.

"Why don't you tell *me*, Janna. Talk to me."

She stared into the fire, a faraway look in her eyes. "I never told anyone this," she began, "but ever since I was a child I was aware that I was somehow different to everyone else."

"In what way?"

"I could see things that other people couldn't."

"What kind of things?"

"Images, forms, faces—people standing in rooms that no one else could see. I could often even sense what other people were thinking. But whenever I told my parents about this they dismissed it. They said I was imagining it. Before long I was told to stop telling lies."

Janna nervously ran her hand through her wavy blonde hair, pushing it behind her ear. Clearly, this admission was difficult for her. Janir waited for her to continue. "I began to realize that this inner vision, or whatever it was, was a bad thing. I learned not to speak of it. It became my shameful little secret, something that made me feel so different, so alien to everyone else. I was just a child and I wanted to be like other people. I wanted to be normal. Over the years I actually became quite good at tuning out these impressions. They were still there much of the time, but I managed to push them to the background and more or less ignore them. And now..."

"Now?"

"I don't know what Letanta did to me but it's intensified everything. This thing, this 'gift' as she called it—is stronger than ever. I can't ignore it any longer. You were there with me back at Sekyr. Other beings were talking *through* me! At the time it felt profound and special, but the more I think about it, the more it terrifies me." Her face tightened. "It's still happening, too. I can see and hear things—but it's all unfocused; a jumble in my head. I've been trying to ignore it as best I can but it's not easy."

"It must be overwhelming right now," Janir said. "It will get easier, though. It may not seem like it right now, but Letanta was right, Janna. What you possess is a gift, not a curse. Aspirants train for many years to develop the kind of clairvoyant abilities that come to you so naturally."

"But why? Why am I like this?"

"I don't know for sure, but I suspect you may have some Starlanian blood in your veins."

"Starlanian?"

"The Starlanians were an ancient race of telepaths. Gifted with extraordinary psychic powers, they lived on Alanar many millennia ago."

"What happened to them?"

"Because of their power to read others' thoughts and their ability to see beyond the veils that separate dimensions, they were feared and distrusted by a great many people. In fact, they were often hunted and killed."

Janna listened, wide-eyed and attentive as Janir continued. "In the face of such danger, they dispersed. Concealing their identities they intermarried and interbred with many other races throughout Alanar. So while the Starlanians as a race gradually disappeared, their blood runs strong through a number of people—and with it, their powers of telepathy, clairvoyance, and clairaudience."

"If that's true and there's Starlanian blood in my family, then why didn't my mother or father exhibit these powers?"

"These psychic powers largely remain dormant. It's only every second or third generation that develops their Starlanian powers to any degree. So you see, what you possess is a great gift. It's now time that you embraced that gift and learned to use it."

"Use it? How?"

"There are some exercises I can teach you; techniques I learned when attempting to develop my own extrasensory abilities. I can help you through this transition, Janna. This has been a great burden you've carried all these years, but I want you to know—you're no longer alone."

"Most my life I've been afraid to get close to anyone in case they found out the truth about me—that I was different, that I wasn't normal..."

"You *are* normal, Janna. This is normal for you, and a great many others. All you must do is learn to accept this gift—and to accept yourself."

"You think Darien will understand all this?" Her voice was hushed. "I mean, he's not really known what to say to me since we left Sekyr..."

"He's just worried about you. He cares about you deeply. I'd even go so far as to say he loves you."

"He doesn't *love* me. He doesn't even know me. If he knew what I'd just told you, he'd most likely run for his life."

"I think you're underestimating him. I know he can seem a little brash and overbearing at times, but there's a much deeper side to his nature."

"On New Haven I always thought he was a bit immature," she admitted.

"He has a certain bravado to be sure," Janir said. "He's the youngest of four brothers. I suppose he's always felt the need to prove himself. But there's a much deeper side to his nature. He's a young man with a good heart and exceptional loyalty. Regardless of what happens, I know that he'll always be there for you."

"You may be right. But I think I need some space to myself right now, to deal with this in my own way."

"If you like I can have a word with him."

"Could you?"

"I'll do that now. I'm sure he'll understand."

Janna smiled, relieved. Janir could tell that a huge weight had been lifted from her. He reached out and gave her a comforting hug. He felt a great empathy for her. She'd been harboring a tremendous secret for so many years. He knew exactly what that was like.

Leaving the warmth of the campfire, Janir found a brooding Darien pacing the periphery of the camp, each footstep stirring up dust from the parched land. Wearing only a sleeveless shirt and trousers, Darien stopped and folded his arms, shuddering in the cold night air.

When pressed by Janir, he claimed that Janna had shut him out and was barely talking to him. Janir assured him that she was going through a time of transition and needed a little space and a lot of patience and understanding.

Darien nodded but said little. Realizing that there wasn't much more he could say, Janir encouraged Darien to get some sleep, for they would start moving again at first light.

Returning to the campfire, they found Mariane and Janna already asleep. Even Chari, who needed far less sleep than the rest of them, had settled down on the ground. Janir placed another log on the fire and arranged his sleeping mat and blankets, lying down with a weary sigh.

Looking upward, he watched the stars sparkling in the sky; the reflected light of aeons gone by, shining across the universe—a universe now threatened by what was happening on this very world.

He found it impossible not to think of David. He knew that Zhayron would be doing everything in his power to break him; to corrupt, coerce and manipulate him into carrying out his will. Janir found himself again racked with guilt and unable to shift the feeling he'd failed David as a mentor. But it wasn't over yet. He would do everything in his power to save him and complete their original mission. This he vowed, no matter the cost to himself.

When morning came, the travelers wasted little time readying themselves for another day of hiking. They trudged across the desert, sweltering amid the heat and struggling against the dust storms. Their spirits were lifted upon catching sight of mountains upon the horizon—the mountains of Rastayan.

It was another full day's travel before they neared the reddish-brown mountains lining the edge of the desert. As they approached, the weather changed. For days it had been hot and dry, with barely a cloud in the sky. Now the sky was thick with ominously churning cloud, obscuring the suns and darkening the land. When the rain began, the land thirstily lapped up the water. But the deluge continued until rivers of water pooled across the plains.

The lashing rain stung and their waterlogged clothes clung to their skin as they moved. There was nowhere to shelter, so they had no option but to keep going.

It was difficult to see far ahead. But as they neared the mountains, they noticed a structure of some kind—perhaps an old castle or fortress.

The storm intensified. Thunder and lightning set the darkened sky ablaze.

"Keep going," Janir called, pointing ahead to the fortress at the foot of the mountains. "Perhaps we can find shelter!"

They pressed onward, their water-filled boots squelching with every step, the ground muddy and slippery as the rain continued sheeting down.

Nearing the fortress, Janir was disappointed to discover it was in a state of semi-ruin. What in a bygone age had clearly been a structure of imposing majesty now stood in disrepair. The redbrick battlements and ramparts were crumbling, although many of the towers and turrets remained intact. But derelict or not, it would still provide shelter from the storm.

They maneuvered across rocks and boulders, staggering over rubble and through pools of water. The ground sloped upward as they came to the barbican—its arched entrance wide open. "You think it's safe?" Mariane said as a flash of lightning lit up the fortress.

"I'm gonna take my chances," Darien said, stepping past and entering the building.

The others followed. Mariane shrugged and joined them.

Relieved to finally be out of the rain, they found themselves inside a grand hall. Like the exterior of the fortress, it was constructed of ancient bricks of the same reddish hue as the surrounding mountains. The only light came streaming through the entrance.

"What do you suppose this place is?" Darien wondered.

"I'm not sure," Janir said. "I'm just glad we have somewhere to wait out the storm. It looks like it's not stopping anytime soon."

"I thought we were going to drown out there," Mariane said, wringing the water from her sleeves.

Janir was about to say something when he noticed Janna jump, as though startled by something. "What is it, Janna?"

"This place isn't as abandoned as it looks," she said, narrowing her eyes as she peered across the darkened hall.

"I'm not sure I like the sound of that," Darien said.

Mariane concurred. "I definitely don't—"

A flash of lightning illuminated the hall, revealing a dozen or so figures emerging from the shadows. Tall and imposing with large silver batons, they were clad in red and silver hooded robes, their faces concealed in the dim light.

Chari drew his rifle. One of the hooded men leapt through the air and with one strike of his baton, knocked the weapon clear from Chari's hand. As the gun hit the ground, the robed men closed in on them, batons raised.

Janir motioned for his friends to leave. But as they turned to exit, more of the hooded men appeared from outside, their robes dripping with water as they stood in the doorway, blocking the exit. They were surrounded. Janir couldn't believe it. They'd finally reached Rastayan as the Guardians had directed only to fall straight into a trap.

# CHAPTER TWENTY FIVE

# Dark Enchantment

David awoke to find himself lying upon a metal bed. He was naked, with only a blanket draped over him.

The Key—? He reached up to his chest. He was relieved to find the crystal amulet still hanging around his neck.

Fighting a wave of dizziness, he got up from the bed.

His clothes were nowhere in sight. He did however find a gray robe neatly folded at the foot of the bed. He picked it up and slipped it on. To his surprise it was a perfect fit. The soft, delicate fabric felt smooth against his skin.

He tried to focus his mind and recall the last thing he could remember. He had a vague recollection of being led here through the darkened streets by a mysterious woman. Or had that been part of his dream—?

The room in which he found himself was small and sparsely furnished with smooth granite walls and a high ceiling. Candles burned upon a table at the far side of the room, above which hung an oval mirror.

Stepping forward, he gazed into the mirror. His face, illumined by the candlelight to ghostly effect, looked pale and tired. His head and body had been smeared with some kind of oil, making his skin glisten. His hair had grown quite a bit these past few weeks, and now fell over his shoulders. But what struck him the most were his eyes. They looked different somehow— unfamiliar, alien to him—as though he was looking at someone else's reflection.

The door creaked open.

He turned to see Zhayron enter the room. The darkly elegant, robed man reached up to a panel on the wall and turned on the ceiling lights. With a flicker the room lit up in a reddish luminescence. "I'm glad to see you're awake," Zhayron said.

"Barely," David said.

"You were asleep for some time."

"I was—?"

Zhayron nodded, his eyes fixed upon David. "You needed much rest. It takes time to recover from such traumas as you've experienced."

Though his memory was patchy, he recalled the traumas of which Zhayron spoke—the loss of his home, his mother, his friends. Though distant and half-formed, the memories burned nonetheless—memories he'd been forced to relive over and over in his dreams.

"You found the robe I left for you," Zhayron noted.

"Where are my clothes?"

"I had them thrown out. They were tattered and worn."

David glanced around the womblike room. "Where are we?"

"In the citadel, remember?"

"Yes...I think so."

Zhayron strode to the table beneath the mirror. He lifted a glass chalice filled with an orange colored liquid and handed it to David. "Here, drink this. It'll help revive you."

David took the chalice, but part of him was wary. He knew nothing about this man. Was he certain he could trust him?

*Don't resist*, a voice reverberated through his mind—a voice that sounded curiously identical to Zhayron's. *Zhayron is not your enemy.*

David lifted the chalice to his mouth and took a sip of the sweet liquid. The moment it passed his lips, he felt a wave of dizziness. He stumbled; the chalice slipping from his hand and smashing on the ground. His legs buckled and he was about to topple when Zhayron reached out to steady him, helping him back to the bed. As David sat, the dizziness subsided and his head began to clear. A strange sensation lingered, however. His body felt light and his mind spaced out.

"Don't worry, you'll be fine," Zhayron assured him.

David wasn't so certain. Strangely intoxicated, he found himself unable to think clearly. He was in the citadel—but why?

What had happened to his friends? "Janir and the others...where are they?"

Zhayron's face darkened at the mention of Janir's name. "Do not concern yourself with *him*. You're rid of him now and for that, you should be glad."

"Why?" Although David recalled some kind of argument between them, Janir had been his friend and mentor...

"Janir is a dangerous man," Zhayron said. "He has deceived and manipulated you for years now—poisoning your mind with lies and twisted half-truths. He made you believe that everything he was doing was in your best interests, but it certainly was not. He was using you."

"Using me?"

"Yes. All so he could have the Key of Alanar for himself."

The voice in his head implored him to heed Zhayron's words: *You must listen to him. He speaks the truth.*

Zhayron's words were carefully measured; softly spoken yet filled with fire. "The moment that man set foot on New Haven he sought you out, David. He made you trust him and believe in him. It was an expert game that he played; all based on lies and deception. The whole time he was after but one thing."

"But why? What did he want with the Key?"

"Power, David. Some men crave power all their lives. But those who crave it most are those who've had it and then lost it. The Key of Alanar—with its ability to open and seal inter-dimensional gateways—can easily be used as a weapon; one that would grant untold power to whoever wields it. Think of it, David; the ability to unlock the universe itself."

"But everyone—Janir, Balaska, Naranyan, the Enari—they said it was the Alliance that wanted the Key, and that they were working for the Narssians."

"As I said, you've been lied to." Zhayron was calm and collected, yet his green eyes seared with intensity. "Contrary to what you've been told, it's Janir and the Guardians that are in league with the Narssians—not the Alliance. This I can assure you. The Alliance was trying to stop them; to safeguard this world. We knew the terror Janir would unleash if he got his hands on the other half of the Key." Zhayron stepped forward. "We are not your enemies, David. It's Janir who's your enemy. He deceived and used you, all so he could harness the power *you* possess in order to overthrow Alanar and unleash the deadly force of the Narssians."

"But why would he do that?"

"Because he's one of them, David. His mind is infected. The Narssians offered him power and dominion over all of Alanar. All he had to do was retrieve the other half of the Key and use it—use *you*—to reopen the gateway."

David could scarcely believe this. But whenever he found himself questioning Zhayron's words, he felt a tightening sensation in his head; a feeling of pain and discomfort.

*Listen, David,* the voice in his mind assured him. *It's time you embraced the truth.*

"But if that's true," David whispered, "then everything Janir ever told me was a lie?"

"Sadly, yes. He never told you about his past, did he? He never told you why he had to leave his homeland?"

"No."

"And with good reason. You see, I know Janir. I come from his homeland, the kingdom of Taribor. In Taribor, Janir was a sorcerer—a powerful sorcerer of great renown. Students from all across the land sought his tutelage...and I was one of the lucky few to be accepted as his apprentice."

"You were Janir's apprentice?"

"Indeed. I trained under him for many years, learning everything that he knew. But alas, that was not all that I learned." He began pacing. "I came to realize that the power and prestige of being Taribor's Great Mage had corrupted his mind. He became obsessed with wielding ever more power and authority, and after a time his thirst for power escalated into madness. Something in his mind snapped, and when his push for absolute dominion over Taribor failed, he embarked on a rampage of fury. He killed our leaders and many innocent civilians—among them, my own mother."

Zhayron's mask of controlled calmness slipped and David saw a look of vulnerability in his eyes. But he quickly regained his composure and continued relating his astonishing tale. "The only way of stopping Janir was for us, his students, to band together and attempt to overpower him. This we did. We succeeded in driving him from Taribor, banishing him into exile. Enraged by the defeat, he swore that one day he would return to overthrow not only Taribor, but the whole of Alanar."

David was stunned. He thought he'd known Janir. Yet it was true that he'd refused to divulge any of his past. "So what happened?"

"I was elected to keep watch over him; to monitor his activities and ensure that he never got the opportunity to carry out his threat. So I used my powers to observe him from a distance. I watched as he traveled from land to land, maintaining anonymity and never staying too long in one place; all the while seeking the means by which he could reconquer Taribor and the rest of the world. It was on his travels that he happened to come into contact with the Guardians.

"The Guardians are not what you have been told. They are a race of parasitic entities that seek to manipulate and control the people of this realm to further their own agenda. It was through the so-called 'Guardians' that Janir encountered the Narssians. You see, the Guardians are in league with the Narssians. They are two offshoots of the same race, and together they seek to invade and decimate our realm."

David felt his stomach tense as Zhayron continued. "Knowing that Janir was a powerful sorcerer, they enlisted his help, telling him of the Key of Alanar and how they needed it to fulfill their plans. They traced the Key and its Custodian—you, David—to the island of New Haven. Janir journeyed there at once, setting up home on the island and quickly gaining your trust and compliance. He then patiently bided his time, waiting until you had come of age, at which time you would take possession of the Key and be able to use it."

It somehow all made sense...

"The moment you inadvertently activated the Key, I knew Janir would be quick to make his move. I knew that with the assistance of his Enari accomplices, he would rush you off the island to find the missing half of the Key. Knowing that he had to be stopped, I enlisted the help of the Alliance."

David felt a shudder at the mere mention of the Alliance.

"Contrary to what you've been told," Zhayron said, "the Alliance is not your enemy. The Alliance is actually a benevolent peacekeeping force. They seek to promote and maintain peace across the kingdoms of Alanar."

David had listened attentively to everything Zhayron had said, but he couldn't stand to hear this. "You expect me to believe the Alliance is *peaceful?* Did you see what they did to New Haven?"

David felt a contracting feeling in his head as he challenged Zhayron. Though his mind remained fuzzy and unclear, the memories were still vivid—the Death Troops, the burning buildings and the sea of corpses.

"That was deeply unfortunate, I know," Zhayron said. "Their orders were to capture and apprehend Janir."

*Listen to him,* the voice in David's implored. *He speaks the truth.*

David got up from the bed, overcome with anger. "Well, they failed, didn't they? All they succeeded in doing was killing dozens of innocent people. Why? *Why* did they have to kill so many people? People that had nothing to do with any of this—"

"It was a grave mistake. I can assure you that those in charge of the operation were severely punished."

"That doesn't bring back the dead, does it?"

"No, it doesn't," Zhayron said, "but I know what can."

"What are you talking about?"

"Death is no obstacle to a sorcerer, David. The shedding of the physical form is but the end of one cycle of existence. Consciousness lives on—and under certain, unique circumstances, it can be reunited with the body. Death itself can be reversed."

David stared at him, incredulous.

"Under normal circumstances, when a person dies it's because their *zhian* is ready to depart the mortal realm. In other words, it's their time to go. But that is not always the case."

"It's not?"

"Sometimes the body is mortally damaged before the zhian is ready to leave. When this happens the soul becomes suspended in a state of purgatory—frozen in eternity, unable to progress as it painfully mourns the premature loss of its physical form."

"Why are you telling me this?"

"Because your mother is one such soul. Along with others that died in New Haven, your mother was young and healthy—and was not ready to depart this realm. She can't let it go. Her zhian is frozen in a state of torment."

"No," David growled. "You're lying..."

"Then see for yourself."

Zhayron placed the palm of his hand on David's forehead. A pulse of energy shot from his hand into David's head. David's mind and senses unravelled—slipping from him like sand through outstretched fingers.

An image appeared in his mind. He saw dozens of ghostly forms trapped in a void of darkness—frozen in what looked like a sea of black ice. Among them was his mother, suspended in the deadened expanse of blackness. Though imprisoned and unable to move, she was conscious and in pain.

"Help me," she cried. "Please. Help me..."

Unable to bear this, David's eyes snapped open and he pushed Zhayron away from him. "Why did you show me that?"

"Because she needs your help. She needs *our* help."

"How—?"

"It won't be easy."

"I don't care. I can't leave her like that! She and the others died because of me. I'll do whatever it takes."

"*Whatever* it takes?" Zhayron's voice lowered. "Do you mean that?"

"Yes..."

"With my powers we can free her and the others from this astral prison. And then, because it was not yet her time to pass from the mortal realm, we *may* be able to bring her back."

"How?"

"There are ways, David. But it'll take much time and effort. We'll have to work together closely. I'm willing to share the secrets of my power with you. But you have to trust me. You must let down all your defenses and obey my every directive. Only then, together, can we save her." He looked to David questioningly. "Are you with me, David?"

After a momentary hesitation, David nodded.

Zhayron extended his hand and David reached out and took hold of it.

With a single handshake, David knew that he'd sold his soul. But he'd done so in order to save his mother's. What Zhayron was offering him was the power over life and death, and that was an offer he simply couldn't refuse.

# CHAPTER TWENTY SIX

# Broken Oath

"Stand aside," Chari growled.

"I think not," one of the hooded ambushers responded. He stood blocking the doorway, baton raised.

Chari was prepared to put up a fight. Darien stood by his side ready to assist. But Janir motioned for them to stand down. Outnumbered and outmaneuvered, he saw little option but to surrender.

"A wise choice," the man said.

"Who are you people?" Darien demanded.

"You will find out soon enough."

Without another word, they were rounded up, disarmed and led through the ruined fortress. Their footsteps echoed as they were marched along a series of fire-lit passageways. Their assailants wore the robes of monks, but Janir knew of few monks likely to arm themselves and take prisoners—even if those prisoners did happen to be inadvertent trespassers.

Coming to the bottom of a series of winding stairways, they found themselves in a metallic underground chamber. Completely unlike the fortress above, the sleek curving walls were lined with computer panels and flashing lights.

"A spaceship," Janir whispered.

"You're serious?" Darien said.

"It has to be—an ancient craft, by the look of it, hidden beneath the fortress."

Ahead of them, an enormous crystal dominated the center of the chamber. Tetrahedron-shaped, the crystal pulsated waves of violet-tinged light, illuminating the entire ship.

Their hooded captors led them forward, past the crystal, to the far end of the chamber. There, upon a silver throne, sat a man clad in robes of red, silver and black. He smiled as they came to a stop before the throne. "I bid you welcome." Janir noticed a strangely transparent quality to him—as though his body wasn't entirely solid. His almond-shaped head and delicate features had an almost feline quality; his skin a golden hue and his eyes cobalt blue. Embedded in his forehead was a triangular crystal, pulsing like a miniature version of the crystal behind them. Flowing white hair fell down his shoulders, and his expression was one of dignity, serenity, and forbearance. "My name is Elas, last monarch of the Jinerans."

*Jinerans—?* Janir recognized the name immediately.

Elas motioned for his men to back off and lower their weapons. "You are guests here, not prisoners," Elas told them. "You have traveled a long way and will be accorded the respect you are due."

"Thank you," Janir said. He introduced himself and his comrades, although he got the feeling that Elas already knew exactly who they were. "I have to say," he added, "I never thought I'd ever encounter a Jineran. I was led to believe your people were all gone—that your race was extinct."

"Nearly, but not quite. What you see here is all that remains of my people, on this world at least."

"What happened to the rest of your people?" Darien asked.

"Our mission nears completion," Elas said. His voice was strong and deep, yet somewhat wavering. "When at last it has been fulfilled and all debts are repaid, we will be free to depart this realm. Most of my people have already left this world. Yet we, my men and I, have remained to complete our final task."

"Which is what?" Chari had a clear note of distrust in his voice.

"We are protectors of the realm."

"Protectors?"

"It is not a role we sought through choice. My people have been tied to Alanar for many millennia, until the sins perpetrated by a certain faction of my race have been atoned for."

"I don't understand," Janir said. Although legends of the mighty Jinerans were widespread across Alanar, very little was actually known about this most mysterious of races.

With a silver scepter in hand, Elas rose from his throne. "Long ago, certain wayward Jinerans arrived on Alanar and caused great damage to this world."

He came to a stop before the crystal; the violet light reflecting upon his increasingly translucent form. Images began appearing in the heart of the crystal, as though the crystal itself was a repository of ancient memories.

It showed three alien starships: immense triangular vessels soaring across the star-filled heavens. This sight of majesty and wonder turned to terror as the ships arrived in orbit of a blue-green planet and unleashed a nightmarish fury upon the unsuspecting world. Weapons fire rained down upon the planet, destroying entire cities. Ground troops then landed, overthrowing any remaining resistance.

"We Jinerans are a powerful race," Elas said. "A power that has on occasion been abused by factions of my people. However, the Jineran High Council did not stand idly by. My men and I were sent to undo the damage caused by the rebels and to repay the debt they incurred. That is our duty here, and here we have been for millennia."

The crystal showed another Jineran starship arriving in orbit. A battle ensued as warriors from the new ship landed on the planet and fought to defend Alanar from the attackers.

"We dealt with those who committed the infraction, and we remained, attempting to undo the damage by offering ourselves as immortal custodians of the peace." He sighed, the weariness of the ages evident in his face. "Needless to say, we have not always succeeded. Over the centuries, this world has become an increasingly dark place, rife with war, conquest and subjugation. Most of this can be traced back to a single event, occurring some ten thousand years ago..."

"The fall of Lasandria," Janir said.

Elas nodded. The image of a golden city appeared in the crystal. It lay amid a valley at the foot of a cloud-capped green mountain. In a violent flash of light, the entire city was consumed by an explosion that tore across the entire continent.

The image faded, replaced by the mirrored reflections of Janir, Elas and the others. "We failed to see it coming," Elas said. "Once it happened there was little we could do. Yet now, as our final task lies before us, we stand ready to correct the mistakes of the past."

"Am I right to assume this task somehow involves us?"

"That is why you were sent here by the Guardians." Elas lifted his hand. "Observe the Crystal of Elandaan. The wellspring of our life-force, it allows us to sustain physical form on Alanar. At one time it blazed so brightly you would have had to shield your eyes to avoid blindness. But now, as you can see, it grows increasingly dim. As the energy of the crystal fades, so too does my physical form. I struggle to maintain cohesion in this realm, yet I resolved to hold my form just long enough..."

"For what?" Darien ventured.

"Your arrival. I have long been expecting you. I know of all that has transpired—of your escape from the Alliance, your quest to find the City of Lorden and to reunite the Key of Alanar with its missing half. Yes, I know everything—including the collapse of your noble mission. The Custodian of the Key, the boy named David, is now in the hands of the enemy; a dark sorcerer named Zhayron. A man you know only too well, Janir."

Again the mere mention of Zhayron's name had a profound effect on Janir. It brought back a flood of painful memories; ones he'd spent many years trying to bury in the deepest recesses of his mind.

Elas continued, "Zhayron is as skilled a sorcerer as his old mentor. As we speak, he continues to corrupt David's mind, tainting him with dark incantations; blinding him, filling him with poisonous lies and deceit. David will soon lead him to the City of Lorden. There, the Key will be made whole—and will be used to reopen the gateway to the Narssians' dimension. The incursion will begin and this entire realm will *burn*."

Janir looked up in desperation. "What can we do to stop this?"

"Unless the dynamics of the situation are changed, nothing can be done. Zhayron has not only the might of the Alliance at his disposal but also the Narssians."

"We must stop them somehow!"

"But do you really think we can?" Darien said.

"Loathe though I am to agree with Darien," Mariane said, "I'm afraid we have to face facts, Janir. We've all seen the might of the Alliance. It seems impossible that the five of us could have any hope of defeating not only the Alliance but these Narssians too..."

"Nothing's impossible," Janir said. "But you're right. We can't do it alone."

Elas concurred. "Help you most certainly need. For even if you manage to travel to the City of Lorden and intercept Zhayron, you would be hopelessly overpowered by the Alliance. That is why I now pledge my remaining men to aid you in this task. You will need an army, and though my men are few in number, their skills in battle are unparalleled. They will fight with you until the very end. And should victory be attained, the last of the Jinerans will finally be free to leave this realm; all debts repaid."

Elas gestured to his men, who removed their hoods to reveal their faces. With golden skin and blue cat-like eyes, they resembled their sovereign, although they were younger and stronger, and their physical forms still fully solid. Despite wearing the garb of a religious order, Janir knew that these monks were formidable warriors. "You have my deepest gratitude, Sovereign," he said.

"Do not thank me yet," Elas said. "Because for you to have any hope of defeating Zhayron, you must be able to fight him on his terms. To do that, you must relinquish your oath."

How did he know about the oath?

"What's he talking about, Janir?" Darien asked.

"You have not told your comrades of this," Elas noted. "Perhaps now is the time."

"Perhaps it is," Janir whispered. In the ten years he'd lived in New Haven he'd divulged virtually nothing about himself or his past, and with good reason. For he held a crushing secret too painful to even contemplate—one that he'd tried so hard to forget. Yet they were about to head into battle and the outcome was uncertain at best. These were his friends and comrades. They'd been through so much together and they had a right to know. All eyes were upon him. As he met their bewildered gazes, he struggled to find the right words. "David is now in the hands of Zhayron," he began. "Zhayron is a powerful sorcerer and an agent of the Alliance..."

"As we've learned," Mariane said with a nod.

"Well, what you don't know is that Zhayron and I...we know each other. We know each other very well."

"How?" Chari asked blankly.

"I never told you any of this, but many years ago, back in my homeland, I was a sorcerer."

"A sorcerer?" Darien echoed.

"Indeed, I was renowned as the most power sorcerer in the land. When I was a child, I grew up fascinated by the feats of the Great Mage, the head sorcerer of Taribor. All I wanted was to become like him, to learn the secret of his powers and to become a sorcerer myself. The moment I came of age, I went through the application process and after many rigorous trials I was honored to be accepted as his apprentice." A smile played upon his lips as he recalled those days. "I was a diligent student, but it took many years of study and practice before I came anywhere near his level of mastery. When my master eventually died, I was appointed his successor as Great Mage."

"Not being familiar with sorcery," Mariane began, somewhat skeptical, "just what did that entail?"

"I had a great many skills and powers. I could control the weather, improve harvests, heal the sick, advise government leaders and use my power to protect our borders from neighboring aggressors."

"Such powers sound almost godlike," Chari remarked.

"Not godlike, no. I was certainly no god. The powers of the sorcerer are simply the application of an ancient esoteric science. My Master taught me the law of the primordial essence;

the unmanifest aspect of Infinity. After much training, I learned to manipulate that power and bend to it my will."

"Fascinating," Chari rumbled.

The others said nothing, waiting for him to continue. Clearly this was a great surprise to them. Although they'd known him as a healer, the notion of him as a powerful sorcerer was something that would take some getting used to. His words reverberated throughout the metallic chamber as he continued to relate his tale. "After a number of years it came time for me to select an apprentice. Although I had many pupils to whom I taught the rudimentary healing arts, my apprentice would be the one protege to whom I would teach all my secrets and who would one day succeed me as Great Mage. My chosen apprentice was a young man named Zhayron."

Registering the look of shock upon his comrades' faces, Janir had to force himself to continue. "In retrospect, I should never have inducted him into the art of sorcery. Even when he was a boy I could sense within him the seeds of anger, vanity, and desire. But there was a bond between us and, giving him the benefit of the doubt, I spent many years teaching him as my Master taught me. He was an exemplary pupil; bright and so eager to learn. To my own credit, I was a good teacher—albeit a blinded one. For I never saw what was happening within him; how his increasing thirst for power was slowly twisting his mind. No, I never saw that until after his training was complete...by which time it was too late."

"What happened?" Janna asked.

"He betrayed me. No longer content to serve under my shadow, he went before the Council of Taribor and petitioned to have me step down as Great Mage in order that he could replace me. He wanted nothing more than to take complete control of our people. He'd had a taste for power and it was like a drug to him; an insatiable addiction.

"Needless to say, his petition was dismissed by the Council. Zhayron was a man driven by a narcissistic need to be admired, revered—even worshipped—by others. In his eyes, the Council and the people of Taribor had rejected him. In a fit of rage, he murdered the Council and burned the entire capital to the ground. As he rampaged across the land, determined to make all tremble before his might, it fell to me to stop him. It was I who'd created the monster he'd become and only I who could defeat him."

Though so many years had passed, the memories remained fresh in his mind. He could see it all so clearly—the burning cities, scorched fields, and people running, screaming, dying. Devastated that he had been too late to prevent this from happening in the first place, Janir had confronted Zhayron amid the rubble of the city of Serantha, engaging him in a fierce battle of sorcery. Zhayron had thrown everything he had at his old mentor; including an army of wraithlike shadow men, projections from Zhayron's own consciousness, staggering toward him through the fiery battlefield. Janir had quickly defeated these phantoms and was ready for everything else Zhayron unleashed upon him.

"I managed to defeat him, although I was unable to kill him. His power had escalated and he was now in league with dark entities who granted him a measure of protection. All I could do was banish him from Taribor, using a protective seal to prevent him from ever returning. But my victory was tainted by blood."

"What do you mean?" Mariane asked.

"Zhayron was enraged that I had turned against him," Janir's voice was now but a hoarse whisper as he stopped and stared into the crystal. In spite of all these years of trying to forget, the wounds were still raw. "I returned home to find Zhayron had taken revenge on me...by murdering my wife."

He fell silent, casting his eyes to the ground and trying so hard to erase the dreadful image of Chaldana's burnt and broken body from his mind.

Mariane was first to react. "Janir," she said softly. "Why did you never tell us any of this?"

"Because some things are simply too painful to speak of."

"I'm so sorry..."

Janir straightened his back and took a deep breath. "The people of Taribor didn't blame me for Zhayron's actions. But I did. The Master is always responsible for the student. I'd failed to see how twisted he'd become and what a danger he posed. I was responsible for everything that happened, including my wife's death and all the other deaths."

"Janir, listen to me," Mariane said. "You can't possibly hold yourself responsible."

Janir shook his head. He knew she meant well, but she didn't understand. How could she? "I stood over her body," he continued, "and in that moment I vowed to stand down as Great Mage and renounce my powers. Such power carries tremendous responsibility; a responsibility I was no longer fit for, as demonstrated by my tragic lack of judgment.

"I imposed exile upon myself. I could no longer stand to be in that land, for everywhere I looked I saw reminders of my past. I packed some belongings and left; traveling aimlessly across different lands, over mountains, and through valleys... finally building myself a raft and setting out into the ocean, allowing the fates to guide my way. I decided that wherever the current took me—there I would stay and live out the rest of my life."

"So that's how you came to New Haven," Darien said.

Janir nodded.

Elas stepped toward Janir, his translucent form shimmering with a pale golden light. "We do what we must as we journey through life. We respond to what life brings as best we can, knowing the result is never in our hands. You must now let go of your burden of blame and guilt."

"But by your own account, Sovereign, you have spent millennia upon this world attempting to atone for the actions of the rebel Jinerans. There has to be accountability. I was Zhayron's Master. I was responsible for him. I should have..."

"Done exactly as you did."

Janir opened his mouth to speak but no words came out.

"One cannot second guess the fates," Elas continued. "If you could but imagine life through the eyes of an immortal. Over eons I have witnessed so much: the creation and dissolution of stars and galaxies, the rise and fall of interstellar empires and the birth and death of so, so many beings. From the perspective of an immortal, this realm is but an unfolding play; a tapestry of duality woven by threads of dark and light. There are no isolated events, for everything is the result of an immense and unfathomable chain of cause and effect. The rebel Jinerans had to attack Alanar all those millennia ago, just as we had to stop them and atone for their misdeeds. Zhayron had to become the man that he did. He had no other choice. It was his nature—the song that life gave him to sing—just as your nature, your song, is to stop him."

"But I didn't stop him and that's the problem. I tried, and the best I could do was simply to displace him. And what did I do after that? Did I try to hunt him down and finish things? No, I ran away. I hid away on an island for a decade, in which time Zhayron only grew stronger and more dangerous."

"It happened as it had to happen. You ended up in the right place at the right time. The Guardians have seen all eventualities and have planned accordingly. As you know, it was by no accident that you arrived in New Haven when you did. They sent you there to seek out the Custodian of the Key and prepare him for the dark times ahead."

"And I failed him. Look where David is now."

"In time you may find you helped him more than you know. For now, you must let go of the past and relinquish this misdirected grief. It serves you not." The ghostly Jineran began circling Janir. "Right now your powers are greatly needed. You must relinquish your oath. You made the vow out of misplaced guilt when your judgment was impaired by grief. The time approaches when you must face Zhayron once more and this time defeat him—and for that, you must be free to use your powers again."

"I can't break my oath."

"You must. The only way you can hope to defeat Zhayron is by using your powers of sorcery. He will not hesitate to use his powers against you, and you must be willing to fight back. You know what is at stake here, Janir. Step into your power again, sorcerer—and *use it*."

Janir found himself staring into the shimmering crystal. The long-suppressed memories of that time—the pain of Chaldana's death and the terror and grief wrought by Zhayron's betrayal—overwhelmed him. It had almost destroyed him back then. He'd blamed it all on his powers and that was why he'd sworn never to use them again. While he'd used some rudimentary spells such as protective incantations and healing invocations, it had been many years since he'd consciously tapped into the power of Infinity and bent it to his will.

Yet he knew Elas was right. He recalled trying to convince David that his guilt over the deaths of the New Haven victims was misplaced. Perhaps his own guilt was similarly erroneous; a self-indulgence that he could no longer afford. Chaldana was gone and there was no bringing her back. But the future was not yet decided.

"Very well," he said. "I'll use my power again—but only when absolutely necessary and only until Zhayron is defeated."

Elas smiled, satisfied. He raised his scepter aloft as he spoke, his voice deep and resounding: "I, Elas, last of the Jineran sovereigns, now pledge my men, under the command of Centurion Castan, to serve as your army. Although their time grows short, I will give them the remainder of my energy to sustain them. My men know where the City of Lorden is and they will take you there. You must make haste! David will soon lead Zhayron to Lorden—and when your paths intersect I foresee a great battle. It will be neither an easy or a fair fight. But you must fight without fear and without relent. For, Alanar is the keystone world. If this world falls, an entire universe will fall."

A silver radiance emanated from Elas's shimmering form, mixing with the pulsing light of the crystal. It soon became almost impossible to distinguish his physical form from the light consuming it. "My promise is fulfilled," he declared. "The covenant nears completion. I leave you now, my men. Take my remaining strength and let it sustain you in the days to come..."

Janir watched in wonder as the angelic form of Elas dissolved into a brilliant burst of light. All that remained were waves of effervescent silver light, surging across the underground ship.

Tendrils of the energy danced around the remaining Jinerans, penetrating their foreheads and merging into their bodies. The chamber dimmed as the remaining wisps of light were absorbed by the crystal.

"That's one way to make an exit," Darien whispered.

One of the Jinerans stepped forward. "I am Centurion Castan. True to the word of our Sovereign, my men and I now pledge ourselves to your service."

"You honor us, Centurion," Janir said. "With your help, we now at least stand a chance of defeating Zhayron and the Alliance."

"We set off tomorrow at first light. The journey will take several days and there is little time to waste. I suggest you prepare yourselves for the ordeal ahead. For as our Sovereign said, a great and terrible battle now lies before us. Our enemy is Death itself and I promise you, it will not be easily defeated."

# CHAPTER TWENTY SEVEN

# Promises and Lies

His was a shattered world, the broken shards bound by a lingering grief over a tragedy he could barely remember. David stood in front of the grand fireplace, watching as flames devoured the logs, crackling and spitting sparks and embers as smoke spiraled up the chimney. Outside the storm continued raging. Rain and wind battered against the windowpanes; thunder booming in the distance and occasional forks of lightning flashing through the room. David barely registered any of it, for his mind was far elsewhere.

Though his memory had become increasingly hazy—his past blurry and indistinct—he found himself unable to shake the image of his mother trapped in a tormented state of purgatory—calling to him, begging him for help. That was the one thing he did remember and it haunted him without relent. He'd let her down somehow. He'd been responsible for some great tragedy and he had to make things right.

David had spent the past few days alone. Much to the outrage of the Sekyrian monarchy, Zhayron had ordered the Sekyrian palace to be cleared. There he and David had stayed for an indiscernible amount of time—days, or perhaps weeks. With the lavish palace at his disposal, David quickly became accustomed to living in luxury. Yet what good was luxury when he had never felt more alone? He found himself yearning for human contact, if only to distract him from the dreadful images in his mind.

He didn't know where Zhayron had gone or when to expect his return. The only people he'd seen were the Sekyrian servants who were on hand to prepare his meals and tend to his every whim. But they'd been of little company. For some reason they seemed to be afraid of him; visibly cowering in his presence and scurrying off the moment they'd attended to their duties.

The only other presence he was aware of was the shadow people. David had no idea who or what they were, but he'd encountered them on numerous occasions since arriving in the citadel. There seemed to be five of them in all, both male and female. Darkly mysterious beings with pale skin and jet black hair, they looked similar in appearance, clad in long black robes with an ethereal, ageless quality to them. David usually caught sight of them in his peripheral vision, silently watching him from the corners of rooms, hallways and in the shadows (hence the reason he called them the 'shadow people'). Upon seeing them, the ghost-like beings tended to vanish as mysteriously as they had appeared. Ordinarily, that might have disturbed David, but he found their presence strangely reassuring, as though he had the comfort of knowing that someone was watching over him.

A knock at the door made him jump. He took a deep breath, again becoming aware of the rain rattling against the windows. "Come in," he called.

Although it was surely just one of the palace attendants, for some reason he felt on edge. He turned and watched as the door swung open and a Sekyrian man—one of the smaller, ruling cast—entered with an imperious stride. Dressed in a frilled shirt with a green cape and a silver crown upon his head, David got the impression that he knew this man.

Devlan. His name was Devlan.

Although the memories seemed distant and far removed (why was it such a struggle to remember?), he vaguely recalled having traveled with him for a time.

"Ah, it *is* you," Devlan said, fixing him with a slightly perplexed, penetrating glance. "I'd heard you were here. Although for a second I didn't recognize you."

"Why?"

"You look different."

David wasn't quite sure what to say. He looked down at the Sekyrian, struggling to piece together his memories. He got the impression he'd never quite trusted this man. Zhayron had mentioned something about a change of circumstances in the Sekyrian royal family. The existing king had been deposed and banished into exile following the return of the legitimate heir to the throne.

"Where's your Master?" Devlan asked.

"My Master?"

"Zhayron," he snapped, his rounded, reddish face darkening as he spoke Zhayron's name.

"Zhayron's not my *Master*."

"No? Then what is he?"

"I don't know. He's my friend, I suppose."

"Really? Then I must say I don't much care for the friends you're keeping these days."

"What do you mean?"

"I mean you should watch yourself. I've never had any problem with the Alliance until now, but believe me when I say that he's not a man to be trusted. He's dangerous."

What did he mean—in what way dangerous? David was about to respond but Devlan preempted him. "I came here to find out just how much longer Zhayron will be occupying *my* palace."

"I'm not sure. He's not here right now. He's been away for a few days."

"This is all most irregular and highly inconvenient," the Sekyrian king fumed. "I finally return home after all this time, rally my forces and depose my traitorous brother—only to have my palace commandeered! Ordering the royal family to vacate the palace is the ultimate humiliation. In all my years I've never heard of the like—and it will not be tolerated much longer."

Before David could respond, Zhayron stormed into the room, his fury at Devlan's intrusion palpable. "Oh, it will not be tolerated, will it?"

Although initially startled by Zhayron's sudden entrance, Devlan quickly regained his resolve. "No, it will not." Zhayron loomed over the Sekyrian king menacingly, but what Devlan lacked in height he made up for in attitude. "This is the residence of the Sekyrian monarchy and it has been for over a thousand years! It is unacceptable for you to simply barge in here and—"

"I ordered the palace cleared until further notice and my orders stand," Zhayron cut in, his voice a low growl. "I have complete jurisdiction here. Need I remind you that Sekyr is Alliance-controlled territory and within the Alliance hierarchy my authority is second only to Zhylan Tyraah himself. You'd do well to remember that the Sekyrian royals are here only at the whim of the Alliance. Do you understand me, your highness?"

Although clearly enraged, Devlan could do nothing but dutifully nod.

"Now leave us at once," Zhayron commanded. "And please be aware that next time you barge in here uninvited, the celebrated 'lost prince of Sekyr' may mysteriously disappear a second time—only next time your departure will be a permanent one."

Devlan glowered at Zhayron but said nothing. He turned for the exit, making brief eye contact with David. His eyes seemed to convey a warning. The Sekyrian departed, slamming the door behind him, leaving David and Zhayron alone in the fire-lit room.

David found himself unnerved by Zhayron's hostile response to Devlan and his barely concealed threat.

"Is something wrong?" Zhayron asked sharply.

"No."

"Good. The Sekyrians can be such a tiresome people, don't you agree?"

David mumbled noncommittally.

"Sekyr would be a fine place were it not for its inhabitants."

Uncomfortable with the direction of the conversation, David decided to change the topic. "Where have you been?"

David could tell from the look that flashed across Zhayron's face that he didn't care to be questioned, but he responded nonetheless. "I've been away consulting my guides, the Lords of Abidalos. I needed their guidance as to how we should proceed; how we should rescue your mother."

"What did they say?"

"We'll discuss it in the morning. It's late. You require rest."

"I'm fine. We can discuss it now..."

"I don't appreciate being contradicted, David. I sense you're tense; distracted; out of sorts." Zhayron marched forward, his piercing green eyes drilling through David. "What have you been doing in my absence?"

"Nothing really. There's not much to do here."

Zhayron reached down to a nearby table, picking up a chalice of liquid. "Have you been drinking this as I told you?"

"I keep forgetting. In fact, I keep forgetting everything..."

"It doesn't matter, David. Drink it now."

David didn't know why Zhayron was so adamant that he keep drinking this 'mutah nectar' but he didn't see the harm in obliging. He took a sip as Zhayron watched. With a sweet, fruity taste, the juice always had a curious effect on him. Warm waves of relaxation washed over his body and mind.

"Keep taking it," Zhayron urged. "It'll ease the pain of the past."

Indeed, it almost seemed to erase the past altogether.

"Now, I suggest you go back to your chamber and get some rest."

David nodded and took another sip of the drink. With each drop his memories dispersed in a pleasantly narcotic haze of forgetting. His mind became strangely still; the tensions brewing inside him disappearing like waves folding back into the ocean.

"Tomorrow will be a momentous day," Zhayron said. "But you can relax now, David. I promise you—everything is being taken care of..."

# CHAPTER TWENTY EIGHT

# The Sulyahn

"Why did you never mention your powers before?"

Taken aback by Darien's question, it took Janir a moment to respond. "Having disavowed them I saw little point," he said as they continued through the glade. "It was a part of my past I'd chosen to leave behind. I wanted my life on New Haven to be a new life, unencumbered by the shadows of the past."

"Just how great a sorcerer are you?" Darien continued. "Could you have stopped the Alliance from attacking New Haven?"

Janir didn't reply.

"Could you?"

"Darien, I don't think that's helpful," Janna said.

"I'm just asking."

"Yes, at one time I probably could have," Janir admitted.

"Then why didn't you?"

"I took an oath to renounce my powers—and even if I'd broken that oath, so many years had passed since last I'd used them, the results would most certainly have been mixed."

"Did you consider trying?" Mariane asked.

"Of course I did. But in the end it would probably still have amounted to too little, too late. If I'd been ready for them, then perhaps, but the Alliance had the element of surprise, not to mention far superior force. As it was, I used some simple tricks and incantations along the way to get us to safety. If I could have done more I certainly would have." He came to a stop. "Indeed, if I had my life to live over again, I'd do a great many things differently."

"I think that's true of most people," Janna said.

"So when will we get to see these powers of yours in action?" Darien asked.

"Probably sooner than you might think," Janir said. "And the circumstances will not be pleasant, that I can assure you."

Janir and the others continued across the valley. Three days had passed since leaving the Jineran base at Rastayan. The Jinerans had led them along the Britak Mountain pass, a trail zigzagging along the mountains. The desert seemed far behind them now; for the landscape around them was lush, green and verdant.

Janir watched as all sixteen Jineran warrior-monks strode ahead. Tall and lithe, their every moment was elegant and graceful. Prior to leaving Rastayan they'd cast off their priestly robes and attired themselves for battle. They were clad in gold and silver armor and armed with metal batons, swords, and shields. As fierce yet noble protectors of the realm, tales of their bravery, honor, and skill in battle were still told throughout Alanar.

Their leader, Centurion Castan, radiated a sense of controlled power, tempered by an evenness of mind and quietude of spirit. Janir had taken an immediate liking to him and although he knew virtually nothing about the man, trusted him implicitly. True to their enigmatic reputation, the immortal warriors rarely spoke unless spoken to, never volunteered information and very much kept to themselves. Men of unyielding discipline, strict ceremony and few words, Janir got the impression that they were eager to reach the City of Lorden and complete their mission as quickly as possible. Understandable perhaps, for Elas had said that their time upon Alanar was limited and their power diminishing. As immortals who'd lived on Alanar for millennia, it seemed ironic that their greatest adversary should now be time.

They were all intrigued by their new comrades—none more so than Darien, who'd been attempting to strike up a rapport with them. Thus far the Jinerans had been unresponsive to his efforts, but Darien persisted. Janir suspected that he may simply be trying to impress Janna, who for her part barely seemed to have noticed his attempts. Instead, she appeared to be enjoying some space to herself now that Darien's attentions were elsewhere. Though Janir hadn't spoken to her privately since their conversation in the desert, she seemed more at peace with herself.

After a time they came to a wide river splitting the valley in two. Realizing that their best option was to cross it rather than finding a way around, the Jinerans found a relatively narrow part of the river scattered with rocks and boulders. Taking the lead, they gracefully stepped across the boulders until they reached the other bank. Janir and the others followed.

Upon reaching the other side, Darien was the first to notice a series of large fissures in the ground. There were over a dozen holes, each several feet in diameter. "What do you suppose caused these?"

"They don't look natural," Janir said. "They've been dug by someone...or something."

"I wonder how deep they are." Darien picked up a large rock. Before Janir could stop him, he tossed the rock down the nearest hole.

"Darien, why did you do that?"

"To see how deep it is."

"That was not advisable," Chari warned.

"Why?" Darien shrugged. "What's the worst that could happen?"

"I do wish you wouldn't keep saying that," Mariane grumbled.

"Let's not stay around to find out," Janir said, motioning to the Jinerans, who were already several paces ahead.

Just as they were about to move, they were startled by a loud hissing sound.

"What is that?" Mariane gasped.

The sound continued, loudening and accompanied by a scuffling, scraping noise. "I don't know," Janir said, "but I don't like the sound of it." With a growing sense of alarm, he realized that the noise was coming from underground.

Chari, having reached the same conclusion, glared at Darien as he raised his electro-pulse rifle. "You should not have thrown that rock. You have disturbed whatever lives down there."

Darien looked up sheepishly. "Something *lives* down there?"

They watched in horror as an enormous insect crawled out of the nearest tunnel. At least the size of a grown man and armored with a prickly brown exoskeleton, the creature had six legs, two oversized pinchers and an upraised, spiked tail, swinging from side to side.

"What in the twin suns is that?" Mariane cried, staggering back.

"A scorpion," Janir exclaimed. "A *big* scorpion."

It wasn't alone. More of the monstrous insects clambered out of the underground lairs until over a dozen of them encircled the travelers. Initially angered by the disturbance, the scorpions now appeared to be anticipating a hearty meal.

Chari raised his rifle, took aim and fired—only nothing happened. He tried again, to no avail. Realizing that the Alliance rifle had finally run out of charge, he tossed it to the ground and stepped toward the advancing scorpions, ready to defend himself and the others.

Now aware of the commotion, the Jinerans rejoined them and sprang into action. "Get back," Castan barked at the others.

Hissing and wailing with fury, the scorpions initiated their attack. Castan and the Jinerans retaliated, attempting to drive them back underground. Every bit as skilled as Janir had been led to believe, the Jinerans were clearly adept at multiple forms of martial art—their movements graceful yet decisively powerful. They used their weapons minimally but with precision as they leapt in and out of the attacking beasts, avoiding each swipe of the creatures' tails and claws and striking blows to their most vulnerable spots. Within moments they'd disabled several of the predators, but more of the creatures were scrambling out of the underground nests.

As the Jinerans fought, Chari joined them, weaponless yet using his mighty hands to restrain one of the scorpion's snapping claws as he pushed it back and tried to batter it against the trunk of a nearby tree. Lacking the agility of the Jinerans, one of the other beasts knocked him down with a swipe of its tail. Mandibles snapping wildly, it let out a snarl and was about to tear into the fallen Kellian when one of the Jinerans came to his aid. Leaping at the attacking beast and stunning it with a kick to the head, the Jineran felled the scorpion with only two moves of his blade.

Mariane turned to Janir. "Janir, you're a sorcerer, is there anything you can do?"

"I can try," he said with a measure of uncertainty. So many years had passed since he'd used his powers. Raising his arms aloft, he mentally reached out to the force of Infinity. Once certain that he'd tapped into the all-pervading ocean of unmanifest energy, he consciously pulled a thread of it down, drawing it through his body, grounding it and directing it into the palms of his hands.

"Stand clear!" He took a deep breath and unleashed the energy. A surge of crackling blue energy shot from his hands, hitting the scorpions, immediately knocking a half dozen of them to the ground.

"You did it," Darien cried.

"But there are plenty more of them," Mariane cautioned.

Janir repeated the process again. His powers hadn't deserted him after all, but years without practice had left his skills as blunt as a rusted blade. In times past he could have wiped out every single scorpion without so much as a blink. Perhaps it would just take him time to hone his skills again.

More and more of the creatures were streaming out of the nests, seemingly undeterred by the onslaught. Chari and the Jinerans continued battling the oversized insects but Janir, now unaccustomed to channeling so much raw energy through his body, soon felt exhausted and weak.

All of a sudden a flaming arrow—seemingly appearing out of nowhere—struck one of the scorpions, impaling its thorax. The creature shrieked and thrashed about as it ignited in flames.

A flurry of arrows followed; fire raining down upon the startled creatures. The scorpions reacted in alarm, scampering for cover, withdrawing and disappearing back into their nests. Soon all that remained were the fallen bodies and the burning remains of those hit by the arrows.

"Who fired those arrows?" Chari growled.

"We did," came a woman's voice.

A group of armed warriors emerged through the trees. Chari instinctively bristled and the Jinerans readied themselves for possible conflict.

Muscular and dark-skinned, the strangers wore simple clothing comprising embroidered earth colored tunics, leather belts, and sandals. An even mix of male and female warriors, their dark hair was either braided or tied back, although most of the men were shaven-headed. Armed with swords, spears and bows and arrows, several of them carried fire torches.

Their leader appeared to be a tall, lean woman. Formidable-looking with black, close-cropped hair and striking dark eyes, she strode toward them carrying a bejeweled spear. "The scorpions are a damned menace in these parts," she said, surveying the carnage. "But we find they have a particular aversion to fire."

"So I see," Janir said with a gracious nod. "We are most grateful for your assistance."

"You obviously disturbed their nests. Perhaps you'll be more careful in the future."

"We certainly shall. I confess we're unaccustomed to this region."

"That much is obvious. What brings you here?"

"We're traveling east. In search of the City of Lorden."

"Really?" She looked at him with a mixture of incredulity and amusement. "I wish you luck, then. You'll need it. I take it seeking mythical cities is a pastime of yours?"

"Something like that," Janir said with a pleasant smile, ignoring the barbed nature of the comment. "I'm Janir, by the way. And these are my friends."

"Dutshyana," the woman introduced herself. "Second of the Sulyahn."

"The Sulyahn are your people?"

Dutshyana nodded. "We are the Sulyahn of Arnashen." She paused, her eyes settling upon Chari. "This Kellian—he's with you?"

"Yes," Janir said. "Chari is a friend and ally."

"I didn't know Kellians had friends—and I've never seen one allied to anyone but themselves."

"Chari is not like other Kellians."

"So it would seem."

Chari glowered at the warrior woman.

"Well, since you're in the vicinity," Dutshyana said, "why not come see our kingdom for yourself? We have few visitors so I'm sure our king will be happy to meet you."

"I'm afraid we have little time to spare."

"It's nearing sun-fall. Why sleep down here in the mud when you could join us for evening meal and stay in our guest quarters?"

Whilst certainly a welcome offer, Janir found it strange that Dutshyana would invite a group of complete strangers to her kingdom. Perhaps, he supposed, it was simply the way of her people. Dismissing his reticence, he knew that it was too good an offer to refuse. "Perhaps you're right. I appreciate the kind offer. We'd be honored to join you."

"Then come. Our kingdom is not far from here." Dutshyana turned and with a wave of her hand beckoned her men to head back the way they had come. Janir motioned for his comrades to follow.

The Sulyahn led them across the valley, through the forest-land, and up a well-worn mountainside track. Though rocky and uneven, the ground was carpeted by moss and scattered with fragrant pine needles.

As they climbed the mountain trail, Janir asked Castan what he knew of the Sulyahn. The Sulyahn were a simple mountain-dwelling people, Castan answered. They were generally peaceful and kept very much to themselves. Janir nodded thoughtfully. The Jinerans obviously trusted the Sulyahn. That ought to be good enough for him. Yet he found himself unable to shake a lingering feeling of unease; the sense that something wasn't quite right. Or was it possible that their long and fraught journey had simply hardened him and made him distrustful of strangers?

The mountain trail grew steeper and narrower, and the air thinner as their altitude increased. Stopping to catch his breath, Janir turned and found himself awestruck by the view that greeted his eyes. The blue-green mountains rose to majestic snow-capped peaks, like the pillars of an ancient world holding the cloudless pink sky aloft. At the foot of the great mountains sprawled a carpet of lush valleys interconnected by crystalline rivers wending their way across the land.

By the time they reached Arnashen, the suns were setting upon the horizon, lighting the trees and mountainside in a pale orange glow. Janir caught glimpse of a large tower peeking through the treetops. Constructed of white stone and built partly into the side of the mountain itself, the elaborate tower was a monument of beauty. As they neared, he saw dozens of white stone houses and buildings clustered around its base. The golden-orange glow of the sunset and the thin wispy clouds surrounding the mountaintop plateau lent the place a dreamlike quality.

"Welcome to Arnashen," Dutshyana called, the pride evident in her voice. She led them up a stone walkway into the heart of the mountaintop abode. With dusk fast approaching, it was perhaps unsurprising that the streets of Arnashen seemed fairly quiet, although a number of men and women still went about their business, looking up at the newcomers in curiosity. Dark skinned with even darker hair, both the men and women wore long tunics with trousers and animal hide vests; some carrying baskets of food, a few leading mountain ponies or goats along the walkway.

A hunched old woman in a shawl sat outside a doorway drinking a mug of steaming liquid, her wrinkled face dominated by a pair of penetrating eyes as she stared at the strangers. Janir smiled at her as he passed. Unresponsive, she simply took another sip of her brew.

A group of children played across the street, carefree and joyous as they ran and shouted. Upon catching sight of the strangers, they stopped their game and looked on in wide-eyed wonder. As Dutshyana herself had said, the Sulyahn had few visitors to their kingdom. Janir again dismissed a creeping feeling that they shouldn't have come here; that this was a diversion they could ill-afford.

They came to the entrance of the white tower. At Dutshyana's command, the Sulyahn warriors left, and she led the guests up a flight of marble steps to an elaborately sculpted doorway guarded either side by shaven-headed Sulyahn men with jewel-studded spears. Inside was an expansive foyer. The elegant architecture reminded Janir of his homeland, Taribor. The high ceiling, dominated by a glass chandelier, was held aloft by sturdy columns, with two winding stairways ahead of them leading up into the heart of the tower. Two other guards stood on duty at the foot of the marble stairways; one of whom Dutshyana ordered to fetch King Rushtaan immediately.

"Your kingdom is beautiful," Janir said to Dutshyana.

"You are right, it *is*," she said. "We Sulyahn are fiercely protective of our home. We love what we've built here and would do anything to protect it."

Janir found this a curious comment. In their isolation here, he couldn't help but wonder who they would have to protect it from.

A man descended one of the staircases. Someone of clear importance, he wore a brown cape fastened by a gold brooch on his shoulder, with a headband encrusted with sparkling gemstones. His muscular torso was bare and beneath his cape, he wore only a loincloth, belt, and sandals. Necklaces and bracelets of precious stones adorned his neck and arms. Trailing behind him were two young, scantily clad women.

Dutshyana bowed before him. "King Rushtaan, please allow me to introduce our guests. I found them in the valley, under attack from scorpions. They've traveled a long way, in search of the mythical City of Lorden. I felt it appropriate to offer them our hospitality."

"Good," Rushtaan said, his rounded face twisting with a wide, toothy grin. "Good!"

"Your majesty, we're grateful for your hospitality," Janir said.

"Think nothing of it," Rushtaan said. "We Sulyahn are nothing if not hospitable. Few travelers pass through this land, so I'm always eager to welcome them when they do. I enjoy hearing stories of far-off lands, and it looks like you may have some interesting tales to tell. As honored guests, you must feel free to stay as long as you wish."

"Thank you. We're on a mission of some importance, however, so we cannot stay long."

"Very well. Though you must at least stay the night, I do insist. As it transpires, the timing of your arrival is perfect. We're soon to commence evening meal in the banquet hall. Join us! I should most like to hear about this mission of yours."

The travelers were hungry. Not having eaten all day, their hearts leaped with joy at seeing the glorious feast laid out for them in the banquet hall. There were several varieties of meat along with trimmings and sauces, and an assortment of vegetables, grains, and bread. The guests were seated at the banquet table, which was of such size that it provided ample room for all of them, including the Jinerans. Rushtaan sat at the head of the table accompanied by his two female consorts, Dutshyana and several Sulyahn officials and noblemen. A handful of guards lined the hall entrance.

After uttering a prayer to the mountain spirits in gratitude for their meal, Rushtaan urged his guests to begin. As they ate, their gregarious host told them about the history of the Sulyahn people. There were dozens of Sulyahn kingdoms dotted across the mountains, where they had lived peacefully for many centuries. Each kingdom, he explained, was self-governing, self-sustaining and largely self-reliant. Living in the mountains, remote and isolated, they had little contact with outsiders and lived simple lives.

"Alas, times are changing," Rushtaan said with a note of resignation. "Whilst we've lived here peacefully for many generations, there are those that would seek to destroy our way of life."

Janir, taking a bite of bread, looked over at Rushtaan and saw that his face had darkened. "Oh?" he said, eager for him to elaborate.

"Our historic adversaries are the Kellians." Rushtaan glanced over at Chari. "But our kingdoms are well fortified and we've always managed to repel them from our lands. Now there are other, far more deadly threats to our existence—such as the Alliance, who would seek to wipe us from the face of Alanar."

Janir found it curious that the Sulyahn had encountered the Alliance. What possible interest would the Alliance have in the Sulyahn? Rushtaan abruptly changed the conversation. "So tell me," he said, taking a sip of wine. "What is this mission you speak of? Dutshyana mentioned the City of Lorden. I'm most intrigued."

Perhaps against his better judgment, Janir told Rushtaan of their quest to find the City of Lorden and to stop the Alliance from unleashing a great horror upon the planet. Rushtaan remained silent, nodding thoughtfully every so often as he listened to the wondrous tale. When Janir had finished, the Sulyahn king smiled and held his glass aloft. "Well, may the mountain spirits bless you in your quest. To defeat the Alliance is indeed a noble goal. A noble goal indeed!" He took a gulp of wine, let out an involuntary belch and grunted in satisfaction.

"If you share our desire to defeat the Alliance and safeguard Alanar, then why not join us, King Rushtaan? We need all the help we can get."

Rushtaan's smile faded. "You would have us go against the Alliance? I think not. Though I certainly wish their defeat and pray to the mountain spirits accordingly, I cannot be seen to act against—"

"If you join us, you will aid us in defeating them," Chari cut in. "The greater our number, the greater our chance of success."

"I heed your words, Kellian. But I cannot and will not send my forces into battle with you. To do so would be to leave Arnashen unprotected and vulnerable."

"Which is out of the question," Dutshyana agreed.

"You don't have to send all your forces," Janir said. "Even just a handful of soldiers would be of immense help to us."

"No," Rushtaan declared. "No! We will not involve ourselves in this. If your mission is met with failure, as it most likely will, the Alliance will certainly seek retribution. And if the Sulyahn are seen to be part of this strike, then that retribution shall be taken upon us!"

"But, your majesty..."

"My decision is made!" He slammed his fist on the tabletop. "We will speak of this no more!"

The matter was closed. They finished their meal in awkward silence.

Following the banquet, Rushtaan bade them a cordial good night and departed with his mistresses. Dutshyana ordered two of the guards to show the guests to their accommodation. Led along the winding white tower and up several flights of stairs, they were shown to a corridor where four rooms had been prepared. The Jinerans took three of the rooms, while Janir, Darien, Janna, Mariane, and Chari took the fourth.

Entering the room, they were surprised to find they were not alone. Around ten Sulyahn men and women, all young, attractive and wearing little in the way of clothes, stood around the door, waiting for them.

"Can we help you?" Janir said.

"No," purred one of the women. "We're here to help *you*."

Another of the women stepped over to him, placing her hand on his back. "You're our guests. We've been sent for your pleasure and gratification." She smiled as she ran her hand down his spine.

"I don't think that's such a good idea," he said, pulling back with a polite shake of his head.

However, they were reluctant to heed his refusal. They closed in on their guests like spiders advancing on their prey. The women flocked around Janir, Darien, and Chari, while the men approached Janna and Mariane. But much to their surprise, their amorous attentions were not reciprocated. Chari was resolutely failing to succumb to his prospective suitor's charms and

Darien was clearly unhappy about the two handsome young men whispering in Janna's ear and caressing her neck and back. Riled with jealousy, he was oblivious to the two beautiful women competing for his attention. "Janir's right," he declared. "It's definitely not a good idea."

One of the men began stroking Mariane's arm as another whispered something in her ear. "I beg your pardon?" she exclaimed. "I'm old enough to be your grandmother!" Staunchly disgusted by the whole notion, she cleared the room with Janir's help. "Get out please," she demanded as she shooed them away with a wave of her hands and closed the door behind him. "It's a pity there's not a lock on this door."

"I'm sure they've got the message," Darien said.

"I certainly hope so. In all my years, I've never been propositioned in such a way. Outrageous."

Free from the unwanted advances of their Sulyahn hosts, they settled into their room. Everyone was tired from their long hike and comfortably full after their meal. It took little time for them to wash and settle down for the night. Janir told them that come morning they would set off without delay.

As the others got into bed, Janir took the opportunity to speak with Janna. "What's your impression of Rushtaan?"

"I don't know," she said. "He seems like a good man, but there are two sides to him, and he's holding something back. It's not just him, either. I can feel it from all the Sulyahn. Something's happened here—quite recently too. It's like there's a cloud of darkness over everything." Her face creased. "I can't fathom it. But there's definitely something wrong here."

"I sense much the same," Janir said. "The sooner we're out of here, the better."

*Janir dreamt of David again. He saw him in the clutches of Zhayron, ensnared in a web of deception; helpless and unable to protect himself from Zhayron's dark and invasive spell.*

*He found himself helplessly wandering the labyrinthian corridors of the citadel. The further he went, the more lost he became as the walls began closing in on him. He was desperate to get to*

*David; to rescue him—but he couldn't. David needed his help, but there was nothing Janir could do. He was lost and in mortal danger himself.*

*His dream suddenly shifted and he became aware of Balaska standing before him. "Awaken, Janir!" she shouted. "Awaken now!"*

Gripped by sudden alarm, Janir jolted awake.

While ordinarily the twilight between sleep and waking was characterized by hazy disorientation, this time he came to his senses with lightning speed. He opened his eyes to see a man standing over him with a knife, poised to strike.

It was Rushtaan.

He was aware of other men in the room, standing over his friends' beds, also with knives in hand.

He had no time to think. In one fell swoop, Rushtaan would plunge the dagger into his chest.

He connected himself with the power of Infinity. With a flash of light and a sound like thunder, he ensnared the Sulyahn assassins in a net of crackling blue energy. As their bodies jerked and twisted in shock, their daggers fell to the ground and they cried out in fright.

Janir rose to his feet. Raising his hand, he lifted all five Sulyahn clear off the ground.

The others, awoken by the commotion, leaped out of their beds. "What happened?" Chari demanded.

"Janir?" Mariane cried.

Janir stood, hands raised, continuing to focus all his attention upon the energy net. Rushtaan and his men howled in terror, frantically trying to wrestle their bodies free of the electrified forcefield.

"What's going on?" Darien cried, bounding to Janna's side.

"They were going to murder us as we slept," Janir growled. Consumed with rage, he intensified the energy net and lifted his hands higher, elevating the Sulyahn even further above the ground, the entire room lit up by the crackling energy.

"Let me go," yelped Rushtaan. "Please...I can explain! I can explain!"

Janir released the energy net. Rushtaan and his men fell to the floor. "Then explain!" he shouted, towering over the fallen Sulyahn. Chari retrieved the fallen daggers and stood by Janir's side. The only source of illumination in the room now came from silver streaks of moonlight streaming through the window.

Rushtaan began sobbing like a child. "Please, I didn't want to hurt you, truly I didn't! We're a peaceful people..."

"You have a strange way of showing it," Chari said.

"It wasn't my intention to harm you. But *he* arrived...and he demanded that I kill you...all of you."

"*Who* arrived?" Janir demanded.

"A sorcerer...as powerful as he was brutal. His name—his name was Zhayron."

Every time he heard that name, Janir felt his stomach seize up in dread. He eyed Rushtaan warily. "Go on."

"He came here several days ago. He knew you'd be coming this way. He demanded that I find you, lure you here and...dispose of you."

"What exactly did he say?"

"He described you to me, all of you. He made it clear that I had to kill you. At first, I refused, of course. The Sulyahn are a peaceful people. We have no desire to harm others. I told him this. He became enraged! He threatened to destroy my kingdom and kill every man, woman, and child in Arnashen." A teardrop rolled down his face. "But in spite of my fear, I stood up to him. I challenged him! Who was he to appear in my kingdom and make such terrible threats? But as punishment for my impudence, he destroyed our neighboring kingdom, the kingdom of Ushtan, ruled by my own brother, Saljaht."

Rushtaan stared at the ground, his body shaking. "He showed me images of my dear brother's kingdom. It was in ruins...smoldering ruins! The houses and buildings, all burnt to the ground; not a soul left alive. All that now remains of Ushtan is dust! Dust and bones. The bones of my fellow Sulyahn, and my dear brother..."

Janir felt sickened. What Rushtaan described was genocide.

"I didn't want to harm you. But I had to save my people! I know the mountain spirits will never forgive me for agreeing to commit an act of murder but it was the price I had to pay for my people. I couldn't let Zhayron destroy my kingdom as he had my brother's." He paused. "But now I've doomed us all. He'll return and he'll punish us for my failure."

"No, Rushtaan, he won't. He won't get the chance. For I swear I will destroy him and end his tyranny."

"But he's much too powerful. Who could ever hope to defeat a sorcerer of such power?"

"Only the man who taught him everything he knows. I was his Master and only I can stop him." He offered his hand to Rushtaan. Initially hesitant, Rushtaan took hold of it and Janir helped him to his feet. "We're going to find the City of Lorden," Janir said. "There we expect to encounter Zhayron and his forces—and a battle will be fought. Come, Rushtaan. Come join us! Help us defeat him. Only then can you safeguard your people from his terror."

"But if we fail and he sees the Sulyahn standing against him in battle—"

"Cast aside your fears, Rushtaan. They are ill-befitting a king. You were right about one thing: the mountain spirits will frown upon your actions here tonight. Appease them, Rushtaan! Redeem yourself—join us. We need your help and we will not leave without it."

Rushtaan paused to consider this. "Very well. We'll join you on your mission to defeat the dark sorcerer. I only pray my people do not live to regret it."

"Pray all that you like, Rushtaan. Our cause is noble and righteous, but all the same, I'd feel happier knowing the gods are on our side."

The Sulyahn monarch nodded. Janir found it ironic how allegiances could shift with such swift unpredictability. Whereas moments ago the Sulyahn had been intent on murdering them as they slept, they now stood as allies, united in their quest to defeat Zhayron and safeguard the future of Alanar.

# CHAPTER TWENTY NINE

# Falling Deeper

*"David...listen to me..."*

*A voice echoed amid the darkness.*

*"David..."*

*As it repeated his name, the voice became louder and clearer; the only glimmer of light amid a void of nothingness.*

*Out of the dark appeared a girl he'd seen in his dreams so many times before. In her late teens, with striking blue eyes and brown hair falling to her shoulders, hers was a regal beauty matched by an almost tangible inner strength.*

*"Who are you?" David whispered.*

*"My name's Eladria. I've come a long way to help you."*

*"Help me? How?"*

*"All I can do now is warn you, David. You're in danger here— terrible danger. You have to leave. You have to resist him and ignore his lies—and leave now."*

*"But how? How do I leave?"*

*"Any way that you can. But you have to go, David. You have to!"*

*David reached out, but his hand moved through her. She seemed so real to him, but was ghostly and ephemeral.*

*Her warning reverberated through his mind as he felt the pull of consciousness drawing him back to the waking world.*

*"You have to leave, David, you have to leave now..."*

David opened his eyes and rolled over in the bed. Daylight filtered through the curtains, only barely illuminating his chamber. With a pang of alarm, he realized he wasn't alone. A figure in a dark robe stood several paces from his bed.

"Zhayron," he murmured, squinting in the dim light, still struggling to throw off the lagging heaviness of sleep.

"It's time to rise," Zhayron said.

David propped himself up on the bed. Thirsty, he reached to his bedside table and picked up the chalice of mutah nectar. He took a gulp of the sweet liquid. Almost immediately he felt it soothe his nerves as a feeling of warmth swept through his body, and with it a wave of pleasant forgetting. The dream, so fresh in his mind—the girl and her stark warning—dissipated like wisps of vapor.

"I was beginning to think you'd sleep all day," Zhayron said. "We have work to do."

"What kind of work?"

"As I said last night, I have consulted my Masters, the Lords of Abidalos. They've advised me how we can rescue your mother."

"What must we do?"

"There's only one way we can help her, David. We must create a gateway to the astral realm."

"A gateway?"

"Yes, and for that, we need the Key of Alanar."

David looked down at his amulet.

"The Key must first be made whole," Zhayron continued. "In its current state, it is useless to us. We must travel to the City of Lorden and find the other fragment of the crystal. Once the Key is whole, we can use it to access the astral realm, where your mother's life essence is trapped in its purgatory state. Only then can we bring her back to the mortal realm."

"We can really do this—?"

"It'll take much effort and a tremendous amount of power, but together I believe we can..."

A combination of drugs, dark magic and a rekindled sense of hope deafened David to the alarm bells ringing somewhere in his mind. The warning in his dream now forgotten, any last vestiges of resistance were falling away. What reason did he have to resist anyway? What Zhayron said made sense. Maybe this was why he'd been given the Key in the first place?

"So, David, are you willing to do this?"

"Of course."

"Good. The City of Lorden is hidden and shielded. Even the Watchers have been unable to trace it. But I believe, with the Key, you have the ability to locate it. Am I right?"

David had a distant memory of having used the Key before, as a compass leading him across foreign lands. He nodded, fairly certain that he'd be able to use it again.

"Excellent. I have an airship primed and ready to leave. All you need do is use the Key to determine our trajectory. Soon it'll be made whole—and with it, we'll have the power to change the destiny of an entire world."

"And save my mother and the others?"

"Yes, yes—of course. Now I suggest you get ready. We'll leave the moment you've dressed and eaten." As Zhayron made for the door, David could hear him mutter under his breath: "Finally the wait is over."

# CHAPTER THIRTY

# The Gatekeeper

They raced through the forest, scrambling over rocks and fallen logs—the Kellians in close pursuit. Janir knew that running was futile. No matter how fast they ran, the Kellians were bigger, stronger and significantly faster. Rounding a twist in the forest path, his heart sank upon seeing a dozen more Kellians ahead.

The animalistic warriors swung their maces and raised their machetes and axes as they closed in. They were after blood—and it appeared to be Chari's blood they were particularly interested in. "Traitor," they bellowed. "Death to the traitor!"

"If I surrender," Chari said, "they may spare the rest of you."

"No," Janir said. "We're in this together, Chari. You saved us from the Kellians and now it's our turn to repay the favor."

Janir turned to Castan and Dutshyana. With nowhere to run, their only option was to fight. The pair nodded, understanding his unspoken directive. Drawing their weapons, the warriors sprung into battle.

The Kellians hadn't anticipated such resistance. They momentarily hesitated as the Jinerans and Sulyahn charged at them. But their hesitation didn't last long. They retaliated and a full-scale battle commenced.

The Jinerans dizzied their opponents with their speed and agility. Leaping into the air, their golden armor glinting in the sunlight, it was with only minimal use of their swords and batons that they began to disarm and disable their attackers.

Although lacking the Jinerans' power and speed, Dutshyana and her Sulyahn warriors nevertheless fought valiantly as they engaged the Kellians. Armed with a hefty Sulyahn axe, Chari joined in the combat. Despite his understandable apprehension at having to fight his own people, he refused to hold back.

The battle was fierce and violent. Janir had never before seen the Kellians engaged in battle and it was a chilling sight. With thundering war cries, the gargantuan, rhino-skinned savages fought with every last ounce of their strength, laying into their opponents with terrifying ferocity. Although heavy and lumbering in their movements, their sheer strength gave them a decided advantage.

Janir, Darien, Janna and Mariane kept their distance from the fighting. Although armed with swords given them by Rushtaan before departing Arnashen, they had no training or combat experience—and not a chance of holding their own against a Kellian. Darien stood ready to defend them, however; his sword drawn.

Although still hesitant to use his powers, Janir knew he had to do something to sway the battle in their favor. Attuning his mind to the power of Infinity, he conjured a ball of lightning. As it took form in the palms of his outstretched hands, he projected the lightning ball at the Kellians. The blast knocked a dozen Kellians clear off the ground, their weapons flying as they collided with the forest floor.

Janir knew that would get their attention, but their response was even better than he'd anticipated. Although adept at armed combat, such wizardry was more than they could handle. They looked around in stunned confusion.

Janir took advantage of this and unleashed a barrage of lightning balls. Uncertain how to respond to this supernatural onslaught, their resolve deserted them and they retreated like spooked animals, shouting in alarm as they disappeared through the trees and up the mountainside.

"You did it, Janir," Darien cried. "They're gone!"

"For now," Chari cautioned, lowering his bloodied axe. "But they will be back, angered by this humiliation. And they will not soon forget about me."

"Why were they calling you a traitor?" Janna said. "We're so far from your tribe. Surely they had no way of knowing what happened back there?"

"Any Kellian seen to be consorting with so-called 'lesser races' is automatically deemed a traitor. The punishment for such treachery is death. As I said, they will return, eager for revenge. Kellians have an instinctive fear of the supernatural. Janir's powers may have stunned them, but they will not be so easily deterred a second time."

"With any luck, we'll be long gone from here by then," Janir said.

"I should hope so," Mariane said. "I'm telling you, my nerves can't take much more of this."

With a grim sigh, Janir looked over at the scene of the battle. Through the lingering screen of smoke, he saw a number of Kellian corpses strewn across the forest floor. By the look of it, the Jinerans had escaped with only minor injuries, but four of the Sulyahn had been knocked down, three of whom were dead.

Dutshyana and her warriors, many of whom had sustained injuries themselves, tended to the fourth casualty, whose leg had been slashed by a Kellian blade. The young man lay clutching his leg, groaning in agony. Janir knelt by his side. "Here, let me help."

Initially reticent, Dutshyana stepped back and urged her men to do likewise. Janir decided to use an ancient healing incantation. As the words streamed from his mouth, he pulled down a stream of healing energy and directed it into the wound. After a few moments, the man's face relaxed. "The pain...it's gone," he gasped. The torn skin had almost completely healed up.

"You'll be fine" Janir said, helping him slowly to his feet. All the young man could do was nod, staring at Janir with an expression of awe.

Dutshyana and her fellow Sulyahn began performing a death ritual over the bodies of their fallen. It was a poetic invocation to the mountain spirits to safeguard their departed souls. Janir and the others kept a respectful distance as the Sulyahn completed their ritual.

Although shaken by the ambush, the group wasted little time setting off. Pressing onward, they journeyed ever deeper into the valley. The sunlight flickered as it shone through the forest canopy. The valley was alive with sound: from the trickling of a nearby stream to the ever-present symphony of birdsong and the chattering and cooing of small arboreal creatures.

After a time they came to an obstruction in their path. A great golden wall stretched across the valley and all the way up the mountainside. Constructed of thick sandstone and the height of at least four grown men, the wall had clearly been here for a great many years, yet showed little sign of weathering or decay.

"Impressive construction," Chari remarked.

Dutshyana and the other Sulyahn appeared visibly reticent. She'd told them before that the Sulyahn never came this way, for there were accounts of their ancestors simply disappearing when venturing as far as the wall. The Jinerans, however, seemed unperturbed. Castan stepped forward. "Behold, the Golden Wall of Lasandria. All that now remains of the Lasandrian heartland."

"The Golden Wall," Janir exclaimed. "I can't believe it's still standing! According to the ancient legends, it encircled the entire Valley of Baltaz."

"Why would a valley need a wall?" Darien asked.

"This wasn't just any valley. At its heart stood the City of El Ad'dan, the capital of Lasandria."

"Along with another city," Castan said.

"The City of Lorden—?"

Castan nodded.

"I had no idea the two cities were in such close proximity..."

"Few people do. We Jinerans only know the secret of Lorden because we ourselves were here at the time of Lasandria. In ancient times, the two cities were connected. But as Lasandria fell into decline the link gradually severed, until one day the City of Lorden was said to have simply vanished."

"How does a city vanish?" Mariane wondered.

"We're soon to learn the secrets of Lorden." Janir ran his hand along the seamless brickwork. "We're so close now, I can feel it. But our immediate problem is getting past the wall."

"There's no way we can climb over it," Darien said. "It's too high and the bricks are too smooth."

"Then we have to go through it." Chari lifted his axe and took a swing at the wall. The impact of his blade sent sparks flying but failed to make so much as a dent in the brickwork. The Kellian grunted as he stepped back and lowered his weapon.

"There must be another way," Janir said. "Perhaps we could—"

A sudden flash of light drew his attention to the sky.

Streaks of gold light shimmered above them, coalescing to form a shape in midair. Janir was stunned to see a living creature take form before his eyes—a gigantic, four-legged reptilian with red scales, a long spiked tail and mighty outstretched wings. Now solid and tangible, the airborne creature hovered above them, letting out a roar that echoed across the valley.

It had them in its sights. With a twist of its body, it swooped down. Chari and the Sulyahn drew their weapons as the others retreated. Birds shot up from the surrounding trees, squawking as they darted to safety. The creature landed on the ground ahead of them with a resounding thump. Almost the height of the wall itself, the lizard-like creature lowered its long neck, its black eyes fixing them with a piercing stare. Its tail flicked from side to side; its dagger-like claws digging into the ground. It now stood between them and the wall—and it wasn't about to move.

Dutshyana turned to the others in amazement. "Is that what I think it is?"

"A dragon," Janir whispered.

"But that's impossible. Dragons are extinct."

"Well whatever this is, it's clearly far from extinct..."

To everyone's amazement, the dragon then spoke, in a voice that boomed like thunder. "Who disturbs the Gatekeeper from his slumber?"

Castan moved forward, lowering his head in prostration. "Please forgive us, noble one. We meant not to disturb you."

"Then why are you here?" the dragon bellowed.

"We seek entry to the Valley of Baltaz."

The dragon arched its neck and let out a snort of air. "Many have come seeking entry into the Valley of Baltaz. But as Gatekeeper of Lasandria, they must first get past me."

Janir now recalled the ancient legends from the Chronicle of Alanar. The Valley of Baltaz was said to have been protected not only by the Wall but by an enchanted creature known as the Gatekeeper. Yet that was thousands of years ago. Why was this dragon still guarding a kingdom that no longer existed?

He decided to appeal to the Gatekeeper. "Please, we mean no harm. Our mission is one of utmost importance. We must pass the Golden Wall and travel beyond to the City of Lorden. Great Gatekeeper, you must have witnessed firsthand the terrible carnage that occurred when Lasandria was destroyed all those years ago?"

"Never have I seen such devastation before or since."

"I can't even begin to imagine what that must have been like."

"I recall it as though it happened yesterday. This entire land was reduced to barren wasteland. Everything stripped of life. Aside from the mountains, all that remained standing was this Wall."

"How did it manage to withstand the cataclysm?"

"The Lasan who built the Wall enchanted it, as they did me. Nothing could destroy it. It was built to withstand the ravages of time and fate. Alas, in their oversight they neglected to enchant the very kingdom around which it was built."

"I have to tell you, Gatekeeper, that as terrible as that was, it will be nothing compared to what will happen if you do not let us pass. Dark forces seek to reopen the gateway that destroyed Lasandria. If they succeed our universe will be breached once again—and a force of unspeakable evil will stream forth. We're here to stop that from happening. So, please, you must help us. You must allow us to pass."

"So wearisome is my task. Lasandria has long gone, and along with it, my entire race. Yet my duty must continue. So I will say to you as I say to all who seek to enter the valley of Baltaz—present the password now, or leave."

"I know of no password..."

"Speak the words now."

Janir turned to Castan. As protectors of the realm, surely the Jinerans had been entrusted with the password to the valley. Castan shook his head. "The password was changed in the final days by King Dua-ron. My people were not among those entrusted with it."

"Tell me we've not come all this way for nothing," Darien sighed.

Janir looked up at the mighty dragon. "Gatekeeper, I implore you. Although we have no password, you must let us through!"

The dragon lowered its head. "If you do not have the password, then I present you with a second option. Offer your hearts to me for judgment. If I judge you and your comrades to be of pure heart and noble intent, you will pass through the wall and emerge safely on the other side. If, however, I sense darkness in your hearts, you will not be permitted entry. Your bodies will be trapped inside the wall and you will die."

Although hesitant to subject his comrades to such danger, Janir could see no other option.

"Know the risks," the dragon cautioned. "Only the worthy will be permitted entry to the valley. Over the centuries many have agreed to this test, desperate to seek whatever treasures might lie beyond the wall and, driven by their avarice and deceit, none have survived."

"I assure you it's not treasure that we seek. Our motives are pure and our quest is righteous."

"We shall see." The dragon stepped aside and a section of the wall began to shimmer and glow. The golden bricks melted into a swirling liquid light; a fluidic tunnel leading through to the other side. "Who will be first? Step forward now."

Janir turned to the others. "I'll understand if anyone doesn't want to go through with this."

"We've come this far," Darien said. "I don't think any of us has anything to hide..."

"All the same, if anyone would rather turn back and return to Arnashen I won't stop you."

Dutshyana strode forward. "We Sulyahn have nothing to fear. We are honorable warriors and gladly accept judgment." She motioned to her men to follow and without any trace of fear, marched through the shimmering aperture. Her tall, muscular form disappeared into the light and her warriors followed behind.

The Gatekeeper nodded its head as all twenty of the Sulyahn passed through the great wall. "Warrior hearts. Dutiful, brave and fearless," the dragon murmured, deep in concentration, somehow reaching into the hearts and minds of the Sulyahn. "Mistakes have been made and a dubious deal struck with the darkness. Yet I sense a willingness to atone for this and a determination to aid the planet in a time of crisis. I allow you to pass."

Janir let out a sigh of relief. If there was any lingering doubt as to whether the Sulyahn could be fully trusted, it had been nullified. Castan and his men now stood before the wall and the dragon beckoned them forward. As they stepped through the shimmering tunnel, the dragon passed its judgment. "Jinerans. Yes, I am familiar with your race. Long have you walked upon this world. I recognize only too well the burden carried by an immortal—the weight of having seen and experienced so much over time immeasurable—the silent sadness, the weariness, the subtle yearning for release." The dragon paused, his shining black eyes narrowing. "Your time upon this world grows short. But I sense your determination to fulfill your final mission and attain release. You may pass."

Darien insisted that he go next. Approaching the wall, he passed the towering dragon, glancing up nervously before taking a deep breath and plunging into the fluidic tunnel. "So much to prove," the Gatekeeper remarked of Darien. "A great need to be recognized, to be validated and loved. I sense unexpressed fear in your heart and gnawing self-doubt. But there is no malice; only loyalty, concern and a growing spark of self-sacrifice. I allow you to pass."

Janna was close behind Darien. She entered the wall and the Gatekeeper passed his verdict. "I sense great strength and power in you. Lifelong fear and denial of your own nature has obscured your light and diminished your strength. But the cloud lifts, and day by day, you blossom into a full expression of your true potential. I allow you to pass."

By the time the dragon finished speaking, Chari was already at the wall and ready to step through, clearly unafraid of the impending judgment. As his muscular form dissolved into the light, the dragon expressed some surprise. "Your people I have encountered before. Many times have they tried to pass this wall—first by attempting to attack and kill me, then by agreeing to undergo this test of their souls. In each case, I deemed them unfit to enter the hallowed Valley of Baltaz."

The dragon expelled a puff of steam. "Their hearts were violent, primitive and hateful—their minds dull, covetous and aggressive. Yet in you, I sense something quite different—a seed of hope for the future of your race. Though you still must repress the impulse to react with violence, your heart is noble and your mind is clear. You harbor regret and anger over your alienation from your people, which in time must be resolved...but I deem you worthy of entering the great valley. You may now pass."

Mariane glanced at Janir, a rueful expression on her face. "I'd really rather he kept his opinions to himself, but let's get this over with." Janir put a hand on her shoulder and smiled.

The proud matriarch marched forward and passed through the wall as the Gatekeeper cast his verdict. "Forthright and determined, willful and stubborn...yours is a heart filled with grief, yet tempered with strength and resilience. Beyond this burden of pain, there is no darkness in your heart. Pass now."

It was his Janir's turn. As he walked by the enchanted dragon, he looked up and, with a respectful nod, turned his attention to the glimmering tunnel ahead of him.

Funny that he should feel so nervous. Was there something in his heart that he didn't want the dragon to see—some hidden darkness that might cause the Gatekeeper to deem him unworthy?

He stepped into the wall, finding himself passing through a churning tunnel of light. He could sense the Gatekeeper reaching into his mind and heart; penetrating his psyche and sifting through its many layers.

Janir still held secrets that he couldn't bear the others to hear. He'd made mistakes in life and lapses of judgment that had caused unbelievable suffering. Part of his mind, a deeply rooted defense mechanism perhaps, tried to shield these from the Gatekeeper. But he found himself unable to resist the dragon's all-seeing gaze.

"You carry much pain and regret," the dragon's voice echoed. "Secrets and burdens you have spent years attempting to deny, repress and bury. You cannot hide them from me. A cloud of darkness covers your heart, a darkness you have tried so hard to ignore. You can run halfway across this world and still not escape the demons of the past."

His body suddenly felt weak and heavy, yet Janir resisted the urge to stop and kept walking. He found himself overcome by the fear that the Gatekeeper, having now seen into his naked soul, would declare him unworthy. If that was so, he would die here and now.

"You have made mistakes," the dragon continued, "yet are resolute in your determination to correct them. This is your time of atonement. Do not falter now. You were right, for I can see that your mission holds immense importance. This world needs you. I, Gatekeeper, allow you to pass. Go forth and enter the Valley of Baltaz. It is there you will fulfill your final destiny, sorcerer."

With another step, Janir exited the wall, his feet landing upon the solid forest floor. He exhaled deeply, his eyes stinging with held-back tears. The others stood a little ahead of him, having all made it safely through. Behind him the opening in the wall sealed; the swirling passageway again replaced by the solid brickwork of the ancient, otherwise impenetrable barrier. He uttered a silent word of thanks to the Gatekeeper.

"So," Darien said, "now it's established that we're all worthy, what now?"

"We move on," Castan said.

Ahead stretched several more miles of forestland. Blue-green mountains encircled the valley—including the majestic snow-capped peak of Mount Alsan. According to Lasandrian legends, it was from the foot of this great volcano that the City of El Ad'dan had sprawled across the valley.

Janir used his powers to scan ahead but could sense nothing but barren, earthy plains at the heart of the valley, scattered with rubble and ruins. El Ad'dan was long gone, but Castan was adamant that it was here they would find the other great city— the City of Lorden.

The Jinerans were quick to set off. Janir motioned for his comrades to follow. He found himself filled with both excitement and trepidation. After all this time, after all the distance they'd traveled and friends they'd lost, they were finally on the verge of their destination. Even so, he knew this was no time for celebration, for the real trial was about to begin.

# CHAPTER THIRTY ONE

# The City of Lorden

"Where are we going?"

"You'll see."

The elevator lurched into motion. Wearing similar clothing to David—a dark gray shirt, black trousers with boots and an overcoat—Zhayron cut a darkly imposing figure as he stood, arms folded, eyes fixed ahead.

The elevator stopped and they exited into an underground hangar. The expanse of concrete stretched for what looked like miles beneath the citadel, its curved ceiling dotted with rows of lights. Dozens of stationary aircraft lined a central runway. Built like black metallic birds of prey, the mere sight of them made David shudder. He was certain he'd seen them before somehow. The specifics eluded him, but he knew it hadn't been a pleasant experience. Why had his memory become so hazy? The past was slipping away from him like fragments of a barely remembered dream.

He tried to banish his feeling of unrest as Zhayron proceeded toward one of the hawklike airships. Technicians and engineers appeared to be preparing the craft for departure.

His sense of dread only increased upon seeing a stream of soldiers marching through the hangar toward the vehicle. Covered in thick-plated black armor, he could sense little humanity about them as they marched in rigid, mechanical fashion. The mere sight of them elicited a potent sense of terror. He'd seen them before somewhere—

"Is something wrong?" Zhayron said, sensing the boy's apprehension.

He motioned to the soldiers. "What are they?"

"Eloramian Troopers—foot soldiers of the Alliance."

"What are they doing here?"

"There's nothing to worry about, I assure you. The Alliance has provided the means by which we'll travel to Lorden. This is the airship Galzodian. It'll take us where we need to go."

"But why all the soldiers?"

"It's merely a precaution. Now, come."

David wasn't entirely convinced. Zhayron led him up a series of boarding steps, into the craft. Passing down a narrow corridor, they entered what was evidently its command center.

To the best of his admittedly poor recollection, he'd never seen such incredible technology. Filled with bleeping consoles and flashing lights, the circular two-tiered room was dominated by a raised platform upon which sat three control booths. The officers manning the craft were curious-looking, with long white hair, pale skin, clad in black and silver uniforms. Like Zhayron, most of them had black tattoos winding down one side of their faces.

"Commander Traylat, report," Zhayron called, climbing the steps to the main platform.

"Ready for immediate departure, sir." A man, somewhat older than the others, stood hunched over one of his men's terminals. "The last of the troops have boarded. Fueling and preparatory checks are complete. Technicians report green status."

"Then, let's make haste. The City of Lorden awaits."

An enormous window dominated the forward wall. David watched as a series of lights blinked on along the runway, revealing an inclined ramp ahead. The craft began to move.

"Initiating thrusters," Traylat called above the roar of the engines.

In moments a burst of acceleration propelled them across the runaway. Reaching out to grab hold of the nearest railing, David watched as the hangar sped by in a dizzying blur. The airship scaled the ramp, passing through a tunnel before emerging above ground, shooting into the air like an arrow.

David blinked in amazement. Seconds ago they'd been underneath the citadel and now they were airborne—gliding across the sky with the effortless ease of a bird. Beneath them the citadel stood tall, dwarfing the city encircling it. Both stood propped upon the edge of the ocean, the craggy headland stretching far into the distance.

"It's time, David," Zhayron said. "Use the Key to determine our trajectory."

Sensing Zhayron's impatience, David lifted the amulet from his neck. Holding it in the palm of his right hand, he vaguely recalled having used it as a compass before—but that seemed like a lifetime ago. Focusing on the semicircular crystal, he inwardly asked it to guide him to its missing half. Alive and responsive to his command, the crystal began glowing. One part of its circumference shone particularly brightly.

Zhayron smiled as he looked over David's shoulder. "Traylat, set course...thirty degrees east."

"Yes, sir."

David placed the Key back around his neck. He watched as the lands zipped by below—the various towns and villages of Sekyr, farmland and fields, expanses of forest and hills, and beyond that a long stretch of desert.

Zhayron paced the room restlessly. Every so often he ordered David to recheck their trajectory. David had noticed a change in his behavior. In the citadel, Zhayron had almost acted like an older brother to him. But now any warmth he'd shown had been replaced by an air of coldness and impatience. It almost seemed he was no longer interested in David at all—only in his ability to use the Key. "Check again," Zhayron commanded.

David complied. "We're still on the right course."

"Intriguing," Zhayron muttered. "We're headed straight for the heartland of the old Lasandrian empire..."

"What does that mean?"

Zhayron didn't answer. The fact he was now being ignored increased David's growing sense of alienation.

They were soon flying over a snow-capped mountain range; a maze of green valleys tucked beneath the majestic peaks. After a time, David noticed some kind of partition cutting through the land. It appeared to be a golden wall, stretching over an immense radius.

"Commander Traylat," called one of the female technicians. "There's an object ahead."

"Identify."

"A *flying* object of some kind," she responded, squinting her eyes as she studied her console. "I can't be more specific from these readings, but it appears to be *alive*...and it's coming straight for us."

Traylat marched over to her console to check the readings himself. Zhayron did likewise. "What is it, Traylat?"

"I'm not entirely sure." He called to one of his men on the mezzanine level, "Prepare weapons."

David stared out the window. He could see it now: some kind of huge, flying reptile. Dark red in color, it had a long neck and spiked tail, its powerful wings flapping as it shot toward them.

"A dragon?" said Traylat. "It can't be..."

"It is," Zhayron said, without a hint of surprise.

"Your orders, sir?"

"Destroy it."

"Weapons officer, target pulse cannon and open fire."

"But why?" David interjected. "It doesn't pose any threat to us. Why kill it?"

"Don't question me, David," Zhayron said. "I know what I'm doing."

David watched helplessly as the Galzodian opened fire; bombarding the creature with a round of electrical weapons fire. The dragon struggled as it resisted the assault, yet quite miraculously it appeared unharmed. As the weapons fire ceased, the dragon advanced, opening its mouth and releasing a stream of fire.

"Impossible," Traylat shouted. "Nothing should have survived that."

The dragon's entire body lit up with an intense golden light. Waves of the light shot toward the airship, causing it to lurch in the sky, almost knocking David and Zhayron to the ground.

"I should have known better," Zhayron growled. "We're dealing with no ordinary creature."

"What is it?" David asked.

"An obstacle," Zhayron said. "One that'll take a little more effort to deal with, but deal with it I shall..."

A sudden voice boomed through the command center: *"Present the password, offer your hearts for judgment, or leave here now! I, Gatekeeper of the valley, command it!"*

Zhayron's face was set in an expression of contemptuous resolve. "Command all you like, beast. I will not comply."

Another wave of golden light shot from the winged creature, causing the Galzodian to again lurch in the sky. "Cut the engines," Traylat barked.

"Enough of this," Zhayron said. "You may have the power of the ancients, beast, but so do I—and I assure you, I'm far stronger. You're but a sorry echo of an age long past. It's time to consign you to oblivion along with it."

Zhayron closed his eyes. David could sense the energy shift around him; an electrostatic charge that made the hairs on the back of his neck stand on end. Snapping his eyes open, Zhayron raised his hands aloft, his body now crackling with blue-white light. The energy collected into his outstretched hands as balls of lightning. Zhayron released the lightning energy. It shot outward, passing through the Galzodian and into the sky, where it slammed into the dragon. The dragon struggled to hold its own as Zhayron continued the offensive.

Traylat ordered his weapons officer to again open fire. The poor creature seemed unable to deal with the two-pronged attack. In spite of whatever supernatural force it possessed, Zhayron had the upper hand. The dragon struggled but eventually succumbed. A flash of gold light rippled across the sky as the creature combusted into a ball of flames. Seized by the force of gravity, the dragon's flaming form fell to the ground beneath.

David turned to Zhayron, filled with indignant fury. "Why did you do that?"

"It had to be done, David." As the energy around him dissipated, Zhayron's expression was cold and rigid. "That creature stood between us and our destination. It would not have let us past. You *do* want to save your mother, don't you?"

"Of course I do."

"Then you must trust me. Now, check the Key again. I believe our destination may be close at hand."

Still reeling from the creature's execution, David tried to set his feelings aside as he again asked the Key to point the way. This time the entire crystal glowed brilliantly, pulsing like a heartbeat. He'd never seen it do that before but he instinctively knew what it meant. "This is it," he announced. "We're here."

"You're certain?"

"Yes."

"Traylat, bring us to the center of the valley."

"You're sure this is the place?" Traylat asked. "According to the readouts, there's nothing here—nothing but some old ruins."

"The Key wouldn't lie. If it says the City of Lorden is here, then here it must be. Now take us forward—and notify the troops to prepare for immediate landing. I want a full legion to secure the valley."

"Secure *what?* I assure you, sir, there's no one down there."

"You're mistaken, Traylat. There *is* someone down there. I can sense him clearly now. We've not crossed paths for many years, but his presence is unmistakable..."

Although tired and hungry, the knowledge they were close to their destination lent Janir and his comrades a renewed vigor. It became clear, however, that time was not on their side. A mechanical drone punctured the quietude of the valley.

"Please tell me that's not what I think it is," Darien said.

"An Alliance warship," Janir confirmed.

They stopped, watching as the black airship passed over the treetops; the entire forest rumbling.

"How did they find this place?" Mariane gasped.

"David," Janir answered grimly. "David has led them here using the Key."

"Then he's aboard that ship?" Janna said.

"With Zhayron—?" Darien added.

"You can be sure of it," Janir nodded.

Darien shook his head. "I still can't believe David would willingly help Zhayron. The David I know would never—"

"But he's not the David you know—not anymore. His mind is no longer his own. Zhayron is a powerful sorcerer and you can bet he'll have David deep under his spell."

"If that's true," Janna said, "and he's now on Zhayron's side, that means he'll be fighting against us?"

All Janir could do was nod.

"What is your plan?" rumbled Chari.

"The plan is simple. We defeat Zhayron and break his hold over David."

"And if we cannot?"

Janir had tried not to think about such an eventually. "If that happens, then I'll have no choice...but to kill David."

"What?" Darien blurted.

He and the others stared at Janir, aghast.

"I can't let him use the Key to aid the enemy. If he unleashes the Narssians, then everything is over."

"You'd really kill him? You'd really kill David?"

"It'd be one life to save billions. But I pray it won't come to that. We'll do everything in our power to avoid it."

He turned to Castan and the Jinerans. Like their sovereign Elas, the mighty cat-like warriors now had a translucent quality to their bodies. He knew that their time on Alanar was finite. "Castan, how much farther to the City of Lorden?"

"We are very nearly there."

"Right, let's keep moving, people! We have to prevent Zhayron from reaching the City."

The Galzodian deposited its passengers and hovered above the valley. The Alliance troops, of which there were dozens, spread outward, securing the perimeter of the valley.

David and Zhayron marched across the plains toward the heart of the valley, the ground beneath their feet curiously barren. Nothing grew here: no trees, plants and barely any grass. David got the sense that something terrible had once happened here. They came to the remnants of some ancient ruins: charred ochre bricks and rubble scattered across the land, all but pounded to dust.

The sky was crimson and the suns bathed the land in a fiery glow as a hazy mist rolled in across the valley. Standing amid the ruins, David found himself overcome by vague, barely distinguishable fragments of memories, accompanied by a potent sense of loss and despair. What was it Zhayron had called this place—El Ad'dan...?

*El Ad'dan.*

Why did that name sound so familiar to him? He found himself unable to throw off an inexplicable sense of déjà vu. He didn't know how or why, but he was certain that he'd been here in some distant time. An image flashed through his mind of a grand city—the golden streets, temples, and domes glistening in the sunlight. It was so beautiful. Yet now it was all gone. Nothing remained of this wondrous city but rubble and charred ground. The loss of this place had somehow wounded the entire planet.

Zhayron came to a stop, his arms folded and brow furrowed. "This is *it?*"

David said nothing.

"There must be some mistake. Use the Key again."

David saw little point, but he placed the talisman in his hand and again asked it to point him toward the City of Lorden. "There's no doubt," he said as the Key pulsated in his hands. "According to the Key, this is it."

"But there's nothing here. I certainly see no City of Lorden, do you?"

"You said it yourself, the Key wouldn't lie. It's here somewhere. I can almost feel it."

"Good, then I suggest you *find* it."

David looked around helplessly. The City of Lorden had to be here and he was determined to find it—and not for Zhayron, but for himself. A sudden insight struck. What if the City of Lorden was here, but simply invisible? And what if he somehow had the power to reveal it? Acting on impulse he lifted the Key, inwardly commanding it to reveal the hidden city.

The crystal pulsated frenetically, becoming so hot he almost dropped it.

The air became charged and a gust of wind swept through the valley. A light drew his attention upward as the sky exploded in a brilliant flash of light. Initially forced to shield his eyes, the intensity subsided and David looked up to see waves of golden-white light streaming across the heavens. The energy danced and crackled as it illuminated the entire valley. An aperture formed to reveal something extraordinary—a gleaming city floating amid the clouds.

The light faded, and David stood transfixed by the magnificent sight. Built on a bed of crystalline rock, the city itself appeared to be constructed of crystal; its many towers, domes, and spires reflecting the crimson sky and shimmering with an ethereal radiance. A filament of light shot down from the city. Landing some way ahead of them, bridging sky and land, the thread of light widened to reveal a swirling golden tunnel; a portal to the city above.

"Finally!" Zhayron's anger of moments ago was supplanted by an ecstatic glee. "The City of Lorden—just as the ancient texts described. The key to power beyond mortal comprehension."

David stared at him.

"Well done, David. Now, come! Our enemies will be upon us at any moment. We must enter the City. It's time to reclaim the missing fragment of the Key. After all these millennia the Key of Alanar will be whole once more."

David again found himself questioning Zhayron's sincerity. This wasn't about him or about power. Although his memory was hazy, he knew this for sure—it was about saving his mother and the others whose souls were trapped in purgatory. That was why they were here and that was all that mattered.

Sensing David's reticence, the sorcerer forced a smile and stepped toward him. David backed off. The smile faded from Zhayron's face. He reached out and grabbed David's arm. David tried to break free. Zhayron placed his other hand upon his forehead and a wave of energy shot from his hand into David's head.

His mind and senses suddenly numb, David relinquished all struggle.

His doubts of only seconds ago now erased, he again accepted Zhayron as his sole authority—and he would willingly obey his every command.

Janir watched as the dreamlike City of Lorden appeared above the land. His heart sank upon realizing what this meant. Zhayron had done it. He'd found the city. Now was the moment of truth. They had to intercept him before he could get his hands on the other half of the Key.

They were finally at the edge of the forest. Ahead lay the heart of the valley, a barren plain stretching all the way to the foot of Mount Alsan. The magnificent city floated high above the land and not far from it the Alliance warship hovered stationary above the valley. Janir spotted Alliance Death Troops encircling the valley. The nearest were just beyond the forest.

They were vastly outnumbered. They'd need nothing less than a miracle to get past the Alliance. He turned to his comrades. "Darien, Janna, Mariane—you three stay here in the cover of the forest."

"Why?" protested Darien. "I can fight!"

"No, you can't. You have no fighting skills and no experience in battle. This is for real, Darien. Stay here with Janna and Mariane."

Darien's face fell but he knew better than to argue.

"The rest of you, arm yourselves. On my mark, we charge at the enemy. As I'm sure you know, the Death Troops are powerful, ruthless adversaries, but I have the utmost faith in your abilities. I'll help you as much as I can, but my priority is to reach Zhayron and David. Once I do, I'll have my own battle to fight."

As they readied themselves to fight, Mariane reached out and kissed Janir on the cheek. "Janir, please take care of yourself."

"You can do this, Janir," Darien said.

"I know the Guardians are with you," Janna added.

Janir mustered a smile. "Take care, my friends. Stay low and keep back from the fighting."

"We have company," Castan warned.

The nearest of the Death Troops had spotted them and were closing in. Janir took a deep breath. This was it. "Arm yourselves! We charge on three. One...two...three!"

Their fates uncertain yet their fortitude unwavering, Janir and his army charged at the robotic soldiers, weapons in hand, shouting with indignation—

"For Alanar!"

Zhayron and David made their way to the city portal, only to be stopped by one of the Alliance soldiers. The metallic trooper marched toward them and came to a stop, lowering his visor-plated head. "We are under attack, my Lord," he said, his voice a guttural, mechanical rasp.

Zhayron's eyes narrowed and his mouth tightened. Following his line of vision, David saw that the Alliance troops were indeed under attack. From this distance, he couldn't make out the attackers. Zhayron, however, clearly knew who was behind the assault. "*Janir...*"

David instantly recognized the name.

"Well, what are you waiting for, General?" Zhayron barked. "I want them dead—all of them."

With a nod, the General moved into action, tapping the side of his metal visor, sending a signal to his troops.

David turned to Zhayron. "Janir...I know him. But I can't remember how. Why can't I remember?"

"Because, David, some things are best forgotten."

"But who is he?"

"It doesn't matter. He'll be dead in moments. He may have gathered a pathetic little army, but there's no way he can stop us now. I assure you, this battle is already won. Now, come. The City of Lorden awaits."

# CHAPTER THIRTY TWO

# The Last Stand

Charging at the enemy with screams of fury, the Sulyahn released the first round of fire. A volley of flaming arrows sliced through the air, bouncing off the Death Troops' thick-plated armor with impunity. The soldiers advanced, raising their rifles and opening fire. The Sulyahn took the brunt of the fire; several falling to the ground, screaming in agony.

The Jinerans dodged the weapons fire and propelled themselves into the air, leaping at the mechanical soldiers. Their forms shimmering with silver radiance, the Jinerans fought with balletic grace, weaving in and out of the enemy lines, disarming and disabling the soldiers with deft strokes of their swords and batons.

As the Sulyahn fired another round of arrows, Chari lunged forward, knocking several soldiers down with the sheer might of his bulk. The instinctive violence of his people igniting his blood, the Kellian laid into the enemy, his axe striking against the metal armor of his adversaries.

The Death Troops continued firing their electro-pulse rifles, the energy blasts striking down their opponents and setting the nearby trees and ground alight. The Sulyahn were falling fast and by now some of the Jinerans had sustained injuries.

Having shielded himself with a protective incantation, Janir was impervious to the weapons fire. He gazed across the battlefield. At least half a dozen Sulyahn lay severely injured or dead. He knew that as long as the Death Troops had their energy weapons they had the upper hand.

Summoning the full force of his power, Janir directed it at the Death Troops with a simple intent. A stream of energy surged from his hands, engulfing the oncoming soldiers. Though the energy quickly dissipated, the Death Troops hesitated, uncertain what had happened. Taking advantage of their momentary indecision, the Jinerans and Sulyahn hit them hard. The Death Troops lifted their rifles, preparing to open fire. But this time nothing happened. They checked and re-checked their weapons, but—nothing. Their weapons were useless.

Janir smiled. He'd successfully evened the odds. But even without their rifles, the Death Troops were strong, powerful and hugely outnumbered them. The fight would be a brutal, bloody one, and victory by no means certain.

David and Zhayron observed the battle from across the valley. With Zhayron's attention elsewhere, his hold over David was slipping. David found himself confused and conflicted. Janir's name had brought back a flood of distant memories, blurry and indistinct, yet impossible to dismiss. Janir had been a friend to him; a mentor.

His trust in Zhayron had been shaken. He had a darkness and anger that caused David to question the sincerity of his motives. But how could he resist Zhayron when the mere touch of his hand could numb his mind and melt away all doubt and resistance? And there remained a relentless voice in his mind—Zhayron's voice—urging him to relinquish his doubts and trust Zhayron implicitly and without question.

"I don't know what he's done," Zhayron fumed, "but he's managed to disarm my men. They're discarding their weapons and engaging in hand-to-hand combat." Zhayron tapped a mechanical bracelet on his wrist, evidently a communication device, and opened a frequency to the Galzodian, which remained stationary above the valley. "Traylat. Lock target on those intruders and open fire."

"Affirmative," came a crackled response.

"It's time to end this."

David watched as the airship sent a round of missiles raining down upon the battlefield. The shells detonated on impact, tearing the ground apart, sending both turf and bodies flying. David strained to see through the rising cloud of smoke and dust. Could anyone have survived that?

* * *

Janir forced himself to his feet, spluttering as smoke filled his lungs. Though unharmed for the most part, that was more than could be said for many of his comrades. The dust began to settle and he saw a number of Jineran and Sulyahn warriors strewn across the battlefield, dead or gravely wounded. Fortunately, at least a dozen Death Troops had also been caught in the blast. At his foot lay one of their dismembered arms. A mass of wires and cabling spilled from the metallic limb, along with traces of blood and organic tissue.

The moment the shock of the bombardment wore off, the battle resumed. Largely unperturbed by the blast, the Death Troops fought relentlessly. Even without their weapons they remained formidable adversaries. Larger, sturdier and more powerful than their opponents—and having long since lost any last vestige of their humanity—the cyborg soldiers knew no fear.

But with seemingly limitless energy, the Jinerans flung themselves at the Death Troops, using their acrobatic skills to maximum effect; disorientating and dizzying the soldiers, before knocking them to the ground and finishing them off with their swords. Janir was relieved to see that Chari was also unharmed, for he rejoined the battle, using sheer brute force to his advantage, slamming the soldiers to the ground and hacking into them with his axe.

Janir held back from the fighting, assessing his next move. One of the wounded Sulyahn lay at his feet. The young man cried out in agony, as did some of the other wounded. Janir wanted to stop and help them but there was nothing he could do right now. He had to remain focused and plan his next move, or this would all end in defeat.

He found his attention drawn upward. The Alliance warship appeared to be powering up to release another round of missiles. He had to stop it—and fast.

A momentary doubt flashed through his mind. Was he powerful enough to disable an entire warship?

Reaching out to the universe, the electrified energy of Infinity again surged through his body, igniting in alchemical brilliance. Molding it with his intent, he released it and a wave of energy shot upward, blasting through the air and striking its target; the stationary black craft. He released another wave of energy and then another.

The warship initially seemed unaffected. But soon a series of explosions consumed its hull, tearing it apart from the inside out. Rocked by the explosions, the ship gradually disintegrated, burning up like a log consumed by fire. Janir watched as the craft was finally devoured by one last explosion. Erupting into a fireball, it plunged downward, colliding with the ground not far from the battlefield. The wreckage combusted, lighting up the valley in an orange blast, spewing out ash and debris.

Janir struggled to catch his breath. The effort had taken considerable energy. Back on the ground, the Death Troops were increasing in number as they closed in from across the valley. Undeterred by the loss of their warship, they marched forward, determined to vanquish their enemy. His comrades were struggling. The Sulyahn were falling fast and only a handful of Jinerans remained. How could they ever hope to defeat the Alliance? They had neither the manpower nor the strength.

Janir became aware of a commotion from behind. Turning, he was astonished to see—

Kellians!

Dozens of the rhino-skinned warriors were charging onto the battlefield, armed with axes, crossbows, and knives, howling war cries as they advanced.

The Kellians must have followed them through the valley, silently stalking them the whole way. He didn't know how they'd managed to get past the Gatekeeper, but they were here, no doubt looking for revenge following their earlier defeat.

Janir stood ready to defend himself as the Kellians stormed onto the battlefield. But to his surprise, they charged straight past him. It was then he realized that the one thing the Kellians despised above all else was the Alliance. The Alliance had destroyed countless Kellian homelands and exterminated entire tribes. Their initial plan may have been to take revenge on Janir and his comrades but upon catching sight of the Alliance, they now had a new, better target.

"Death to the Alliance!" the Kellians roared as they plunged into battle, giving Chari, the Jinerans and Sulyahn some much-needed backup. Who would have thought the Kellians would come to their aid?

Not far behind, Janna, Darien, and Mariane approached the battlefield, swords drawn, eyes blazing with indignation.

"What are you doing here?" Janir called. "I told you to stay back!"

"No," Darien said. "We're part of this war, Janir, and we'll fight. You clearly need all the help you can get."

"No, I don't want you getting hurt."

"Let us worry about that," Janna said. She stood before him, sword raised, her face lit with determination and passion. Janir saw that she had finally tapped into the inner fire he always knew she possessed. She was a changed person. They all were.

"Very well," he conceded. His eyes fell upon Mariane. She was so much older than the others and had probably never even held a sword before, much less used one. This was no place for her. "Mariane, I think—"

She stopped him short. "We're all risking our lives today, Janir. And we're doing it for something greater than ourselves. Besides, none of us will live forever and maybe it's better to die for something worthwhile than to live a life crippled by pain and regret."

Janir nodded. They'd made their decision. "Take care, all of you," he said, "and stay behind the—"

An Alliance soldier had broken through the lines and was about to pounce on Darien from behind. "Darien, look out!"

Darien span round but had no time to react. Instead, it was Janna that came to his aid. She thrust her sword at the attacking soldier. The cyborg deflected it with its arm, sending it flying and knocking Janna to the ground.

But the distraction gave Janir just enough time to summon his powers. He conjured a lightning ball and threw it at the sol-

dier. The Death Troop staggered back, its entire body electrified. The soldier slumped to the ground, a cloud of smoke rising
from its motionless body.

Breathless and stunned, Darien reached out to Janna.
Helping her from the ground, he held her tight, kissing her
cheek. "Janna, I love you!"

She smiled, her eyes twinkling.

"Perhaps we could save this for a more appropriate time,"
Mariane said with a roll of her eyes.

"With the Kellians on our side we have an opportunity,"
Janir said. "Now the Death Troops are fully occupied, I'm going
to take this chance to slip past and get to Zhayron and David.
That's where my battle will be fought. All of you: watch your
backs and look out for each other. Take care—and stay alive!"

"And you," Darien said.

"I'll do my best." Drawing his sword, Janir placed an invis-
ibility screen around himself. Vanishing from sight, he slipped
past the fighting, knowing only too well that the real ordeal lay
ahead of him.


Zhayron was incensed by the destruction of the Galzodian and
the arrival of the Kellians. David stood back, keen to avoid the
brunt of his fury. Zhayron turned to him, his eyes filled with
rage. "They won't stop us, David. We've waited too long for
this. Victory's just within our grasp. Come, let's proceed to the
city."

Zhayron clearly sensed the boy's reticence, for he grabbed
David's arm and pulled him toward the gleaming portal leading
up to the city in the sky. Just before they could step through it,
a voice halted them.

"Stop! You will never enter the City of Lorden as long as I
draw breath!"

Even before David turned, he knew who'd spoken those
words. It was Janir. Although the memories were still blurry,
the mist obscuring his past began to lift the moment he laid eyes
on his old mentor.

The last time Janir had seen Zhayron was over ten years ago and it had been in the heat of battle. He found the agony of that tragic day instantly rekindled upon setting eyes on his former protégé—the man who'd so cruelly betrayed him; who'd renounced everything he'd been taught—and who had murdered his beloved wife.

Zhayron had changed over the years. With a slender, spidery frame, his face was narrow and his skin pale. Janir barely recognized his eyes, for they were cold and deadened yet burning with rage and hatred. An elaborate black tattoo snaked down one side of his face and neck; inscriptions in ancient Eloramian, the language of the Alliance hierarchy. It pained Janir to see him like this—the boy he'd known so many years ago, now a man filled with hate and twisted by the darkness.

"Janir," Zhayron growled.

Janir steadied himself. He knew he had to set aside his personal feelings. "You may have got this far, Zhayron," he said, his voice filled with determination. "But I promise you, you will go no further."

Janir turned to David and saw that he too looked different. Like Zhayron he was dressed in black with a leather overcoat and boots, his hair tied back and his complexion pale. Janir could see that his mind was still ensnared in a net of Zhayron's making. He had to get through to him and break Zhayron's spell. "David, I don't know what Zhayron's said to you, but you must not trust him. He doesn't care about you. He has his own agenda and he'd be willing to say or do anything in order to get you to help him."

"He's lying, David," Zhayron said. "And listen to you speak of agendas, Janir. We all have our agendas. And contrary to what you might tell yourself, you and I both seek the same thing. We are sorcerers. We seek *power*—the power of life and the power of death."

"You know nothing of me."

"Don't bother denying it, old man. It's always about power. We live in a universe abundant with power. You yourself taught me that! It's everywhere, hidden in every moment, just waiting to be tapped; to be utilized and bent to the will of the sorcerer."

"I see you've been selective in your recollection of my teaching. Perhaps you no longer recall the first rule of sorcery? Power is of no use unless one's intent is tempered by wisdom and right action."

Zhayron's lip curled. "Don't try to impose your self-righteousness onto something that's beyond such meaningless dogma. Power is power!"

Sword in hand, Janir stepped forward, eyes fixed upon his former apprentice. "Tell me. What happened to you, Zhayron? What happened to the harmless young boy I remember? When did he become a monster capable of committing murder and genocide—and willing to destroy an entire world? Where did it all go so wrong? Where did I go wrong?"

"Don't underestimate yourself, Janir. You were an exemplary teacher. Everything that I am now, I owe to you."

"That's what pains me most. The power—you weren't ready for it. I should have seen that. It overwhelmed and intoxicated you, leaving behind an unbearable, unquenchable thirst. An addiction..."

Zhayron maintained his steely gaze, his eyes searing with hatred.

Janir continued moving toward him. "And somewhere, somewhere along the way you lost all sense of right and wrong. Morality was conveniently discarded. All so you could satisfy your lust for power and prestige. How could I have been so blind? How could I not have seen it? Alas, it was my greatest failing in this life. I should never have accepted you as my apprentice."

"Yet you did, for which I'm eternally grateful. But you're no longer my Master. I now serve the Lords of Abidalos. They offered me far more than you or your precious Guardians ever could."

"What could they possibly have offered you? The Shadow Lords and Narssians are parasites—they live only to destroy and consume. When they tear down the dimensional barriers and come exploding into this universe, they'll devour everything in their path. What do you suppose will remain once they're done with this realm?"

"You don't understand. I hear their song, old man. It plays in my ears endlessly, echoing through my mind, and it's beautiful! So beautiful. This is their time—it's coming. It has to!"

"They've infected your mind, Zhayron. They're using you! You and the Alliance are nothing but puppets to them! When the Narssians start stripping this world apart, you'll be among the first to die."

"Oh, I fear not death, for I'll achieved the ultimate power. I'll be one with Death itself!" He paused, his eyes narrowing. "But you'll never understand, Janir. Spoon-fed only what the Guardians wanted you to hear. This discussion serves no purpose! As touching as it's been, this little reunion is now over."

Zhayron raised his arms, his outstretched hands crackling with electrical charge. With a malevolent glint in his eye, he discharged the energy, projecting it straight at Janir.

Caught off guard, Janir had little time to defend himself. The lightning struck his torso, knocking him to the ground. Electricity surged through his body and he cried out in pain. Though the energy faded, he remained slumped on the ground, breathless and weakened.

Zhayron closed in and unleashed another blast of electricity, and then another.

Struggling to ignore the pain, Janir constructed a forcefield to deflect the assault. The balls of lightning bounced off the invisible shield, fizzling out into the air. Now protected, he forced himself to stand up, reaching down to pick up his fallen sword.

Zhayron had clearly grown in strength. That was only natural, for he'd had ten years in which to develop his powers. Janir, on the other hand, had renounced his and spent the last decade trying to forget he'd ever possessed them. As a result, his connection to Infinity was tenuous and his skills rusty. He knew he had little hope of defeating Zhayron this time. But perhaps he didn't have to. Perhaps all he needed to do was distract him...

David stood back from the dueling sorcerers. Janir and Zhayron stood facing each other, eyes locked, neither moving. They were both calculating their next move and summoning the power with which to defeat the other. The very atmosphere seemed electrified. Storm clouds rolled in across the sky, darkening the valley.

He didn't know who to trust anymore. Janir had used and betrayed him, all so he could harness the power of the Key for himself—or so he recalled Zhayron telling him. As for Zhayron, he'd promised to help David rescue his mother from her astral purgatory and bring her back. David wanted to trust him, for he'd promised so much. Yet why was he filled with so much doubt? The doubt hurt; it physically hurt. Each time he questioned Zhayron he could feel a tight, constricting pain in his head, and the voice in his mind cried for him to—

*Trust Zhayron. He's your ally. Trust him.*

As a fork of lightning streaked across the sky, accompanied by a roar of thunder, the battle recommenced. Zhayron shot a bolt of electricity at Janir, who deflected the blow with a sweep of his hand. Angered, Zhayron targeted him with another blast of energy, and then another.

Struggling to deflect all that was being thrown at him, Janir had little opportunity to retaliate. When he did, he raised his hand aloft, reaching up to the storm in the heavens. David watched in astonishment as Janir brought the lightning down from the sky and channeled it through his own body, lifting his sword and pointing it at Zhayron. The lightning blasted from the tip of the sword, crackling through the air and shooting into Zhayron's chest. Zhayron yelled as the electricity surged through his body and knocked him back several paces. But in spite of the impact, he remained on his feet.

Out of nowhere, a group of men and women suddenly appeared by Zhayron's side. Pale-skinned with long black hair falling over their shoulders, they were coated in black armor, wielding swords and maces. David immediately recognized them as the shadow people—the mysterious, ghostlike figures he'd seen so many times in the palace. Zhayron had seemingly conjured them out of thin air. The wraithlike figures swarmed around Janir, weapons raised. Janir for his part seemed unconcerned and, with a wave of his sword, he destroyed the shadowy figures; each of them dispersing into the air like ash.

This was a mere distraction, however, allowing Zhayron time to unleash the full force of his might. Lightning-like sparks of energy surged across his chest and torso, collecting in his outstretched hands as spinning vortices of light. His face twisting in a smile of malice, he unleashed the energy.

Janir's protective shield had worn off and the impact sent him flying. He fell back, the sword slipping from his hand. He landed on the ground with a thud.

Zhayron's entire form still crackled with light. He marched forward and unleashed a web of energy that ensnared Janir, pinning him to the ground. Janir struggled to escape but was caught like a fly in a spider's web, immobilized and helpless.

Zhayron let out a satisfied laugh. He released a pulse of energy that wound around Janir's body like a coiled snake, constricting and suffocating him.

David looked on helplessly. He didn't want to see Janir harmed. But what could he do? He couldn't go against Zhayron. He couldn't!

"Look at the mighty Janir," Zhayron jeered. "If only the people of Taribor—the people who so revered you—could see you now. But don't feel bad, old man. For there always must come a time when a son eclipses his father—and that time is now."

What...? Janir was Zhayron's father?

"You're no son of mine," Janir rasped as he struggled to drawn breath. "My son died a long time ago. He died the day he gave into the darkness!"

"No, old man," Zhayron hissed. "Your son died the day you turned against him—the day you tried to drive him from his homeland. That was the day he died, and it was *you* that killed him."

"It was you that turned against me, Zhayron; against everything I ever taught you..."

"I offered you the chance to join me. Together we could have ushered in a new era for our people. We could have made our land strong again; a beacon of light across the whole of Alanar. It would have been glorious!"

"It would have been tyranny. You know you'd never have been content to share power. You'd have destroyed everything that was good and noble about our land. I didn't want to harm my own son, but I had to stop you. You left me no choice, Zhayron. I couldn't stand by and allow you to conquer and subjugate our people..."

"Don't try to justify your betrayal."

"It was you that betrayed me, and the sacred powers with which you'd been bestowed."

Zhayron towered over his father, his body still blazing with sparks of blue-white light. "I wanted only to use my gift to its full potential. I was your son and you should have stood by me. And for that treachery I had to punish you...by destroying that which you held most dear."

"By killing her? By killing your own mother? Nothing can ever justify that!"

"The old Zhayron died; killed by an act of betrayal by his own father. In order to emerge unhindered by the shadows of a dead past, I had to cut myself free of all ties. First it was her—and now there remains but one link to my past..."

Suspended in the energy web, Janir was helpless, gasping for breath and unable to move. Zhayron was about to unleash another round of assault that would surely finish him off.

David couldn't let that happen. Ignoring the stabbing pain in his head and the raging screams of his inner voice, he bounded forward to intervene. "Don't kill him!"

"Stay out of this, boy," Zhayron growled. He turned his attention back to Janir and was about to deal his mortal blow when David reached out to stop him.

Zhayron reacted swiftly. With a swipe of his arm, he sent David flying to the ground. David struggled back up, determined to fight him hand-to-hand if necessary. Zhayron didn't give him the chance. The sorcerer unleashed a lightning bolt that slammed into David's chest. The impact sent him crashing back to the ground. Overcome by pain, he convulsed in agony as the electrical charge blasted through every cell of his body.

Moments later he was dimly aware of Janir having taken advantage of Zhayron's distraction to break free of the energy web. Once freed, Janir struck out at Zhayron with all the force he could muster and the cataclysmic battle resumed. Maybe he'd succeeded in helping him, after all.

David struggled to stay conscious but found his mind slipping into a semi-conscious state of delirium.

Part of him was still aware of what was going on around him. The devastating battle between Zhayron and Janir continued. High above, thunder and lightning ignited the heavens. Rain began falling; the drops stinging his skin as he lay upon the ground.

David could see how wrong he'd been to trust Zhayron. Zhayron had never intended to help him. He'd been lying to him all along; twisting his mind and corrupting his soul.

At least with Zhayron's attention fixed on Janir, the spell had lifted. As David lay paralyzed, he felt an anger of such intensity that it nearly eclipsed the pain searing through every nerve of his body. He was angry at Zhayron for having deluded and manipulated him so perfectly, and angry at himself for having been so blind as to let him.

But he knew that regret was futile now. Perhaps it was all futile. Was there really any hope of defeating a sorcerer as powerful as Zhayron?

Despite his best efforts to stay awake, David's eyes closed, consciousness slipped away, and darkness consumed him.

# CHAPTER THIRTY THREE

# Redemption

*David found himself back in the place he'd dreamt of so many times before. Why did his mind keep pulling him back here, to this bleak underworld of emptiness? Alone in the darkened cavern, he could sense some dark force searching for him amid the endless tunnels. It was only a matter of time before it caught up with him.*

*"What is this place?"*

*He didn't expect an answer, which made it all the more surprising when one came—*

*"It's you."*

*A teenage girl appeared before him. He'd seen her many times now, always in the twilight of his dreams. With shining, fierce blue eyes and locks of shoulder-length dark hair, she had the toughness of a warrior and the refinement of nobility.*

*"Eladria," he whispered, recalling the girl's name. "What are you doing here?"*

*"I've come a long way to find you, David. I'm here to remind you."*

*"Remind me of what?"*

*"Of who you are and what you must do." She gestured around the cavern. "This place is a reflection of your psyche; your mind and heart. It's dark right now because you're afraid—and you should be, because there's someone here—someone who's not meant to be here."*

*They could hear the enemy approach. "He's on his way now," she said. "You have to break free of the darkness and there's only one way to do that."*

*"You don't understand," he said. "I failed. I turned my back on Janir and let myself be deceived by Zhayron. There's no hope left, and no way I can possibly make things right..."*

"Listen, David. My entire world was lost because of me. I know what it's like to fail. But you can't afford to give up now. Yes, he broke you; he distorted your mind and used it against you. The spell has lifted now and you can see things for what they are. But he's still in your head, trying to regain control of you—and you can't let him."

"Do I really have the power to stop him?"

"Yes, you do. You're more powerful than you can possibly imagine. You have to give up this self-doubt and believe in yourself..."

The enemy drew closer. "This world needs you," Eladria continued, "in ways you can't even begin to imagine. You have no idea how important you are: how far you've come, and how far you will go. You're here for a reason, David. You have a destiny to fulfill and you have to see it through. In spite of all that's happened; all that you've done and all that's been done to you, you still have something to offer this world—something they want and are determined to take from you. You have a power—a power that will determine the fate of not only this world but everything beyond it. This is the moment, David. The moment that decides everything."

David's pursuers emerged from the shadows. Gargoyle-like creatures staggered toward him like animated corpses, their features gnarled and distorted; half-formed, burned, puss-covered and melting. They closed in on him, reaching out to him with clawed hands, howling, groaning and shouting. David backed off in horror. Eladria was gone, having vanished the moment the shadow creatures appeared.

Knowing he had no option but to run, David sped through the cavern, stumbling over rocks as he raced onward.

But as before he came to a gaping chasm blocking the path ahead. With no way around it and no way to cross, he was forced to stop. Within seconds, his pursuers caught up with him. They reached out and grabbed him with long, their nails clawing into his skin.

As they restrained him, Zhayron emerged from the darkness.

"There's no escaping, David." Zhayron's voice was but a low rumble. "Stop resisting me. I'm stronger than you and we both know it. Your soul belongs to me."

"No!" Fire ignited David's soul. "You're wrong. You tried to steal my life from me, you tried to mold me into the perfect puppet; and for a time, I let you. But it's over, Zhayron. This is my mind and I'm taking it back."

"Really? Just what are you going to do? Look around you. There's nowhere to run; nowhere to go. There's nothing here but oblivion. You have two options. You can either embrace me—or you can die."

With a sudden burst of energy, David broke free of the shadow creatures. He caught sight of Eladria standing on the other side of the chasm. In that moment he knew what he had to do.

He looked into Zhayron's cold, heartless eyes. This was the man that had raped his mind and tried to steal very his soul from him. "I'm not playing by your rules any longer." David slammed his fist across Zhayron's face, causing the sorcerer to stagger back into the shadows. The shadow men attempted to grab hold of him, but he was no longer afraid. They weren't real. They were just projections of Zhayron's mind.

David began running. Only this time he wasn't running away from his demons. This time he was running toward his destiny.

The time had come to take his fate back into his own hands. He'd given up so many times before, stopping in his tracks and letting the enemy catch him. But not this time.

His mind single-pointedly fixed on freedom, he ran ahead—and as he came to the mouth of the chasm, he leapt.

He knew that if he didn't reach the other side he'd fall and most certainly die. But even death no longer scared him. Alive or dead, his destiny was his own. Whatever happened now, he was finally free of his tormentor.

An indomitable sense of empowerment flooded his being. With this newfound power and determination, he successfully crossed the chasm, his feet landing firmly on the other side.

Eladria stood before him, smiling.

He had done it! He had crossed the abyss. His enemies could no longer reach him. He was finally free.

David opened his eyes. He lay in a puddle of water. His senses were unfocused and his entire body throbbing with pain. The rain continued streaming down as lightning blasted across the heavens.

How easy it would have been to simply roll over and concede defeat. But he wasn't going to take the easy option. He was alive and determined to fight until the end. Through gritted teeth, he forced himself up from the ground.

Zhayron had again overpowered Janir, who hung suspended in mid-air. David was shocked to see how old and weak he looked. Zhayron had somehow drained his very life-force, robbing him of his strength and vitality. He looked frail and helpless, gasping for breath as blood trickled from his eyes, nose, and mouth.

Zhayron laughed as he taunted his victim. "What a pitiful sight! Look at the brave and noble Janir now..." His entire form irradiated with crackling light, Zhayron was moving in for the kill.

David caught sight of Janir's sword lying in a puddle. He picked up the blade and edged forward. Zhayron's back was turned to him, the entire focus of his attention upon Janir. "Let him go!" David shouted.

Zhayron turned. With his focus now broken, Janir fell to the ground. His eyes blazing with fury, Zhayron fired a bolt of energy that struck David's torso, causing him to stagger backward and yell with pain.

"Don't make me kill you," Zhayron growled.

"You wouldn't dare," David shouted, doing his best to bear the pain as the electricity surged through his body. "You need me!"

"There comes a time when everyone outlives their usefulness. Simply ask Janir..."

David braced himself for another assault, knowing that Zhayron could kill him in an instant. But just as Zhayron was about to strike, the dark sorcerer staggered and fell, hit from behind by a fork of blue lightning. It was Janir. From where he lay, Janir unleashed another bolt of energy that engulfed his son's body.

It wasn't enough to stop him, however. Zhayron got to his feet and turned his attention back to Janir. Raising his hands, the energy pulsated furiously as he prepared to deal a mortal blow.

Before he had the chance to strike, David leapt forward and plunged the sword into Zhayron's chest. A current of electricity passed from Zhayron's body through the blade into David. David cried out but refused to let go of the sword.

Howling in agony, Zhayron tried to dislodge the blade.

David pulled the weapon from Zhayron's body. In a state of shock and rapidly losing blood, Zhayron fell to his knees, the energy around him evaporating like mist.

David stood over the fallen sorcerer. He had a look of bewilderment on his face. Clearly, he hadn't expected David to pose any threat to him; an act of underestimation that would now cost him his life. For David knew that he couldn't let Zhayron live. He had to die.

David steeled himself to strike once more. Lifting the blade high in the air, he swung it toward Zhayron's neck. The sword swished through the air, decapitating Zhayron in one swift move.

Zhayron's head dropped to the ground and his body, jerking in uncontrollable spasms, slumped down. Within moments all movement ceased and the corpse lay upon the rain and blood-soaked ground, limp and lifeless.

David dropped the sword and stared down, nauseated by the grisly sight. He'd never taken a life before. As he withdrew in alarm, he only half-noticed that the thunderstorm had ceased. Although the battle between the Alliance Troops and Janir's allies continued toward the edge of the valley, a strange quietude spread over the ruins of El Ad'dan. The storm clouds parted to reveal a chink of sunlight in the sky.

David turned his attention to Janir, gripped by a feeling of dread. He stumbled over to his fallen mentor and knelt by his side, feeling for a pulse. He was alive, but only just. "Janir, can you hear me?"

Janir nodded his head ever so slightly.

"He's gone, Janir. It's over now. It's all over..."

"Over..." Janir murmured.

"Janir, I'm so sorry. I can't believe I let Zhayron fool me like that. I can't believe I ever trusted him...that I ever doubted you."

"We all make mistakes." Janir's voice was hoarse and weak. "Zhayron was not only yours but mine as well. When it really mattered, you emerged triumphant...you made things right."

"Zhayron said that my mother's soul was in torment. He showed me her in some kind of purgatory, in terrible suffering. How do I help her, Janir?"

"He lied to you, David. He took your grief and used it against you." Janir paused, his every word clearly a struggle. "Believe me when I tell you: your mother may be gone, but her zhian lives on. And when I leave here myself, when I cross the great void, I promise I'll find her and ensure that her soul is safeguarded."

David's eyes moistened with tears. "What can I do to help you?"

"I'm beyond help, David. There's only one thing I ask you to do for me..."

"What? I'll do anything."

"Let go of all grief and blame. As we've both learned such things only serve to undo us. Let it all go, and be strong."

David nodded.

"It's time," Janir said with a cough. "Time for you to go..."

"Go where?"

With some effort, Janir pointed to the sky. The City of Lorden was again visible above them, its ethereal light shining through the storm clouds. Extending down from the city, the thread of light connecting it to the land terminated a little way ahead of them.

"That can wait," David said. "I have to take care of you first."

"No, you must go now..."

"I can't just leave you."

"You must. Zhayron may be gone but there are still Alliance Troops here. The moment they see what's happened, they'll try to stop you. So, go! You have to make the Key of Alanar whole. Only then can you save this world and defeat the enemy. Don't worry about me. My time in this realm is at an end. I can feel it. I accept it, and so must you..."

"There's so much I want to say, Janir. I just—I don't have the words..."

"Then say nothing...and go."

David wanted to argue but the words drowned in his throat. He knew that Janir was right. It was time to enter the city. He could somehow feel it calling to him. This had been the object of their quest all along—and he'd finally made it, albeit at immense cost. He knew his friends were out there caught in the battle, and he wanted to help them. But the only real way to do that was to fulfill his mission.

He knelt down and kissed his mentor's forehead. Overcome by a storm of emotion—grief, sorrow, guilt and remorse—he tried to do as Janir said and set these feelings aside. He would not let them consume him. He'd made that mistake before and it had nearly destroyed him.

By the time David was on his feet, Janir's eyes were closed. He lay unmoving yet still struggling for breath. David bowed his head, feeling a teardrop trickle down his cheek. "Goodbye, Janir."

He turned and made for the city portal.

Leaving Janir to die alone was one of the hardest things he had ever done. But he knew there was no other option. Janir had sacrificed himself to free him from Zhayron, and David vowed his sacrifice would not be in vain.

Lying on the ground, choking back tears, Janir grieved for Zhayron. Not for the monster that he'd become, but for the son he'd once known—the little boy he'd loved, cared for and tucked into bed every night. That seemed like a lifetime ago. That it had come to this, that they had fought so brutally to kill each other, pained him more than any of his broken bones. But it was over now.

He watched through misty eyes as David made his way to the City of Lorden. He was now free to save Alanar. Janir had done his part, and as the life drained from his body, he felt content in that knowledge.

David stood before the portal. After a lingering backward glance, the boy stepped forward and disappeared into the whirlpool of light.

That was the last sight Janir's physical eyes were ever to behold.

His consciousness drew inward and lifted from his body. With a sense of breaking away, like a seedling bursting through the soil, he felt himself exit the shell of his physical form.

Unbound and free, his consciousness seemed to rise higher and higher. He was aware of his body lying in the mud like a disused garment.

From this increasingly higher vantage point, he could see from the scattered ruins of El Ad'dan to the edge of the valley, where the battle had now ended.

Although the Kellians had retreated in the face of heavy losses, the last of the Death Troops had been defeated. The odds had been heavily against them, but the allies were victorious. He was relieved that his friends—Darien, Janna, Mariane, and Chari—were alive and largely unharmed. The protective incantation he'd placed around them had obviously held.

Many of the Sulyahn had died in combat. The remaining Jinerans were triumphant and content that their mission upon this realm had finally ended. Now free to leave, they vanished in a glorious flash of light, ascending to the higher realms to join their sovereign. After millennia of service, the last of their kind had now departed Alanar.

Janir watched as his friends stumbled across his lifeless body. He could sense their despair and grief. He wished he could reach out and assure them that he was still here in some way.

For this wasn't the end. One part of his existence had ended, but a whole new chapter opened before him. A new beginning—one filled with infinite potential.

Drawn to a brilliant expanse of white light, he felt himself merging back into the welcoming embrace of Infinity. His destination was, as it always had been...

Home.

# PART THREE

# GATEWAY

*"You have a power: a power that will determine the fate of not only this world, but everything beyond it. This is the moment, David. The moment that decides everything."*

# CHAPTER THIRTY FOUR

# Unity

Stepping through the portal, David found himself in an unearthly realm; expansive, dreamlike and strangely fluidic.

The panorama greeting his still-tearful eyes was one of enchanting beauty. The crystalline towers, cathedrals and domed temples sparkled with prismatic color. Parks and courtyards stretched for miles, lush with blossom-heavy trees and plants and flowers of infinite variety and color. Everything around him shimmered and danced with life: the trees, flowers and even the buildings. A single star shone amid a clear lilac sky, bathing the City of Lorden in a hazy glow.

Behind him, the edge of the city gave way to steep drop. Through patches of cloud, he could see the valley and mountains below. It seemed a world away from him now. He was fairly certain that whatever this place was, it wasn't part of Alanar as such.

The portal that had brought him here had now gone.

*So,* he wondered, *what happens now?*

His unspoken question was answered when two robed figures, a man and a woman, approached. Shining with a serene radiance, they exuded a quietude and purity of spirit. That was when it struck him. These people were Guardians! He was sure of it.

"Welcome," the woman said, smiling.

"Please accompany us," the man added. "Balaska wishes to see you now."

"Balaska's here?" he exclaimed. Overjoyed at the prospect of seeing her again, he followed his guides through the city, across the quartz courtyards, through the gardens, down marble walkways and past the magnificent buildings.

The city inhabitants shone with an unworldly radiance that quite matched their surroundings. The overriding feel was one of timeless serenity. Strolling down the streets and gathering in the gardens and courtyards, their voices carried through the air, along with a melodious hum permeating the city like the sound of a distant choir.

Energy and light danced around him, the very air tingling and buzzing. Once again he got the impression that everything was alive here. No shadows fell upon the city. The light was constant and unchanging, and it seemed to radiate from within everything. The only hint of darkness came from his own clothing, for he still wore the garments given him by Zhayron.

They arrived at a temple near the heart of the city. Circular and white, the gleaming structure rose to a domed peak. Ascending a flight of steps, David's heart leapt with joy upon seeing who stood in wait for him at the entrance.

"Balaska!"

"David, welcome."

It seemed a lifetime ago since they'd last met. She looked exactly as he remembered her. Wearing gold and white robes, her face shone with an ageless beauty; long locks of dark brown hair cascading down her shoulders. The two escorts departed and with a smile, she ushered him into the temple. A pinkish light streamed down from the high ceiling, illumining a grand marble entrance.

"I had no idea the City of Lorden was in your realm, Balaska."

"The City exists in the fifth dimension. It serves as a bridge between our two dimensions—the focal point of my people's contact with the mortal realm."

He recalled Zhayron telling him that the Guardians were a malevolent race intent on manipulating the people of Alanar for their own ends. How foolish he'd been to heed Zhayron's deceitful words. Now that he was actually here, he could sense only beauty and benevolence.

"I know it has been a long and painful journey, David."

He nodded. Although Zhayron was gone and he was now free, a residue of pain still lingered inside.

"The last time we met I told you that I would be with you always. I stayed true to my word, David. Even though you could neither see nor hear me, I was watching over you and attempting to help you along your path."

"Even when I was with Zhayron?"

"Especially then."

"I tried to fight him, Balaska. But he was in my mind and I—"

"You need not explain yourself. Zhayron latched onto you at a time of intense grief, invading your mind and psyche. He was a sorcerer of immense power. That he succeeded is no reflection on you. But the fact you eventually broke free of him is a testament to your strength and courage."

"Janir said that Zhayron was lying when he told me my mother's soul was suffering and in need of help..."

"Every word Zhayron uttered was a lie. All designed to manipulate you into complying with him. Rest assured, your mother's life essence is free, David; free beyond imagining."

"And Janir—?"

"You need not worry about Janir either. Though his time upon the mortal realm has ended, his consciousness has returned to the endless ocean of Infinity. As I once told you, all waves return to the ocean. Where else can they go?"

David felt an immediate unburdening.

"You must now let go of all that has gone before," she said. "Cast it aside. It is but the trail that has led you here. It is time to look ahead. For as you know, your mission is not yet over."

"The Key," he said. "You yourself sent me here, all that time ago—to find the other half of the Key."

"And here you are. What was broken must now be made whole."

David felt a surge of excitement as she led him along the cathedral-like corridors. He'd been through an immense physical and psychological ordeal, but his arrival in the realm of the Guardians had given him a boost of energy and somehow eased his aching body. Although still concerned about his friends back in the valley, the stresses of Alanar somehow seemed a long way off.

They came to an elaborately sculpted green doorway lined either side by emerald pillars. Balaska pushed the door open and beckoned him to follow as she stepped inside. David hesitated. He knew something momentous was about to occur.

Stepping through the door, he found himself in a glistening emerald hall. Circular in shape, the hall was lined with columns and arches and crowned by a glass domed ceiling. Hundreds of glowing orbs floated around the ceiling like iridescent bubbles of white light. A single ray of light shone from above, striking a pedestal at the center of the room.

Balaska led him across the hall to the pedestal, upon which sat a single gold box. "How did the Key end up broken in the first place?" he asked.

"It was deliberately broken."

"Deliberately—why?"

"As a safeguard. If it had been whole, you would have been able to use it at any time. Which clearly would have been disastrous, for until now, you were not yet ready to use it. Because you first had to find the other half, it was assured that you would end up here. It was a necessary journey for so many reasons. You had to be *ready* and responsible enough to wield the power of the Key."

"You think I'm ready now?"

She held out her hand. "Give me the Key, David."

He felt a strange reluctance to part with it. He nevertheless complied, lifting the amulet from around his neck and placing it in her hand.

Bathed in the light streaming down from the roof, she opened the gold box and lifted out another semicircular piece of violet crystal. She placed the two fragments together and smiled. They were a perfect fit. Holding them together, she raised her hands and began chanting words David had never before heard: *"Icasta rahn notodah...rahkuna tam mana...esta do ram."*

The chant reverberated through the hall, and her body became engulfed by the light shining down from above. The light spiraled out in waves, illuminating the hall in a brilliant white radiance. David watched in wonder, feeling the hairs on his arms and neck prickle as the energy in the room continued to build.

"*Antahna esta rah tashyana rahkuna masyan Alanar!*"

The energy reached a peak. A fork of lightning shot down and struck the Key, sending sparks flying across the room. David staggered back.

As the energy subsided, Balaska opened her eyes and lowered her hands. She appeared unharmed. Indeed, she smiled in delight as she opened her hands to reveal the Key of Alanar—now whole once more. The two halves had seamlessly knitted without so much as a crack. David felt a wave of excitement as he stared down at the gleaming spherical amulet.

"Take it," she said. "It is yours, David, and yours alone."

Warm to the touch, he held it in his hand and ran a finger along the outer rim. He somehow felt that now the Key had been made whole, so too had a part of him. Strange that he should feel so connected to an inanimate object; although he knew it was much more than that. It was alive in some way. He could feel its power surging through him as he placed the silver chain back around his neck.

"Do you recall the last time we met on Alanar," she said, "at the Enari encampment, prior to my departure?"

"How could I forget?"

"You came to me that night with questions—questions which, at that time, I could not answer for you."

"I remember."

"Well, you are here now, David. The Key has been made whole. And it is finally  time you learned the truth."

"The truth—?"

"About who you *really* are..."

# CHAPTER THIRTY FIVE

# Destiny

"Your birth was by no means accidental." Balaska began circling him, hands elegantly clasped behind her back; her footsteps echoing across the emerald hall. "Your very existence was ordained."

David could barely believe what he was hearing.

"The Key of Alanar was created by the Council of Elders; the council upon which I myself sit. As I think you already know, you and the Key are connected. It is a part of you and you of it. Just as the Key was created by the Guardians, so too were you. You see, David, you were born like no other mortal."

"I wasn't?"

"No, for you have a specific function, a task you were always destined to perform. You were born with a gift, David; a unique power unlike any the world has known. This was not by chance. It was part of a dispensation given by the Council to the mortal realm millennia before you were even born..."

"So the Guardians somehow arranged my birth?"

Balaska stopped and nodded.

"How...?"

"You were born to a mortal woman; an Enari as it happens. Your father, however, was no mortal."

"But if he wasn't mortal he must have been—"

"A Guardian. A Guardian who briefly assumed physical embodiment, encoded with the cellular patterning that would enable you to be born as we had intended."

"Then I'm half-Guardian..." It seemed inconceivable, yet his entire life he'd somehow felt different to those around him, and now it all suddenly made sense. "What does that even mean? What does it mean to be a Guardian?"

"That you will learn in time. Until now your powers have lain dormant; in seed form, yet to germinate. But rest assured they will, and sooner than you might think. There will come a time when you must claim the fullness of your birthright."

There was so much he wanted to know, but there was one thing he wanted to learn above all else. "Who were my birth parents? Tell me about them."

"I can do more than tell you."

She raised her hand and one of the orbs of light hovering above the hall began floating toward them. Expanding as it drifted down, the golden-white bubble enveloped both of them as it touched the ground.

Their surroundings changed. No longer in the temple hall, they were now in a dense forest. Gnarled old trees stretched over the moss-covered land, forming a thick canopy through which only glimmers of daylight could penetrate. The sound of rustling amid the undergrowth alerted David to someone nearby.

He turned to see a band of Enari tribesmen and women marching through the forest. The tribe's hunters led the way, carrying fire torches. Just behind them strode an imposing man wearing a feather headdress. Evidently the tribe's leader, the rugged, middle-aged chieftain wore a buckskin shirt and fur-lined trousers, with a long cloak trailing behind him. His gait was urgent and purposeful; his olive-skinned, chiseled face betraying a mix of concern and silent resolve.

The rest of the tribe followed behind: men and women of all ages, along with children and even some animals, including goats and horses. Each carried backpacks. This tribe was clearly on the move, relocating their home along with them.

Balaska said, "Behold the Tahlumar; an Enari tribe living in a remote part of Alanar."

"Why can't they see us? We're right ahead of them."

"What we witness is but an echo of events that occurred in the past; nearly twenty years ago in your world's chronology."

"They seem scared."

"They have every reason to be. They are fleeing for their lives."

"From who—the Kellians?"

"The Alliance."

"What would the Alliance want with an Enari tribe?"

"The Alliance hierarchy is headed by master occultists working in league with the Shadow Lords of Abidalos," Balaska explained. "Zhayron was one such individual. We call them organic portals; those mortals influenced and controlled by the shadow forces. They are familiar with the ancient texts and acutely observe the prophecies of old. That is how they knew this particular Enari tribe possessed something—something they wanted at all costs."

"What?"

"Observe."

The scene shifted. Though they were still in the heart of the forest, it was now dark and the Enari had set up camp for the night. Guards patrolled the perimeter of the camp. While the adults prepared a meager evening meal, groups of children played by the campfire; carefree, merry and oblivious to the clear jeopardy they all faced.

David's attention was drawn to the edge of the camp. A single cone-shaped tent had been pitched at a discrete distance from the others. Feeling drawn to investigate he moved closer and Balaska followed. A man and woman stood outside the tent deep in conversation. David recognized the man as the tribe's leader. "That is Garadanti, Chief of the Tahlumar," Balaska said. "He was great and wise man whose faith in the prophecies, and in us, was unerring."

"Who's he talking with?" David asked in a hushed voice. He didn't know why he felt the need to whisper, for it was clear that the Enari could neither see nor hear him.

"That is Parethka, the tribe's healer and medicine woman."

With long locks of braided graying hair and a kindly face with sparkling dark eyes, Parethka wore a tasseled brown dress with moccasins. Balaska and David were now close enough to overhear their conversation. "She is doing well, At'tah," Parethka told Garadanti as she wiped the sweat from her forehead. "Which is a miracle given the circumstances."

"Circumstances are beyond my control, old friend," Garadanti said. "How much longer will it be?"

"She is now entering the second stage of labor. Though I cannot say with certainty, I expect we will have another member of our tribe by dawn."

"Good. We can stay here no longer than is absolutely necessary. We must set off as soon as the baby is born."

David leaned toward Balaska. "The baby. It's me, isn't it?"

Balaska nodded. She stepped past Garadanti and Parethka and disappeared into the tent like a ghost. His heart racing, David followed.

Inside the tent, a heavily pregnant woman lay upon a mattress of blankets and cushions. "My birth mother," David exclaimed, his eyes fixed upon the beautiful young Enari. Little older than he was, with wavy black hair and tan colored skin, she lay in the delivery position, her face beaded with sweat. Even though she was in clear pain, she radiated an air of serenity. An older woman sat by her side, applying a compress to her head. "What's her name?"

"Enkatia." Balaska pointed to the woman's neck. "And look..."

David hadn't noticed it at first, for it lay partly concealed in the folds of her white dress, but around her neck was the Key of Alanar. It was the same broken fragment that David had taken possession of on his birthday.

"So the Key was hers? How did she come to have it?"

"It was given to her by the man who fathered her child."

"What happened to him, Balaska? Is he still here?"

"Yes, he is still in your realm, but far from here."

"How did they meet?"

"Enkatia was alone in the forest one day when she met a handsome stranger with whom she felt an immediate and strong affinity. Though their encounter was brief, their connection was immediate and the consequences, as you know, far-reaching."

David gazed down at his mother, wishing he could somehow reach out to her and make his presence known. But he was nothing more than a ghost here. The barrier of time had placed an impenetrable wall between them. He looked back up at Balaska, eager to know what happened next. Balaska raised her hand and the scene shifted.

Though still in the same tent, time had jumped ahead. The first thing David heard was a howl of pain from Enkatia.

"Push, Enkatia," came Parethka's voice. "You can do this. Push!"

David and Balaska stood at the side of the tent, watching as Parethka delivered Enkatia's baby. Garadanti looked on in concern, while the other woman remained by Enkatia's side, holding her hand and whispering words of encouragement.

Enkatia's face was creased with pain, her breathing rapid and uneven as she pushed with all her might. Her screams of pain were soon accompanied by another sound—the unmistakable cries of a newborn.

"You have done it, Enkatia," Parethka called. "It is a boy—a beautiful baby boy!"

Parethka lifted the newborn and cut the umbilical. Checking the baby was in good health, she passed the child to Enkatia. Enkatia smiled as she looked down at her newborn son.

David could barely believe what he was seeing. He'd just witnessed his own birth.

"Enkatia, he is beautiful," Garadanti said with a proud smile.

There came a call from outside the tent. One of Garadanti's men was summoning him in a voice full of urgency. With a nod, Garadanti exited the tent. Balaska followed, motioning for David to join her.

Garadanti stood outside the tent with his subordinate. "What is it, Tienanthi?"

The young man pointed to the sky. "See for yourself, At'tah."

Far beyond the treetops, amid the black star-filled sky, rays of light streaked across the heavens, leaving rippling trails across the sky. "Hershala be blessed," Garadanti exclaimed. "The Acosta Sari!"

The tribesfolk gathered to watch as the stars continued blazing across the heavens. A wave of excitement swept over the tribe. Those that had been sleeping emerged from their tents to see what the commotion was about. "Behold," Garadanti called. "Behold the Acosta Sari! The sign we have been awaiting!"

"What does it mean?" one of the men asked.

"It means that in spite of all that has happened, we are on the right path. As foretold in the Chronicle of Alanar, the Acosta Sari, the dancing stars, will herald new hope—and new life for us all!" A smile played upon his rugged face; his eyes sparkling with reflected starlight. "And indeed, our dear sister Enkatia has just given birth!"

"Then it is true?" Tienanthi said. "If Enkatia's baby has been born to the dancing stars, then her child must be *Aharan?*"

"Yes!" Garadanti cried, raising his voice so all could hear. "The child is Aharan, as foretold in the ancient Chronicle!"

As the crowd erupted into cheers, David looked to Balaska, confused. "What does that mean? What's 'Aharan'?"

"Aharan is an ancient Enari word that roughly translates as *the timeless.* It was foretold by the ancient mystics that in a time of darkness, when all hope seemed lost, a gift would be granted to the people of Alanar. In the year of Atania, a child—half-mortal, half-Guardian—would be born to a people on the run from a deadly enemy. The child, Aharan, would grow up to fight a great force of evil and was destined to save the planet at its time of greatest need. According to the ancient prophecies, his birth would be heralded by the Acosta Sari, a shower of stars dancing across the night sky."

"And that's me...I'm Aharan."

Balaska nodded.

"What happened next?" He was eager to learn the fate of his people; his family.

"The Guardians directed Garadanti to take the child from the tribe to a place of safety, a place that we had arranged. This was not easy for him, but he knew he had to heed our words.

With the Alliance just around the corner, it was clear you were not safe here."

Again the scene changed. David and Balaska were once again inside Enkatia's tent. Although exhausted from labor, she seemed radiantly happy as she cradled her son. Garadanti sat by her bedside. "Enkatia," he began. "I owe you an explanation. The Alliance is pursuing us for a reason. That reason is...your baby."

"My baby?"

"They want him, and they must never get him. This may be hard to believe but the Acosta Sari confirmed it. Your child is—"

"Aharan."

"You knew...?"

"Not at first," she said. "But the moment I fell pregnant I knew there was something different about this child; something special."

"He has a future ahead of him, Enkatia; a great future. According to both the Chronicle and the Guardians he is destined to do something incredible; something that will save us all and bring hope to this dark and troubled world. Beyond that, I cannot begin to imagine what fate has in store for this little boy." His eyes fell upon the sleeping child. "All I know is that it is our duty to ensure he does not fall into the hands of the enemy. And to do that..."

"You're going to take him away?"

Garadanti could only nod. "It is the only chance, Enkatia. The only chance for your boy—and for us all."

"Where will you take him?"

"According to the Chronicle, he is to be taken to the summit of Mount Ahdral. The Guardians have confirmed this. As it happens, Ahdral is only a day's walk from here."

"Why there?"

"That I do not know. But when I last communed with the Guardians, they were very specific about this, and thus far they have not been wrong. They promised that he would be safe there."

"Then I will go with you."

"You are too weak, Enkatia. You need rest. It will be a long and hard climb and I cannot postpone my departure."

"You're leaving now?"

"I must."

Enkatia's eyes welled with tears. "Will I ever see him again...?"

"That I cannot say. All I know is that this must be done. The Alliance is almost upon us and could catch up with us at any moment. Your child must not be here when that happens." He placed his arm around her. "I am so sorry, Enkatia, but I have to take him from you now. I wish there was another way."

Wiping the tears from her eyes, Enkatia gazed down at the infant resting so contentedly in her arms. "Several nights ago I had a dream. I dreamt about my child, only he was no longer a child. He was a grown man: a shaman, a warrior, and a crusader; fighting against impossible odds to defeat a force of evil that chilled my very soul. The images kept shifting and I could not hold onto them. I could not hold onto *him*. I wanted to with all my heart, but he was not mine to hold. A woman appeared in the dream, a woman who shone like suns. She told me that I had to be willing to let him go; that she would take care of him until the time was right...

"There was more. I cannot remember it all, for the moment I awoke the dream began to fade. But what did not fade was the knowing that my son would be taken care of as long as I had the courage to let him go. I know I have to. I have to for his sake..." She broke into sobs, clutching the baby to her chest.

David reached down and tried to touch her face. His hand passed straight through her as though she was made of nothing but air. He wanted her to know that he was here; that she had made the right choice and that everything would be all right.

For a moment she lifted her head and looked up in his direction. Was it possible she had somehow been able to sense his presence? She quickly, however, returned her attention to her baby. The tears still streaming down her cheeks, she lifted the crystal amulet from around her neck and placed it over her child's head. The Key of Alanar was now his.

* * *

In a flash, David and Balaska were back in the forest at the edge of the Enari encampment. With dawn approaching, Garadanti prepared to depart with the child. He left his subordinate Tienanthi in charge and directed them to head to the nearby town of Rodasar, where they would find safety and shelter. It was a difficult and emotional farewell as he left behind his tribe.

"Why did Garadanti have to take me away?" David asked. "What's so special about this Mount Ahdral?"

"At the summit of Ahdral was a gateway," Balaska said, "a conduit to our realm. It was decided that once born to the mortal realm, you would be taken to a place of safety. If you had remained with the tribe you would almost certainly have been captured by the Alliance, and we could not let that happen."

Scenes of Garadanti's perilous journey flashed before them. He set off through the forest, the baby strapped to his chest. The Alliance was soon on his trail, with over a dozen Death Troops in close pursuit.

Fueled by desperate resolve, Garadanti made it to Mount Ahdral. He scrambled up the mountainside, the Alliance soldiers never far behind. Nearing the summit, Garadanti was careful to keep his footing as he inched his way up the mountain ledge.

Now an open target for his pursuers, the Alliance troops opened fire. A blast from one of their rifles hit his leg. While a lesser man may have given up at this point, Garadanti struggled on. The baby screamed as the weapons fire continued, pounding the nearby rocks to dust. Behind him, the Death Troops scrambled up the ledge like metallic insects.

Watching helplessly, David wished there was some way he could assist. But he knew that was impossible. He was but a passive witness to an echo in time.

Garadanti made it to the summit, where he was greeted by a spinning vortex of light. The screaming baby in his arms, he limped toward the gateway.

As the Death Troops closed in from behind, Garadanti stepped into the swirling pool of liquid light. But just as he was about to disappear into the vortex, one of the soldiers shot him in the back. With a flash of light, everything dissolved.

David blinked in disorientation. He and Balaska were now back in the emerald hall. "What happened? Garadanti—did he make it?"

"Yes, and no," came Balaska's response. "He was killed as he entered the portal. Fortunately, you were unharmed, David. The portal was sealed the moment you got through. Garadanti was a great man who sacrificed his life to bring you to safety."

David's mind and senses were racing. "So I ended up here, in the realm of the Guardians?"

"It was the only way to safeguard your life. Under the directive of the Shadow Lords, the Alliance leader, Zhylan Tyraah, wanted you found and captured at all costs. They knew that the child born to the Acosta Sari would grow up to one day threaten their plans for domination. So it was decided by the Council of Elders that upon your birth, you would be taken here and safeguarded from those that would harm or exploit you."

"What of my mother and the rest of Garadanti's tribe? Did they manage to escape the Alliance?"

"Sadly not. Knowing you were now lost to him, Tyraah initiated a rampage of destruction, attempting to kill every single Enari. Few tribes escaped the ensuing annihilation. The Enari, for so many millennia the keepers of the land and the ancient lore, were near-decimated. I am afraid Garadanti's tribe were among the first victims, with only a handful of survivors."

"My mother?"

Balaska shook her head.

David felt a pang of grief for a woman he'd never even known. For so many years he had wondered about his biological parents. He could never have imagined how tragic the circumstances around his birth had been. "What happened to me after I arrived here?"

"We had already selected a home for you, somewhere far from the grasping claw of the Alliance: a remote island called New Haven. We knew the people of New Haven would adopt you and raise you as one of their own. So, you were returned to Alanar and taken to the edge of the mainland where a group of islanders found you. To ensure that you would remain protected and could be guided when the Alliance inevitably arrived, we also sent a guide to New Haven: a sorcerer from a far-off land—"

"Janir!"

"The rest, of course, you know."

It all made sense now; pieces of a puzzle finally slotting into place. But there was still so much he wanted to know. He looked down at his chest, over which hung the violet crystal. "Balaska, tell me about the Key."

"Yes, it is time you learned more about the Key. And for that, you must cast your mind back ten thousand years."

"To Lasandria..."

She nodded. "As you know, during the final days of that civilization, the science ministry, under the authority of King Dua-ron, stole the technology of the ancients and used it to create their own gateway, a conduit capable of accessing other dimensions."

How could he forget?

"The High Priest Ardonis beseeched us to intervene. Although it was not permissible for us to prevent the fall of Lasandria, we were able to bend the rules and offer a promise of hope for the future. We did this by creating the Key of Alanar. The Key, capable of opening and closing inter-dimensional gateways, was used to seal Dua-ron's gateway. By that point, tremendous damage had already occurred. The civilization of Lasandria was destroyed and the Narssians came streaming through the portal the moment it opened."

"I remember seeing it, but what happened afterward?"

"The Key was used to seal the gateway. Once sealed, the Narssians were cut off from their own realm. Mercifully, only a small number of the demonic beings made it through the portal. If the gateway had remained open, the catastrophe, not only for Alanar but countless other worlds, would have been beyond imagining. Nothing less than universal armageddon was averted by creating the Key of Alanar and sending its Custodian to Lasandria."

"You told me his name was Arran; the man who used the Key to seal the gateway."

He could tell by the look on her face that she was about to tell him something important. "David, Arran is an ancient world dating back to the First Age of Alanar. It translates literally as the *timeless one.*"

"Timeless one?"

Wasn't that what the Enari word Aharan meant? And wasn't *he* Aharan?

David was struck by a sudden, shattering realization. Aharan and Arran were the same word—and they referred to the same man. It was *him.*

But how was that possible?

"We Guardians exist beyond time," Balaska explained. "Here in the fifth dimension, past, present and future exist as one. If we so choose we could step into your distant past or your far future. Time is no barrier to us."

"What are you saying?"

"Your birth was orchestrated by the Guardians. You are the Custodian of the Key; the only person that can and ever shall be able to use it. It is patterned into your bio-energetic code. In the hands of anyone but you, the Key is useless."

"Why?"

"To prevent it from ever being used by the enemy. You were born to use the Key to save your world. No one else can play the role for which you have been chosen. There is a war being fought: a battle between darkness and light; a struggle that has been waged since the dawn of phenomenal existence. It now comes to a climax. Alanar is the keystone world, upon which the fate of an entire universe will be decided. You must ensure that your world never falls. This nearly happened when Lasandria was destroyed and the Narssians invaded. And it still will, if you do not go back in time and fulfill your destiny—by sealing the Lasandrian gateway."

"Then it was *me* that sealed the gateway...millennia before I was even born?"

"Therein lies the paradox. In order to safeguard the present and save the future, you must first go back and save the past."

"You're saying I play a part in my own world's history?"

She nodded.

"In my time, it's already happened. History records it. The gateway was sealed. Which means I succeeded—or I will succeed?"

"Success is by no means determined. Timelines fluctuate and either outcome is possible. If you should fail, the present day as you know it will be changed in an instant. Alanar and many other worlds will long since have been destroyed. A new timeline will exist."

So the fate of his world now rested with him? Past, present, and future converged upon a single moment in time—and a decision he now had to make.

"Balaska, you told me before that Arran died upon sealing the gateway. Does this mean that—"

"I am afraid it is a fixed event in time, David."

"A fixed event?"

"It has happened and it *will* happen. In order to save your world—"

"I must die."

# CHAPTER THIRTY SIX

# Full Circle

David awoke feeling strangely calm. Perhaps it was because for the first time in as long as he could remember, his dreams were unperturbed by the shadows of darkness. Zhayron was gone from his mind, and he finally felt free.

Balaska had insisted that he get a good night's sleep. With a yawn and stretch, he got up from the bed and gazed out the window, marveling at the crystalline rooftops, temples, and spires of the wondrous city. He felt safe and protected here. The strife of Alanar and the threat of the Narssians seemed so far away.

That was all about to change, however.

Although no stranger to death, his own mortality was something he'd never given much thought. In spite of all the peril he'd faced along his path, he was still only a teenager and had always assumed that his entire life lay ahead of him. But now the end was in sight, he was shaken free of his complacency.

Should he embrace his destiny, he'd be sent back in time to the Kingdom of Lasandria, where he'd have to sacrifice his own life to stop a full-scale Narssian invasion of his realm.

It was the only way, Balaska had told him. Whether he succeeded or failed, his death was inevitable.

But what was *one life*—? Surely a small price to pay for saving a universe.

He found some clothes laid out for him upon a silver railing—a sleeveless white top emblazoned with an eight-pointed star and dark navy trousers. He put them on, along with the belt, wristbands, and boots beside them. The clothes were a perfect fit, as though they'd been tailored just for him. Grabbing a piece of orange fruit from a bowl on the table, he left his private chamber and made his way along the temple corridors.

Balaska was already waiting for him in the emerald hall.

"You have made your decision?" she asked.

"Yes. I'm ready to do this. I figure even if I refused I'd be dead anyway, along with everyone else..."

"Indeed, your world would have long since have destroyed by the Narssians, and their poison spread halfway across the galaxy."

"Then I guess I save the future by saving the past. I just won't be around to see it..."

The Guardian moved closer, her face softening; the fondness she felt for him clear in her sparkling brown eyes. "Your path was never going to be an easy one, David. It is one of sacrifice. I wish I could change that..."

"There were so many things I wanted to do and experience in life. I don't suppose I'll ever get the chance now—to fall in love, have a family, grow old watching the suns rise and set each day. I guess I just wanted to find my place in the universe..."

"And you have. It was not the life you would have chosen, but it was the life you were born to live. Often the harder the path, the greater the gift can be offered."

"What do you mean?"

"Life is given to all, but it is neither an entitlement or an unqualified blessing. All beings live that they may contribute to the totality. Just as trees give the air that you breathe, the rivers yield water to quench your thirst, plants offer food and the suns, light and heat, nothing exists entirely for its own sake. Life contributes to life."

"Then we should be no different?"

"Exactly. We are all part of the symphony of existence. Each of us has a gift to give; a unique song that only we can sing. Some are faint and barely heard, while others are a cacophonous roar. But some—some are of such tremendous power that they echo throughout eternity, never to be forgotten."

He understood what she was trying to tell him: that his death mattered and would be for a reason. He could feel the fear inside him. But he wouldn't let his feelings blind him to the path of his destiny. If all that Balaska had revealed was true, then this was his entire reason for existing. He'd been searching for the answers his entire life. Now he finally knew who he was and why he was here. He had a purpose—a mission—and he was determined to fulfill it.

"So what happens now?"

"I will take you before the Council of Elders. There you will meet Ardonis and he will accompany you back to the mortal realm."

"To Lasandria?"

"Where you must seal the gateway and prevent a full-scale Narssian incursion."

"But how do I even do that, Balaska? I don't know have a clue how to open or close gateways..."

"You and the Key are one. As you have already demonstrated, you have an intuitive understanding of how to use it. When the time comes, you will know what to do."

He could only hope she was right. He mustered a smile. "Balaska, I wanted to thank you for everything; for all that you've done for me. After a lifetime of wondering, I finally know who I am, and it's because of you."

"We all have our part to play, David," she said with a warm smile, "and this was mine." She paused. "Are you ready?"

"As ready as I'll ever be."

"Then may Hershala light your way..."

She raised her hand, reaching to one of the orbs of light floating above the hall. The orb descended, enlarging as it touched the ground, enveloping David in an iridescent bubble of energy.

His heart quickened as his surroundings disappeared in a flash of light.

The temple was gone and Balaska along with it. He now stood in the Court of Shanadon; a vast cylindrical chamber. Beneath his feet, a crystalline platform branched into four walkways like the spokes of a wheel. Below it a sheer drop spiraled into a seemingly bottomless precipice. A vertical shaft of energy dominated the chamber. Blasting down from above, it sent waves of silvery-white light dancing outward.

Beneath the pillar of energy sat the Council of Elders; a dozen robed Guardians gathered around a semicircular table. He was astonished to see Balaska sitting among them.

One of the Guardians—a man with long silver hair—stood, his hand outstretched toward David. The name *Malkiastan* somehow impressed itself in David's mind. Clearly the leader of the Council, he was a being of immense power and radiance.

Another man stood before the Council. His eyes were locked upon David, a look of curiosity and surprise upon his bronze-skinned face. A mortal, like David, he was dressed in a loincloth, with sandals, a blue cloak, and a golden headdress.

*Ardonis.*

David didn't know how or why, but as he gazed into the High Priest's turquoise eyes, it was as though looking into a mirror. He felt such a strange, inexplicable familiarity with him. Strong in both body and spirit, Ardonis exuded a wise, understated power. Yet this was a man who knew his kingdom was about to be destroyed and the pain was written upon his face.

"Behold *Arran,* the timeless one," Malkiastsan said. "He is your future, Ardonis. He alone has the power to save your world. Only he can safeguard your future."

Ardonis opened his mouth to speak. Before the words could come out, a spark of light shot from Malkiastan's palm, engulfing the High Priest in a spiraling cocoon of energy. Seconds later it dispersed, but Ardonis seemed different somehow. His confusion had lifted and there was a newfound clarity in his eyes.

Malkiastan placed a hand upon David's shoulder and beckoned Ardonis forward. "It has been decided," he said. "The future now rests in your hands. It is time to go forth. Go forth and fight for it."

David had a feeling that Malkiastan was talking to him. He still had doubts, however, and a wave of uncertainty spilled to the surface. "It's a great task that's been placed before me, and I'm willing to do it...but I don't know if I'm ready..."

Malkiastan smiled. "If you were not ready, you would not be here."

David wasn't so certain.

"Have faith," the Guardian continued. "With faith, courage, and resolve, you will not err. You have been prepared for this your entire life, in ways you cannot begin to imagine. Everything that has ever happened to you has been necessary to bring you here, to this point, when at last you are ready to embrace your birthright and fulfill your destiny."

David looked into Malkiastan's sky blue eyes, which glistened like diamonds. He nodded, somehow feeling the Guardian's strength and conviction seeping through him, easing his doubts.

A spinning portal of light appeared before them—the gateway that would take them back to the mortal realm.

"It is time," Malkiastan said.

David turned to Balaska. She smiled sweetly at him, but her eyes were tinged with sadness. He knew this was probably the last time he would ever see her.

Ardonis bowed before the Council and gestured for David to enter the gateway. David did so, striding forward and disappearing into the swirling vortex of light. His time among the Guardians at an end, his fate now lay in the twilight of a dying kingdom.

"Welcome to Lasandria," Ardonis said.

The gateway vanished behind them. In its place stood a hexagonal mirror set into the base of a towering amethyst crystal. David glanced around in wonder. A crystalline cavern unraveled before them.

Ardonis continued, "This is the sacred Temple of El Ad'dan; for thousands of years home to the Lasandrian Priesthood."

"It's an honor to be here."

Although the place looked not unlike the realm of the Guardians, David knew he was most definitely back in the dense physicality of the mortal world. The whole time he'd been in the City of Lorden, his body had felt as light as air. Upon stepping through the gateway, he immediately felt several pounds heavier.

"It can take a moment to adjust," Ardonis noted, sensing the boy's disorientation. "Come, allow me to show you around the Temple."

"I'd like that."

David found it hard to believe he was now in the Kingdom of Lasandria, some ten thousand years before he was even born. He was filled with wonder as Ardonis led him through the temple. A simple, elegant sanctuary, the walls were constructed of sandstone with statues of saints and sages lining the halls. Candles illuminated the corridors; the air scented with incense.

The place was surprisingly quiet. The only person they encountered was an elderly monk draped in an indigo robe. Ardonis stopped to confer with him in hushed whispers. David watched the High Priest, again overcome by a strange sense of familiarity. They'd obviously never met before, but he recognized something of himself in Ardonis—in his face, his voice, even the way that he moved.

The monk departed. Ardonis led David onto the temple rooftop. From here they could see the whole of the valley. Whereas in David's time all that had remained was scattered debris and charred ground, here the great golden City of El Ad'dan stood in all its splendor, spanning almost the entire valley. The morning suns shone amid the lilac sky; sunlight sparkling upon the river and reflecting upon the houses, halls, towers and domes of the city.

"It's so beautiful." The moment David uttered those words a terrible sadness fell upon him. He knew that by the time this day was out, the city would be no more.

"It is magnificent," Ardonis said. "At its height, Lasandria was a beacon of civilization. Its light shone across the globe. Alas, my people have lost their way; tainted by their lust for power, dominance and material acquisition, their minds poisoned and their hearts empty. But even now, as it stands upon the verge of its own demise, one can see echoes of its past glory."

"It must be awful for you—knowing what's going to happen."

"I grieve for all that has been lost, and for all that will yet be lost."

"I come from the future, and even in my time, thousands of years from now, the loss of Lasandria continues to scar the whole of Alanar. Janir once told me that time heals all wounds, but I'm not so sure. I think some wounds never truly heal."

"I promise you it is not yet over. Of the future, the Council of Elders was adamant. There will come a time when all that is lost will be restored. The Lasandrian people will one day rise up and reclaim their heritage; their birthright—their destiny. In my heart, I know this to be true. And I know it is you, Arran, who will be responsible for our eventual return."

"Me?"

"The Council was clear on this. The future lies in your hands. Though I know not how, *you,* my young friend, hold the key to our redemption."

Even if that were true, David knew that he wouldn't be around to see it. "What will you do now?" he asked the High Priest.

"The Council has directed me to gather as many of my people as possible and bring them to the temple. I will lead them through the gateway to a place of safety."

"And you'll accompany them?"

"That is my intent. Although I cannot shake the feeling that my life is soon to end, and that it will end here, in the temple. Should that be the will of Hershala, then I accept my fate. All that matters is that I get my people to safety. If even a handful of us survive, our legacy shall endure."

Interesting that Ardonis had foreknowledge of his own death as well. Maybe that was why David felt their destinies were linked in some way. They were both fighting to salvage what they could in the shadow of an impending apocalypse, and both destined to die in the process.

"When will they activate the gateway?" David asked.

"The crowds are already gathering. The ceremony is scheduled to begin mid-afternoon."

"Then I should go now. I have to be there when it happens."

David recalled Balaska taking him back in time to witness the activation of the gateway. It was a moment of horror forever etched in his mind. He knew exactly what was going to happen the moment the gateway exploded into life. A wave of destruction would demolish the city, killing everyone in the vicinity. He wasn't sure how he'd even survive the blast. Perhaps the Key would protect him somehow? Surely the Guardians hadn't left anything to chance.

"I will have one of my monks take you down the hill and direct you to the city," Ardonis said. "I must go and make preparations myself. There is much to do and so little time."

"With luck, we'll have all the time we need."

Ardonis placed his hands on David's shoulders. "It has been an honor to meet you, Arran. I know so little about you. I know not where you are from or why you were chosen for this unenviable task. But from the depths of my heart, I thank you for what you are about to do. It is a dangerous path you now tread, but, in spirit, I will be with you. I also feel that, in some strange way, you will be with me as well. May Hershala grant you the strength you need and guide you to victory."

"And you, Ardonis."

Ardonis left the rooftop, disappearing back into the temple.

David's attention returned to the valley and the city glistening in the morning light. It was soon to be destroyed and nothing could prevent that. History had recorded the destruction of El Ad'dan and the obliteration of the Kingdom of Lasandria. All he could do was fight to save the future, and he vowed to do that with all his might. His death would be for a reason and his sacrifice would count. He would make certain of that.

# CHAPTER THIRTY SEVEN

# Hour of Annihilation

The monk moved with surprising speed and agility for a man of his advancing years. His name was Jarado and he'd been sent by Ardonis to escort David from the temple to the outskirts of the city. As David followed him down the mountain trail, a haze washed over the valley. Aside from birdsong, all that could be heard was the ringing of distant bells. The valley seemed tranquil, yet with every step, David's apprehension grew.

Reaching the foot of the mountain, the monk directed David to the city, which was now visible beyond the edge of the forest. They parted company and David set upon his journey with haste.

He couldn't help but contemplate what lay ahead of him. Although part of him had accepted his fate, another part felt cheated. He was only seventeen years old. He'd barely tasted life, and it was all about to be snatched away from him.

*Come on, David, stay focused.* This was a self-indulgence he couldn't afford. If he was to have any chance of succeeding, he had to remain unwavering in his determination.

At last, he reached the edge of the forest. Just beyond the river stood the City of El Ad'dan. He stopped for a moment, overcome by a mixture of awe and dread. Stretching as far as he could see in either direction, its grand temples, halls, towers, archways and spires glistened as the suns shone through the mist. At the heart of the city the metal pylons of the gateway towered above the metropolis.

A bridge led him across the river to the gates of the city. Sentinels in gold armor stood watch as people filed through the open gates. David did his best to blend into the crowd as he passed under the golden archways. The bells, growing louder with every step, chimed with hypnotic repetition.

The streets were filled with people making their way to the heart of the city. As he joined the procession, David noted the air of celebration and excitement. People laughed and joked, speaking excitedly of the 'new era' that was about to begin.

*If only they knew. If only they knew they were marching to their deaths...*

He saw a group of children playing on the steps of a nearby temple. Their laughter carried above the chatter of the crowd. They were so young; so innocent. It pained him to know that these children, along with everyone else here, would soon be dead, and there was nothing he could do to save them.

Or was there?

Perhaps he didn't have to wait until the gateway was open before sealing it. Perhaps he could find a way to prevent it from being opened in the first place...

*Why hadn't the Guardians thought of this?*

He had to do something to save these people.

Yes, history had recorded the annihilation of El Ad'dan, and the Guardians seemed to think it was impossible to avert the catastrophe, but he couldn't just stand by and watch them all die. There were so many people here—men, women, and children of all ages—their faces beaming with excitement. They didn't deserve what fate had in store for them.

David eventually reached the central plaza. Thousands of people already filled the city square. Awash with color, the buildings, temples, and pillars were adorned with flags and garlands. Dominating the entire plaza, the gateway stood upon a raised platform: a colossal metal obelisk with two smaller pylons either side, connected by a stationary wheel. It was all so familiar to David. Everything was just as it had been when Balaska had brought him here before.

Beneath the gateway a team of scientists busily prepared the device for activation, oblivious to the horrors they were about to unleash.

King Dua-ron stood at the forefront, overseeing the activity. A short, stout man dressed in regal attire, he was accompanied by a wiry woman in black who even from this distance exuded a bitter coldness. David recognized her as Mailyn, the dark sorceress Balaska had told him about. It was her that had sabotaged the gateway in order to unleash the Narssians.

It took some time for David to maneuver his way through the crowd, but he was determined to get as close to the gateway as possible. The generators powered up with an oscillating hum, and the crowd grew increasingly excited.

He eventually made it to the front of the crowd. A metal barrier had been erected to keep people back. King Dua-ron stood ahead of him upon the podium, readying himself to address the crowd. If David was to do anything, now was the time.

"Dua-ron!" he bellowed at the top of his lungs. "Don't do this! If you activate the gateway the city will be destroyed. Please, listen to me!"

David felt a stirring amongst the crowd. Dua-ron had evidently heard his protest as well. The portly monarch stepped forward, scanning the crowd through squinted eyes. Mailyn leaned toward Dua-ron and whispered in his ear, pointing at David. Dua-ron dispatched two of his guards to deal with him.

David stood defiantly, hands against the railings. "Listen to me! You must not open the gateway! You don't know what you're doing!"

The guards were soon upon him. They grabbed hold of him and dragged him away from the podium. "Let me go!"

Eager to allay concern after David's dissent, Dua-ron addressed the crowd, his voice booming through some kind of sound amplifier. "There is nothing to fear, my people. We stand upon the threshold of a glorious new dawn. All the wonders of the cosmos now stand before us. This is the crowning achievement of the Lasandrian people—a day that will be remembered for all of history!"

The crowd roared in applause.

David found the irony bitter. *Yes, this day will be remembered for all of history.*

"Now, stay out of trouble," one of the guards grunted as they deposited David at the far end of the plaza. From here the entire podium was visible above the heads of the spectators.

"You have to listen to me," David pleaded. "You have to get Dua-ron to stop this. He must not activate the gateway!"

"Keep quiet," one of the men warned.

"You don't know what's going to happen once that gateway opens. But I do. I've seen it! Everyone here is going to die! You hear me? Please, you have to go to Dua-ron and tell him to—"

Abruptly losing patience, the first guard slammed his fist into David's belly. "I told you to be quiet!"

David's reflexes were dulled by the unexpected blow. As he tried to strike back, the guard preempted him, punching him in the face. He fell back, the breath knocked from his lungs.

"What is wrong with you, boy?"

"Just another adolescent troublemaker," the other guard muttered. "Probably had too much honey wine."

"I could be doing with some myself."

"Look, they are about to activate the gateway—"

David straightened up, wiping the blood from his nose. They were right. The countdown had been initiated. Overcome with excitement, the crowd began chanting in unison: "Lasandria!... Lasandria!...Lasandria!..."

At the wave of Dua-ron's hand, the scientists activated the gateway. The rumbling generators caused the ground to shake. Surging electricity leapt up the pylons, setting the metal wheel into motion. With a screeching hum, the wheel spun ever faster until it was a blur to the naked eye.

"No," David whispered.

A dazzling vortex of light and color exploded into life at the heart of the wheel. Sparks rained outward as the aperture grew in size. The pulsating pool of light was a thing of strange beauty. It wasn't dissimilar to the other gateways David had seen, but on an altogether grander scale. Stretching from sky to ground, it dwarfed the surrounding buildings, bathing the city in an electric blue haze.

"Behold the gateway!" Dua-ron cried, arms outstretched as he stood before the portal. "The gateway to our liberation!"

The crowd erupted into frenzied applause and howls of delight and awe.

David braced himself. He'd seen it all before and knew only too well what was about to happen.

Sure enough, the gateway exploded.

David crouched down, burying his head between the knees.

In what seemed like a split second, a wave of annihilation consumed the entire city; stripping it apart and instantly incinerating those around him. The crowd—all of them—were killed before they had the chance to realize what was happening.

David was swept from his feet and flung into the air like a piece of flotsam. Yet he was still alive and somehow protected from the cataclysm. A protective bubble of energy surrounded him. He knew it was the Key. The Key was protecting him. A tornado of annihilation swept through the city. He fell to the ground in its wake, breaking his wrist and several ribs. Wincing in pain, he forced himself to rise from the fiery rubble.

Observing the devastation around him, he let out a cry of horror. The city was gone. All that remained of the grand golden temples and towers was rubble and in place of the tens of thousands of men, women and children—nothing but smoldering clouds of ash.

He stood amid the nightmarish scene, choking as smoke filled his lungs, tears streaming down his blackened face. An impenetrable cloak of blackness enveloped the city, obscuring the sky and blotting out every last trace of daylight.

Amid the desolation, all that remained was the gateway. David stared up at the swirling portal and watched in horror as an airship emerged through the opening. It was a spiked predator with outstretched black wings; not unlike the Alliance warships he'd seen, only bigger and mightier. First came one, and then another, and another—gliding over the ruins like demonic birds of prey.

That wasn't all, The ships were accompanied by ground troops. An army of wraith-like soldiers spilled through the gateway, swarming into the city.

The Narssians. They were here—and it was up to him to stop them.

# CHAPTER THIRTY EIGHT

# Endgame

David crouched down behind the remains of a fallen temple. The ruins of El Ad'dan burned and smoldered. The sky was obscured by clouds of ash and black smoke. The gateway remained open, like an eye piercing the blackness, impassively observing the devastation around it. What bitter irony that all that should remain of the Lasandrian people was the instrument of their annihilation.

David could do nothing for the city or its inhabitants now. But the future of Alanar rested with him. He had to carry out his task and seal the gateway before any more of these monsters could get through.

He wiped the dust from his stinging eyes and winced as waves of pain throbbed from his arm and ribs.

*Ignore the pain.*

The air was smoky and blisteringly hot, scalding his skin. Cradling his broken wrist, he noticed that the bone had penetrated the skin; blood spilling down his hand and arm. His shirt now torn and blackened, he pulled it off and wrapped it tightly around his wrist in an attempt to stop the bleeding. The Key of Alanar still hung across his chest, glowing faintly. He owed it his life, yet he knew that this was only a temporary reprieve.

The Narssian warships hovered above the ruins, rows of lights along the fuselage only just penetrating the consuming blackness. By now the last of the Narssian infantry had emerged through the portal. A couple dozen of the creatures sifted through the rubble. It was just a scout party; the prelude to a true invasion.

From this distance, all he could make out were shadowy creatures—tall and powerful, armed with rifles and an assortment of blades hooked to their body armor.

As they spread out, advancing through the wreckage, he could sense them somehow feeding off the death and destruction around them. Balaska had told him that they were parasites; scavengers that fed off the life force of not only people but entire worlds.

David stayed down, peering over the rubble and debris. Much to his alarm, several of the Narssians were getting closer. As they approached he was gripped by an icy chill. He could see them clearly now, their faces lit by the flaming ruins: greenish-black reptilian creatures with gnarled faces, piercing red eyes, large jaws and sharp, twisted teeth. Beneath spiked armor, their arms rippled with oversized muscles; their long scaled hands tapering into sharp claws. But it was more than just their appearance that horrified David. They exuded an aura of malevolence: a death-like poison that seemed to seep through the air around them.

David's heart froze upon realizing that the nearest of the Narssians had spotted and were headed straight for him. His immediate response was to get up and run: to run as far from here as he possibly could. But he wasn't going anywhere. He had a mission to accomplish. He knew that this was just the first wave of the assault. More of these creatures would soon come pouring through the gateway. Millions, possibly more. They would obliterate Alanar and then spread out to other worlds: a parasitic, deadly plague.

Ignoring his impulse to flee, David got to his feet and stood to face the reptilian invaders. While most of the Narssians had spread out across the ruins, drinking in the death and desolation, five of them had their sights on David and were closing in fast.

David knew that he had to get past them in order to reach the gateway. But there was no way he could fight them and win. They were too big, too powerful and heavily armed, whereas he was unarmed and barely able to move without wincing in pain. The only way he could get past was to try and distract them.

With the vaguest of plans taking shape in his mind, he turned and ran in the opposite direction. With each step, his body shot with pain but he kept on going, never once daring to glance behind. He knew that the Narssians were in close pursuit, for he could feel their venomous presence bearing down on him.

He didn't know where he was running. He didn't suppose it mattered. All he had to do was distract them long enough to loop round and reach the gateway. Raging fires consumed what little remained of the city. The rubble and debris slowed David's escape, and the heat was almost unbearable. The fiery air singed the hairs in his nostrils as he breathed it in, while his skin was burning and blistered.

He made his way down what had been a side-street, alight with flames. What little remained of the buildings were collapsing to the ground either side of him. Stumbling through the rubble, he moved as fast as he could, choking as smoke filled his lungs.

It was all he could do to dodge the ruins as they crumbled around him. Gaining on him, the Narssians now had him in their sights. They opened fire, the blasts from their rifles only narrowly missing him but singeing his skin. It was all so hopeless! It was only a matter of time before—

A deafening crash from behind made David stop in his tracks.

Shielding his eyes from a wave of dust and hot ash, he saw the remains of a large building had toppled to the ground behind him. So close. Had it fallen a split second sooner he'd have been caught beneath it. His pursuers hadn't been as fortunate. They'd been trapped beneath the falling wreckage. He uttered a silent prayer of thanks.

He carefully navigated through the ruins back to the central plaza, still struggling to breathe without choking on the smoke. It was a miracle that he was able to function at all amid this apocalyptic nightmare. He suspected that the Key, still glowing around his neck, must be keeping him alive and shielding him from the worst excesses of this fiery hell.

David set his sights on the gateway. He had to get to it, but it wouldn't be easy. The city was still crawling with Narssians and high above, barely visible through the dust and smoke, the Narssian warships circled like vultures.

Clasping his broken wrist to his chest and keeping his eyes fixed ahead, he bolted forward. Running fast as he could, he had to leap across all kinds of obstructions: the remnants of buildings, boulders, fiery rubble and shards of metal.

Onward he continued, determined that he wouldn't stop until he'd reached the gateway. All that kept him going was sheer determination. His body was broken and his mind teetering on the brink of despair, but a fierce determination burned in the core of his being.

More Narssians were soon upon him. Fortunately, they seemed less inclined to fire their rifles, perhaps due to their proximity to the portal. They obviously didn't want to risk damaging the instrument of their emancipation.

The podium had been damaged but largely stood intact. Climbing the steps to the portal, David stumbled on some debris and fell to the ground.

Before he could get up, one of the Narssians grabbed his leg.

A chill swept through him the moment it touched his skin. He could taste death—his own death—the deaths of everyone on this planet—and the death of entire worlds and universes.

He tried to break free, but its grasp was tight and unrelenting.

It pulled him back, snarling as it reeled him in. Several other Narssians closed in with blades in hand, ready to slice him apart.

David's mind froze and he was overcome by terror. But it was a momentary hesitation. He knew he couldn't give up now.

As the Narssian dragged him down the steps, he caught sight of some shards of broken metal. With his good arm, he reached out and grabbed a sharp piece of metal. He lunged forward, stabbing the Narssian between the eyes.

The Narssian shrieked, releasing him as it tried to dislodge the metal from its head.

David clambered to his feet, tears of pain rolling down his face.

The gateway was just ahead of him and he didn't have a second to lose.

The other Narssians shot after him, determined to prevent him from entering the portal. One of the creatures grabbed his arm, its claws digging into his skin as it pulled him back.

Struggling to break free of its grasp, David mustered all of his strength and pushed the Narssian aside. Staggering forward, he leaped headfirst into the gateway.

Inside the portal, everything changed. Like being immersed underwater, the energy flowed like a river, swirling around him, blue-silver in color. David's immediate reaction was one of relief. He'd stepped from the hell of the dead city into the relative peace of this energy conduit.

But looking ahead, he was filled with horror.

They were coming. A stream of black warships was shooting through the gateway en route to Alanar; with legions upon legions of Narssian troops marching beneath.

David couldn't let them reach his world. They'd already done enough damage. He wouldn't let them destroy Alanar.

He grabbed the Key from around his neck with such force that the metal chain snapped in his hand. Holding it tightly, he directed his entire focus upon it, mentally directing it to seal the gateway.

Nothing happened.

*Come on! Don't fail me now...*

He tried again, directing the full force of his will at the Key, imploring it to fulfill its function—to close this doorway before the Narssians could reach his world.

Nothing.

But just as panic was about to set in, he felt the crystal come to life. It began pulsating and glowing; brighter and brighter, until it became like a radiant star, shooting rays of white light from the palm of his hand.

Though the approaching Narssians were nearly upon him, the light of the Key intensified, eclipsing all else. He could feel the immensity of its power surging through his being, igniting every cell of his body.

It continued intensifying: growing stronger by the second; building and building—an imminent storm about to burst into thunderous life. David couldn't control it. It was too powerful.

The Key of Alanar finally ignited, exploding in his hand.

David screamed as lightning energy blasted throughout him, tearing his body apart from the inside out.

In a single moment, everything was consumed by a violent implosion of energy.

The entire universe seemed to collapse in on itself.

And there was silence.

# CHAPTER THIRTY NINE

# Infinity

Time was ended.

A single moment now stretched into an indefinable eternity.

Everything was suspended; an entire universe frozen.

David was no more. Yet something of him remained.

His fragmented consciousness, scattered across an infinite void, began to coalesce. He stirred from a dormant twilight of oblivion, as though awakening from a sleep lasting eons.

Awareness illumined his mind. It was the same awareness that had looked out of his eyes throughout his entire life—a silent witness, ever-present and unchanging.

Something was different, however.

It was no longer encased in a body of flesh and blood.

What remained was but a formless consciousness, adrift upon the oceanic cosmos.

He experienced a strange and profound sense of liberation.

He was free! Free to move about the entire universe. Carried by mere thought, he could go anywhere and do anything.

Filled with excitement and growing curiosity, he danced about the heavens with the exuberance of a timeless child—innocent, fearless and filled with the joy of simply existing.

So many wondrous things appeared before him. He witnessed the birth and death of stars; and the spinning of galaxies, solar systems, suns, and planets—many dormant, but some bursting with life.

He became aware of a multiplicity of dimensions; interpenetrating yet existing at different frequencies. Exploring these tiers of reality, he peeled back the layers of existence with his mind. Each revealed yet another level, from the densest to successively higher and more rarefied states of being.

Truly, there was so much to comprehend. It now seemed there was not just a single universe, but an infinite number of universes.

To witness the creation and dissolution of entire universes was like watching the cells in some vast cosmic body; blinking into existence then dissolving, only to be replaced by others.

The tapestry of existence was a dance of perpetual motion—a never-ending cycle of birth, expansion, and decay.

The very fabric of the multiverse seemed alive.

Everything was alive!

\* \* \*

His consciousness soaring, he now could taste Infinity itself. It was the base essence of everything; the ocean upon which the waves of phenomenal existence arose and subsided.

He was struck by a profound sense of interconnectedness.

Before he'd always felt alone, separate and cut-off from the rest of the universe. But from this elevated vantage point, all boundaries were gone. All distinctions and spatial separations seemed illusory. Whether at one end of the cosmos or another; it was the very same creative force responsible for the creation and dissolution of stars and galaxies.

Infinity, he realized, wasn't some inert force. Ever-present and ever-shining, unlimited and ungraspable, it was everywhere, and in everything! It seemed to be the very core of existence.

Shining upon countless bodies and minds, by themselves just inert matter, it animated them; granting them life, motion, and consciousness. In essence, all beings were the same—all emanations of a single light. This boundless life-giving force shone eternally, playing a multitude of roles—billions upon billions of beings.

*But why?*

Did it simply desire to experience itself—to express and know itself?

Was it possible that reality was some kind of grand cosmic play; a dream allowing Infinity to experience a multitude of forms and experiences?

If it was all some kind of cosmic dream, it was certainly an immersive one. Beings lived and died like fireflies flickering on and off through eternity, bound by a sense of fear and desire.

Forms came and went; birth and death dancing hand in hand across time. But it was all one. Life was an unbroken continuum. There could be no end.

\* \* \*

Having expanded to encompass the entire cosmos, he now experienced a painful contracting. He could feel his attention being pulled back to the mortal realm. He was still connected to it somehow.

Close to his own realm, he could sense the dimension of the Narssians, a universe of perpetual darkness. No stars shone there and deadness pervaded. The Narssians and their formless counterparts, the Shadow Lords, were driven by an insatiable hunger; the burning desire to break free of their dimensional prison and feed off life itself.

He knew what would happen if they succeeded. The contents of this dark dimension would spill into other universes, and the entire tapestry of life would unravel. It would be the death of all things.

Everything became so clear to him now. Light flooded his awareness as a kaleidoscope of images and scenes flashed before him.

Becoming aware of his own world, he saw the entire history of Alanar unfold before him; countless millennia passing by in a flash.

From the birth of Alanar to the rise and subsequent fall of Lasandria, he witnessed it all. He saw how seeds of corruption, born of Narssian interference, sent Lasandria spiraling into an era of darkness. Ardonis fought to avert the impending disaster, going before the Council of Elders and pleading for their intervention. The Key of Alanar was created: destined to, if not save Ardonis's kingdom, then at least safeguard the future.

While David had made his fateful journey to El Ad'dan, Ardonis managed to get a handful of Lasandrians through the temple to a place of safety. Once activated, the gateway destroyed the entire city, and Ardonis was killed as he ushered the last of his evacuees to safety.

But this wasn't the end for the noble High Priest. Though he didn't know it at the time, Ardonis was a Guardian in physical embodiment, and following his death, he returned to the realm of the Guardians.

An age of darkness engulfed Alanar as the centuries rolled by in dizzying succession.

The Guardians had meticulously planned everything, setting David's birth and destiny into effect millennia after the arrival of the Narssians.

Ardonis again returned to the mortal realm, this time in the form of an Enari male. A lone traveler, it was in the forests of a remote land that he one day encountered a young woman named Enkatia. Their connection was brief yet immediate.

David was astonished, yet it somehow made sense. Ardonis was his father. No wonder the High Priest had seemed so strangely familiar to him.

He saw the Tahlumar tribe on the run from the Alliance, and Enkatia's despair at having to part with her newborn son. He again witnessed Garadanti's journey to Mount Ahdral, where he sacrificed himself to get David to safety. From Ahdral, the Guardians took the child to the forest of Senrah, in a distant part of Alanar, where he was discovered by islanders from New Haven.

David's own life flashed before him; from the day he learned that he didn't belong on the island, to the day he was given the gift that would forever change his life. The moment he took hold of the Key, a tragic chain of events was initiated, culminating in the arrival of the Alliance and the destruction of New Haven.

He could see how his grief and guilt had festered inside him, clouding his judgment and distorting his mind. It was amid his despair that Zhayron had reached out to him, planting a seed of darkness that would gradually poison his mind.

There was still a remnant of shame that he had succumbed to Zhayron's pernicious influence. But he had more than redeemed himself: breaking free of the dark enchantment, killing Zhayron and entering the City of Lorden where his destiny was finally revealed to him.

He'd done what he had to do—what he, as David, was born to do.

* * *

Having witnessed his entire life from this elevated state of consciousness, he finally felt able to let it go.

Everything had been part of an unbroken chain of causation. All of his experiences, both joyous and painful had served to make him who he was, enabling him to become stronger, to grow in power and wisdom; and allowing him to fulfill the mission he'd been born to carry out. The happiness and pain, as intertwined as day and night, had balanced out to serve a greater purpose.

The grief that had torn him apart now seemed misplaced. He could feel the presence of his lost loved ones—his parents and Janir. Although their bodies were gone, their essence remained; liberated from their broken bodies and freely traversing the boundless cosmos.

He wanted to reach out to them, but some force prevented him.

It no longer mattered. Infinity was everything, everywhere. From this perspective, there could be no death, no separation; only unity.

This knowledge lifted an unspeakable burden. The ghosts of the past now resolved, he felt free, liberated and, for the very first time, at peace.

His consciousness expanded. He wanted nothing more than to merge back into the limitless expanse of Infinity—

But something held him back.

He felt himself contract further and further. Some unknown force had grabbed hold of him and was pulling him downward. He was unable to resist it. It seemed Infinity had a different destiny in mind for him.

# CHAPTER FORTY

# Crossing Point

He found himself on a lifeless moon. Stars shone amid the endless expanse of black; twinkling, pulsating and shooting across the heavens.

To his surprise, he now occupied a body of sorts. It looked much the same as the body he'd had before, but it had a translucent, dreamlike quality to it.

Ahead of him was a gateway; rays of silver light shining from a spherical nucleus of light.

He felt an almost irresistible urge to step through it. He didn't want to be here. He wanted to go back to where he'd been. He wanted to soar free.

"David."

He turned. "Balaska—?"

The Guardian smiled as she stepped toward him, her graceful form leaving a trail of light as she moved.

"Where are we?"

"A crossing point. A junction between realms."

He motioned to the silver gateway. "And this? What's beyond it?"

"Everything. It is the bridge to all you have just experienced—the totality of all universes, dimensions, and spheres of existence."

"I felt like I was part of it all. Like there was no division. Everything was one."

"Freed from the boundaries of mortal consciousness, you had a taste of Infinity; an experience of reality as it truly is."

"Why am I here? I want to go back, Balaska." He stared into the gateway, yearning to merge back into the oceanic bliss. He could already feel it slipping away.

"You cannot, at least not yet."

"Why?"

"We pulled you back. Your journey is not yet over. You are still needed."

"I am?"

"The Council of Elders wishes to see you."

David was hesitant.

"You will return here someday, David, and you will enter the silver gate and never look back. But it is not yet your time."

In spite of his reticence, he knew she was right. He could feel something pulling him back to the mortal realm. His world was still in danger, and so too were his friends. He couldn't forsake them. As much as he wanted to stay here, he knew he had to leave it behind.

He recalled Balaska telling him that all beings had their own song to sing in the grand symphony of existence. Perhaps his song was not yet over.

He could sense his loved ones—his parents and Janir—just beyond the silver gate, in dimensions so close yet just out of reach. Although he wanted to reach out and be with them, he knew he had to finally let them go. He had to let it all go.

*No separation, remember.*

He vowed to never forget that.

Uttering a silent farewell, he stepped back from the silver gateway, turned to Balaska and gave a nod. He was ready to go.

David again stood before the Council of Elders. Malkiastan sat at the center of the table, bathed in the light pulsating through the heart of Shanadon; Balaska again seated to his left.

"*You have done well, timeless one,*" the Council addressed him in a unified voice echoing throughout the chamber like celestial music. "*You successfully sealed the Lasandrian gateway, preventing a full-scale invasion of your realm. Universal containment is upheld—for now.*"

David lowered his head.

"*Your mission, however, is not yet complete. There are further challenges you must face as Custodian of the Key.*"

"What kind of challenges? I've done everything you asked of me."

*"You have restored the past, yes. But you must now consider the present and future, as you perceive them. We told you about the war being waged; the war between Life and Death.*

"Its origin is not of your realm. It began here, in our dimension: a never-ending battle between the Guardians and Shadow Lords. We regret it has long since spread to encompass many other realms. Your world is one of many now caught in the crossfire."

David had sensed something of this: a current of darkness rippling through the multiverse, affecting countless spheres of existence. "Alanar's still in terrible danger, isn't it?"

*"The enemy has been thwarted but they are far from beaten. They grow stronger and more powerful, and they will stop at nothing. The mortal realm is soon to be eclipsed by a reign of darkness such as it has never known. Unless, that is, the dark forces that threaten your world can be defeated."*

"Tell me more about these dark forces; about this war you speak of."

Malkiastan rose from the Council chamber. He moved toward David, his every movement elegant and graceful. "What we fight," he said, "is nothing less than Death itself—the Shadow looming over all of creation. While living beings are born and die according to natural law, the continuity of all life is under threat." He paused. "All beings cherish life, yet there is a force that is inverse to creation—a force of anti-life—that seeks to consume *all* until nothing remains. These creatures are the children of Death."

"The Narssians," David said.

"Yes. In their original, incorporeal form they are known as the Shadow Lords. Though they exist on these two levels, physical and nonphysical, they are essentially one and the same. We Guardians simply refer to them as the Shadow."

"Where did they come from?"

"Believe it or not, they were once Guardians, like us."

David stared at Malkiastan, aghast. "What happened to them?"

"We Guardians are caretakers. We oversee the multiplicity of dimensions and universes. Containment must be maintained. If cross-contamination occurs, the natural balance is disrupted. Damage to one universe can shatter the equilibrium of the multiverse."

"That doesn't explain the Shadow Lords and Narssians..."

"The Guardians are largely bound by an oath of noninterference. Direct intervention in the affairs of a universe is only permissible when damage would threaten to spill outward, causing a chain reaction across the multiverse. The Shadow Lords were a faction of our people who believed that we should disregard our oath and take a more active involvement in universal affairs. This ignited within them a burning lust for power, which eventually consumed them. There is no greater poison than greed, David. These wayward Guardians presented themselves as gods to the mortal realm...and over the eons become wraith-like creatures that fed off the very life-force itself."

"They became Death..."

"As their hunger grew, they began stripping an entire universe of life, eventually decimating it. Until that point, we remained bound by our oath of noninterference. But we could not stand by as they sought to move on to other universes. Thus, the war began. After much struggle we succeeded in sealing them in the very universe they had annihilated. There they have been imprisoned throughout time, and from there they have been desperately trying to escape, usually by manipulating susceptible individuals in the mortal realm."

"As they did in Lasandria, with Mailyn and Dua-ron..."

"Indeed. This incursion has been a problem on many worlds."

"The ones that made it through into my universe," David said, "they're back—in my time, they're back on Alanar and determined to reopen a gateway to their universe..."

"Yes, and with or without the Key of Alanar, they are close to succeeding. They believe they can converge your realm with their own. Once your universe is overrun and destroyed, they will seek another, and then another. The chain of reality will collapse."

"That can't be allowed to happen."

"Agreed. That is why you were brought back, David. The world needs you."

"Because of the Key?"

"Because you *are* the Key. The crystal is but a means of directing the power you already have within you. This power is yours, and it always was."

"Then I have to use it. I have to save my world."

"You were given life that you might fight for life."

He looked down at his ghostly form. "But how do I go back? Wasn't my body destroyed when I sealed the Lasandrian gateway?"

"We have the ability to clothe you in another. The cellular patterning of your body was stored in the Key at the moment of your death." David had assumed the Key was destroyed when he sealed the gateway. Malkiastan continued, "When you leave here and return to the mortal realm, you will receive a new form, precisely patterned on your old one. Though born anew, you will be the same as before."

"No. After all I've seen and experienced, I can never be the same."

"Indeed," Malkiastan smiled. "The same and yet different."

"What am I to do when I return to Alanar?"

"Follow the signs. Your mission will be made clear in time."

"Before I go, there's so much I need to know," David said. "My father was a Guardian—which means that I'm half-Guardian. What does that even mean? What does it mean to be a Guardian?"

"You will learn much, timeless one, and you will *become* much. We will guide you for as long as we can, if only in your dreams."

"My dreams," David whispered. "In my dreams I've seen someone over and over again, for years now—a girl. She's been getting clearer and clearer. She even helped me defeat Zhayron. Her name's Eladria..."

"Yes. Eladria."

"Who is she?"

"She is of a different universe, from a world twinned with Alanar."

"Then she's real? I knew it."

"She is indeed real. A link has existed between you throughout your lives, connecting you from across two universes. Together you share a unique destiny."

"Then I'll meet her—in person?"

"You will. She has been sent by us to aid you in your mission, to safeguard Alanar and defeat the Narssians."

It was a relief to know that he wouldn't have to shoulder this burden alone.

"The time has come for you to return to Alanar, but before you go..." Malkiastan held out his hand. There, in the palm of his hand, appeared the Key of Alanar. He smiled as he handed David the crystal amulet. "This belongs to you."

# CHAPTER FORTY ONE

# Rebirth

David found it hard to say goodbye to Balaska. They stood at the edge of the City of Lorden. It was the exact spot at which he'd arrived what seemed like an eternity ago. Beneath the violet sky, the crystalline buildings glistened like prisms, reflecting beams of rainbow light. He wished he could stay here. There was so much he still wanted to learn.

A gateway appeared before him. He looked up at Balaska. "I don't know what to say. You've helped him through so much. I owe you a debt of gratitude I can never repay."

"You need not thank me, David. I have been assigned by the Council as your guide, and I will do my utmost to help you in every way. I will maintain the line of communication as long as possible, although how long that will be I cannot say."

"What makes you say that?"

"Do not let the peace of Lorden fool you. We are at war, and the battle intensifies. Some of my people believe the Shadow Lords are about to gain the upper hand. I fear our connection with the mortal realm may soon be severed."

"Whatever happens, I swear I'll do all I can to stop them."

"I know you will. You have the power within you, David. Never forget that." She gestured to the golden portal. "Now go. Your world needs you."

He bowed his head. Not wishing to prolong this difficult departure, he moved toward the portal. After one last backward glance, he turned and stepped into it.

As soon as he entered the river-like energy conduit, he felt the Key of Alanar begin to vibrate. A strange sensation took hold of him. The light of the Key grew brighter and more intense, until it enveloped him in a cocoon of energy, penetrating his entire being.

He could feel himself become heavier and denser—an uncomfortable and alarming sensation. The free-flowing expansiveness he'd experienced in the Guardians' dimension was now gone.

With staggering rapidly the energy around him coalesced to form atoms, weaving together to form a new body. The Infinite was becoming finite once more; the immortal again shackled to the bonds of mortality.

Ordinarily, a mortal form developed in a mother's womb over a period of months. In this case, the energy of the Key was the womb and the process had been sped up exponentially.

Painful and disorientating, David found himself resisting the sudden transformation. Yet he'd agreed to his. He'd accepted his destiny and all that came with it. And like all things, the experience ended.

Catapulted out of the portal, David landed on the ground with an unceremonious thump. Lying in the mud, he drew a lungful of air and began coughing.

He'd just been born anew and it felt as though he was trapped in somebody else's body. It felt alien to him; tight, constricted and uncomfortable. It would probably take time for him to adjust to being encased in solid matter again. The clothes he wore were the ones the Guardians had given him in the City of Lorden: navy trousers and a sleeveless white shirt embossed with an eight-pointed star.

Still struggling to deal with the denseness of his reconstituted body, he pushed himself off the ground. He was definitely back on Alanar, in the Valley of Baltaz. Judging by the scattered ruins of El Ad'dan, he was back in his own time.

He looked up to see the City of Lorden, hovering above the land in dreamlike splendor, begin to shimmer and fade. He'd been there only moments ago, but it now vanished before his eyes, along with the portal that and brought him here. He felt saddened, as though his bridge to the Guardians was gone.

He had no idea how much time had passed since his departure. Bodies littered the battlefield. Toward the east side of the valley, the wreckage of the Galzodian burned; smoke still rising from the crashed warship. He could see no sign of the Alliance, the Kellians, or Janir's army. Surely there were some survivors—?

He turned, and his heart jumped as he caught sight of his old friends: Darien, Janna, Mariane, and Chari, along with some dark skinned warriors he didn't recognize. Overjoyed, he bounded toward them.

Their reaction was not what he expected.

Chari raised his weapon, a large axe, and the warriors beside him took aim with bows and arrows.

"Wait, it's me!" Didn't they recognize him?

He now saw they were gathered around a body on the ground. It was Janir.

"We can see it's you," Darien said, the distrust clear in his voice. "But whose side are you on?"

"What—?"

"You betrayed us to join Zhayron. And look where it got Janir..."

"No." David shook his head. "It's true I fell under his influence, but that's over now, I promise you. Zhayron's dead."

"We saw the body..."

"It was me. I killed him."

Silence. All eyes—and weapons—were trained on him.

"You have to trust me."

"Trust is earned," Chari said.

Janna had been kneeling by Janir's side. She moved toward David, her eyes locked on him. David got the impression she was gazing into his mind, somehow trying to intuit his intent. "It's all right," she said, her voice filled with relief. "There's nothing to fear."

"You're sure we can trust him?" Darien said.

"I'm sure."

"You can lower your weapons," Mariane told Chari and the archers.

Darien's face lit up with a relieved smile. "David, I can't believe it. After all that happened I didn't think we'd ever see you again."

"You almost didn't."

"Where were you?" Janna asked. "There was no sign of you anywhere."

"I made it to the City of Lorden."

"Up there?" Mariane motioned to where the city had been.

He nodded.

Darien caught sight of David's amulet. "The Key—it's whole. You found the missing half!"

"I did."

"Well, what happened?"

"It's a long story. Believe me, I've got so much to tell you." David found himself staring down Janir's body. He knelt by his mentor's side. The unmoving form seemed barely recognizable as the man David had known. He felt a pang of grief; one clearly shared by the others.

"I can't believe he's gone," Darien whispered.

After a moment's silence, David shook his head. "He's not. Not really."

"How can you say that? He's not moving; he's not breathing. Look at him—"

"But this isn't Janir. It's just his body." David stood up. "There's so much *more* to him than this—more to *all* of us. Janir himself tried to tell me that many years ago, the day my father died. Death is just the shedding of one layer of our being. This realm, these bodies and everything we count as real is just one facet of existence. I should know, because I died."

Darien's eyes widened. "You *died?*"

"They sent me back in time, to the day this city was destroyed. I died saving this world ten thousand years ago."

His friends stared at him, at a clear loss for words.

"As I said, there's so much to tell you," David continued. "I saw and experienced so much. I just wish I could share it with you. Because I don't want to forget it. I don't want to lose it..."

"Well," Mariane said, "I don't quite know what to say. But I certainly look forward to hearing more."

"And I thought *we'd* had a crazy time of it," Darien said.

"If you died," Janna said, "how are you back here?"

"I was brought back by the Guardians. The battle is won, but the war is far from over." His eyes fell upon the disheveled warriors standing at a discrete distance. Virtually all of them had sustained injuries in the conflict. Some were in very poor shape. "Who are our friends here?"

"Of course," Darien said, "you haven't met the Sulyahn."

"They joined us in our battle against the Alliance," Janna said.

"They fought valiantly," Chari said. "We would not have succeeded without them."

One of the warriors, a formidable looking young woman, strode forward. "I am Dutshyana, Second of the Sulyahn. If it was indeed you that killed the dark sorcerer, then it is to you that my people owe our freedom. In which case, I offer you a place in our Kingdom—where you may stay for as long as you wish."

David smiled. "Thank you, I appreciate the offer."

"Their Kingdom is beautiful," Janna said. "High up in the mountains, with a view you'd have to see to believe."

"Sounds perfect. I think we all need somewhere to rest and recover after all that's happened." David again looked down at Janir's body. "But first, we must give Janir a proper burial."

"Agreed," Darien said.

"Is it safe to linger?" Mariane cautioned. "What do you suppose the Alliance will do when they find out what's happened here?"

"I imagine they won't be happy," Darien remarked.

Chari concurred, "One of their warships has been destroyed, a sorcerer killed and a legion of Death Troops defeated. It is likely they have never suffered such a defeat. They will be quick to respond."

"We certainly haven't seen the last of them," David said.

"You think they'll send reinforcements here?" Janna asked.

"It's possible," David said. "But even if they do, we'll be long gone from here by then."

Fashioning metal spades out of wreckage from the Galzodian, they dug a grave for Janir, while the Sulyahn tended to their own dead. They chose a spot at the foot of Mount Alsan, amid a grove of firs. As they gathered, the suns set over the mountain peaks, setting the sky alight with ever-changing hues of red, gold, and orange.

Each stepped forward in turn, laying flowers upon the grave and speaking a few words in remembrance. When it came David's turn, he laid down the sweet-scented violets he'd picked from the mountainside and stared down at the grave. "I don't really know where to begin. No matter what I say it'll never come close to describing just how much Janir meant to me. He was my friend, my mentor, my confidante...and in many ways he was like a father to me. I can't believe I ever doubted him..."

This wasn't the time for regret. The past was gone.

He began again, his voice stronger and more assured, "I'll miss Janir beyond words. We all will. Our lives will never be the same without him. He held us all together and did everything he could to keep us on the right path. He sacrificed so much for us.

"The loss we feel is a tangible one; a hole in our lives and in our hearts; a void that nothing can fill. Nothing perhaps but time. We grieve not for Janir, but for our own loss. For I know that he's free now." He bowed his head. "Soar free, Janir—and until next we meet in the great ocean of Infinity...goodbye."

He felt a teardrop roll down his cheek. He now realized the importance of this ceremony. It wasn't just for Janir. It was a memorial for all those they'd lost back in New Haven. In their haste to escape the Alliance, they'd been forced to put their grief on hold. By now honoring their loss and acknowledging the pain they'd endured, perhaps they were finally ready to move on from it. None of them could face the future while still anchored by the pain of the past. It was time to let it go.

*No separation, remember.*

David felt a sudden wave of peace and comfort wash over him. It was as though the pain in his heart had opened a doorway within him. His heart felt lighter and a sense of joy arose within.

Perhaps it was misplaced. After all, he was standing over his mentor's grave in a valley that had known more death than anywhere on Alanar. Why then was he overcome by a strange feeling of peace—an inner sense of boundlessness and freedom?

Maybe it was because after all that had happened, and all that he'd been through, he'd been given a second chance at life. Perhaps what he now tasted was the joy of simply being alive and at last liberated from the shadows of the past.

# The Beginning

David watched from his balcony as a new day dawned. Heralded by a chorus of birdsong, the suns edged their way above the snow-capped mountains, lighting the sky with striking shades of red and gold.

He recalled the day after New Haven had been destroyed. Naranyan had taken him to the edge of the forest to watch the sunrise. There he'd recounted an old Enari legend about how the gods had pledged to always shine their light upon the world, offering the suns as beacons of life, light, and hope. No matter what happened, Naranyan said, he'd always found comfort in the knowledge that each night the suns would set only to rise again the following morning. Life was a dance of light and dark, but the darkness would always yield to the returning light. David vowed to remember that in the days ahead.

"It must have been hard," came a voice.

He turned to see Darien enter the chamber.

"What?"

"Coming back—from where you were. You know, when you died…"

They'd been at Arnashen for three days now, and this was the first time Darien or any of the others had asked him about it. "I didn't want to," he admitted. "I'd never felt such freedom. It was like my mind had expanded and merged with the entire universe, and everything beyond. It's so hard to explain, but I saw it all; the birth and death of planets, civilizations, stars, galaxies and entire universes. It was like this amazing dance of creation, and I was somehow *one* with it all—with everything. It was all happening in me like some kind of endless cosmic dream."

Darien's brow furrowed. "You sure you hadn't been smoking hampa weed?"

David smiled. "I'm sure."

"If it was all so great, then why did you come back? I'm not sure I'd want to."

"I had to. The Guardians made it clear that my place is here. I admit it was hard at first." He turned back to the mountains. "But I forgot how beautiful it is; how beautiful life is. I don't know if I ever really appreciated it before, but life is so precious. Maybe we don't really appreciate it until we're staring death in the face; until it's about to be snatched away from us. But being here, just being *alive,* is the most wondrous gift. And I'm going to try to never take a single moment of it for granted. Life's a thing to be embraced, cherished; and it's worth fighting for; it's worth saving."

"Well, whatever happened, you seem like you're at peace with yourself now."

"I think I am. I think I finally am."

"I'm glad." Darien smiled, placing his hand on David's shoulder. "Enough of the deep talk, huh? I'm starving! Why don't we go see what the Sulyahn have cooked up for us this morning?"

"Lead the way."

The boys made their way through the palace toward the dining hall. The atmosphere in the palace remained subdued. These had been difficult times for the Sulyahn. Their army had been decimated at the battle of El Ad'dan, and the entire kingdom was in mourning. In spite of this, King Rushtaan had been generous to a fault, affording David and his friends every luxury the Sulyahn had to offer, including full run of his palace.

"Where were you last night, by the way?" David asked.

"I'll let you figure it out," Darien said. "I wasn't with Chari and I certainly wasn't with Mariane."

"Janna?"

Darien nodded, his face lighting with a giddy smile.

"You and Janna—?"

"Yeah..."

"What happened?"

"We just talked, the whole night."

"About what?"

"Everything I guess. But we spoke a lot about us—about our feelings. Turns out she's never really been close to anyone. She's always kept people at a distance, mainly because she didn't want them to find out about her powers. She said I'm the first person who's ever totally accepted her for who she is and—"

"Her powers?"

"Yeah, I keep forgetting, there's still a lot you need to catch up on. Anyway, I guess what with all we've been through together, it's brought us closer. She admitted there's an attraction between us. I mean, everyone knows I've always been attracted to her..."

"Yes, we kind of got that impression," David laughed.

"Well, she likes me too," Darien smiled. "She actually likes me too."

"So what now?"

"I don't know. We agreed to take things slowly and see where it leads. But it's like a dream come true. I've never felt like this for anyone. I just can't believe it!"

"I'm happy for you, Darien."

Rounding a corner they reached the dining hall. Their Sulyahn hosts had laid out another exquisite banquet. There was more food than they could ever possibly eat, but thankfully David was hungry. In the weeks since departing New Haven he'd eaten little and lost a fair amount of weight, but now his appetite had kicked back into overdrive.

He and Darien seated themselves at the table. Sunlight streamed through the tall windows, illuminating the feast in rays of golden light. They were joined by Chari, Mariane and Janna, followed by their Sulyahn hosts, including King Rushtaan and Dutshyana. Aware that this would be one of his final meals here, David was keen to savor every last bite. After eating as much food as he felt able, he thanked Rushtaan for his unceasing kindness.

Once Rushtaan and the other Sulyahn left to attend to their duties and the servants busily cleared the dining table, David opened the veranda doors and invited his comrades onto the balcony. From here they had a view of the entire kingdom and the surrounding mountains, valleys, forests and rivers.

"I wanted to talk to you alone," David said.

"About what?" Mariane said.

They all looked at him. He could sense an undercurrent of apprehensiveness. "We've been fortunate here," he said. "Our Sulyahn friends have blessed us with every courtesy. In some ways, I wish I could stay here. But I can't. Since we arrived at Arnashen I've been having these dreams..."

"Dreams?" Janna echoed.

"Yes, only I'm certain they're much more than just dreams. It's almost as though when I'm asleep my mind is free to return to the realm of the Guardians. Each night I find myself back in the City of Lorden, with Balaska. And last night—last night she had a warning for me."

Darien shifted nervously. "What kind of warning?"

"She told me there's a new wave of darkness rising. While we may be safe here for the time being, that'll change." He paused as he considered his words. "As I told you, I was sent back in time to defeat the Narssians and seal the gateway that brought them to our universe."

"It's hard to quite get my head around that, but yes," Mariane nodded.

"Well, the past is restored, but I've yet to deal with the very real threat they pose here, in the present. The Narssians that made it through the gateway all those millennia ago are back, and they're a dying race. Working with the Alliance, they're fighting for their survival. That makes them more dangerous than ever. They'll stop at nothing to reopen the gateway and converge both universes. If that's not bad enough, the Narssians are also trying to smash their way through from their own realm. It's an assault on two fronts."

"Well, I don't know about the rest of you, but I suddenly feel a whole lot worse," Darien muttered, putting his arm around Janna.

"How can we stop them?" Chari asked.

"I rather think the question is, *can* we stop them?" Mariane said. "We beat the odds the first time around, and even with the Sulyahn, Jinerans and Janir's sorcery to help us, we were lucky to escape with our lives. Now I'm guessing the Alliance and the Narssians have countless warships and troops at their combined disposal."

Chari nodded. "They have technology far in advance of anything else on Alanar. And they control a vast portion of the planet."

"So what possible hope do we have of defeating them?"

"I don't know," David admitted. "But all I do know is that they must be stopped. You've never encountered the Narssians, but I have. The thought of those monsters invading this universe is beyond any nightmare you could imagine. They live only to kill and destroy, and they would—everything, everywhere." An uncomfortable silence followed. "But we can't let ourselves be overwhelmed by the immensity of what lies ahead. Fortunately, at the moment there's a kind of pause."

"A pause?" Janna said.

"Yes, I can feel it. It's almost like the whole planet is holding its breath: watching, listening...waiting."

"For what?"

"For the enemy to make its next move. All we can do now is to be strong, and be ready."

None of them had wanted to hear this. After all they'd been through, they'd clearly hoped their ordeal was over. David continued, "In my dream, Balaska told me to travel south, beyond the mountains to a place called Dalzyon. There's a school there. Some kind of academy of sorcery and magic. She said they're expecting me and that upon my arrival the next stage of my mission would be revealed. So I'm to leave for Dalzyon as soon as possible."

"What about us?" Darien said.

"That's up to each of you. If you want to join me I'd certainly be grateful for your company. But you've all been through so much already. I'll understand if you decide to stay here in

Arnashen. In fact, I'd recommend it. I'm sure Rushtaan would be happy for you to remain, and you'd certainly be safer here."

Chari, ordinarily a man of few words, was first to respond. "This is not my home. I will never be able to return to my people, but I now have a purpose, and that purpose lies with you. I will join you and protect you with all my might until we reach our destination and defeat our enemy."

"Chari's right," Darien concurred. "Our place is by your side. We started this together and we're going to finish it together."

Darien turned to Janna, who gave a resolute nod. "You're not alone, David. We're with you all the way. As nice as it is here, I know our destinies lie elsewhere."

David smiled, glad of their support. The only person yet to respond was Mariane, who appeared noticeably reticent. "I don't even know how I made it this far," she said. "I'm much older than the rest of you and I'm feeling my age most pronouncedly. It would be much easier if I just stayed here."

"I understand, Mariane," David said. "I'm grateful you've come as far as you have. I know it can't have been easy for you."

"No, it certainly hasn't. But even so...I don't belong here. As nice as the Sulyahn are—at least now they're not trying to murder us in our sleep—I don't particularly want to spend the rest of my life here." She paused, staring across the mountaintop vista. "I remember telling Janir not so long ago that Jadan, my husband, was an adventurer at heart. His whole life he yearned to set off into the wilderness and explore the world. I think the only reason he stayed in New Haven was because of me, for I certainly had no desire to go traipsing off into the unknown. Well, Jadan's gone now, and in some strange way, I feel I owe it to him to live out his dream—for him, and also for myself. I don't know if that makes any sense..."

"It makes perfect sense," Janna said.

"So whilst I have no doubt I'll soon live to regret this, I'll join you," Mariane added. "After all, *someone* has to keep you all in order, and it may as well be me!"

"It means so much that you're all willing to join me," David said. "You're more than just my friends. You're my family now. I must admit I've no idea what lies ahead of us—"

"Indeed, when do we ever?" Mariane interjected.

"Well, whatever happens, we'll take this journey together— and I know that together we can make it."

The following morning they departed Arnashen. Having packed enough supplies to see them through the weeks ahead, they said farewell to their Sulyahn hosts and set off.

Descending the mountain path, their feet crunched on the twigs, leaves and fir needles. David's eyes drifted across the blue-green mountains, sculpted into perfection by the passage of time; the silent witness of uncountable centuries. A pinkish-violet light from the sky lent the landscape a warm glow as sunlight illuminated the valley and sparkled upon the winding river.

Marveling at the beauty of his world, David knew that he had to do everything in his power to save it. While it seemed inconceivable that he had any hope of defeating the combined power of the Narssians and the Alliance, he would no longer allow fear or doubt to hold him back.

His journey had changed him. He was no longer a lost and confused boy, tortured by the loss of his home and crippled by a burden of misplaced guilt.

He'd been forced through the flames, and in death's embrace had witnessed everything burn away: his old life, his understanding of reality, and every concept he'd ever held about himself. There'd been nothing he could do but allow it: allow himself to be burned, dismembered, and eventually reborn.

For only birth could conquer death, and from the ashes had been born the fruits of knowledge; knowledge of who he was, why he was here, and of the illusory nature of death and limitation.

Although the memory now seemed hazy, the experience of merging into Infinity remained with him. He'd experienced reality from an elevated vantage point, transcending entire universes and every perceivable dimension.

He recalled that life was but the unending cosmic dream of Infinity; a play of light and dark; a chain of birth, death, and resurrection, with universes rising and falling like waves. All beings had their parts to play, from the littlest sparrow to the mightiest of kings, each contributing their own note to the symphony of existence.

Filled with a courage and certainty he'd never before known, David now knew who he was, and with that knowledge came a sense of peace, power, and purpose. He was ready to play his part in the great unfolding—to embrace his destiny and safeguard his world from those that would endanger it. He was a man reborn—a man who no longer feared death, and perhaps more importantly, who no longer feared living.

# Afterword

As I write this, I'm aware that this is not only the end of an era, but also a significant chunk of my life. 'The Key of Alanar' began as the faintest wisp of an idea when I was barely a teenager. To say it's a story that's been with me most of my life is, therefore, no exaggeration.

If I'd been more expedient I could probably have written a dozen other novels by now. Instead, it took me a number of years to develop the story, characters, and themes, as well as to learn the craft of writing.

I finished the first edition a decade ago (ironically, before my first published novel 'Eladria' was even conceived of). Although a tale that captivated my heart, I was never satisfied with it, even when I released a more expanded second edition a couple of years ago. If it had been any other book I'd probably have simply shrugged, learned what I could from the experience, and moved on to some other work.

I found I simply couldn't do that. 'The Key of Alanar' is a special story to me, and I wanted to know that I'd finally done it some justice. That's why I went back and stripped it down, removing significant chunks, while adding, polishing and refining a number of elements.

This final edition is the culmination of not only years of work, but years of life. It's the fruit of much inquiry, reflection, and experience. I think I had to experience some crashing lows and soaring heights before I could possibly hope to write David's journey in a way that felt emotionally genuine to me.

'The Key of Alanar' was never written to be just a fantasy story. I hope people will enjoy it on that level, but what I wanted was to tell a story about life: about human nature, existence, loss, purpose, failure, and redemption.

David's story is about what happens when we fall—when life breaks us and we lose touch with who we are; when we're wounded, hurt and swept off course, and completely unaware of the true light and power that's within us.

I believe the most powerful stories are stories of transcendence. Transcendence is the alchemising key of human experience. It's the ability to overcome suffering and pain, to find love where there was hate, to transform ignorance into knowledge and bondage into liberation. That's the spirit in which this book was written and in which it is now offered.

This story has been part of my life for over twenty years. I'm not sure how many more books I'll write, but I have a feeling this is the one that'll always be closest to my heart. It was the book I needed to write, if only to heal myself.

Its core message is one I intend to live by for the rest of my days: that we are capable of dealing with whatever life brings our way, for at essence we are more powerful and expansive than we ever dared imagine. We are Infinity in radiant expression, and as Balaska said, we each have our own song to sing in life.

I'd like to express my gratitude to everyone who has supported me along this journey. I'm especially grateful to my Mum and Dad, my sister Holly, and my grandparents. They've always been my support team. They believed in me ceaselessly and encouraged me to pursue this work in spite of all adversity. I'd likely have given it up long ago had it not been for their endless love and support. I feel blessed beyond measure to have them in my life.

Finally, I'd like to thank whoever is reading this now (that's you!) for being part of this and allowing me to share the world of Alanar with you. If you enjoyed the book, I'd be very grateful if you would leave a review on Amazon or elsewhere!

Thank you, and thank you to Infinity, that essential creative force through which this book, in keeping with all creative endeavors, was born. In a sense, I think we are all sorcerers.

*Rory B Mackay*

Lightning Source UK Ltd.
Milton Keynes UK
UKOW03f0637160517
301301UK00005B/503/P